Praise for *Mr. Darcy Ta[*

"A wonderfully unique Jane Austen re-imag[
Get ready to laugh."

— Mary Simonsen ~ Author of *The Second Date , Searching
for Pemberley* and *Anne Elliot, A New Beginning*

"Mr. Darcy Takes The Plunge is definitely a story that I will read over and
over again when I am in need of sunshine! My sides hurt, my cheeks
hurt. Thank you for such a good laugh!"

— Marg

"I laughed, snorted, smiled, and groaned. *Mr. Darcy Takes The Plunge* is
a delightful story!"

— Karen A

"I would much rather have my soul tried with your puns than my soles
tried by poor times. I laughed out loud - I truly love this story!"

— Rachel P

"Uproarious! I threw my head back and howled with laughter!"

— Mischa

"It was certainly no PUN-ishment to read this funny, delightful story!"

— Brenda

"My sides hurt from all my laughing. I can only hope that this 'deranged
authoress' has more stories up her sleeve to bring us, and soon."

— Pat M

"Absolutely magnificent! It's so unique, clever, witty and delightful."

— Jo Y

"A very enjoyable romp!" — Margaret F

Mr. Darcy Takes The Plunge

~ A pun-filled tale featuring Austen's *Pride and Prejudice* characters~

*with some
added or addled,
missing or missish,
modified or mortified,
healthier, wealthier or wiser*

J. Marie Croft

Rhemalda Publishing

Rhemalda Publishing
Rhemalda Publishing, Inc. (USA)
P.O. Box 2912, Wenatchee, WA 98807, USA

First American Paperback Edition

ISBN 13: 978-0-9827437-0-6
E-book ISBN 13: 978-0-9827437-1-3

Library of Congress Control Number: 2010931827

PRINTED IN THE UNITED STATES OF AMERICA.
10 9 8 7 6 5 4 3 2 1

⊗ The paper used in this publication meets the minimum requirements of the American National Standard of Information Services - Permanence of Paper for Printed Library Materials, ASNI Z39.48-1992.

Visit J. Marie Croft at her author website http://prideand.weebly.com or at her blog http://prideand.wordpress.com/.

Visit Rhemalda Publishing at http://www.rhemalda.com.

In memory of two special ladies who were well
loved by a sister:

Jane Austen
An inspiration in my life and in this story
She died in Cassandra's arms July 18, 1817.

Judith Padmore
An important part of my life and of this story
She passed away May 8, 2010.

PART I

Darcy in a Meadow at Pemberley
or
A Man's Field (in his) Park

A tribute to Austen's *Mansfield Park*

Chapter I

Whilst Enduring the Heat of the Summer Sun,
a Gentleman Still Wears His Coat — and Pants

Pemberley's revered housekeeper, Mrs. Esther Reynolds, graciously entertained, in her own comfortable private quarters, three genteel ladies, one of middle age and two much younger. Once they had finished their tea and the older women had caught up on all the latest news and gossip, Mrs. Reynolds inquired as to whether her guests would care for a guided tour of the grand estate's public rooms and its immediate lawns. The visitors had anticipated such an invitation and quickly and eagerly agreed to the scheme. The housekeeper was mightily proud to show to advantage her employers' excellent taste and elegance, for the rooms were richly furnished and tastefully decorated with the very finest-quality pieces without pretension.

Mrs. Reynolds was highly efficient at her job and had held the esteemed position for the past three and twenty years. As a native of nearby Lambton, the young Esther Bentley had begun work at Pemberley as an upstairs maid. She had even met her husband, Owen Reynolds, at the stately estate when he was but a burly footman; and the loving couple had progressively worked their way up through the ranks of servants to their present important positions of housekeeper and butler.

Both fiercely loyal and protective of Pemberley's Master, Mistress, and their offspring, Mr. and Mrs. Reynolds had no complaints about serving the distinguished family; although they could not quite understand the family's propensity to allow a motley assortment of dogs, rabbits, hedgehogs, and other sundry critters the freedom of the manor. Not that the housekeeper and butler disliked animals, nonetheless, their jobs, and those of their underlings, would be made much easier if the beasties were kept outside where, in their humble opinion, God intended them to live. From the time they had each been in leading strings, the Darcy progeny brought home countless stray and wounded creatures of the furred, feathered, and scaly persuasion; and they had never entirely outgrown performing such rescue missions.

As Mrs. Reynolds guided her dear friend and the two young ladies through Pemberley's public rooms, she kept a constant and wary eye out for anything flying, slithering, crawling, creeping, hopping, or racing through its corridors, especially the first four categories; and she involuntarily shuddered. When the indoor portion of the tour was nearly complete, Esther Reynolds breathed a sigh of relief that no critter encounters had occurred. Over the years, the housekeeper and her staff had suffered countless unexpected and heart-stopping discoveries of birds, snakes, spiders, turtles, and toads whilst performing their duties. They had learned the hard way that boxes hidden under beds were an especial reason for suspicion and caution.

When the party neared the music salon, it became apparent they would have to bypass that room, as from behind its closed doors came the sound of scales being practiced on the new pianoforte. As they started down the hall to the portrait gallery, the musical training ended, the door opened, and a young lady appeared at the doorway and said over her shoulder, "Do continue, dearest, and I shall return in just a moment. You are progressing well, Anna. I am so very proud of you." As she exited the room and spotted the others, she rushed forward and exclaimed, "Oh, Mrs. Reynolds, I understood you to be off duty today. Are you conducting a tour?"

An indistinct white shape dashed out of the music room, followed by another blur of fawn and black; the objects skidded across the highly polished hardwood floor of the hallway and ended up in a heap together at the feet of one of the visitors. That astonished young lady gathered her skirts, stepped aside, peered down, and smiled in delight at the two small balls of fur, which proved to be a sweet, silky Maltese and a cute, cuddly Pug.

From the direction of the music salon, a girl's voice urgently called, "Dust Bunny! Pug-Nacious! Come back here at once, you little scamps!" A pretty young woman of approximately six and ten years appeared in the doorway and looked to the left and then to the right. Upon seeing the assemblage in the hall, her eyes widened, she blushed, and covered her mouth with an elegant hand. "Oh, I am so very sorry. The rapscallions were both sleeping so peacefully until Georgiana left, and then they just suddenly careened across the floor and out the door after her. I should have been attending them, but ... "

"Anna, do not fret, dearest. As you can see, no harm has come to these ladies; and the puppies are fine," the older girl reassured the younger.

Mrs. Reynolds also stepped in to soothe the girl's unease and spoke kindly. "Yes, Miss Anna, we were momentarily startled but have come to no injury. The little beasts are relatively harmless, except perhaps to the finish on the floor." The housekeeper spared a brief scowl for the two canines, which were by then sitting at Georgiana's feet, staring up at her with rapt adoration. A pretty lady of about twenty years, Miss Darcy had pale blonde hair and lovely azure eyes, whereas Miss Anna had darker blonde hair and captivating eyes of hazel. The sisters were both quite tall and had light but well formed figures.

The senior female servant then began her introductions. "Madeleine, Miss Bennet, Miss Elizabeth, please allow me to introduce to you Miss Georgiana Darcy and her younger sister, Miss Anna. I was just about to show you their beautiful portraits in the gallery, but here they are in person." She smiled lovingly at the girls and then introduced her dear friend, Mrs. Madeleine Gardiner, from London, though formerly of Lambton, and the lady's nieces, Miss Jane Bennet and Miss Elizabeth Bennet, from Hertfordshire. Curtsies and smiles were exchanged, and polite small talk ensued until Mrs. Reynolds suggested she and her guests should continue with their tour.

The kindly housekeeper was pleasantly surprised when Miss Darcy made a suggestion. "Mrs. Reynolds, perhaps you and Mrs. Gardiner would enjoy more time to chat together. In the meantime, Anna and I would be delighted to take a turn in the garden with the Misses Bennet." Georgiana paused and frowned at the two furry creatures at her feet. "As for these little rascals, I believe they would benefit from a tiring romp outside."

Agreement was immediate; and bonnets, gloves, and parasols were brought to the four young ladies, while the two older women continued on to the impressive portrait gallery. The Darcy sisters each scooped up a pooch and accompanied the Bennet siblings through the doors and down the front steps. As soon as they were on the garden path, the dogs were released. Miss Darcy explained, "These are my newest pets, Dust Bunny, the Maltese, and Pug-Nacious, obviously the Pug. Mother and Father presented the puppies to me on my twenty-first birthday, several months ago, and I am still endeavouring to train them. Do you have any other siblings or any pets, Miss Bennet and Miss Elizabeth?"

Elizabeth spoke first. "We have no pets, at least none allowed inside our house; but our father raises hounds for hunting, and there are a number of barn cats at Longbourn."

Jane scolded, "Lizzy, perhaps you should have first mentioned our siblings before alluding to any animals."

"Oh, of course, yes. There is only one year between Jane and I; however, the rest of us are all spaced about four years apart. We have three younger sisters, Mary, Catherine, and Lydia, and a darling baby brother, who is but three years of age and the pet of our entire family." Elizabeth smiled fondly and continued, "Our parents waited so long for an heir, I am afraid little Robert Thomas Bennet is quite spoiled by all of us. I understand you ladies have an elder brother."

Georgiana plucked a plump rose from a bush and replied, "Yes, Fitzwilliam is five years my senior; and Anna is five years my junior, which means I, alas, am the poor, neglected middle child."

Anna Darcy gasped. "Georgie, you are neither poor nor neglected. Mother and Father dote on us all equally, as you are well aware; although dear Fitzwilliam, being the heir, is held up to very exacting standards and great expectations."

Jane asked whether their parents and brother were presently at home. Miss Darcy answered, "Mother and Father were called away rather suddenly to take care of an urgent family matter in Kent." Georgiana furtively rolled eyes at her sister and continued, "But Fitzwilliam is expected later this evening or early tomorrow with a party of his friends."

Miss Anna added, "It is unfortunate you will most likely not have the opportunity to meet the young men, for they are all quite attractive and dashing. Our cousin, Richard, is an army officer and has earned a rather suspicious nickname. We have heard him referred to as Colonel Stu … " She had been about to reveal the sobriquet but caught her sister's disapproving glare and quickly changed the subject. "Um … and I may not be totally impartial; nevertheless, I believe our own brother to be the most handsome of men, as do many of the ladies, both young and old, in Derbyshire and in London. However, Fitzwilliam does not much care for Town society, except for attending the theatre, opera, museums, and art galleries. He prefers the bucolic country life but is still *always* impeccably dressed and proper, even here at home."

"Dearest Anna, our guests do not care to hear so many details about our perfectionist brother and please refrain from ever mentioning Richard's scandalous nickname. But now, Miss Bennet and Miss Elizabeth, you must tell us about your summer travels. Is this your first visit to Derbyshire, where are you lodging, and how long will you be staying?"

Jane answered, "You have already met our aunt, and we are also here with our Uncle Gardiner. He is in the import-export trade and is conducting business in the area, so our aunt took the opportunity to accompany him in order to visit with some of her dear friends, Mrs. Reynolds being one of them. Lizzy and I were fortunate to be invited along to enjoy the rugged beauty of Derbyshire. It is our very first visit to your breathtaking county. We are staying at the inn at Lambton for two more nights. We will travel home to Longbourn after a brief stop in London."

"Do you spend much time in the city?"

"Not really, Miss Darcy," Elizabeth replied. "Similar to your brother, although we enjoy the arts and entertainment available in Town, our family also favours the peaceful country life." She plucked a small stick off the ground and tossed it down the path. The little dogs fetched it and scampered back, side by side, with the twig held between them. Their tails wagged in unison, and the four young ladies laughed at the delightful sight.

"You mentioned Longbourn," Miss Anna said as she walked carefully between the puppies while they frolicked around her feet and wrestled for the stick. "Is that your family's estate, Miss Bennet?"

Jane looked down, also taking care not to step upon tiny paws, as she replied, "Yes, it is one of the county's largest and has been in our family for many generations. Papa is a very attentive landowner and is responsible for a large number of tenants and workers, with the help of our steward. Have you ever been to Hertfordshire?"

"I believe we have passed through after visiting Kent or London, but I regret to say we have never stopped," Miss Darcy responded.

"Well, now that you have such interesting new acquaintances there, you must promise to visit and not simply pass us by next time," teased Elizabeth.

In the twinkling of an eye, the four genteel young women were sufficiently comfortable with one another to use first names, chat, and laugh as though they had been friends of some longevity rather than mere acquaintances of an afternoon's duration. When the beauty and fragrance of the estate's gardens had been enjoyed to everyone's satisfaction, they decided to take a leisurely stroll around Pemberley's manicured lawn toward the river. As they walked, they twirled their parasols and giggled at the antics of Pug-Nacious and Dust Bunny.

Five miles in the distance at the grand estate's boundary, four overheated young men arrived earlier than expected on horseback and in a cloud of dust. They had been riding hard since mid-morning from the Fleming estate farther north in Derbyshire and, as a result, were uncomfortably sweaty and grimy. Mounts were reined from a canter to a walk upon entering the park, making repartee easier for the chaps.

When the blue-eyed, fair-haired Bingley realized they would soon reach the spot where the house came into view, he exclaimed, "I say, Darcy, I am quite looking forward to soon being able to slake my thirst with several pints of Derbyshire's finest ale. In fact, I daresay Pemberley's brewer can attest to producing the best in the kingdom."

"Really, Bingley? I know your fondness for our barley and hops; all the same, can you honestly boast of having sampled enough brews across the land to be an expert and make such a claim?"

Fitzwilliam, the eldest of the four, spoke up. "Sample is certainly all Bingley can handle, cousin. The chap is entirely in his cups before a third serving."

Charles Bingley came to his own defense. "Aye, I am not such a seasoned old elbow-crooking imbiber as you, Fitz. I have only ever been half-sprung and, unlike you, certainly never as drunk as a wheelbarrow. Nevertheless, I would always prefer to have good quality ale in my cup before quaffing enough to get me in my cups. I could not abide the swill I am certain you, as a military man, are forced to guzzle. Your love of drink, my friend, is an ale-ment."

"Enough talk of ale, gentlemen, for my throat is positively parched. Blast this insufferable, sweltering heat!" Ellis Fleming wrenched at his neckcloth and continued, "How much farther until we finally reach your home, Darcy? I am afraid I shall appear at your illustrious parents' doorstep a sopping dishrag if we have to travel much longer. I had much rather make a good first impression and sincerely hope my accoutrements have preceded me to Pemberley. A good washing-up and fresh clothing are very appealing right now."

"I am sure your valet has your belongings awaiting you in a guest room, my friend; and you have, in fact, been on Pemberley's grounds for some time now. My parents are presently not in residence, so you only have to worry about impressing my impressionable younger sisters. But I share your discomfort, Fleming. Hell, 'tis hotter than Hades today." Fitzwilliam Darcy doffed his hat, wiped his brow with his handkerchief, and gave his cousin, Colonel Richard Fitzwilliam, a challenging look. "Too bad we are no longer carefree youths, for the pond is but another ten minutes afar."

"Youth is a relative term, Darcy; and I am not yet eight and twenty. As for being carefree, are we not all gentlemen of leisure, or at least on holiday or leave?"

"To the pond, then?"

"To the pond. Charge!"

Pemberley's heir and his army-officer cousin left their friends in the dust as they galloped off. Bingley and Fleming exchanged grins before urging their horses to follow the others around the bend. The four then veered off and, at a trot, followed a narrow path through the woods; within minutes they emerged into a grassy clearing edging a small lake.

If the gentlemen expected to behold pristine, fresh water, they were certainly disappointed. The lake was partially covered with a film of slimy pea-green scum. Dragonflies and a variety of other insects droned, dipped, and danced above the putrid soup. The four dismayed gentlemen dismounted, saw to the comfort of their horses, and gazed in disgust at the stagnant pond.

"You cannot be serious, Darcy! I can certainly believe it of Fitz. But you, Mr. Meticulous, actually swam here?" Ellis Fleming wrinkled his nose in repugnance and exclaimed, "Well, I, for one, absolutely refuse to submerge my body in *that*!"

Bingley nodded in agreement. "Ugh! Is that unpleasant odour actually emanating from the water?" He bent his head to take a wary sniff beneath his clammy armpit.

Colonel Fitzwilliam told the two youngest men not to be so fastidious and turned to Darcy. "I do not believe this pond has been tended since we used to swim here years ago, cousin. Nevertheless, are you game?"

"Are you daring me, Richard?"

"Last one in is both a chicken and a rotten egg; and no, I do not know which came first, so do not bother to ask."

The others watched in amazement and disgust as the cousins quickly divested themselves of hats, cravats, coats, waistcoats, and riding boots in preparation for a plunge into Pemberley's polluted pond.

The meticulous Fitzwilliam Darcy ensured each and every piece of his clothing was neatly folded – or it may simply have been a delaying tactic – so Richard Fitzwilliam was the first to disrobe down to shirt and breeches. The Colonel dashed toward a small, decrepit wooden pier that extended from the bank several yards into and over the murky water hole. The rickety boards creaked and groaned under his weight as he ran; and with a shout and a running leap, he cannonballed into the middle of the pond. When he surfaced, green slime oozed down his head and dripped back into the lake. He grinned and slicked back his sandy hair while he treaded water. His three companions stood at the water's edge, arms akimbo, and shook their heads.

"I always knew Fitz was a slimy fellow. Absolute pond scum!"

"Slimeball!"

"Scumbucket!"

Colonel Fitzwilliam paddled toward the others and said, "So happy to be of service to you by way of providing such am*ooze*ment. I admit this pool could use a good dredging, but you fellows could use a good … drenching!" He launched a dousing spray of water toward Bingley and Fleming and lunged for his cousin. Darcy realized what Fitz was up to just a moment too late; the hand that clutched his ankle suddenly jerked the young man off balance; and, with an ungentlemanly oath, Pemberley's distinguished heir was yanked into the muck.

The friends on shore were surprised when Darcy proceeded to the deeper middle instead of rejoining them on clean, dry land. Their algae-covered host shouted to them, "Come, you two blokes. I must have you swim. I hate to see you standing about on the bank in that stupid manner. You had much better swim."

Colonel Fitz added, "For wat-er you waiting? Just jump in, you rotten-egg chickens."

Bingley and Fleming looked at one another, shrugged their shoulders, and stripped down as far as propriety dared. If the slime-surfaced water met with the persnickety standards of Fitzwilliam Darcy, then it should certainly be acceptable to them. They raced to the dock and enthusiastically launched themselves into the scummy pond. They surfaced, spitting and sputtering, and pointed and laughed at the goop and gunk adhered to each other's hair and linen shirts. Ellis Fleming started to fuss again about appearing as a slimy and foul-smelling dishrag in front of Darcy's siblings. Bingley assured him it would not be a problem; but he suddenly stopped and cried out in alarm, "Bloody hell! What was that?" Bingley frantically tried to see, with wide, panicky eyes, below the lime-green surface. "Good God, Fleming! Something vile just latched onto my foot!"

Fleming floated on his back in a clear patch of water and calmly said, "Probably just vile Fitz again, kicking up a lark."

"No. Fitzwilliam and Darcy are on the other side, wisely climbing out of this godforsaken hole."

"Then probably just vile leeches feasting on your blood and sucking you dry."

"Very funny, Mr. Phlegm-ing."

"Well, Bingley, duck underwater and detach the nefarious sucker."

"Swim underwater in this turbid … phlegm? Do not hold your breath, Fleming. Fiend seize it! There it is again!" Bingley began to thrash about and pant. "I am not staying another second in this foul murky soup! Who knows what sinister denizens of the deep reside beneath this scum!" He splashed toward the shore, slipped and slid in the mud, and scrambled up the bank to safety with an anxious Ellis Fleming close on his heels. Firmly entwined around Bingley's right ankle and trailing behind were several strands of slimy aquatic grass.

The friends spent a few moments drying themselves out in the sun and ribbing Bingley, who insisted he quite easily might have drowned. The four then donned their boots, gathered their belongings and mounts, and squished and squelched their way, on foot, the short distance toward the manor. Two stable boys met them at the edge of the meadow and took the horses. With algae-tinted hair and clinging, revealing shirts and breeches, the sodden, malodorous gentlemen continued across the lawn, on a direct trajectory to four genteel and unsuspecting young ladies.

The gentlemen, for they were still worthy of that distinction even though they did not appear to deserve it at that moment, strode onward, four abreast, and continued to tease Bingley about his hair-raising encounter. The victim, an easy-going chap, took it all in stride. Fleming suggested they should search the shelves of Pemberley's library for information on plant life so they could identify the lank specimen from the abyss that had latched onto their friend.

Darcy's smirk belied his serious tone when he said, "I do not believe we would succeed in finding such books, for our family has not recently botany."

Colonel Fitzwilliam added, "That is a shame, for Bingley will be unable to weed 'em and reap. Fortunately, our friend has his feet firmly planted on the ground and, like a mushroom, he is a fungi."

The good-natured Charles Bingley shot back, "Fitz, unlike you, grass grows up; and with fronds like you, who needs anemones. I think you should make like a tree and leave."

"Oh, for pity's sake," groaned Ellis Fleming, "enough already!"

"Yes," Darcy agreed. "Incorrigible punsters should never be incorriged."

"Darcy, I swear you are behaving just as badly as Fitz and Bingley today. You are, you know, quite a different fellow in public settings, always so perfect and proper and notoriously picksome, with a stiff upper lip and all. I am still trying to recover from the awful shock of seeing you in your current unkempt state. I sincerely hope we can all avoid detection until we have had an opportunity to put our appearances to rights. It would simply not do to be observed as we are now."

From behind a seven-foot neatly trimmed hedgerow, four very elegant and pretty young women suddenly appeared before the four creatures from the green lagoon. The ladies had their backs to the men while they searched the bushes for the puppies and did not initially notice the swamp savages.

"Bloody hell! Look," whispered Richard Fitzwilliam as he grabbed his cousin's arm to halt forward momentum and pointed in the direction of the females.

Darcy glanced toward the hedge and the colour drained from his face. Nonplussed, he frantically swung his head around looking for a place to hide but saw no options for concealment and was brought to point non plus. "Oh God," he groaned. "They cannot *possibly* be allowed to see us like this," he hissed, "and who *are* those ladies with my sisters?"

The other two men froze in their tracks and Charles Bingley muttered out of the side of his mouth to Ellis Fleming, "Perhaps if we stand absolutely still, they will not even notice us."

"Bingley, sometimes you are as thick as two short planks. We are obviously quite highly visible out here in the middle of the lawn, I foresee no possible way to salvage this unacceptable encounter and my chance of making a good first impression is now certainly dashed." Fleming spoke in a quiet undertone, not wanting to draw the ladies' attention.

"By golly, your mention of pieces of wood and 'dashed' has just given me an excellent idea, Fleming. I shall gather some twigs, toss them behind the bushes and while the ladies investigate the sound, we shall all make a mad dash for cover."

Fleming looked at Charles Bingley as if he had grown a second head. "*Mad* is right, my friend; for you are certainly as mad as a March hare. Egad, man, I have always suspected you were dicked in the nob!"

Bingley picked up two projectiles and quite precisely lobbed them over the hedge. To his friend's amazement, the ruse actually worked, for the young women disappeared behind the bushes. Fleming hissed and frantically gestured, "Psst, Darcy! Fitz! Make haste! Bingley has created a diversion so we can run and hide. Come, let us remove ourselves from this horrible hobble."

Bemused Fitzwilliam Darcy and befuddled Richard Fitzwilliam stood momentarily rooted to the spot and looked at their friends in bewilderment. Unfortunately, a moment was all Dust Bunny and Pug-Nacious needed to each snatch up one of the sticks and bound toward Darcy, overjoyed to welcome him home and to play fetch with the toys that had fallen from the sky. This action, of course, alerted the ladies to the fact they had unexpected company.

PART II

A Mad Derbyshire Cat
or
Northern Angered Tabby

A tribute to Austen's *Northanger Abbey*

Chapter I

"I Have a Bone of Contention to Pick With You!"

The first to retrace her steps from behind the tall hedge, Miss Georgiana Darcy was curious to determine why Dust Bunny and Pug-Nacious had so suddenly bolted. Her eyes followed their pell-mell progress across the manicured lawn until four pairs of tall leather boots arrested both her vision and the puppies' motion. As she glanced further upward, Miss Darcy saw a most incredulous and alarming blot on the landscape. She gave a little squeal, the colour drained from her face, and she lost her grip on the parasol and very nearly on reality. In spite of her angst, Georgiana stubbornly refused to give in to a missish swoon; instead she muttered an unladylike oath and quickly turned around to prevent the other three females from witnessing the humiliating and scandalous spectacle.

Miss Darcy was too late. When the elder Miss Bennet re-emerged, her gaze immediately came to rest on four damp and raffish ruffians frozen in front of her. "Good Lord in heaven," she gasped and immediately lowered her eyes. A furtive second glance verified the wild green-tinged rogues were, indeed, not a figment of her imagination. There they stood, not moving one obviously well-toned muscle. Jane clamped down on her rising panic; and, face flooded with colour, she spun around to protect the two younger ladies from observing the jaw-dropping sight.

Miss Bennet was too late. Her sister gasped and blushed. To Elizabeth's utter amazement, four handsome, earthy specimens of masculinity stood immobile on the lawn before her very appreciative eyes. *My goodness! Perhaps the crass truly is always greener on the other side of the hedge.* She was, of course, properly embarrassed; just the same, Elizabeth was also mesmerized by the way their revealing clothing clung quite indecently to rather impressive bodies. She knew it was wrong to stare; still, her only familiarity with the male form came from changing her baby brother's nappies and from artwork and statuary. Although the specimens in front of her were as inanimate as statues, they were actual flesh and red-blooded full-grown men. She only looked, therefore, for purely educational purposes. Elizabeth did, however, have the presence of mind to try and shield the youngest member of their party from the scandalous exhibition; and she quickly turned to give a warning.

Miss Elizabeth was too late. Miss Anna stepped out from behind the massive hedge and wondered why the others had either grown pale or coloured up so quickly. A bizarre image caught her notice; she screamed, swooned and would have fallen had Miss Elizabeth not been instantly at her side. Anna had recently finished reading a Viking novel that caused her vivid imagination to run wild, so she thought the barbarians on the lawn had come to plunder and pillage Pemberley and perhaps to ravish young maidens. When the youngest Darcy regained consciousness, Georgiana whispered in her ear; and Anna's reaction turned to chagrin when it was revealed she was actually well acquainted with three of the four brutes. She narrowed her eyes at the low-life hooligans across the way; and the awful truth was confirmed, for there stood the impeccable brother she had earlier boasted about to the Misses Bennet. For the first time ever, Fitzwilliam was shamefully scruffy, wretchedly rumpled, and most inappropriately attired for polite company. Her cousin Richard, the amiable Mr. Bingley, and another young fellow were in no better condition. Anna was miffed because her dear new friends were exposed to such impropriety on Pemberley property.

Dust Bunny and Pug-Nacious sat in front of their hero, their tiny tails and ears twitched whilst they waited for Darcy to play fetch. The puppies soon lost interest in being totally ignored, dropped the sticks, and bounded off in search of adventure. Fitzwilliam Darcy, still rooted to the spot, was absolutely horrified and mortified; and he knew there would be the devil to pay for his reckless actions. Nevertheless, he began to sheepishly speak, "Georgiana … Anna … "

Georgiana abruptly overrode him. Although the young lady was neither timid nor reserved, she usually projected a very gentle and genteel mien; however, her rather infamous temper, once provoked, was both fearsome and fierce. She snatched up her parasol, marched toward the delinquents, stopped in front of her elder sibling, tapped her foot, and glared. Miss Darcy's blue eyes flashed as she poked her brother in the chest with the point of her folded bumbershoot and launched a tirade.

"Fitzwilliam Darcy! Do you, by chance, have a maggot in that bacon-brained head of yours? How *dare* you arrive at our home so indecently attired? You must certainly be touched in the upper works to display such blatant disregard for propriety. You have incontrovertibly disgraced our family in front of my new friends while making a cake of yourself. I swear you have more hair than wit; and speaking of hair, I wonder what cork-brained whim resulted in this smelly green slime you are all sporting so prominently. Whatever the foul substance is, it must have seeped through your thick skull and addled your feeble mind."

The victim winced at the warranted criticism and tried to raise his hands in supplication, but they were filled with hat, riding crop, wrinkled cravat, coat, and waistcoat. Darcy turned to his cousin for moral support before attempting an explanation. Georgiana noticed the fleeting look between the two and became suspicious. She shifted her glare, and her ire, to her cousin. "Richard! I might have guessed. You, Colonel Mud-stuffin must be behind this … this … *this!*"

The army officer's military training instinctively kicked in. He stood at attention under her glower and eloquently gave his self-justifying defense. "*He* thought of it first, Georgie," accused the soldier as he twitched his head toward Darcy.

Georgiana continued to seethe and fume. "Richard Fitzwilliam! I very much doubt that *thought* played any part whatsoever in whatever rowdiness you *boys* have been involved in. Shame on you!" She turned her scorn on a new victim, pointing her frilly pink weapon at him. "And you, Mr. Bingley! I would have expected better of you, sir."

Charles Bingley hung his head in shame. In doing so, he caught sight of his form-hugging shirt and inexpressibles. The coat and waistcoat he had earlier flung off with wild abandon were quickly utilized to shield his torso from further scrutiny by the wide-eyed, innocent young women.

Ellis Fleming was entirely miserable, for he had so wanted to favourably impress Darcy's esteemed family. He might have been somewhat mollified, however, to know his sculpted body and handsome face had actually already made quite a fine impression on at least one of the ladies.

Jane Bennet, whose face was still flushed, had modestly dropped her gaze to the ground; and she had endeavoured not to glance up again. Miss Bennet spared a quick sideways glimpse at her sister and caught Elizabeth staring, chest level, at one of the men. "Lizzy," she hissed, "lower your gaze!" Miss Elizabeth obediently lowered her eyes, but not to her sister's satisfaction. When Jane peeked at her once more, she scolded, "Lizzy, not *there*! I meant lower your gaze to the ground!"

During Georgiana's dressing-down of her brother, Elizabeth was surprised to discover the male she had been ogling was, in fact, the always proper and impeccable Darcy heir. He certainly seemed far removed from the perfect specimen described by his youngest sister and more closely resembled a very good-looking barbaric buffoon; therefore, further observation was definitely warranted.

Fitzwilliam Darcy gradually regained his dignity and decided to also gain control of the situation. Determined to ignore the fact he and his companions were indecently attired, he squared his broad shoulders and stood proud and tall. Darcy noticed this slight movement again drew the attention of the pretty brunette's fine eyes, but it could not be helped. "Fleming, please allow me to introduce my charming sisters to you." He gestured with his riding crop and grimaced slightly as he said, "This dear, sweet, dulcet-toned gentlelady is Miss Georgiana Darcy." He gave them time to bow and curtsey before he beckoned his youngest sibling and continued. "And here is Miss Anna Darcy. Ladies, this is Mr. Ellis Fleming from farther north in Derbyshire. He and I enjoyed many a friendly rivalry on opposing sides of chess, debating, and fencing matches at Cambridge."

The visitor bowed again and said, "It is a pleasure to make your acquaintance, Miss Darcy and Miss Anna. Please accept my apologies for not gracing your presence with the decorum it deserves. We had truly expected to have ample opportunity to make ourselves presentable before being in such refined company."

Miss Darcy blushed, smiled, and responded sweetly, "Mr. Fleming, I am heartily convinced the fault was in no way yours." Again Georgiana looked daggers at her brother, thus providing her eyes a place to rest other than the direction to which they were involuntarily drawn, namely Fleming's tantalizing indigo eyes, thick, feathery black hair, exposed neck, and clinging shirt that hugged broad shoulders, muscled arms and chest. "Welcome to Pemberley. I hope you will enjoy your stay, sir. Gentlemen, please meet our delightful new friends, Miss Jane Bennet and her sister, Miss Elizabeth, who are visiting from Hertfordshire with their aunt, a dear friend of Mrs. Reynolds, our housekeeper."

Georgiana moved along the row of malodorous young men as she made each of them known to the Misses Bennet. Between each presentation, while those being introduced bowed, curtsied, and made polite small talk, she daintily took a whiff of her perfumed handkerchief to counteract the dank, fusty odour that permeated the air surrounding the gents. When she lastly introduced her brother, Miss Darcy emphasized the fact he had not been expected home any sooner than the evening. Georgiana shot her elder sibling an ominous look that unmistakably implied he was definitely not welcome in his present deplorable state. In his own defense, Darcy tersely explained he had received an express from their parents urging him to hasten the arrival of his party.

Indeed, whenever duty called them away from home, George and Lady Anne Darcy did not like to leave their two beloved daughters without the caring protection of their elder brother, albeit Georgiana was of age and quite capable of running the estate for a few days. Even though Mr. and Mrs. Reynolds were totally dependable and Pemberley had an excellent steward in Hugh Wickham, George Darcy was always more at ease when the strong, decisive heir was available to take over the reins in his absence.

The heir was predictably strong and decisive that very afternoon; and the strong odour, Fitzwilliam Darcy decided, would be washed away just as soon as enough hot water for four baths could be made available. He spoke on behalf of the other gentlemen when he said, "Please pardon us, ladies. We must repair to the manor and attempt to, uh, repair our appearances and, hopefully, our sullied reputations. We trust the damage is not irreparable." He bowed, as did the other fellows, and they made their way across the lawn with as much dignity as they could muster.

Charles Bingley's sullied reputation suffered further defilement when his cravat slipped from his bundle of clothing, wafted toward his boot, and wrapped itself around his ankle. As Bingley walked, the strip of white linen trailed through the grass, unnoticed by the men.

The four young ladies turned to watch the departure and one after another began to giggle. The menfolk immediately stiffened upon hearing the tittering but refused to be cowed by the offensive sound. They raised proud chins and strode toward the house without a backward glance. They proceeded without incident until Bingley's vile neckcloth became entangled around his other foot, which caused him to stumble. Without so much as a glance or stutter in his step, Colonel Fitzwilliam grabbed the chap's arm to steady him and muttered, "Shake a leg, Bingley." The foursome stepped up the pace and could not reach the safety of Darcy's home quickly enough.

Warm water, scented soaps, and crisp, clean clothing did much to restore the four gentlemen to rights. They did not give any thought to the number of servants sent scampering to see to their needs. Indeed, many heavy kettles of water had to be heated and lugged up flights of stairs by overworked chambermaids. Then their invaluable valets had to be summoned to assist with hair, barbering, and attire. Most employers tended to take such service for granted; however, these mannerly men were at least considerate enough to thank the workers for their efforts.

Darcy, Fitzwilliam, Bingley, and Fleming regrouped to lick their wounds and quaff alcoholic beverages in Pemberley's delightfully well stocked library, which benefitted from the work of many generations. The first three gents wholeheartedly agreed Georgiana could be an out-and-out hellcat. However, Fleming defended the lady, saying, "She was quite rightfully provoked by our unseemly appearance and was merely being protective of her younger sister and new friends. I greatly admire Miss Darcy's pluck."

Bingley sniggered and said, "Hah! Pluck reminds me of a chicken, which is just how I felt while being berated by her. I say, Darcy, your sister is absolutely lovely. All the same, if she ever eventually sets her cap at someone, I shall undoubtedly pity the poor chap when she is in high dudgeon. Miss Darcy can definitely raise a breeze. That said, she cannot hold a candle to my sister Caroline for being a harridan."

Darcy apologized on his sister's behalf and added, "Georgiana is a dear girl, though I must admit she has frightened off an alarming number of eligible suitors lately. Nevertheless, those blokes ultimately proved unworthy by not possessing sufficient intestinal fortitude to withstand a bit of temper from a mere chit. Regardless, I rather doubt she will end up as a tabby. Georgie's dowry, accomplishments, and beauty ensure her eventual marriage. Most importantly, she is a wonderful young lady; and I do not say so only because she is my sister. Truthfully, she is a treasure."

"Oh, yes, indeed, Miss Darcy is absolute perfection," Ellis Fleming was quick to agree.

The other three gentlemen shared amused looks; then Charles Bingley enthusiastically asked, "Speaking of absolute perfection, did any of you happen to notice her two new acquaintances?"

Fleming snorted, Darcy raised his brows, and Colonel Fitzwilliam replied, "We *have* eyes, Bingley; so how could we possibly not notice when so much beauty was before us? The Bennet ladies are undoubtedly diamonds of the first water, and I cannot believe I made such a complete mull of meeting them. I would have cut a much finer figure in my red coat than in the green slime I wore today, and you chaps would have been quite invisible to the ladies had I been wearing regimentals."

Darcy rolled his eyes and said, "I rather imagine invisibility would have been preferable over our earlier indecorous appearances. Be that as it may, I happen to know for a fact that I was quite embarrassingly visible to the pretty brunette with the sparkling, intelligent eyes. Miss Elizabeth is obviously not shy," Darcy said with a smirk. Although he grinned, Fitzwilliam Darcy silently reproached himself for the lapse in judgment that had resulted in such an improper encounter with members of the opposite sex. Anything less than perfection was unacceptable to the idealist, and he usually attempted to avoid situations in which he might appear to be flawed. Darcy felt the need to be above criticism; and although he would not admit it, Georgiana's public censure had wounded him. He was quite resolved to do everything in his power to project the image of a perfect gentleman if ever again in the company of his sisters' new friends.

Charles Bingley interrupted Darcy's self-castigation when he said, "Miss Elizabeth may not be shy; however, her angelic sister is perfectly proper and demure."

"And once again, Bingley, you are making a claim based upon a mere moment's observation. Are you such an exceptional judge of character your first impression cannot be mistaken?"

"You saw Miss Bennet, Darcy; she is the most exquisite creature, and I think ... "

A knock upon the library door was answered by Darcy's command to enter. A footman announced, "Mr. George Wickham to see you, sir." Smiles lit up the faces of the four friends as the visitor appeared in the doorway.

"George! Come in, come in, you mangy scoundrel," Darcy invited. "Gentlemen, look what foul vermin the accursed cat dragged into the house."

With a swagger and a wide grin, Wickham entered the room and exclaimed, "Cripes, man! How could you thus pollute the shades of our beloved Pemberley with the likes of this trio of depraved reprobates?"

"Yes, sorry, old chap. As the estate's future steward, I know you only have its best interests at heart. So we must see about having such unworthy degenerates evicted immediately from these hallowed halls," Darcy bantered. Greetings and more teasing ensued as the quintet of comrades settled into the easy friendship of many years' standing.

At five and twenty, the same age as Bingley and Fleming, the devilishly handsome George was the son of Pemberley's steward, Hugh Wickham, a widower. He was also George Darcy's godchild and namesake and had the privilege of being educated alongside the other occupants of the room. They had all attended Cambridge for one overlapping term and became quite a formidable coterie. Wickham was being trained by his father to take over the reins as Pemberley's steward as soon as the elder relinquished the position later that same year after decades of service. Like his parent, the young man was of an honest and hard-working character; however, unlike his father, the son was a skirt-chasing roué.

"Would any of you chaps happen to know the identity of two gorgeous females, a blonde and a brunette? I noticed them stepping into a carriage out front over an hour ago and have been speculating on the purpose of their visit. I suppose they must be the latest conquests of two of you fortunate, although undeserving, blokes."

Richard Fitzwilliam responded, "By coincidence, we were just discussing those very same *gentleladies* when your unwelcome carcass most rudely imposed itself upon our very refined presence here, Wickham. That the ladies have left already is unfortunate news, indeed. I had planned to impress them with my much-improved appearance before they departed."

"Still making a valiant effort to live up to your 'stud-muffin' reputation, I see, Colonel Fitz. It must be quite an arduous struggle for you, but some things never change. Regardless, have you purposely evaded answering my query about the females? Shame, shame, you must share the wealth, you know, gentlemen. I assume the *ladies* were here because your parents are not, Darce."

Pemberley's heir shot out of his chair and glowered. "You know, one must never assume, George. And you are both disgustingly crude and very wide of the mark, my friend. Those genteel ladies are merely newly formed acquaintances of my dear sisters."

"My apologies, then. But are these women of virtue, whom you seem reluctant to name, returning any time soon, perchance?"

Darcy sat back down, crossed his legs, flicked a nonexistent speck of lint from his knee, and nonchalantly replied, "I really have no idea whatsoever, Wickham; and honestly, I do not care a groat."

Edward Gardiner's carriage had returned to Pemberley for his wife and nieces shortly after the disastrous encounter on the lawn. While their aunt and uncle bade farewell to Mrs. Reynolds, Jane and Elizabeth took leave of their new friends. Georgiana and Anna whispered profuse apologies again and were relieved to receive assurances the incident had not tainted the visit. The four young ladies made promises to correspond faithfully and hoped to possibly meet in the near future in London, should their visits ever coincide. The Bennets renewed their invitation for the Darcy family to visit Longbourn the next time they found themselves in Hertfordshire.

On the nearly five-mile ride between Pemberley and Lambton, the sisters enthusiastically praised Georgiana, Anna, and their family's grand estate. Jane gushed, "Oh Uncle, I know your fondness for little dogs, so I must tell you we saw Miss Darcy's two adorable puppies, a Maltese and a Pug."

Mr. Gardiner smiled and said, "Well, Jane, I daresay those fortunate pets, with such a rich mistress, are often sitting in the lap of luxury."

"Now, Uncle, I happen to be aware that even your cat sleeps on a fluffy, down-filled pillow."

"Yes, we have always had a soft spot for Mrs. Sourpuss."

Elizabeth laughed appreciatively and then scolded Jane for mentioning the animals before alluding to the gentlemen they had encountered. She then told the Gardiners they had met the Darcy heir, his army-officer cousin, and two of his friends. Lizzy smiled and arched a brow as she added, "They were all very attractive fellows, were they not, Jane? Although the gents were, perhaps, a little rough around the hedges and a little less than formally attired."

The two young ladies blushed and suppressed giggles whenever they looked at one another for the remainder of the trip to the inn; their aunt and uncle rolled their eyes and grinned at their nieces' baffling and rather uncharacteristic giddiness.

The Darcy sisters wished desperately to atone for the embarrassment the Bennets had suffered at Pemberley, so a hastily jotted note was quickly dispatched to the inn at Lambton inviting and imploring Jane and Elizabeth to agree to return the next day. As their relatives had plans to visit an elderly cousin of Mrs. Gardiner, the recipients gladly sent their acceptance with the messenger and eagerly anticipated spending another pleasant day with Georgiana and Anna at their impressive estate.

So it was that the modest Gardiner carriage pulled up to the magnificent manor's front entry for the second time in as many days. Jane and Elizabeth alit and waved goodbye to their aunt and uncle while Miss Darcy and Miss Anna patiently waited on the steps and their older brother surreptitiously watched from between the curtains of an upstairs hallway window.

"Jane, Elizabeth, welcome back. We are very happy you agreed to return, and Anna and I apologize again for the awkward situation that occurred here yesterday. Please be assured the debacle was the exception rather than the rule at Pemberley, and we shall have a perfect time today to make amends for the fiasco."

Miss Anna added, "Yes, the sun is shining; and we have planned a nice ride around the park followed by refreshments. Perhaps we shall also have an opportunity to play the pianoforte for one another, if time permits. Does this agenda meet with your approval? If not, we can alter it to accommodate whatever activities you would prefer in order to make your stay here more enjoyable."

Elizabeth laughed with delight and said, "Georgiana and Anna, please relax. Jane and I are not, whatsoever, upset over the previous afternoon's … hmm … let us frivolously refer to it as entertainment henceforth, rather than fiasco. There may have been a modicum of embarrassment at the onset; still and all, we are resilient women and have recovered quickly. So you must promise to not think again on the incident."

Jane agreed, "Oh, yes, please do not worry yourselves any further on our account. We are very happy to be here again and shall derive pleasure in whatever occupations and pursuits you have scheduled for our day together."

The four linked arms and made their way to the sitting room, where they chatted and sipped tea while the landau was made ready for their afternoon outing. As Elizabeth brought the delicate teacup to her lips, a mysterious noise erupted from the direction of an overturned sewing basket on the floor next to her chair. She glanced toward the contents but was only able to distinguish spools of embroidery thread.

Purr, whistle, snuffle.

Her eyebrows lifted, her eyes widened, and she looked to her sister as if to ask whether she had also heard the peculiar sound.

"Lizzy, are you well?"

Purr, whistle, snuffle.

Elizabeth gracefully lowered the teacup to its saucer, smiled serenely, and calmly replied, "Yes, Jane, thank you. I am fine."

Purr, whistle, snuffle.

On pins and needles with curiosity, Elizabeth placed her cup and saucer on a nearby table and then dropped her napkin as close to the noise as possible without being too obvious. "Oh, how clumsy of me," she said. A footman started to cross the floor to assist, but she waved him away. The intrepid Lizzy Bennet crouched down beside the basket, peered inside, and inched her hand toward the back, hoping to discover the origin of the curious little sounds no one else seemed able to hear.

Snort, puff, grunt!

"Ouch! Eeek!" Lizzy promptly withdrew her hand and stood up with a startled, bewildered look on her face.

"Elizabeth!" Georgiana exclaimed and came swiftly to her guest's side. "Whatever happened? Have you pricked your poor finger on a needle in my sewing basket?"

"I am uncertain. Does your pincushion happen to purr, whistle, snuffle, snort, puff and grunt?"

Miss Anna rushed forward. "Oh, thank you, Elizabeth! You have found Barbara Thorne. I spent most of the morning searching for her, but ... Oh, I am sorry. Did she startle you? Barb is quite harmless, really. Does your hand require attention? Please allow me to ring for assistance." The flustered girl began to turn away.

Elizabeth stopped Anna with a gentle touch on her arm and insisted she was fine. "Truly, my friend, I was merely startled."

Jane joined them and looked at her sister with protective concern. "Lizzy, are you certain you have not been injured?"

"I am perfectly fine, Jane; and if I am not mistaken, your solicitude should be for a prickly little hedgehog by the name of Barbara Thorne, who is most likely very upset and frightened by now."

Miss Anna retrieved a small ball of quills from the basket, held it gently in her hands and cooed soothingly to the little creature. She then excused herself to return Barb to its proper confinement in her bedchamber.

Georgiana's apology for Elizabeth's distress was dismissed as unnecessary. Just as Anna returned, a footman informed them the landau was ready and waiting. While the ladies donned their bonnets in preparation for the excursion, Fitzwilliam Darcy made an appearance that was remarkably different than the one a day prior on the lawn. The striking young man bowed elegantly and politely inquired about the ladies' health and plans for the afternoon. He was immaculately attired in a soft white lawn shirt and cravat, tan striped waistcoat, nut-brown tailcoat, Nankeen breeches, and tall Hessian boots. Elizabeth was relieved to discover his hair was not actually green-tinged but was a rather alluring rich chocolate colour with thick tousled curls. *So, here, obviously, is the dignified, impeccably dressed brother Anna had so loyally praised yesterday.* Lizzy Bennet thought he just might not be such a barbaric buffoon after all; just the same, she soon came to realize the hooligan had actually been just as appealing as the formally proper, well-groomed, conventional gentleman who stiffly stood before her.

For his part, Darcy simply wanted to make a better impression than he had on their initial meeting; so he had donned his reserved public persona. As his father had taught him, a gentleman must not show his emotions; so Darcy's handsome but unreadable face displayed total indifference, never allowing an iota of his attraction to the younger Bennet sister to be detected. He wished the ladies a pleasant afternoon and informed his sisters that he and his party were going riding and would return to the house later in the afternoon. Should he be needed for any reason afterward, they would most likely be found in the billiard room. Once that succinct information was imparted, Darcy bowed very properly and took his leave.

The ladies insisted the landau's hoods remain folded down as they started their jaunt around the expansive park. Ninety minutes later, they returned to the house with rosy, laughing faces. A light repast of cold meats, bread, cheese, and fruit was enjoyed al fresco at a canopied table on the garden terrace. The two sets of siblings then strolled toward the stables to see a litter of kittens born several weeks previously. The feral striped mother cat flattened her ears and growled if anyone came too close to the babies, so the young ladies left the felines alone and walked in the direction of the orangery.

Unbeknownst to them, Rex and Regina, George Darcy's two rambunctious Dalmatians, had also entered the barn, perilously close to the open stall where the cats had taken up residence. The outraged tabby arched her back, hissed a warning, and then attacked, which caused the spotted dogs to run away with tails between their legs. They raced pell-mell toward the winter-garden glasshouse on a direct collision course with the four women, who were by then headed back to the manor. When Miss Anna saw the Dalmatians barreling toward them, she warned the others. "Stand absolutely still, and the dogs will swerve away from us. Do not move until they have passed." The young lady spoke from first-hand experience; she had once tried, unsuccessfully, to dodge the boisterous dogs.

Miss Darcy and Elizabeth heeded Anna's advice. However, Jane was on the other end; she panicked and took a few steps to her left just as Rex veered off to his right. They collided, and Jane was knocked down and, in fact, knocked out. The impact knocked Miss Bennet's shoe off her foot and sent it sailing through the air. Rex was instantly miserable, for he had not intended to hurt the poor lady; so, as his way of apologizing, he licked her face as she lay unconscious.

Meanwhile, Mrs. Reynolds, who was on a different route to the orangery, noticed an unexpected object on its glass roof. She stopped, with fists planted on hips, and stared upward. As Georgiana ran in her direction, the housekeeper began to question her. "Miss Darcy, do you have any notion why a woman's shoe is up there or how it arrived at such a mysterious final resting place?" She pointed to the enigma but immediately became alarmed by the distressed look on the dear girl's face.

"Oh, Mrs. Reynolds, it is in every way horrible. Please do not mention final resting place, for Miss Bennet is gravely injured and comatose. You must help us. Please make haste!"

Elizabeth knelt at Jane's side as her sister began to groan. "Please, Jane, awaken. Tell me you are going to be fine. Wake up, my darling sister, please. Be well, I pray."

Panic-stricken, Jane opened her eyes and cried, "Oh, Lizzy, I fear I am partially paralyzed. The entire left side of my face is stiff and numb." Tears filled Jane's eyes as she clasped her sister's hand.

Lizzy at once realized what had caused the 'paralysis;' and, partly in reaction to shock but also due to the humour in the situation, she began to chuckle. When Mrs. Reynolds arrived with Georgiana, she found a very giddy Miss Elizabeth and an outraged Miss Bennet. The latter sat up, glared at her sister, and said, "Not funny, Lizzy! My goodness, was I unconscious long enough for dog slobber to actually dry up on my face like that? Oh, do stop laughing, Lizzy! My head feels funny and my funny bone hurts."

The housekeeper, Georgiana, and Miss Anna were relieved Miss Bennet quickly recovered from the impact with the dog and the ground. Still and all, Mrs. Reynolds insisted they immediately return to the house so she could attend the lady's injured elbow.

Miss Darcy felt it necessary to apologize, yet again, to the Bennets for another hair-raising chapter in what seemed to be a savage saga of dastardly Darcy family failings and faux pas. Once more, the visitors made light of the episode. Elizabeth said, "I am very thankful Jane's injuries were no more serious than a scraped arm. Just the same, I cannot help but find the whole incident rather *humerus*." That statement earned Lizzy another indignant glare from her elder sibling.

In the billiard room, Darcy, Colonel Fitzwilliam, Bingley, and Fleming took turns shooting the colourful ivory balls across the green baize of the table that dominated the room. Darcy's foxhounds, Romulus and Remus, were curled up and dozing beneath; and each time the balls clacked above them, the dogs raised their heads.

As the Colonel prepared to take a shot, he addressed his cousin. "Will the lovely Bennet sisters be joining us for dinner?"

"When I last saw the ladies several hours ago, Georgiana had not made mention of it, so I am uncertain."

Bingley, who had been leaning against the wall, pushed himself off and exclaimed, "Darcy, do you mean to tell me now that the exquisite Miss Jane Bennet has been here all this afternoon?"

"I do not mean to tell you now, Bingley; for you have just already gained that knowledge."

"But, blast it, you had concealed their presence from me!"

"I did not conceal the fact. I just never thought to mention it."

"Really, Darcy, I thought I could count on your assistance; but with friends like you … "

"Yes, yes, I know … who needs anemones. All the same, perhaps I was remiss, and I apologize."

"Then I have your approval to become better acquainted with Miss Bennet?"

"Good God, Bingley," interrupted Fleming. "Do you actually *need* Darcy's approval for such a pursuit?"

The young man sheepishly replied, "Most certainly not! Nonetheless, I should like to know I have it all the same."

Fleming rolled his eyes and said, "Oh, just go and get to it, Bungley."

Bingley turned to one of the Darcy family's ever-present footmen and commanded, "Bring me my coat at once. Quickly, man!"

Ellis Fleming put away his cue stick, glanced at Darcy, and said, "I daresay Bingley is right. We should all do the gentlemanly thing and pay our respects to the fairer sex. It might be unseemly for the rest of us not to do so while biddable Bingley makes an appearance." Fleming did not seek assistance but pulled on his coat and hastily ran fingers through his feathery black hair.

"Yes, I do suppose it would be proper etiquette, my friend. However, that is the only reason I can think of for seeking out the young ladies." Darcy hurried to don his coat, straighten his cravat, and check his impeccable image in the mirror over the mantle. The two burly bucks tried to exit the room at the same instant, and their broad shoulders were momentarily jammed together in the doorway.

Colonel Fitzwilliam snickered and shook his head. His cousin and two friends were obviously attracted to women currently residing or visiting at Pemberley. There was no question which lady held Bingley's interest. Fleming had staunchly defended and praised Georgiana, and Darcy referred to Miss Elizabeth as 'the pretty brunette with the sparkling, intelligent eyes'. Richard Fitzwilliam was thankful they were not all attracted to the same Bennet sister; nevertheless, he thought it would be interesting to discover if any real attachments would be formed. He calmly slipped his coat on and followed the others, who were already out of sight down the hallway.

The gentlemen found the fair ladies in the drawing room, and Charles Bingley was dismayed to learn angelic Miss Bennet had suffered an injury. In his opinion, she was the picture of loveliness stretched out on the sofa. At her elbow a bandage was wound round the wound on the creamy white skin of her elegant arm. Bingley fawned over the young woman, praised her bravery, and tried to dance attendance on her; but, of course, Miss Elizabeth, Mrs. Reynolds, Miss Georgiana, Miss Anna, and a houseful of servants were also available to cater to her every wish, if she had any, which she did not, save for everyone to stop making such a fuss.

The ladies chatted enthusiastically about the possibility of meeting in London before long; and promises were exchanged that correspondence would flow freely between Derbyshire and Hertfordshire as well as their residences in London, for each family had a townhouse there. Three of the gentlemen in the room paid particular attention to the location of the Bennet residence and were pleased to learn it was in a fashionable section. Because the ladies all played the pianoforte, they made plans to purchase sheet music from the new Chappell & Co. shop on Bond Street. A lively conversation followed on the merits of their preferred composers. But when talk subsequently turned to shopping for fashions in the city, the men's eyes glazed over. They tuned out the female conversation and turned to a discussion about the Napoleonic War.

During a lull in the ladies' discourse, Miss Elizabeth surprised the gentlemen by joining their debate. She caused utter astonishment by speaking of the expensive military investment in the Lines of Torres

Vedras. Colonel Fitzwilliam was stunned any civilian, especially a woman, knew of the fortifications and fervently hoped the young lady was not a spy. Upon observing the men's shocked expressions, Elizabeth explained she had a very good friend who was a Lieutenant-Colonel, which caused Darcy to wonder just how intimate that fortunate friend might be. The military officer was still unsure whether or not Miss Elizabeth Bennet was involved in espionage and was furthermore quite upset at and disgusted with a certain loose-lipped Lieutenant-Colonel.

The gents were again amazed when the young lady held her own as they conversed on a number of topics ranging from the Berner Street hoax, to the Prince of Wales, and then to the Luddites. Miss Elizabeth spoke eloquently, intelligently, and always with wit and an enticing sparkle in her dark eyes. Bingley and Fleming were out of their league and had joined Miss Bennet, Miss Darcy, and Miss Anna on the other side of the room, pretending to be utterly fascinated by a debate on short sleeves versus long sleeves, with Fleming in total agreement with Miss Darcy and Bingley defending Miss Bennet's preference.

Just as the entire company started to discuss their favourite authors, Georgiana deflected another potential fiasco when her mother's Italian Greyhounds bounded into the room, hard on the heels of Anna's pet rabbit, Herr Stewart. Miss Darcy grabbed Geoffrey Canterbury Tail by the scruff of its neck and directed her brother to do the same with Chaucer Cantering Burybones. A harried servant rushed into the room and regained control of his recalcitrant charges, and Geoffrey and Chaucer were quickly marched out the door. Miss Anna captured the rabbit, Stew, and apologized for the ruckus while Miss Darcy flopped back in her chair and sighed. In Georgiana's opinion, her precious, prestigious Pemberley had suddenly gone to the dogs.

Georgiana noticed her brother staring at something, or someone, rather intently; and she became occupied in observing his surprising attention to Elizabeth. Though he displayed no outward sign of attraction, such as a smile, heightened colour, or, heaven forbid, animated speech, Georgiana saw in her brother's eyes the same affectionate look Fitzwilliam often bestowed upon family members; and she began to speculate. Miss Darcy was far from suspecting she was herself becoming an object of some interest in the eyes of one of her brother's strapping young friends.

Further contemplation was interrupted by the announcement Mr. and Mrs. Gardiner had arrived for their nieces. The couple declined when their party was invited to stay for dinner, as they had to make an early start the next day for their return journey to London. The Darcy siblings and Charles Bingley protested their departure most vehemently; the Gardiners were insistent, and the carriage soon drove away from Pemberley.

Part III

Influence & the Cut Direct
or
Persuade∫ Shun

A tribute to Austen's *Persuasion*

Chapter I

The Town's Population is Dense

Jane and Elizabeth spent several pleasurable days in London with their Aunt and Uncle Gardiner at Gracechurch Street. During that time, they paid a visit to their sister, Mary, who, at ten and five years of age, was attending a seminary for young ladies. Although the girl missed her family, she was perfectly content with her studies in the city and was becoming quite a proficient pianoforte performer. Mary was thrilled to spend time with her older siblings and laughed heartily when Lizzy related, with gestures and more than a little hyperbole, the series of bizarre events experienced at Pemberley. At that moment, somewhere in Derbyshire, four debonair gentlemen's ears must have been brightly burning, because Elizabeth Bennet spared no detail while reciting a particular chapter and verse.

The travelers eagerly returned to their idyllic country life at Longbourn and were welcomed with open arms by their parents and siblings. When the initial excitement of the reunion waned, Thomas Bennet informed his family should he be needed he could be found in his study with Jonathan Whitelaw, the estate's competent steward, for the next three-quarter hour. With a twinkle in his eye, he added, "Following our meeting, Whitelaw and I will be walking down to the stream to communicate with some fish."

Puzzled, his wife asked, "Thomas, exactly how are you going to communicate with fish?"

"I shall be dropping them a line, of course, my dear," he answered with an impish grin. Mr. Bennet then bestowed a loving peck upon his lady's cheek before leaving the room.

Mrs. Bennet shook her head and chuckled, "Teasing, teasing man! I fear I shall never learn, for I have been walking straight into your father's traps since the moment we first met. Still and all, entering into the parson's mousetrap with such a charming and caring man as Thomas Bennet has always been an especial ensnarement I shall never regret." The lady smiled and roused herself from a pleasant, private reverie. "Now, Jane and Lizzy, I shall just ring for Alice to take Robert to the nursery and for Martha to collect Kitty and Lydia for their lessons; and then we three shall have a nice long chat over some tea."

"Oh, Mama, can Robert not stay here with us? It seems ages since I have held him and look, the little poppet has already fallen asleep on my lap. Surely there is no need to disturb him." Elizabeth smiled down at her three-year old brother and kissed his forehead. Their mother gazed fondly at the two heads so close together, one a riot of chestnut ringlets and the other of strawberry-blonde curls. Jane, the eldest, and Robert, the youngest, were tow-headed and blue-eyed like her, while Lizzy, Mary, Catherine, and Lydia were brown-eyed brunettes like their father, although his hair was turning quite grey. Mrs. Bennet smiled as she remembered her husband once said that finally having a son was an heir-raising experience.

Longbourn's mistress rang for tea and also for Miss Martha Edwards, the children's governess, who curtsied and greeted the returned travelers before taking her charges in hand. As the three were about to leave the room, Lizzy asked, "Miss Edwards, has Lydia been living up to her nickname in our absence?"

The governess smiled and replied, "Oh, yes, indeed. Little Miss-Information recently told me geese do not mind fowl weather and find it just ducky. Miss Lydia, please repeat what you told me this morning about your pony."

At seven years of age, Lydia Bennet obviously followed in her father's footsteps and was a constant source of amusement to most of her family. Her dark eyes sparkled mischievously as she took great delight in responding, "I believe Miss Edwards is referring to the fact my pony has lately been giving me a lot of whoa."

Kitty, as the family called Catherine, was much more serious and missish at one and ten years; she rolled her eyes as the others laughed at Lydia's nonsense. In Kitty's opinion, her young sister should not have been allowed to run on in such a wild manner, as she was no longer the baby of the family.

Mrs. Hill, Longbourn's housekeeper, arrived with the rosewood tea caddy; Mrs. Bennet opened the ornate box with a tiny key that dangled from the chatelaine at her waist. A pot of the hot commodity was prepared, and the caddy was locked again and taken away by Mrs. Hill for safekeeping. When the two eldest sisters and their sleeping brother were alone with their mother, Mrs. Bennet said, "It is so pleasant to have you home again, my dears, for you have been greatly missed. I suppose I should prepare myself for eventually losing you both to charming young men. In the meantime, let us always make the most of our time together. So, tell me of your adventures in Derbyshire with my brother and sister-in-law and about your visit with our darling Mary in London, and then you shall hear of Hertfordshire's latest news."

Elizabeth carried the napping Robert to a sofa, gently transferred him, and placed a velvet cushion beneath his head. She then returned to her chair and explained, "I did not want to risk scalding him, which reminds me, Papa once said tea is very beneficial because boiling water raises your self-of-steam."

"Lizzy, for the life of me, I do not know who is the worst, you, Lydia, or your father," laughed Mrs. Bennet. "You are like three peas in a pod, in looks and in temperament. My goodness, speaking of legumes, do you remember the uproar when, at the dinner table, he told you to eat every bean and pea on your plate?"

Jane blushed and exclaimed, "Mother!"

Elizabeth groaned and changed the subject to their visit with Mary and their travels to and from Derbyshire. The 'encounter on the lawn', as the sisters referred to it, was entirely omitted from the narration about Pemberley.

Mrs. Bennet was glad her girls had new acquaintances whose family also owned a townhouse in London, for those friends might prove beneficial when she broached a rather delicate subject to Jane and Elizabeth; but she postponed it to relate bits and pieces of the happenings in and around Longbourn during their absence.

She spoke of the bout of gout suffered by Purvis Lodge's butler. The former army officer, Lieutenant Domo, had been wounded and left the rank and file of the military without being promoted to Major.

Then she told her daughters about the wedding between the young and pretty Miss Greedy and the ancient but very rich Mr. Gerry Atric and how Sir William Lucas kept saying their marriage was "capital, capital."

Lastly, they heard about the evening Miss Sylvana Forester became lost in the woods. "Yes, my dears, it was a horrible ordeal that stretched into the night and wee hours of the morning. A search party was organized to try and locate the poor young woman. There was quite a collection of helpers, you know, as the entire community was involved and desperate for her recovery. Well, your father sent out helpers from Longbourn to search in the dark and one of our young tenants, in particular, carried a torch for her. She was, of course, finally located; and I believe Miss Forester will soon become matched with our own Mr. Cresset, whose name, coincidentally, means torch."

Longbourn's sweet little heir, Robert Bennet, stirred; and the nursery maid was summoned. The boy kissed his mother's cheek, gave his sisters sloppy raspberries, and then readily took Alice's hand. He eagerly anticipated playing with his favourite toys and chattered happily to the maid as he skipped along at her side. The room's three remaining occupants smiled at the little chatterbox's retreating form.

Mrs. Bennet said, "Your father and I have been blessed with five lovely daughters and finally a heaven-sent son. It is our fondest wish you both have families of your own some time soon. We have already promised not to arrange marriages against your wishes. Nevertheless, because our own community suffers from a dearth of eligible young men, we have discussed the possibility of spending some time in London before long in order to broaden your sphere of potential suit … " Jane and Elizabeth interrupted with protests but were cut off by their mother. "Girls, you know better than to interrupt. Please, just listen for a moment; and be assured your father and I will not forcibly push you into the Marriage Mart. He and I long ago agreed we would be heartbroken should any of our offspring end up in a loveless marriage. Even so, you must agree it is time to start considering your futures. So Jane, please tell me of your concerns and wishes."

Jane, unsure how to begin, blushed and said, "Mama, I know you and Papa have our best interests at heart, and I thank you. However, it makes me cringe to imagine being paraded about at Almack's similar to prize horseflesh at Tattersalls. Please tell me you have not arranged a voucher in order for us to attend that exclusive … den of iniquity!"

Lizzy snorted and instantly covered the sound by coughing delicately into her handkerchief. Mrs. Bennet shot Elizabeth a look before addressing her other offspring. "Shame on you, Jane. Almack's is hardly a den of iniquity; in fact, the patronesses are extremely fussy about its members and would never allow impropriety of any sort. Be that as it may, I certainly have no intention of parading any daughter of mine through that … den of inequality and inimitable snobbish elitism of le bon ton. As for you, Miss Lizzy, while we are speaking of impropriety, please do not snort; it is most unladylike. So now then, Jane, how do you envision the course of your future happiness?"

"Truthfully, Mama, I simply want a loving relationship like you and Papa share. I wish to meet an amiable young man, fall in love, and have him return such regard without consideration of my £12,000 dowry. I realize, with so many sisters, the amount is not an overly tempting fortune. Just the same, I would wish to form an attachment that does not have money as its foundation."

"I believe what Jane is trying to say, Mama, is she could never be one of those people who wed only for the matri-money; and before you ask, that is my stance as well."

"Elizabeth Frances Bennet, I realize I have your other parent to thank for that saucy tongue of yours, but please be serious and tell me your thoughts on going to London for the Little Season. I should mention the purpose of today's meeting between your father and Mr. Whitelaw is to discuss the family's potential absence from September to November. It will be of little consequence to our steward if we are not at Longbourn for Michaelmas, and we would certainly return home in time for Christmas. If nothing else, Lizzy, think of the variety of entertainments in which we can all partake during those months in town. Perhaps you could even visit with your new friends while in the city."

"Actually, Mama, I would very much enjoy visiting with Georgiana and Anna, attending a few art exhibits, perhaps the opera, and a Shakespeare play or two."

Mrs. Bennet grinned and agreed. "A little Shakespeare would set me up forever."

Jane slouched down in her seat, crossed her arms, and muttered, "And yet I am unmoved. I do not want to return to London again so soon. Lizzy and I just arrived home, and I would prefer to remain here in the country."

"Oh, do sit up straight, Jane! Good heavens, girls, between the snorting and the slouching, I am beginning to have second thoughts about these new friends you associated with in the north. You both appear to have recently acquired the horrendous manners of barbarians."

Seemingly out of the blue, Mrs. Bennet's two normally ladylike eldest daughters had an uncontrollable fit of the giggles. Their mother hastily excused herself from the room and narrowly escaped succumbing to their contagious rampant laughter.

After collecting Mary at the seminary, two fine carriages, bursting at the seams, arrived at the Bennet family's London townhouse. Each equipage deposited a parent and three offspring as well as a multitude of sundry belongings. Several carts had arrived earlier in the week with the numerous trunks necessary for eight residents to have an extended stay in the city, and many of Longbourn's servants had also traveled to town in order to resume their duties with the happy family. Only a skeleton staff remained behind in Hertfordshire to keep the country estate operating in prime condition. Mrs. Susanna Palmer, the London housekeeper, had suddenly been inundated with questions and requests from many servants hustling and bustling about in order to settle the family comfortably.

Little Robert Bennet was thrilled by the novelty of an unfamiliar residence, as he could not remember being at the townhouse previously. Alice was challenged to keep her energetic little charge occupied in the nursery when all he wanted to do was explore every nook and cranny. Upon their arrival in the city, Mr. Bennet almost immediately went shopping and came home with shiny new metal soldiers for his son, as well as a doll with porcelain head and hands for Lydia, blocks of watercolour paints for Lizzy, and a bundle of books for his other daughters. He also thoughtfully purchased chocolate, which Mrs. Bennet favoured as a drink when mixed with hot milk and cane sugar.

A most welcome letter from Derbyshire soon arrived for the Misses Jane and Elizabeth Bennet explaining the Darcy family would remain at their country estate until early October, at which time they would also take up residence in London and return north in early December. Georgiana and Anna expressed their eagerness to see the Bennet sisters once again, and Miss Darcy happily related she and Mr. Ellis Fleming had formed a strong attachment during his stay at Pemberley. When her parents returned from Kent, Mr. Fleming had asked for, and was granted, her father's permission for them to formally enter into a courtship.

Fleming's family had long ago gained substantial wealth in the manufacture of quality watches and clocks. They had generously donated and installed an ornate new timepiece on the exterior façade of the assembly hall nearest their home in northern Derbyshire, and that clock had become the tock of the town. When the elder Mr. Fleming succumbed to an untimely death the previous year, he left his extensive properties, wealth, and collection of watches and clocks to his only son. The younger Fleming had subsequently spent considerable time winding up the estate.

He was then a single man in possession of a vast fortune and in want of a wife, and it did not take long for the strapping young chap to find a woman of the right calibre. Ellis knew within minutes – nay, seconds – of first watching Georgiana Darcy's face and the precise movements of her hands that she was perfection personified; he was not alarmed by her fiery temper but thought she was rather well adjusted. Georgiana would be the jewel in his crown, their courtship would tick away like clockwork, and they would be happy for the rest of time.

The Bennets settled as best they could in London and were determined to make the most of their time away from the pastoral life they all favoured. Friends and relatives were visited, the youngest children were taken to the park, and the older girls enjoyed expeditions to exhibitions and museums. The family watched acrobats and jugglers on the street and were regular patrons of the opera and theatre.

Miss Edwards, the governess, spoke frequently with her employers regarding her charges, Lydia and Catherine. Mrs. Bennet was, of course, very involved in the daily lives of all her children. Mr. Bennet, to whom the importance of a child's education was a-parent, also insisted on being apprised of his daughters' progress. Therefore, when he was informed both girls were having difficulty with arithmetic, he had a suggestion.

"An abacus might help with their sums, Miss Edwards; though I would not *count* on it." The young governess smiled, thanked him for the recommendation, and waited until she was out of the gentleman's sight before sighing and rolling her eyes heavenward.

Mrs. Palmer, the housekeeper, passing in the hallway, said quietly, "Is Master at it again, Martha?"

Miss Edwards nodded. The two women shook their heads and then went about their daily functions. The family's derivative sense of humour could be a problem at times. All things being equal, the servants realized they were positively fortunate to work in such a cheerful household where voices were more often raised in laughter than in negativity and anger.

One late September afternoon, Jane and Elizabeth excitedly opened a letter from Miss Georgiana Darcy saying her family would finally be in residence at their London townhouse at the very latest by the end of the week. The two eldest Bennet sisters resumed work on their needlepoint projects in the sitting room and discussed the eagerly anticipated arrival of the Darcy family. They did not realize their little brother was behind the sofa, hiding from Alice as he munched on a pilfered biscuit.

Later that same day, Mrs. Bennet perused household accounts and menus while her son played with a spinning top on the floor near her feet.

"Mama?"

"Yes, Robert?"

"Is barberin here?"

"I beg your pardon, dear?"

"Is the barberin here?"

"The barberin?"

He nodded.

"Are you saying barbering, Robert?"

The little boy looked up at her with wide blue eyes, nodded, and then shook his head. Mrs. Bennet put her paperwork aside, lifted her son onto her lap, and said, "Your father's valet is responsible for his barbering, love. So if you are asking about his valet, then, yes, Morris is in the house somewhere. Are you in need of a shave, young man, or perhaps a haircut?" She tickled under his chin and on the back of his neck beneath the blonde curls.

Robert giggled and squirmed, shook his head, and said, "No, no, Mama. The hanson barberin is coming. Libazeth said so."

His mother blinked and repeated, "Elizabeth said 'the hanson barberin is coming.'"

Robert nodded.

"Well, if your sister said so, it must be true, darling. Just the same, perhaps I should confirm the details with her." Mrs. Bennet set Robert back down on the floor, rang for a servant to fetch her second eldest daughter, and glanced through the menus again while she waited.

"You wished to see me, Mama?"

"Lizzy, young Master Robert here has taken it upon himself to inform me of the imminent arrival of 'the hanson barberin.' Pray tell me, is 'the hanson barberin' already here, or do you happen to know its, his, or her expected time of arrival?"

To Mrs. Bennet's surprise, Elizabeth blushed and stammered, "Ah, the handsome ... um ... I mean ... I think ... that is, we ... seem to have a mischievous little eavesdropper in our midst!" She scooped up her brother and cried, "Aha! I have successfully apprehended the spying scoundrel and shall now take him away to be tickled until he confesses!"

Lizzy tried to flee the room, with Robert wriggling and giggling under her arm; but she was halted by her mother's words.

"Just one moment if you please, young lady. I believe we have determined the barberin is handsome; and since Morris could not, by any stretch of the imagination, be considered attractive, I further deduce we are not speaking of a barbering valet but someone else altogether. How am I doing thus far, Lizzy?"

"Rather well, actually, Mama. I believe Jane and I just might have mentioned, in passing, some triviality about a 'handsome barbarian' earlier today." She scowled at her little brother, who sat on the floor with thumb in mouth. "However, it is of no consequence."

"I see," Mrs. Bennet said. "Be that as it may, when should we expect to have the rather dubious pleasure of this attractive barbarian's presence here?"

"We did not mean to imply he would be coming to our *home*, Mama, but rather to London in general," Lizzy said.

"Shall I alert the authorities of the impending barbaric invasion? Perhaps your friend, the Lieutenant-Colonel, might be interested in such military intelligence."

"Oh, good grief, Mother," Lizzy said, wanting the conversation to come to a rapid end. "Really, it is nothing of importance. Jane and I were just being silly. While at Pemberley … uh. Well, when we first met … ah..." Lizzy frowned and held her bottom lip between her teeth.

Mrs. Bennet sighed, rang for a servant to fetch her sensible eldest daughter, and read through the household accounts again while she waited.

When the enchanting story of the handsome barbarian was finally coaxed and coerced from her red-faced daughters, Mrs. Bennet was in possession of the following information:

1. The handsome barbarian had not been alone. There had been a whole horde of four of them.

2. The handsome barbarian was no less than the heir to the illustrious Darcy estate in Derbyshire, meaning

there probably was no need to call in the army after all.

3. The handsome barbarian was temporarily in London and her daughters were quite fond of his sisters.

4. The handsome barbarian and his cohorts had been less than appropriately attired in her daughters' presence.

5. The handsome barbarian caused both her daughters, especially Elizabeth, to blush quite profusely; and, last but not least ...

6. The handsome barbarian's proximity meant the city had suddenly become not only more attractive but also infinitely more interesting.

The following week, an invitation arrived for Jane and Elizabeth to dine Wednesday evening at Darcy House. At the appointed time, the two young ladies traveled the short distance in their carriage in the company of Miss Edwards, who would be transported onward for a short visit with her own family in the city. While the Bennet sisters wholeheartedly looked forward to seeing Georgiana and Anna again, they were also somewhat anxious about becoming acquainted with their friends' esteemed parents. One of the sisters, in particular, wondered whether a certain attractive young gentleman might also be in attendance. She had chosen her dress and had her toilette performed with extra care that evening, just in case.

Fitzwilliam Darcy, too, dressed with extra care that evening and nervously paced in front of the drawing room fireplace as he waited for his sisters' guests to arrive. He had tried not to think about the Bennet ladies after their departure from Pemberley. Despite his best efforts, he had been dreaming, both day and night, about one in particular. When he had learned they were invited for dinner, he quickly changed his plans and decided to remain at home that night. It mattered not a groat to him that his withdrawal from the other engagement left its hostess, a duchess, with an unequal number of men and women at her table. He had a more important duty that evening; for he was still ashamed of his deplorable appearance upon first meeting Miss Elizabeth – and her sister, he reminded himself – and simply needed to impress her – and her sister – with his manners, to correct any low opinion the pretty, corky, fascinating young lady – and her sister – might yet have of him. Darcy twisted the signet ring on his pinkie finger and continued to pace.

Miss Darcy fretted over what might possibly go awry while her friends visited, and she was relieved when her well-groomed brother came downstairs properly attired. Georgiana fidgeted and frequently checked the magnificent new mantle clock, a gift to her parents from Ellis Fleming.

Although the Darcy family had not transported its entire menagerie to the city, Dust Bunny, Pug-Nacious, Geoffrey, Chaucer, and Barb Thorne had accompanied their mistresses; and George Darcy's Dalmatians, Rex and Regina, had also made the trip. Georgiana had ensured each pet was safely secured in an area away from the drawing and dining rooms, and servants were assigned to see to the needs and whereabouts of the dogs at all times.

Anna shared her sister's unease and concern; yet she sat quietly, except for the occasional wringing of her hands, and impatiently awaited the arrival of Jane and Elizabeth.

George and Lady Anne Darcy watched their normally composed grown children with amusement and wondered what special qualities the Bennet girls possessed that they were able to cause such anxiety. The gentleman especially observed his son.

A good father, though not an overly affectionate one, George Darcy had instilled in his children pride in their heritage. He had taught Fitzwilliam to be a proper and reserved gentleman, to exercise self-restraint in the expression of emotion, to always keep a stiff upper lip, and display fortitude in the face of adversity. The senior Darcy was a perfectionist, a trait he had passed on to his only son. In addition to instructing him on how to be an exemplary landowner and earn healthy profits, George Darcy also spent considerable time teaching Fitzwilliam to excel at the game of chess, to shoot expertly, and to ride extremely well. Pemberley's Master and heir were no strangers to their tenants and workers; the two gentlemen, so similar in appearance, could often be seen riding shoulder-to-shoulder across the length and breadth of their grand estate.

George had been an only child and upon the demise of his parents had become full of juice. The Darcy ancestral estate earned in excess of £10,000 per annum, and that income had always been invested wisely. Because of his name, wealth, and good looks, many women were strongly attracted to the magnate; but George Darcy had already set his cap at the lovely Lady Anne Fitzwilliam, one of the Earl of Matlock's two daughters. That young woman was in possession of excellent connections, money, and beauty, in addition to being very accomplished, kind, and intelligent. Before he snared her for marriage, he also, conveniently, fell in love with Lady Anne; however, any displays of affection were strictly confined to private moments between the couple and never in public or in front of the children.

At fifty years of age, George Darcy was still a very distinguished-looking gentleman, an older version of his son, albeit a bit heavier, and with grey gaining dominance over the brown of his thinning hair. His wife, younger by several years, was still quite beautiful with hazel eyes and silver strands barely visible amongst her golden tresses.

Lady Anne Darcy, nee Fitzwilliam, was proud of her station in life, as were her widowed sister, Lady Catherine de Bourgh, and brother, Henry Fitzwilliam, the current Earl of Matlock. Unlike her siblings, Lady Anne had never allowed pride to rule her world or her interactions with its inhabitants. When her father agreed to George Darcy's petition for her hand, their marriage had started out, at least on the bride's part, as one of convenience. The bridegroom, although not titled, was very wealthy and came from an illustrious family; so the match had been a good one. The young wife soon found herself in love with her dashing husband; before their first year together was celebrated, she also found herself expecting a child.

Lady Anne was a good mother and ensured her three children had the best education available and whatever their little hearts desired. More importantly, she cherished and nurtured them and spent more time with her offspring than most ladies of her sphere. From Lady Anne, the children and their father learned to share her love of animals. Pemberley became a haven for not only a growing number of pets but also for strays of many species, sizes, and degrees of suitability. Pemberley's Mistress also enjoyed gardening; and from such a caring and fostering nature, her husband, her three children, the estate's animals, and its flowers and herbs all benefited.

It was also through Lady Anne's influence that her children were taught to have a softer side and to be caring toward family, relatives, friends, tenants, and servants alike. As they grew older, she encouraged Fitzwilliam, Georgiana, and Anna to each seek that special someone they could respect as a partner on their journey through life rather than merely settling for a visually attractive asset to grace their arm and add to their already considerable monetary worth. She told them that pre-arranged marriages pre-pair people for the future, though not necessarily for happiness.

As she became acquainted with the Misses Bennet, Lady Anne hoped Fitzwilliam would heed that advice. She had immediately noticed the admiring look in her son's eyes while he stood in the background and gazed longingly at the pretty younger Bennet sister.

When Jane and Lizzy arrived at Darcy House, Georgiana and Anna met them in the spacious foyer. The four embraced, chatted, and giggled as though they had never been apart. All nervousness was immediately vanquished – the Darcy siblings relaxed, and the Bennet sisters felt welcome and comfortable - until Georgiana said, "Please come to the drawing room and meet Mother and Father; Fitzwilliam is at home tonight as well." A kaleidoscope of butterflies suddenly attacked Elizabeth's stomach. Nevertheless, she smiled bravely and followed behind the other three.

The introduction of the Misses Bennet to Mr. Darcy and Lady Anne went well. Georgiana then said, "Of course, you ladies remember Fitzwilliam. Brother, will you not come forward and welcome Jane and Elizabeth to our home?"

The handsome young man stepped out of the shadows, bowed, and forced himself not to gape at the younger visitor as he spoke. "It is a pleasure to see you both again, Miss Bennet and Miss Elizabeth; and I do, indeed, welcome you to our home."

Darcy had been immediately entranced upon her entrance and bowled over by the effect she had on him. *Obviously, I have not fantasized her image quite accurately at all. Miss Elizabeth is not just pretty but stunningly beautiful.* The infatuated fellow was mortified when his face suddenly began to flood with colour. Staid Fitzwilliam Darcy had always been perfectly capable of schooling his expression and appearing aloof. This time, he could not stop the blush from spreading across his face; she looked so very lovely, smelled so wonderfully enticing, and stood so temptingly near.

This is totally unacceptable! Father is watching, so pull yourself together, man. The chit is merely my sisters' friend, nothing more. Right ... nothing more than completely enchanting and flawless. My God, a man could absolutely lose himself in the depths of those captivating dark eyes. Wit and intelligence, spunk and sparkle, all wrapped up in a most alluring package ... most alluring, indeed! Oh, stop drooling, fool! Is it her tantalizing scent that is wreaking such havoc? Either go away, Elizabeth Bennet ... far, far away ... or come closer ... much, much closer and ...

" ... do you not agree, sir?" Miss Elizabeth's eyebrow arched as she smiled up at him. He had no idea how to answer.

"I beg your pardon, Miss ... " *gulp* " ... Elizabeth." He savoured the sound of her name separated from its social title and wondered whether he would ever have the privilege of dropping it entirely.

Good God! From where did such an utterly ridiculous notion come? Stop, and pay attention to what the bewitching beauty is saying, you cork-brained mooncalf!

Darcy did not understand such an out-of-control feeling. It was an entirely foreign experience for one who had always been proud of his restraint and mastery of emotions. The situation was intolerable to him, especially in front of his father. He jumped when his sister spoke.

"Brother! Has the cat got your tongue?" Georgiana glared at her blushing sibling with annoyance and amusement; yet when he looked to her with desperation and supplication, she took pity and said, "Come, everyone. Please let us all have a seat before my brother agrees with

Elizabeth's remark about the improvement in temperature since they were introduced. It was rather hot that day at Pemberley, if you remember, Fitzwilliam."

Thank you, Georgie! However, I quite disagree about the improvement in temperature. I am actually rather uncomfortably hot again at this moment. The cheek of that feisty little Bennet minx to dredge up the memory of such an embarrassing encounter. Darcy deliberated before he responded to her deliberate provocation.

"Why, yes, Miss Elizabeth, I quite agree. The sultriness of that afternoon may, however, explain certain … unique circumstances."

Everyone had taken seats, and although Elizabeth Bennet and Fitzwilliam Darcy were safely distant from one another, they locked eyes from across the room and continued their private conversation in public.

"You are, of course, correct, sir. There was a certain humidity and dampness in the air which caused a most uncomfortable clinging sensation, if I recall."

"I regret you were made uncomfortable by such steamy conditions at Pemberley, madam."

"Not at all. I assure you it would take considerably more than the heat generated that day for me to become overly hot and bothered."

"Just how close, hot, and heavy would it have to be, Miss Elizabeth?"

Mr. George Darcy cleared his throat in order to put an immediate stop to whatever the two were discussing. To his disgust, he feared it was not strictly atmospheric conditions. Both Bennet sisters were strikingly magnificent women, and he was fully aware of his son's preference for shapely brunettes. Miss Elizabeth certainly qualified as such; though she seemed quite different from the usual empty-headed, fawning, and compliant ladies who constantly dangled after the Darcy heir. This one had some wit about her and did not seem afraid of confrontation. He decided it would be prudent to do a little inconspicuous prying into the Bennet family connections and wealth.

Miss Bennet was surprised by, and ashamed of, her sister's unladylike teasing of the poor fellow. She wondered what on earth had gotten into Lizzy to behave in such a scandalous manner. Jane kept up her end of the conversation with Lady Anne, Georgiana, and Anna while she eavesdropped on what was being said by the room's other occupants.

Elizabeth was, in fact, rather shocked at her own audacity in front of the illustrious, upper crust Darcy family of Pemberley.

What godawful impertinence has gotten into me? For reasons unknown, I am comfortable amongst these elite people. Be that as it may, to behave in such an improper manner within minutes of arriving at their home is unacceptable behaviour, Miss Lizzy Bennet. Shame on you! In front of his parents ... I mean in front of my friends' parents! Really, I am here to see Georgiana and Anna, not some urbane barbarian.

She smiled enigmatically, looked at him from beneath her lovely lashes, and caught her full bottom lip between her pretty teeth. Fixated, Fitzwilliam Darcy was totally and utterly captivated. He shifted uncomfortably in his chair.

Dinner was announced, to the relief of just about everyone. None could fail to see, and almost feel, the attraction between the obviously besotted young man and woman. The hostess had decided on a seating plan before her guests' arrival; she had not given a second thought to placing Fitzwilliam directly opposite the younger Bennet sister. When she witnessed Miss Elizabeth and her son exchanging fervent looks, blushes, and shy smiles throughout the meal, Lady Anne was amused, amazed, and alarmed.

Just what, exactly, went on at Pemberley in our absence? How had it happened that four young men and four young women had been at our estate without proper chaperones, except for a houseful of loyal retainers? The trip to Kent to intervene ... er ... visit with Catherine had been unavoidable, and Fitzwilliam only mentioned Richard would be accompanying him to Pemberley. Yet now Ellis Fleming is courting Georgiana, and my normally stodgy son is ... unrecognizable.

Lizzy's fluttering butterflies had returned to her stomach with a vengeance, and they were not at all interested in food. She did not wish to offend her hostess by not eating; nevertheless, handsome Fitzwilliam Darcy kept distracting her, smiling, and making her toes curl. Every movement he made sent his tantalizing sandalwood scent in her direction.

She wished he would just keep still and not move a muscle, like when she first set eyes on him at Pemberley.

Oh, now, Lizzy, just enjoy the nice, refined view across the table; it is quite sufficient. There is no need to picture him in damp, clinging attire in your naughty little mind's eye. STOP IT!

While her brain screamed abuse at her, Miss Elizabeth smiled back at the sophisticated man who sat across from her. The devious part of her brain recalled the ruffian with an unforgettable wet linen shirt moulded to his rather impressive pectoral muscles.

When the rather awkward meal was over, the five ladies removed to the music room. It had initially been planned the two gentlemen would immediately accompany them there; however, George Darcy wanted to first have a private word with his son. He signalled for a footman to bring the port and asked Fitzwilliam if he would partake.

"What? Oh. Ah, no, thank you. Well, perhaps ... maybe, I should ... yes, of course. Yes, please."

"Good God, son. That bad, is it?"

"I beg your pardon?"

"I have been in your shoes, Fitzwilliam. It is not the end of the world, you know."

"I am sorry, Father, to what are you referring? I do not have the pleasure of understanding you."

"Poor boy, I do not think you understand much of anything tonight, do you?"

The son hastily left his seat, pacing between the table and the window and twisting his signet ring.

George Darcy handed him a glass of port, gave him a quick pat on the shoulder, and said, "She seems a nice enough girl and certainly a tempting armful. Be that as it may, what do you know of her connections?"

A stricken look crossed Fitzwilliam's face as he turned toward his father. "Again, sir, I do not understand. To whom are you referring?"

"Enough, Fitzwilliam. It is sufficient you have behaved like a lovelorn fool tonight. Do not make it worse by denying your fascination with the younger Bennet girl. I realize you may think me a hypocrite, as I always drilled into your head the notion you must hide your emotions. In spite of that, a man *is* permitted to be attracted to a woman, after all." The father grinned at his shocked son and added, "At least if she is an appropriate, eligible, respectful, beautiful, healthy, wealthy, intelligent, accomplished, kind and caring, obedient, virtuous, and well-connected young lady with a considerable dowry. Is she?"

The young man flopped back down in his chair, looked at his father with a smirk, and asked, "Who?"

When the father and son entered the music room, the ladies were in the middle of a conversation about their favourite pastimes while in the country. Jane was saying, " … in addition to playing the pianoforte and reading, I also enjoy needlework as well as drying and arranging flowers."

George Darcy took a seat near the more interesting Elizabeth Bennet while his son preferred to stand at the fireplace, resting his arm on the mantle and enjoying the unobstructed view his strategic position allowed of the same young lady. His mother turned to Miss Elizabeth and asked about the activities she preferred.

"I share Jane's love of music and extensive reading, as does our entire family. Other than that, I must confess my preferences tend toward outdoor activities. I am an avid horsewoman but also enjoy walking, and I usually take along my watercolour supplies in case I am inspired. I have never taken any formal lessons; nevertheless, I do seem to have some natural ability for capturing scenes that tempt me to paint them."

Jane spoke up. "My sister is being modest, for she possesses a rather unique talent. Her technique with the brush is certainly admirable; however, Lizzy has the ability to perfectly recall any person, place, or object, even much later, and faithfully recapture it on canvas. It is quite uncanny, really."

The artist blushed and said, "Scenes I find aesthetically pleasing imprint upon my mind, and it seems nothing escapes notice. Shape, line, proportion, lighting, colour, and texture are all still well defined even long afterward. Each and every detail of a person's appearance, from the covering of a button to the manner in which clothing drapes on their form, is easily recalled. The texture of white linen, hair highlighted by the sun, the expression on his, or her, face … it is all memorized."

Elizabeth was staring at, or through, Fitzwilliam Darcy; and he realized she was recalling his indecent appearance at Pemberley. He was mortified and excited at the same time as he listened to her sultry voice and gazed into the depths of her dark eyes while she continued to speak. " … and whatever my eyes have not actually witnessed, my imagination can usually quite accurately visualize."

The gentleman standing at the hearth suddenly turned crimson, and his observant father suggested he should move away from the heat. Lady Anne was no artist; still and all, she knew where to draw the line.

"My, my, Miss Elizabeth, that is, indeed, quite a gift. But does this ability only manifest itself when you find something pleasing? I shudder to imagine such accurate recall of an unpleasant scene."

"I suppose I have led a rather sheltered existence and have not been exposed to much ugliness, Lady Anne. I only scrutinize a subject if I find him … I mean, it … aesthetically agreeable." Elizabeth arched her brow, and her eyes sparkled as they held Fitzwilliam Darcy's rapt attention.

The young man relaxed and smiled fully at her, and the sight mesmerized Elizabeth. The smile changed his already attractive features from merely handsome to devastatingly irresistible, and his gorgeous dark eyes shone with warmth and liveliness. A flash of white teeth was revealed behind suddenly sensuous lips and dimples appeared on his smooth-shaven cheeks. The aesthetically pleasing image was immediately filed away for future, repeated recollection. The sound of George Darcy's voice requesting some music from the ladies roused Elizabeth and Darcy from their intimate connection.

Before the Bennet sisters departed that night, they received an invitation to go shopping with Georgiana and Anna the next day and another to an art exhibit with the entire family. More importantly, they had been asked to be the family's guests at a ball hosted jointly by the Darcy and Fitzwilliam families at the Earl of Matlock's residence in a fortnight's time. Georgiana was happy to relate that Mr. Fleming, Mr. Bingley, and Colonel Fitzwilliam would all be in attendance.

The Darcy barouche carried the four young ladies to the high-end Ladies Shoe Manufacturer Wood footwear store, where Elizabeth was to try on the specially made sturdy riding boots she had ordered weeks ago.

Georgiana picked up a dainty dancing slipper from the display shelf and said, "Do you know Mr. Bingley's family made their wealth from footwear several generations ago? He and his sister, Caroline, are well heeled due to their ancestors' diligence in the cobbler trade."

Anna Darcy grinned and added, "It is unfortunate Miss Bingley did not take during the last season. Nonetheless, I believe the sole reason she did not get a foot in the door is her relentless pursuit of our brother."

Elizabeth had been about to try on her new boots when one slipped from her grasp and fell with a thud to the floor. Jane turned in her direction, saw the stricken expression on her sister's face, and waited for the other shoe to drop. The younger Bennet asked with a quavering voice, "Does your brother return Miss Bingley's regard?"

"Oh, no, not at all. Fitzwilliam is perceptive enough to recognize Caroline Bingley as a social-climbing fortune hunter. Our family is extremely fond of the amiable Mr. Bingley, but his sister is … "

"Horrid," Anna quickly added.

Georgiana shushed and scolded while Anna unapologetically continued to insist the description was true. The gangly young store clerk who was assisting Miss Elizabeth took the boots from her and walked to another part of the shop where he could escape female conversation and polish the footwear in peace and quiet.

Miss Darcy looked pointedly at the younger Bennet sister and emphatically stated that Caroline Bingley would *never* become Fitzwilliam's wife. Elizabeth breathed a sigh of relief, while Jane hoped the Bingley woman would have dignity in de-feat.

They exited the shoe shop, entered the barouche, and traveled to Bond Street, where they were disappointed by a sign on the door of the new music store that said, "Bach in a Minuet. Doorknob is Baroque. Do not rattle Handel."

"Well, that is certainly disappointing. I had hoped to purchase another copy of the sheet music for the piece I plan to perform at the ball," complained Miss Anna.

"Never mind, dearest, we shall return later; and you have the piece nearly memorized anyway," Georgiana said.

Georgiana explained to Jane and Elizabeth that Anna's pet rabbit, Herr Stewart, had nibbled the edges of her sheet music, making it unfit for use at the upcoming event. Although Anna would be attending until the supper set, she would not be dancing, as she was not yet out. "Speaking of our ball, will you ladies be shopping for new gowns?"

The Bennet sisters told their friends they had each recently purchased a couple beautiful dresses upon their arrival in London, and they only had one final fitting at the modiste before taking possession of the creations. The next step was to decide which of the two to wear. Elizabeth then asked, "What of you, Georgiana? Have you something spectacular to dazzle the eyes of a certain young man who is currently courting you?"

Miss Darcy admitted she was very much looking forward to seeing Mr. Ellis Fleming again. She then rather boldly asked whether Jane and Elizabeth had formed any attachments while residing in Town. Georgiana crossed her fingers and secretly hoped her brother and Elizabeth might make a match; she was, therefore, somewhat surprised and alarmed when Miss Bennet spoke.

"Lizzy certainly has an admirer in the city. Lieutenant-Colonel John Dun has been trying to win my sister's regard for quite a while, though they hardly ever see one another. We do not spend much time in London, as you know. That said, he has already called five times since our arrival last month."

"Oh." The disappointment was evident in Georgiana's voice. *I must find a way to let Fitzwilliam know he had better step up to the challenge before it is too late. Oh no! I wonder whether Richard has invited many of his officer friends to the ball and if this nefarious Lieutenant-Colonel Dun might be one of them.*

The shopping expedition became a search for accessories for the ball, and it continued most of the afternoon with only a brief stop for tea and sweets. Before parting company, the four had each purchased new gloves after a hands-on attempt to find the perfect fit. They discovered the clerk at the jewelry shop had a heart of gold, and they used common scents when purchasing expensive perfume. Georgiana had suggested a certain fragrance to Elizabeth and hoped it would prove to be a powerful in-scentive if and when her pernickety brother asked that particular lady to stand up with him.

I hope Elizabeth's costly Eau de Cologne shall not be wasted on that prosaic, colourless Lieutenant-Colonel Don Juan, er, John Dun, Georgiana thought.

Chapter II

A Picture Hanging in a Gallery is Worth
a Few Off-the-Wall Comments

Jane patiently waited for Rachel, the maid whose services she shared with Elizabeth, to put a few finishing touches on her sister's upswept chestnut curls.

"Those two little blossoms look very charming in your hair, Lizzy. Your handsome barbarian will be quite undone by your pretty flowers and flirty powers."

"Thank you for the compliment, I think. I shall not allow it to go to my head; in fact, I doubt it will even find its way in through all these thick curls. By the way, whomever it is you are talking about, he is certainly not *my* handsome barbarian. Now, which bonnet will best perform the task of hiding what Rachel just spent such a prodigious time and effort perfecting?"

"Decide quickly, silly sister, or we shall be tardy. You would not want to sully the impeccably prim and perfectly proper impression you left on whomever's parents the night before last."

"Oh, do leave off, Jane! I am embarrassed enough already at that absolute bumble-broth. Although Georgiana and Anna said nothing disparaging yesterday, I wonder what their parents must think. What must *he* think of me?"

"Are you referring to Mr. George Darcy or his son? If the latter, it is blatantly obvious what he thinks, Lizzy."

Elizabeth blushed, snatched up a bonnet at random, and hurried down the stairs. She and Jane encountered their father in the foyer as he was preparing to join some London friends at his club.

"Pleasure-bound again, girls?" Mr. Bennet greeted his girls. "I happened to notice a carriage with a certain rather impressive crest on its door parked at our curb. Are you leaving us to spend more time with the rich and illustrious Darcy family?"

When his daughters acknowledged they were, indeed, invited on an outing with those friends, Mr. Bennet said, "As I understand it, George Darcy is richer than Croesus, who, by the way, was the king of Lydia … but I digress. George Darcy is so wealthy … "

"How wealthy is he, Papa?" Lizzy dutifully asked.

"He is so wealthy that when it rains, he spreads out large books for his guests to wipe their feet on; and those are the tomes that dry men's soles."

"I am embarrassed to admit I am not familiar with the reference," Jane said.

Lizzy stopped giggling and explained, "'These are the times that try men's souls' is a quote from *The American Crisis* by Thomas Paine, Jane."

"Well, I do not know of which times that author was speaking, Lizzy. But you and another Thomas are trying my soul right now; so please refrain from being a pain before we cause an English crisis. The carriages are waiting. Make haste."

A footman opened the door to the Darcy barouche, and the Bennet sisters were surprised to find only Georgiana and Anna inside. Elizabeth beckoned her father over and made the introductions. With his easygoing, open and friendly manner, Mr. Bennet quickly gained the admiration of the occupants. He handed his daughters into the carriage, wished them all a pleasant day, and entered his own equipage. The Darcy siblings expressed their delight at having met the gentleman and were further pleased by Jane's next words.

"Our mother also wishes to make your acquaintance, so kindly pass along this invitation to your parents." Jane retrieved the note from her reticule and handed it to Miss Darcy. "In it she asks your family to dine with us within the week, if you have an evening free of engagements. Any night shall be fine with Mama. Your family has been very kind to us, and we hope to return the hospitality."

Lizzy impatiently asked, "Yes, but will your parents and brother not be joining us today?"

"Jane, Elizabeth, I am so sorry. There has been a slight change of plans." An exasperated glance passed between Georgiana and her sister. "Our widowed aunt, Lady Catherine de Bourgh, is rather … unwell. Our cousin, Anne, lives at Rosings Park with her; and there are times when she requires assistance from the family. Mother and our uncle, the Earl of Matlock, take turns attending to the, ah, matter. As it was our mother's time to go to Kent, she and our father were summoned by express just this morning. But as soon as Fitzwilliam completes a couple of errands, he will be meeting us at the Royal Academy."

Miss Bennet said, "I hope the poor dear lady has a speedy recovery from her malady." Her comment was met with looks of skepticism from the Darcy sisters.

Lizzy also expressed her regret their aunt was afflicted and then remarked that the Darcy family and their relatives seemed particularly partial to the names Anne and Fitzwilliam. "I would imagine the similarity might become somewhat confusing."

"Not really, Elizabeth. You see, Anne and Anna were so called after Mother; and I obviously have the feminine form of George, for my father. As to 'Fitzwilliam,' in our family, the heir's Christian name honours his mother's maiden one."

"So, let me get this straight. If your brother married, say, a Miss Darby, would their first-born son be referred to as the darling Darby Darcy of Derbyshire?"

"Lizzy!"

"Jane, I meant no disrespect. All the same, I admit I am quite curious. Please forgive me, Georgiana and Anna."

Georgiana giggled. "It is not an unbendable rule set in stone, Elizabeth, just a tradition. At any rate, I am rather hopeful my discriminating brother will marry someone with a last name that would also serve nicely as a first, such as Grant, Blake, or Nelson. Why, I believe *Bennet* would even be a very nice given name for a boy."

Elizabeth blushed and quickly changed the topic. While they made their way to the Royal Academy, the young ladies discussed a subject that always made them energetic – the upcoming ball.

A dapper gentleman paced at the main entrance of the Royal Academy. When the awaited carriage came to a halt, he waved away the footman and helped his two sisters and Miss Bennet alight. Miss Elizabeth was the last to exit, and he held her hand a little longer than necessary and gently stroked the back of it with his thumb. Even though they both wore gloves, he and she momentarily forgot to breathe while they enjoyed the thrill of that first fleeting caress. He reluctantly released her, bowed, and greeted the ladies politely; but his gaze never strayed long from the pretty brunette with the sparkling, intelligent eyes. Fitzwilliam Darcy considered Elizabeth the very epitome of femininity, and they exchanged admiring glances and shy smiles until Georgiana spoke.

"So, brother, did you successfully complete your errands?"

Darcy grudgingly tore his eyes away from Elizabeth and replied, "Yes, Georgie. I first stopped at Fletcher & Byrd, the new plumassier, and am embarrassed to admit I became quite adrift. The fledgling business is located in a-loft; and one must follow the arrows up several flights of stairs and down a long corridor to the building's oldest wing. I took several wrong terns before entering the correct doorway, which was so low I had to duck. I feathered their nest with a swift purchase of a large clutch of ostrich and peacock plumage but was in a hurry and may have been gulled by their soaring prices. I managed to swallow my spleen and sign my name with an ornate goose quill, and then the owlish Mr. Fletcher perched himself on the counter and had the pluck to say our patronage would be a feather in his cap. Mr. Byrd, the pompous coxcomb, agreed and crowed that customers would soon flock to their shop. To be honest, Georgie, I found both men to be quite flighty; and they may, in fact, have been robin me.

Fortunately, I was also able to obtain the desired cake just one block away. The package is being dispatched tout de sweet, my errands were completed more rapidly than expected, and I was able to meet, at the appointed hour, four very lovely ladies."

His gaze naturally settled upon one particular lovely lady again; and her cheeks grew rosy as he performed a head to foot, and back again, appreciative appraisal of her person. Lizzy was not affronted and thought he was quite justified in his scrutiny in return for the way she had overtly ogled him at Pemberley.

With a glint in her eye, Anna explained, "My brother went shopping today because we are often asked to forward certain items from Town to Rosings Park in order to appease, er, satisfy the rather eccentric demands … I mean, the discriminating tastes of Lady Catherine de Bourgh … a nutty fruitcake … and large bird feathers. You see, our aunt really takes the cake for being plume crazy."

The five entered the Royal Academy building. Lizzy, being a painter, was eager to view J.M.W. Turner's recent *Mercury and Herse* plus several other of his newest works. She and Darcy stood in front of the masterpiece while the others went in the opposite direction to view portraits.

"Are you familiar with the depicted mythology, Miss Elizabeth?"

"Somewhat, Mr. Darcy; I admit I much prefer Ovid's 'Metamorphoses' over alternative versions of the story, as it is less tragic."

"Indeed, madam, for in Ovid's version Mercury, or Hermes, falls in love with Herse upon first seeing her in Athens and asks for her hand, which I agree is highly preferable over an insane Herse leaping to her death from the Acropolis."

Elizabeth nodded. "I always enjoy a tale in which the hero and heroine live happily ever after, sir, even if they do have to suffer some misunderstanding, separation, and angst along the way."

"Ah, but the misunderstanding, separation, and angst are what make the 'happily ever after' more worth the earning, Miss Elizabeth; and a romance story would be quite lacking without it. Shall we move on?"

"Yes, I am rather curious to see why so many people are gathered in front of a canvas in the alcove over there. It is obvious the artist can certainly draw a crowd."

"Is that an intended pun, Miss Elizabeth? If so, I am surprised you would stoop to, as Dr. Samuel Johnson called it, 'the lowest form of humour.'"

"Shamefully, I must confess it was intentional, Mr. Darcy. Please forgive my flippant folly; for I fear I am fated to foolishly follow in the fallible footsteps of my fantastic but formidably farcical father, who is a fancier of the foible and fatuously fond of tomfoolery. Oh, fie! I feel you are fully fed up. I will finally finish with a flourish and thank you for your forbearance. I forthwith promise to forgo and forsake further frustrating frivolity for now but, unfortunately, not forever."

Darcy stared incredulously at Elizabeth, cleared his throat, and said, "Miss Elizabeth, you must allow me to allay and also alleviate any alarm about an altercation over your alacrity for aloud alliteration. Although allegedly always appearing aloof, I actually ardently admire and approve alert and amusing allegorical allusions. All along, it has been apparent our minds are alike and I, alone, am already an ally and offer my allegiance and alliance. I alternatively allude to your altogether alive, altruistic, and appealing allure. Alas, my allocated allotment of allowable alliterations is almost accomplished. All right, shall we amble along to another alcove of artwork?"

They grinned at one another and strolled over to the depiction that had been so admired by the crowd. Darcy contemplated the lavish banquet on canvas and said, "Now, this painting has taste, and the artist obviously used his palette wisely."

"Mr. Darcy! Upun my word, sir! How very unrepentantly unsophisticated and laughingly lowbrow of you, sir."

The gentleman attempted a straight face as he asked, "Whatever do you mean, madam?"

As Lizzy Bennet and her companion turned toward one another and smiled, the room, the Royal Academy building, and then the entire world around them, vanished. Darcy longingly stared at her mouth and thought, *Yes, smile, Elizabeth. It is the second best thing you could do with those luscious lips*. He raised his gaze, dark eyes locked with dark eyes, and he slowly moved in closer, breathed in her enticing scent, leaned slightly forward and said in a low, husky voice, "Miss Elizabeth, you must allow me to … "

"Mr. Darcy! Yoo-hoo, Mr. Darrrceeey." A woman's shrill voice pierced their bubble of sensuous solitude.

He groaned and muttered, "Oh, God. Please, no."

A tall woman of questionable fashion approached with another young lady in tow. The gentleman gritted his teeth, bowed, and greeted the newcomers. "Miss Bingley, Miss Dalrymple, what an unexpected … pleasure. Ladies, may I present Miss Elizabeth Bennet from Hertfordshire. Miss Elizabeth, allow me to introduce to you Miss Caroline Bingley. You met her brother, Charles, at Pemberley. And this is her friend, Miss Sarah Dalrymple."

All the ladies curtsied. The orange-clad Caroline Bingley snootily said, "Oh, have you had the privilege of visiting the magnificent Darcy home, Miss Elizabeth? Is it not the most beautiful and noble place you have ever seen? I keep telling Charles he must make a purchase in that neighbourhood and take Pemberley for a kind of model. There is not a finer county in England than Derbyshire, I have often remarked. Were you on a tour of the grand estate, Miss Elizabeth?"

Caroline looked down her hawk-like nose at the young woman's simple ensemble of an ivory dress of good-quality linen trimmed with ecru ribbon. Over it she wore a pretty fringed beige shawl of fine wool embroidered in metallic threads with tiny flowers in shades of gold, bronze, copper, and green. Fortunately, the soft coppery cloth bonnet Elizabeth had hurriedly grabbed, almost without looking, matched her outfit quite well.

"No. Initially I was visiting Mrs. Reynolds with … "

"Mrs. Reynolds? Why, is she not the estate's housekeeper? You were at Pemberley to visit a *servant*?"

"Why, yes. The amiable Mrs. Reynolds is a dear friend of my aunt, with whom my sister and I were traveling … "

Caroline ignored the rest of the insignificant chit's words, turned her eagle eyes toward her prey, and dug her talons into his forearm. "Are you here unaccompanied, Mr. Darcy?"

The gentleman extricated his sleeve from her clutch and exclaimed, "Miss Bingley! As you can see, I am here with Miss Elizabeth; and her sister and both of mine are roaming about somewhere as well."

"Oooh, dear Georgiana and Anna are here? Where are my dearest friends? I absolutely must pay my respects." The ostrich-feather-festooned, turban-headed woman in the outrageous orange organza outfit swivelled her head in an owl-like manner, searching for familiar faces in the crowd while Darcy dodged being whipped in the face by the long plumage.

"Yoo-hoo, Miss Darrrceeey, Miss Annnaah!" As Caroline waved her fan aloft in an attempt to gain the attention of his sisters, Darcy boldly latched onto Elizabeth's hand and pulled her away from the two unwelcome birds of prey. The startled young lady blushed at his forward action as she was pulled along behind him.

They came to a halt around a corner, in front of an unappealing canvas depicting an unappetizing bowl of fruit and berries. Once again, Darcy very reluctantly and slowly released her hand.

"Good God. What a monstrosity. I do not know which is more disconcerting, Miss Bingley or this painting. Miss Elizabeth, I apologize for that unpleasant encounter, for my impulsive and presumptuous action, and for stopping at this particular piece of cra ... aft. Who would dare have the audacity, not to mention bad taste, to actually create, frame, and hang such a garish eyesore?"

Elizabeth squinted and scrutinized the squiggly signature. "His name is unknown to me; and I must agree the rendering is a rather peculiar piece of cra ... aft, with no depth, no sense of perspective, or lighting. Where is the texture of the strawberry? Er, that *is* supposed to be a strawberry, is it not? And the gaudy colours are all wrong. Perhaps the poor fellow is actually colour-blind. Really, I do not care to boast; nevertheless, I could do better justice to the subject matter than has this painter. I hesitate to refer to him as an artist, because ... "

"Yes, yes, I get the *picture*, Miss Elizabeth; you do not care for his style either. Did I not say our minds are alike?"

"Well, we are certainly in agreement, sir, that such a distorted display of still-life art is not at all moving."

Darcy realized he had never before enjoyed an art exposition as much as that afternoon. In fact, scarcely had he enjoyed any afternoon half as much. He had allowed himself to openly have fun in a public setting and relaxed some of his emotional guardedness … *all because of this quirky, incomparable woman. Elizabeth Bennet, you might not live up to my unreasonably high standards, and you are definitely not the sort of woman I thought I wanted, but my expectation of perfection has thus far resulted in disappointment. I never thought I would find such a paragon in one so lively and lovely. But perhaps …*

Their sisters waved to them from across the way, and it was fairly obvious Georgiana and Anna wished to be rescued from Miss Bingley's peckish attention. Darcy and Elizabeth reluctantly joined their siblings and the other two young women. The expanded group wandered the gallery together, admiring or criticizing everything they saw, and some of the party even looked at the paintings on the walls. Miss Bingley ignored the works of art and especially turned a blind eye to the Bennet sisters. When she did condescend to speak, it was merely to insult or offend them. Although the Darcy siblings took great interest in the exhibit, they were preoccupied with attempts to diffuse Caroline's snide jibes and bitter barbs ruthlessly aimed directly at Elizabeth.

Inwardly, Caroline Bingley seethed with curiosity, jealousy, and pique. *Who are these countrified Bennet hoydens who scamper off to Pemberley, visit a servant, and end up consorting with Darcy and his sisters? He certainly seems to look in the direction of the dark-haired dairymaid a great deal, and Miss Eliza is obviously using her ample armoury of arts and allurements to draw him in. How despicable for a woman to be such a flagrant social-climbing fortune hunter.*

Jane Bennet paid scant attention to either the displays of art or bad manners. She was far too busy stealing glimpses of and glances at the attractive, self-assured man across the room. *Where in the world have I encountered him before? I am positive we are somehow and somewhat acquainted, yet I cannot recall where …* Oh! Jane suddenly coloured and immediately wondered whether her sister's perfect recall might be hereditary because an unforgettable image insistently clung and would not relent. *It was at Pemberley. On the lawn. I met him that sultry and steamy hot summer afternoon.*

Darcy was in no humour to give much consequence to anyone or anything other than the beautiful brunette Bennet by his side. He was quite distracted by her proximity, by an infernal internal impulse, and by protecting Miss Elizabeth from Caroline Bingley's snotty snootiness.

Elizabeth's attention was equally divided between the beautiful works of art on the walls and the statuesque one walking beside her. She took advantage of an opportunity to gaze up at him as she said, "Do you not agree, Mr. Darcy, that artists are colourful people who draw on their emotions and pigments of their imagination?" She was a smidgen disappointed when the gentleman merely nodded and agreed with the comment, apparently deep in thought and unaware of her wordplay.

The object of Jane's study finally spotted their party, and his secret admirer secretly admired the power and masculinity he exuded as he flashed a knee-weakening smile and strode in her direction. Gone was the wild, green-tinged raffish ruffian from Pemberley; although he was more decently attired, there was still considerable evidence of well-toned muscles beneath his tight-fitting maroon coat and embarrassingly impressive bunchage beneath his inexpressible fawn breeches. Miss Bennet's breathing became more rapid as his polished black boots brought him closer with every step.

Darcy: "Fitz!"

Georgiana: "Richard!"

Anna: "Cousin!"

Elizabeth: "Colonel Fitzwilliam!"

Jane began to hyperventilate.

Caroline: "Oh. It is you."

Miss Sarah Dalrymple sighed, giggled, and sighed again. *Hell-o, Colonel Stud-Muffin!*

"Well, well, what a pleasant surprise, Darcy … and all these lovely ladies. Oh, and hello to you, too, Miss Bingley."

Bows and curtsies were exchanged, and Miss Jane Bennet blushed anew. The gallant officer was not dressed in regimentals; still, he was dashing and extremely handsome, and the lady was very much affected by his male beauty.

The Colonel glanced around and asked, "Is Charles Bingley not here with you?" He looked pointedly at Miss Bennet and assumed her charming blush was brought on by mention of the other man's name.

Caroline, who was obviously not affected by so much male beauty, sniffed, and said, "No, my brother is not here; and I might ask what brings you to such an exhibit. I have never thought of you as a connoisseur, Colonel."

"One does not have to be an authority, madam, to appreciate fine art. Otherwise, you would not be here either."

"Well, in the past, you did not appear to recognize beauty when it was right in front of you. Have you improved in the interim? Have you deigned to add ought of civility to your ordinary style? I dare not hope you have improved in essentials."

"Oh, absolutely not, Miss Bingley. In essentials, I believe, I am very much what I ever was."

"How sad."

"I beg to disagree … "

While the two continued to exchange derision, there was something in their countenances that made the others listen with an apprehensive and anxious attention; but Darcy disliked arguments and wanted to silence theirs, so he finally spoke up. "Miss Bingley and Fitz, your argument is too much like a dispute; so if you will both defer yours until you are alone, we shall all be very thankful."

"Well, cousin, I am afraid the argument shall have to be shelved indefinitely then, because I fervently hope I shall never find myself in such an unfortunate situation with Miss Bingley as you have just suggested."

Caroline Bingley retorted, "On that, at least, Colonel, we are surprisingly in complete agreement."

When George Darcy and Lady Anne returned from their mission in Kent, they accepted the invitation to dine with the Bennets; and it was settled between the two families the dinner would take place on Friday evening.

Mrs. Bennet was an excellent hostess; the lady, her housekeeper, the cook, and all the household's servants carried out the preparations for the engagement in a calm and competent manner. The rooms were spotless, the menu superb, and the goblets sparkled. Arrangements of dried and freshly cut flowers, strategically located, added a floral scent to the air; and brand-new candles were set into polished brass holders in the dining and drawing rooms. As she inspected the table settings one last time, Mrs. Bennet was surprised when her husband snuck up behind her and placed a gentle kiss on her neck.

"My dear, you have outdone yourself. As always, everything is perfect, as are you."

The lady smiled up at him but then frowned. "Thank you, Thomas. However, I am undecided. Shall we use our best flatware or the new silverware Edward recently gave us?"

"Well, the decision must be yours, love. All the same, since your brother and his family are coming, I would suggest the latter." He picked up a fork and examined it as he spoke. "And there is no *tine* like the present to make use of his present." He then whispered in her ear something about wanting to spoon later that night, though no one else was meant to hear.

Mr. Bennet's presence was soon replaced with Jane's, as she was summoned to help with the place cards. The eldest daughter had the best handwriting of the family; so, using the diagram her mother had drawn up and the pretty cards Elizabeth had designed and painted, she inscribed the names of the sixteen people who would be seated at their dining room table later that evening. When Jane noticed the placement of her own name, she suggested switching with Elizabeth, to her mother's surprise. "Why would you not care to sit across from the Darcy heir? Does he eat with his bare hands, wipe his mouth on his sleeve, or slurp his white soup? Are his manners truly barbaric, Jane? If so, why would you wish to expose Lizzy to such savage conduct? If not, what objection could you possibly have to facing him across the table?"

"Mama, I know you are not serious; and perhaps I should not say anything at this juncture, but I believe he and my sister are forming quite an attachment."

When Mrs. Bennet gasped, her daughter asked, "Does such a match shock you?"

"Not really, my dear. I had immediately suspected Lizzy was attracted to the … What was it Robert called him? … 'hanson barberin;' however, are you telling me Mr. Darcy has regard for her as well?"

When Jane emphatically nodded, her agitated mother cried, "Lud, what have I done?"

"Mama, whatever is the matter?" Jane was instantly at her side. "What have you done?"

"Oh, Jane, what is done is done."

"Yes, Mama. But *what* has been done?"

Mrs. Bennet wrung her hands. "No, no, not 'done' … *Dun*! Lieutenant-Colonel Dun paid another visit earlier this afternoon while you and Lizzy were out. Since I assumed he would soon officially start courting your sister, I invited him to join us for dinner."

Jane's eyes grew wide. "Oh Lud, Dun! London will not be big enough for a rivalry between John Dun and Fitzwilliam Darcy, let alone our townhouse. What shall we do, Mama?"

"Well, nothing can be done about Dun now, my dear. We shall simply have to make the best of what could prove to be an awkward situation."

Jane nodded. "Yes, it is unfortunate. I fear Lizzy will have to break the poor officer's heart, Mama. I truly believe hers belongs to another, as you shall undoubtedly see for yourself this evening."

Just then Mr. Bennet peeped around the door frame. "I am relieved to see the two of you still at home, for I kept hearing the word 'Lud' and feared you were both running off to join the Luddites."

Although the three youngest Bennet children – Kitty, Lydia, and Robert – would not be joining the others for dinner, they were permitted to remain in the drawing room for a short while to greet and meet the guests. Their Aunt and Uncle Gardiner were the first to arrive with their eldest son. A strapping lad of ten and seven, Evan was enrolled at Eton for the Michaelmas term and was only in town for a brief visit with his parents. His father, Edward Gardiner, was always a favourite visitor to the Bennet home. He often brought the children assorted trinkets from the import side of his business; and that evening he did not disappoint as he presented the three youngsters with a wooden box containing tic-tac-toe, draughts, and marbles. The delighted children obediently put the games away as soon as the next dinner guests, the widower John Burke and his eighteen-year-old son, Daniel, were announced. The Burkes lived in the townhouse across the street and were often invited when the Bennets entertained.

The Darcy family's arrival soon followed, necessitating many introductions; and when the youngest occupant of the room was brought forward, Robert Bennet's parents were extremely proud as the little boy bowed properly and completely charmed everyone while being presented to Mr. George Darcy, Lady Anne, Georgiana, and Anna. They were not so proud, however, when, upon being introduced to Fitzwilliam Darcy, Robert's blue eyes grew wide and he excitedly asked, "Are you Libazeth's hanson barberin?"

The tall, dark, and handsome Darcy heir stood gaping down at the tiny, fair, and adorable Bennet heir, just as a servant announced, "Lieutenant-Colonel John Dun."

The army officer, in his brilliant uniform, made a striking entrance but stopped short at the sight that greeted him. The three eldest Bennet daughters and their lovely mother were all blushing nearly as deeply as the scarlet of his regimental coat.

"I beg your pardon?" Fitzwilliam Darcy asked Robert Bennet in a distracted manner. His attention was divided between the arrival of the soldier and the sweet little boy with his very intriguing question that had caused such embarrassment for nearly half the ladies in the room.

"I beg your pardon," said the confused Lieutenant-Colonel John Dun as he glanced at the occupants of the drawing room, "have I come at a bad time?"

Mr. Bennet immediately put the young army officer at ease by introducing him to the two Burke men, the Gardiners, George and Lady Anne Darcy, Miss Darcy and Miss Anna.

Already a bit discombobulated by the three-year-old Bennet's 'hanson barberin' question, learning the identity of the brawny soldier threw Fitzwilliam Darcy further off balance. Georgiana had warned her brother he might have competition if he wished to pursue Elizabeth Bennet, and at Pemberley the lady herself had mentioned a very good friend who was an army officer. Darcy thought his sister had said he was a dun fellow; and he assumed she meant he was a colourless, importuning sort. Of course, one should never assume.

It is a truth universally acknowledged that in nature, the more colourful and ornate male bird is designed to attract the female of the species. In mammals, however, the male might actually have to prove himself worthy by competing with another in order to win the right to be a certain female's mate.

Lieutenant-Colonel John Dun was an attractive, well-bred man in his mid twenties, about six foot and twelve stone, with a confident gait and posture. Well groomed and impeccably dressed and polished, he exuded youth, vigour, strength, and dominance. As Dun was introduced to each guest that evening, he made direct eye contact and greeted him or her with a warm and bright smile.

His thick and vibrant wavy hair, which brushed the collar of his coat, seemed to change colour depending on how the light touched the burnished strands. Miss Darcy thought it was auburn with gold highlights; Miss Anna called it amber with streaks of bronze; Jane considered it to be more copper with fiery accents; and Lizzy, who was rather hungry as she waited for dinner, would have said it resembled cinnamon, nutmeg, and honey. Fitzwilliam Darcy's opinion of Dun's hair was that it looked like a clay-covered carrot-coloured mop that clashed horribly with the red of the ruddy bloke's uniform.

The women admired his wide shoulders, broad chest, and slender waist and hips. Beneath the dignified uniform, it was evident John Dun's build was muscular, well toned, and very fit; Jane Bennet's thoughts wandered to Pemberley's lawn as she pictured a different handsome officer and wondered how Colonel Richard Fitzwilliam would look with his clothes on … er, uniform on.

"I apologize for wearing regimentals to dinner. I was detained and did not want to risk the time to change into civilian clothes for fear of arriving during the middle of the meal."

Fitzwilliam Darcy mumbled to himself, "Taradiddling popinjay."

The ladies had no complaints whatsoever about Dun being in uniform, and they continued to study the good-looking officer. Madeline Gardiner noticed the Lieutenant-Colonel had a wide brow, a clear and slightly tanned complexion, and symmetrical features, except for a small scar to the left of his broad chin. Mary Bennet sighed, like the schoolgirl she was, and studied his high cheekbones, square jaw, straight nose, and full lips. The fact the officer was clean-shaven and had neatly trimmed sideburns also met with her approval. Lady Anne Darcy admired Dun's lush auburn lashes and eyebrows, neither too thick nor too thin, that framed big, round, deeply set emerald eyes that often sought Miss Elizabeth; and a concerned Lady Anne glanced toward her son.

Fitzwilliam Darcy stood rooted to the same spot where the tow-headed little boy had confronted and confounded him. Robert Bennet was in the process of being whisked off to bed, in company with Lydia and Kitty; and their mother took a few minutes away from her guests to kiss her youngest children goodnight. As they were going out the door, the little lad could be heard saying, "But, Mama, I want to talk to the hanson barberin!"

Darcy moved closer to Miss Elizabeth, turned his mind away from the conundrum of the poppet's words, and redirected his attention toward the popinjay. Lieutenant-Colonel John Dun felt someone's stare boring into his back, and he pivoted toward a tall and aloof gentleman who was standing, much too closely in his opinion, beside the beautiful Miss Elizabeth. Mr. Bennet introduced the two strong young bucks and wondered whether he could actually feel the tension and animosity in the air between them or if it was just his imagination. Fitzwilliam Darcy's nostrils flared when the other man looked him squarely in the face, and the green-eyed monster reared its ugly head. Dun raised his chin, his emerald eyes met Darcy's glare full on, and the two males recognized and appraised their rival.

In medieval times, nobility and knights alike displayed their trust in one another by extending hands to show they held no weapons; and the grasping of hands demonstrated open hospitality rather than hostility or intent to harm. The unexpected handshake between Darcy and Dun turned into a duel of sorts, with each increasing the pressure of his bone-crushing clasp until Mr. Bennet cleared his throat and gave them both a disapproving glare. The host completed the last of the introductions; and, as everyone took a seat, Mr. Bennet was unnerved to discover Lizzy had become sandwiched on a sofa between the dashing Darcy and the dutiful Dun.

Elizabeth was both thrilled and mortified, and every eye in the room seemed to be unnecessarily focused on her particular seating arrangement. The thrill was the result of being almost squashed between two such magnificent male models of masculinity. The mortification was threefold: firstly, from being almost squashed between two such magnificent male models of masculinity; secondly, from said 'squashment' being under the scrutiny of her family and friends; and thirdly, from the knowledge she would soon have to disappoint one of the men whose thigh was tantalizingly pressed against her own.

Chapter III

Are You Well, Dun?

At the dinner table, to Mrs. Bennet's right and left, George Darcy and Madeline Gardiner sat across from one another and spoke of Pemberley's menagerie. Mrs. Gardiner said, "My husband is very fond of small dogs; and he heard so much about Dust Bunny and Pug-Nacious from our nieces that I finally gave in when Edward hounded me about getting a puppy. We decided on a Maltese, because an acquaintance breeds the dear little dogs. Then we had quite a lengthy dispute over which puppy to choose; and it was, after much argument, the pique of the litter."

At the other end of the table, the host was conversing with those closest to him, Lady Anne Darcy, John Burke, Edward Gardiner, and Georgiana Darcy. Mr. Burke finished telling a story about a ladder having been brazenly stolen from his townhouse property, and Mr. Bennet suggested further steps would need to be taken in order to prevent another such theft from their neighbourhood.

As Mrs. Bennet had decided to keep to her original seating plan, Fitzwilliam Darcy was almost as far from Elizabeth as the table could divide them. To his right was Mrs. Gardiner and to his left Mary Bennet, followed by beyond-the-pale Lieutenant-Colonel Dun, who was in the most fortunate position of being seated next to Elizabeth. Because they were on the same side of the table, Darcy could neither see nor hear what was transpiring between the two without leaning inappropriately forward or backward; so he suffered in ignorance and made polite small talk about music with Miss Mary and also with Miss Jane Bennet, who was seated across from him.

From further down the table, the delightful sound of Elizabeth's laughter reached Darcy's envious ears. *Aargh! What are you saying, Dun? Of what is it you are talking? What are you telling Miss Elizabeth? Let me hear what it is. I must have my share in your conversation.* His over-active imagination had Dun leaning in to whisper sweet nothings in Lizzy's receptive ear, and it got the better of him. Darcy leaned backward until, behind the row of diners, he could see the rogue's carrot-topped head next to the cherished chestnut curls; and he was somewhat appeased to note decorum was, at least, being maintained.

When he returned to a forward position, Darcy happened to glance across the table and several seats away to his youngest sister, Anna. It seemed as though she was thoroughly enjoying her position between two strapping young men, Evan Gardiner and Daniel Burke. *Good Lord. Is Anna actually flirting?* Although he was very protective of both his sisters, he was thankful he did not have full responsibility for them and thought it must be rather difficult to keep a tight rein on young women until they were securely, and with any luck happily, betrothed and wed to good men.

Lieutenant-Colonel John Dun had been extremely gratified to discover he would be the fortunate one seated next to the lovely Miss Elizabeth and that the dour Darcy dolt was far away and, hopefully, forgotten. Dun regularly regaled her with regimental revelry and relished her refreshing responses.

Georgiana Darcy, seated betwixt Edward Gardiner and Daniel Burke, was not a very accommodating conversationalist that evening. Instead she concentrated on what was being said between Elizabeth and the handsome army officer, although they were across the table and a couple places away. Georgiana was not shy and could be quite outspoken when her temper was provoked. She looked daggers at the military man who held her friend captive and could no longer hold her tongue. "Lieutenant-Colonel, I believe an army officer is a position for which some people shoot. I have even heard army officers drink in order to be fortified in their position."

Lady Anne was rather appalled at her daughter's forthrightness. She knew her son suffered in silence at the other end of the table and was somewhat amused that Georgiana had taken up the cause on his behalf; nevertheless, she would not stand for impertinence nor hesitate to put her foot down if the situation merited a firm stance.

Dun smiled at the young lady and said, "Miss Darcy, in general, the rumours you hear about the army often have a colonel of truth to them, but not in a major way."

Edward Gardiner added, "I know of one cavalry officer who switched to the navy, and his life took a new tack."

Elizabeth was having a very good time, despite being separated from the handsome barbarian. She turned toward her uncle and asked, "Is he the same naval officer who gave the milliner a stern look because he wanted to purchase a new hat but was afraid of cap-sizing?"

Mr. Gardiner grinned at his niece and said, "I am unsure, my dear; but as to alcohol, I do know he harboured a love of port."

'Port' was the cue taken by the hostess to stand and indicate the ladies should follow her to the drawing room while the eight gentlemen remained behind to enjoy fortified beverages imported by her brother.

John Burke proudly produced his ornate snuffbox and inquired whether any others cared to partake, which they did not; however, John Dun did light up a cheroot. Copious amounts of port, Madeira, and brandy were available; and the four elder gentlemen were content to remain in the room and talk of Tattersall's, horse racing, and pugilism –especially Tom Cribb's victory in the eleventh round at Thistleton Gap on September 28th. Lieutenant-Colonel John Dun easily joined in their discussions, and it was evident he was an erudite conversationalist. Fitzwilliam Darcy, on the other hand, did not have the talent of conversing easily with those he had never met before. He could neither catch their tone of conversation nor appear interested in their concerns. Darcy was more interested in retreating to the drawing room and speaking with Miss Elizabeth, as he found it quite effortless and pleasurable to have intercourse with her.

The two youngest men, Evan Gardiner and Daniel Burke, were already well acquainted; they sat together at the table and amused themselves by watching Darcy and Dun. The latter two gentlemen alternately pretended the other did not exist at all or exchanged glares that indicated they wished the other some grim reaper-cussions.

Fitzwilliam Darcy impatiently waited for his host to signal it was time to rejoin the ladies; but the older men were enjoying their chitchat and showed no interest in leaving. He wanted to see Elizabeth again, to stake his claim, to ascertain her feelings, to whisk her away with him into the night … perhaps to Scotland. Most of all, he wanted John Dun out of the picture. Instead, he settled for another drink.

When Mr. Gardiner noticed Fitzwilliam Darcy imbibing a bit more than advisable, he leaned across the table and casually suggested, "Young man, never drink beyond the pint of no return or you will be sorry the mourning after."

Lieutenant-Colonel John Dun also noticed his rival's distress; and, with a cheroot clenched between his teeth, he raised his snifter of brandy and saluted the Friday-faced fellow. Fitzwilliam Darcy blearily glared back at Dun through the noxious vapours that hung in the air around the blowhard, windbag bloke; and Darcy hoped his dreams of a future with Elizabeth had not all turned to smoke.

When Mr. Bennet finally looked at the clock and realized they should have joined the ladies long ago, it was almost time for the guests to take their leave. Instead of conversing with Elizabeth, Darcy had to settle for gazing at her with a goofy grin on his face, as he was a wee bit foxed.

The next day, Miss Charlotte Lucas arrived at the Bennet townhouse for a stay of several nights' duration. Sir William's eldest daughter, at two and twenty, was a pretty lady with lustrous café au lait hair and large cobalt blue eyes. She was the particular friend of the eldest Miss Bennet but more closely resembled Lizzy in temperament, as she had a lively sense of humour and was more outgoing than Jane.

The females of the family and their guest gathered in the sitting room. As they settled in, Mrs. Bennet, Jane, and Elizabeth picked up their workbaskets, spoke of their stay thus far in London, and asked about the news from Hertfordshire. Some ladies, while sewing and chatting, needle little something to catch the thread of a conversation; however, Charlotte and the Bennets were as close as family and very comfortable with one another.

A servant interrupted their gossip by announcing, "Lieutenant-Colonel John Dun wishes to pay a visit to the ladies of the house." Everyone's eyes shifted immediately to Lizzy. Mrs. Bennet conveyed her permission, and the dashing officer stayed for a full half-hour. Before he departed, Dun requested of his hostess he be allowed to return on the morrow for the purpose of a private conversation with Miss Elizabeth. Dun was done with pussyfooting around while tomcat Darcy lurked in the shadows.

Over breakfast at another London townhouse, George Darcy and Lady Anne discussed their enjoyment of the previous night's dinner with the Bennet family and their guests.

"I must admit, my dear Anne, after meeting the two eldest daughters and witnessing our son's reaction to Miss Elizabeth at our own dinner, I did a little snooping into her family's status. Although they eschew the ton, the Bennets are actually quite well connected and wealthy, despite having some relations in trade."

Lady Anne slipped several slices of ham under the table to her Italian Greyhounds, Geoffrey and Chaucer, and said, "I was rather surprised to discover those relations to be genteel people of fashion. Edward and Madeline Gardiner did not seem at all coarse or crude. In fact, I would say they are more polite and refined than many of the so-called noble aristocracy with whom we are, unfortunately, acquainted … my own family being no exception."

George Darcy slipped several cubes of cheese under the table to his Dalmatians, Rex and Regina. "I agree they are not the money-grubbing, uncouth merchants I had expected and would not be opposed to furthering the acquaintance. I found Mr. Gardiner to be a man of intelligence and good moral character, and the only reservation I have about the entire evening is the trite sense of humour enjoyed by the Bennet family and their relatives."

The couple was soon joined by their three offspring. As Fitzwilliam, Georgiana, and Anna took their places at the table, their parents were concerned the Bennet influence and trite sense of humour may have rubbed off on their eldest as he tucked into his breakfast, grinned, and said, "A boiled egg in the morning is hard to beat, and I believe there are four dogs under the table enjoying a swine and cheese party."

Before long, the two men separately took their leave. Lady Anne, Georgiana, and Anna decided to go for a stroll in their townhouse garden. The three ladies shared their impressions from the night before, and Georgiana expressed her concern Elizabeth might favour Lieutenant-Colonel Dun over her more deserving brother.

Lady Anne replied, "Georgie, from my limited observations, Miss Elizabeth and Fitzwilliam are forming a rather strong attachment; and although the officer is certainly a fine, attractive young man, I cannot believe she would prefer him over your brother. Still and all, as a doting mother, I just might be an impartial judge of the matter."

Her mother's smile went unnoticed by Georgiana because her mind's eye was focused on the future, and that future involved her dear friend becoming her dear sister. She knew, without a doubt, Elizabeth was the perfect match for her beloved brother. "Mother, would you actually approve of Miss Elizabeth as a match for Fitzwilliam?"

"As you know, my exposure to the young lady has been limited to two dinner engagements, but from what I have gleaned, she comes from a good family, is a healthy woman, and seems just the sort of clever wife your brother needs. Miss Elizabeth does bring out his hidden liveliness. Although your father had hoped Fitzwilliam might marry a lady with a title or wealth, you know my wishes are only for your brother's and your own future happiness. So, if she encourages him to loosen up and be jocular, then yes, I would approve wholeheartedly."

Like Georgiana, Anna also rejoiced in her parent's apparent acceptance. "I am very pleased you like Elizabeth, Mother; yet I am afraid there is someone of our acquaintance who does not share our fond regard for the lady."

Lady Anne looked askance at her youngest daughter, and Anna turned to her older sister for support in broaching the subject of Caroline Bingley. Georgiana explained the snub and nasty attitude Elizabeth had graciously suffered through at the Royal Academy. Their mother was not at all pleased to hear of Miss Bingley's catty treatment of the young lady who was her daughters' good friend and just might, possibly, even become part of the Darcy family in the future.

Her vexation was slightly aggravated when Anna said, "Yes, Mother, it was horrid of Miss Bingley to try and steal away Elizabeth's self-esteem that afternoon. Why, it was daylight snobbery!"

Before Lady Anne could open her mouth to chide Anna for such poor taste, a servant appeared and announced Mr. Ellis Fleming had arrived to see Miss Darcy and that he had been shown to the drawing room to wait.

A blissful smile spread across Georgiana's face, and she said, "Finally he is here! It has been such a long time, and I cannot wait another minute. Mother, I have been expecting him for hours so may I please run ahead this very second and greet him?"

"Yes, yes, go ahead, Georgiana; but the drawing room door remains open until one of us arrives to watch over you."

After breakfasting with his family, Fitzwilliam Darcy met Colonel Fitzwilliam for a ride in the park before going to Whites to join their friends. They avoided the throng by taking the road less traveled. When he was sure they would not be overheard, Darcy pulled up alongside his cousin.

"Fitz, do you happen to know a Lieutenant-Colonel John Dun?"

"Yes, not well mind you; still, our paths have crossed on occasion. He is an exemplary officer, from a fine family, an amiable fellow well liked by both his subordinates and superiors, and, I believe, much admired by the ladies. Why do you ask?"

Darcy had hoped to hear Dun was a deplorable and disobedient soldier, held in contempt by his fellow officers, penniless, and a gambling rakish reprobate. He could then have told Georgiana; and she could have, in turn, warned her friend away from such a good-for-nothing rogue. He wished Lieutenant-Colonel Dun far away in Portugal and suddenly remembered the conversation Miss Elizabeth had with them in Pemberley's drawing room. "No particular reason. That said, do you remember Miss Elizabeth Bennet knew about some secret Portuguese fortifications?"

"Thunder and turf! Are you implying this Lieutenant-Colonel Dun has been revealing military secrets or that Miss Elizabeth is involved in espionage?"

"Good God, no! The lady is most certainly not a spy. All the same, what would be the ramifications if an officer divulged such sensitive information?"

"Bloody hell, man! It might well be treason; and the consequences would be damn dire, indeed, Darcy."

"Then, no, I am definitely not implying any such thing."

"Cousin, if you know of traitorous activity, it is your duty to cry rope on those involved so an investigation can be conducted."

"Really, Fitz, do not make this into a Cheltenham tragedy; it is merely a bag of moonshine."

"I find your end of this conversation to be too smoky by half, Darcy. Nevertheless, if you insist there has been no wrongdoing, I shall let it be for now. Regardless, I intend to keep an eye on Lieutenant-Colonel Dun henceforth."

"Is there any chance you could arrange to have the bloody, ruddy bloke shipped to the continent?"

"Gah! Just what, exactly, is your problem with John Dun, cousin?"

"My only objection to the odious officer is that he is an obstruction to my obtaining ... "

"Stop searching, right now, for words that start with 'o' Darcy; or I swear I will plant you a facer and draw your cork. Speak normally and quickly, man. If I do have to draw your claret, I might need to change my bloodstained uniform before we are due at Whites; I have a meeting at headquarters later in the day."

Darcy knew he did not have a fighting chance against his cousin, as the military man could very well land him a facer. Therefore, he succinctly explained his ardent admiration for the alluring Miss Elizabeth Bennet. This information, however, was old news to his cousin, as he had already witnessed it at Pemberley. What vexed Colonel Fitzwilliam was the extent of Darcy's jealousy of Dun. "That is utterly despicable, Darcy. I cannot believe you would stoop so low as to jeopardize an army officer's career simply because you are attracted to his lady."

"That is it, Richard! Dismount immediately and prepare to have *your* claret drawn. How dare you make such an accusation!"

"Calm down, Darce. Cripes, man, you started the whole damn discussion by implying Dun was leaking information."

"Well, if he did let something slip to Miss Elizabeth, I can guarantee the young woman is not passing the information along to Masséna. I have been known to utter utter nonsense while in her bewitching company as well, so I suppose I cannot blame the bloke. And she is not *his* lady, Fitz. The fool has not even asked for permission to court her yet, and that was his first mistake."

"Has he made a second?"

"Yes. He has made me realize I never wish to lose her."

An hour later, Fitzwilliam Darcy, Colonel Richard Fitzwilliam, and their friends, Charles Bingley and Ellis Fleming, met at Whites.

"Fleming, it is good to see you again; and I trust matters went well in Derbyshire. I know my sister has been eagerly awaiting your arrival. Have you visited Georgiana yet?"

"Of course. In fact, I have actually come here directly from your house. I must say Miss Darcy grows more beautiful every time I see her. I am so glad I was able to complete my business and be here in time for the ball. I understand both your sisters have been enjoying the company of the Misses Bennet since your family arrived in Town and they will also be attending the event. How are those lovely ladies?"

The blonde gentleman pounded his fist on the table. "Confound it, Darcy! Do you mean to tell me now that the exquisite Miss Bennet has been in London these past weeks and you did not see fit to inform me?"

"Bingley, my friend, I only learned of their presence in the city over a week ago. When I discovered Miss Bennet and Miss Elizabeth were to dine with us at Darcy House, it was too short notice to include you; and I could hardly inveigle an invitation for you to dinner at their home last evening. They are a delightful family, though; and the two eldest daughters are such good friends for my sisters."

Colonel Fitzwilliam snorted and said, "Ah, yes. They are merely your sisters' friends. Right. Be that as it may, I agree with Fleming that they are, indeed, lovely ladies. I hope to have an opportunity to dance with them both at the ball at least once, but I imagine their dance cards will fill rather quickly. Hmm, perhaps I should call upon Miss Bennet and Miss Elizabeth and make my requests early. Any gentleman interested in standing up with such desirable women must be kept on his toes, otherwise another bloke will step on his toes to have the privilege of stepping on the ladies' toes."

His suggestion caused alarm in two of his friends, as he had intended; and Bingley and Darcy both privately decided they should also call upon the Bennet household before it was too late. Fleming stood and explained he had an appointment with his solicitor; and Colonel Fitzwilliam departed with him, as he had to attend a meeting at headquarters.

"Darcy, do you suppose Fitz really has a meeting or might he actually be on his way to the Bennet townhouse?"

"I know he really has a meeting, Bingley. Stop fretting. I am sure the Bennet sisters will still have room on their dance cards for you. Speaking of sisters, we met yours at the Royal Academy recently while Georgiana, Anna, and I were in company with Miss Bennet and Miss Elizabeth. I must say, Bingley, your sister can be rather … "

"Yes?"

"Rather … "

"Spit it out, man. How do you wish to describe Caroline? Snooty? Snobby? Snotty?"

"Yes, yes, and yes. Sorry Bingley, but you well know what she can be like. Caroline was very disdainful toward my new friends that day, and … "

"Wait one minute. *Your* new friends? I thought Miss Bennet and Miss Elizabeth were merely your sisters' friends, so why have *you* been spending so much time with them?"

"Oh, do stop nitpicking. Seriously, Bingley, you and I have known each other for years; and I greatly value our friendship and hope to never lose it. Nevertheless, what I have to say next may very well jeopardize our relationship."

"This sounds serious, indeed, Darcy. Please be assured you have my full attention, cooperation, and continual friendship, whatever dire information you are about to impart."

"This is difficult to say, and I realize it is not my place to do so. Despite that, something must be done about your sister. One of these days she is going to go too far and offend the wrong person. You jokingly described her as snobby, snooty, and snotty; however, it is no joke, my friend. Miss Bingley truly is a snob; and I certainly do not allude to the slang that I realize may have been hurtful to you while at Cambridge."

"Darcy, I am not ashamed of my background. For many generations our ancestors were cobblers. Caroline and I do, absolutely, owe our current prosperity to a bunch of shoemakers. I know the origin of the word 'snob' started as the nickname for a cobbler or his apprentice. It also meant tradesman, merchant, townsman, or basically any person of low class. I am not ignorant to the fact 'snob' is now beginning to mean one who imitates their betters. You and your relatives have always been our betters, yet you have never looked down upon us, my friend; and I thank you for that.

Thank you also for being a good enough friend to be honest about Caroline. I will certainly have a long-overdue talk with my sister about her attitude. She is not a bad person, Darcy, merely insecure and, perhaps, envious. Because of our wealth, we were thrust into a mostly unwelcoming society. Without the guidance of parents, we have floundered. Please accept my apologies on her behalf. If you think it advisable, I will also, without hesitation, apologize to Miss Bennet and Miss Elizabeth for any embarrassment they suffered because of my sister's actions or words."

"Good God, Bingley. My sphere of society can only benefit from the inclusion of a good man like you. In my estimation, Charles Bingley, you stand head and shoulders above the majority of aristocrats of my acquaintance; and I am privileged to call you friend."

The two young men suddenly became embarrassed by such heartfelt talk and started to joke about their long-standing friendship, their days together at Cambridge, and the people they knew there.

" … and remember Pascal, the mathematics professor? Now there was a cold and calculating man!"

"Yes, indeed, he obviously had a lot of problems."

"If I remember correctly, Darcy, he was cross-eyed and could not control his pupils."

"Then he started to wear spectacles to improve di-vision."

Bingley groaned at his friend's puny pun and Darcy said, "Well, Pascal could certainly multiply well enough. I have heard he and his wife have twelve children. Perhaps he was not so cold after all."

At the Bennet townhouse, Jane, Elizabeth, and Charlotte Lucas were in the music room; and they took turns at the pianoforte while they discussed young men of their acquaintance. Lizzy was at the instrument, quite lost in a lovely piece of music and only half listening as Charlotte spoke. " … and he is certainly an attractive gentleman, Lizzy. You are very fortunate to have such a handsome and amiable suitor."

"Hmm? Oh, yes, Mr. Darcy is very good looking."

"Who?"

"I beg your pardon, Charlotte. Were you not speaking of Mr. Fitzwilliam Darcy?"

"Lizzy, I am not even acquainted with any such gentleman. You, apparently, are and were just now thinking of him. Jane, who is this dreamy man who has your sister now blushing so furiously? Does she actually have *two* gorgeous and amiable suitors?"

"Why, yes, Charlotte. I do believe she does."

"Jane! No, Charlotte, Mr. Darcy is merely an acquaintance. Actually he is the elder brother of our new friends, Miss Georgiana Darcy and Miss Anna Darcy. You simply caught me off guard while engrossed in Beethoven's moving music. I now realize you were speaking of Lieutenant-Colonel John Dun, who, by the way, is also merely an acquaintance."

Jane teasingly reminded, "An acquaintance who is due here at any moment for the purpose of a private conversation with Miss Elizabeth."

Elizabeth quickly arose from the bench. "Charlotte, I have an excellent idea. Why do we not take one of the carriages and go shopping now? Your trip to London would not be complete without an excursion to its fine stores. You plainly cannot return to Hertfordshire without making at least several purchases."

"Sister! You cannot possibly leave before meeting with the Lieutenant-Colonel, and you would merely be postponing your dilemma. You must deal with your quandary today and be done with it. Lizzy, have you decided what you will say to him?"

"Jane, I can hardly decide what *I* will say when I do not yet know what *he* will say. What do you suppose he *will* say? What do *you* think I should say? Oh, why can we not just go shopping? Then neither he nor I will have to say anything to the other at all today."

Charlotte was incredulous. "Elizabeth Bennet! I cannot believe you have any hesitation in regard to that desirable soldier's regard. From what I understand, he is obviously either going to ask to court you or request your hand in marriage. I would certainly jump at either of the officer's offers, you awfully fortunate girl!"

"You saw him for a half-hour here yesterday, Charlotte. That is not quite enough time to make you understand his character."

"If you were to marry him tomorrow, I should think you had as good a chance of happiness as if you were to be studying his character for a twelve-month. Happiness in marriage is entirely a matter of chance, and sometimes it is better to know as little as possible in advance of the defects of the person with whom you are to pass your life."

"You make me laugh, Charlotte; but it is not sound. You know it is not sound."

They were startled by the sound of a servant as he cleared his throat and announced the arrivals of Mr. Fitzwilliam Darcy, Mr. Charles Bingley, and Lieutenant-Colonel John Dun. Elizabeth Bennet abruptly sat back down and turned as pale as the embroidered white muslin dress she wore.

Chapter IV

How to Accept or Reject a Marriage Proposal:
In One Easy Liaison

Three eager gents had separately presented themselves at the door of the Bennet townhouse within seconds of one another; and an astute servant, by the name of Sharp, recognized friction between at least two of the ar-rivals. Mr. Fitzwilliam Darcy and Lieutenant-Colonel John Dun swapped the same sort of jealous, resentful glares Sharp and another footman, Baines, who was the bane of Sharp's existence, frequently exchanged because of a rivalry over a charming chambermaid. He wisely had both the Master and Mistress summoned to the music salon; and when Mr. and Mrs. Bennet met in the hallway, they rolled eyes at one another and entered to find six stylish young people sitting in awkward silence. The couple took control of the situation, ensured everyone had been properly introduced, and initiated the usual polite small talk.

Ten minutes later, Sharp announced to the assemblage yet another gentleman caller; and although the servant was quite amused, he projected a proper outward mien of composure. "Sir and madam, a Colonel Richard Fitzwilliam wishes to pay a visit to Miss Bennet and Miss Elizabeth."

Mr. Bennet said, "Why, this is an afternoon of wonders, indeed! Very well, Sharp; and if twenty such callers should come into our neighbourhood, send them in, for we are quite at leisure."

The footman was often confused by the Master's remarks, and he wondered whether the family actually did expect a score of eligible young males to arrive at the door. He would not be surprised if that were the case, because the two eldest daughters were remarkable women, both beautiful and kind. Later when no further callers arrived, Sharp second-guest that his employer had not been serious about such visitors after all.

Colonel Fitzwilliam was amazed to find Darcy, Dun, and Bingley all in attendance; and he thought the visit could prove to be quite entertaining. As he looked around the room again, the soldier caught Miss Jane Bennet staring brazenly, and somewhat appraisingly, in his own direction. Fitz glanced behind his shoulder to see if someone else was there; and when he looked back, her face was red and her gaze lowered. *Well, well, now. That was certainly uplifting. But why is she not bestowing such admiring glances on Bingley? I thought ... hah! ... well, too bad, old chap; and thank you, indeed, Miss Beautiful Bennet, for such flattering regard.*

Darcy was not surprised his cousin had called, and, for that matter, neither was Bingley; the latter, however, was not at all happy about his presence.

As for Dun, he was taken aback at the arrival of a superior officer and sincerely hoped Colonel Fitzwilliam was not there as well to see Miss Elizabeth.

Mr. and Mrs. Bennet sat together on a settee, and the husband clandestinely reached for his wife's hand and gave it a quick squeeze as he whispered, "An Englishman's home is his castle, in a manor of speaking; yet this home seems to be suddenly suffering from a surfeit of suitable suitors, specifically soldiers. Whatever were we thinking, my dear, in bringing our lovely daughters to Town? It is all your fault, you know, for Jane and Lizzy received their good looks and fine qualities from you."

Even after all their years together, Mrs. Bennet blushed and whispered back, "Such flattery will get you somewhere later, Thomas."

The observant Charlotte Lucas could hardly contain her laughter at all the little comedies and dramas being played out in the room. Mr. and Mrs. Bennet flirted with one another; Jane was red because she had been caught mentally undressing one of the brawny soldiers; Lizzy was still ashen due to the prospect of a marriage proposal; Mr. Darcy and Lieutenant-Colonel Dun held a staring contest over which had the biggest … ego; Mr. Bingley enviously glared at Colonel Fitzwilliam for having the gall to receive Jane's regard; and the latter gentleman was obviously very pleased about being the recipient of same. When the civil whiskers ground to another uncomfortable standstill, four gentlemen, speaking at once, broke the silence.

Dun: "Mrs. Bennet, yesterday, as you remember, I requested a private … "

Darcy: "Miss Elizabeth, would you do me the honour of standing up … "

Bingley: "Miss Bennet, may I request that you save your supper … "

Fitz: "Miss Bennet, please may I have the very great pleasure of you … "

Dun and Darcy looked daggers across the room at each other; Bingley glowered at Fitz, who smirked back at him.

Mr. Bennet caught the scowls between Mr. Darcy and the Lieutenant-Colonel and bestowed a fond gaze upon his second-eldest child. *Are we to lose one of our precious girls so soon? Where has the time gone? It seems like only last year Lizzy was still climbing trees. Oh, wait. Of course, it was just last year.*

He went out on a limb and said, "Mrs. Bennet, I believe you did, indeed, promise the Lieutenant-Colonel a private audience with our cherished Elizabeth. Perhaps those two should proceed to the drawing room, where the door will remain open." He gave Dun a look the young man could not fail to understand.

Elizabeth's smile wavered as she shakily stood and proceeded across the floor in the direction of the officer. She started to glance backward to another gentleman, but Dun quickly offered his arm, which she took as they moved toward the door.

Fitzwilliam Darcy sat in absolute agony and watched his world fall apart. *No, no, no! Do something, you bumbling buffoon. Immediately if not sooner! Do not allow this attachment to happen. She is mine, and I love her! Stop them! Now! Before it is too late! Quickly, man!*

He stood, cleared his throat, and … sat back down. He could think of no sane reason to halt their departure; and, in fact, he could not think at all, except for what his subconscious had just revealed.

I love her? Good God, yes, I do love her; and that blasted army officer is walking away, both literally and figuratively, with my perfect woman. Be that as it may, I certainly cannot declare myself in front of the present company.

He was utterly devastated; and for the first time in his adult life, he felt his wretched stiff upper lip begin to falter and his lower lip begin to tremble. Darcy was just about to arise again, pace to the window, and hide his emotions as he had been taught, when suddenly Elizabeth spun around and looked directly at him. Their eyes locked; hers silently asked a question of him, and Darcy allowed his to openly express everything he felt. She smiled reassuringly and made his heart skip a beat, and then she turned back to the other young man who impatiently awaited her. As they walked out of sight, Darcy hoped against hope he was reading her expression correctly and all was not lost.

Elizabeth sat rigidly on the edge of a wingback chair and watched Lieutenant-Colonel John Dun pace. He finally came to a halt in front of her, flashed a warm, gorgeous smile, and said, "I must admit I am more nervous facing one beautiful young lady than I have been facing a whole horde of enemy soldiers; and in both situations my life has been in the other's hands. Miss Elizabeth, we have been acquainted for nearly a year and a half. You know I am respectable, have easily earned promotions, and can provide for a family. We are quite compatible; and although the life of a soldier is not always an easy one, I would very much like to share mine with you. I confess, as recently as twenty minutes ago, I merely intended to ask permission to court you; but I have grown impatient to make you mine." He reached for her hand, placed a gentle kiss on her bare knuckles, and looked deeply into her eyes. "Miss Elizabeth Bennet, will you do me the great honour of becoming my wife?"

Elizabeth felt a momentary thrill rush through her body. John Dun was extremely handsome, his touch excited her, and his emerald eyes held such hope and promise. A marriage proposal was a heady experience, indeed, and Lizzy grew quite woozy. The fact she was suffering from a lack of oxygen suddenly occurred, and she released the breath she had been holding. Still and all, she also realized he had not once expressed his regard or feelings for her; and although she would not have accepted even if he had, she was still a bit disappointed and perturbed.

"Sir, I am overwhelmed and flattered by the compliment you are paying me; and I thank you for the offer … "

Dun captured her other hand, pulled her from the chair, and shouted with elation, "Oh, Elizabeth, you have truly made me the proudest man in the world!"

Because both the drawing room and music salon doors were open, the occupants of the latter could not help but eavesdrop on the young man's enthusiastic, if premature, exclamation of joy. The overheard words proved too much for heartbroken Fitzwilliam Darcy; he quickly choked out his excuses, bowed, and made haste for the door. No one heard Miss Elizabeth's next words except John Dun.

Lizzy was momentarily distracted by the sounds of long, hurried strides along the hallway, the startling slam of the front door, and a carriage quickly pulling away. *Mr. Darcy, no!* As she was about to speak, another footfall was heard; and the door to the street had scarcely shut, when more footsteps meant the third visitor was also exiting. She turned back to the final young man; and she knew, although he was certainly not the last man in the world whom she could ever be prevailed on to marry, he was not the first and only such man.

"Sir, you are too hasty. You forget I have made no answer. Let me do so without further loss of time. Please accept my thanks, for I am sensible of the great honour of your proposal; but it is impossible for me to do otherwise than decline."

Lieutenant-Colonel Dun lost colour, released her hands, and staggered backward. "You are … refusing me?"

Lizzy sat down and spoke very softly. "I am truly sorry, sir. It would not at all be proper or fair for me to enter into a marriage with you under the circumstances."

"Do these circumstances involve another man?"

The young lady turned crimson, looked down at her lap, and refused to answer.

"I have my answer, then. Blast it! Pardon me, Miss Elizabeth. I am afraid I must take my leave. I would not be very good company right now. Please extend my apologies to your family and friends for my sudden departure." He curtly bowed, donned his hat, and strode toward the open door.

"John, please wait."

The young officer was startled and halted by the use of his name, and he turned back to face the woman who had wounded his pride. The fact his heart was neither engaged nor broken did not occur to him.

Elizabeth Bennet stood and looked at him with tear-filled eyes. Her voice trembled as she spoke. "Sir, please, stay just a moment longer. I do not wish to part from you in this manner. We have been friends for too long to allow this awkwardness to come between us. I beseech you to understand I did not intend to hurt you. Nevertheless, only the deepest love could persuade me to enter into matrimony. I do care for you and hope you are still somewhat fond of me. Despite that, I know we do not truly love one another."

"Miss Elizabeth ... Elizabeth ... of course, I am, indeed, very fond of you. So I hope you will, someday soon, find the perfect love you are seeking." Dun was unaware the other gentlemen callers had departed; and so he said, "Perhaps you do not even have very far to look. I begrudgingly suggest you begin your search in the music room." He gave her a slight smile and a bow. "Good day, my dear friend."

Had Charles Bingley not postponed his long-overdue talk with his sister, he might have prevented Caroline from experiencing the most mortifying and cataclysmic moment of her life. He fully intended to have the important discussion with her but spent far too much time trying to find the most non-confrontational way of broaching such an unpleasant subject with his rather volatile sibling. He had already removed any breakable objects from the room in case she decided to throw a tantrum. Bingley sat in his study and studied the blotter on his otherwise empty desk. Not finding inspiration there, he stood and stretched, straightened his spine, and rang for a servant. "Fossett, please have my sister immediately summoned here. Quickly, man!"

Bingley wanted to have done with the disagreeable task so he could get on with the important business of ... Well, as a gentleman of leisure, he really did not have any important business with which to get on; but he still wanted to have done with such an unpleasant episode. *Then,*

perhaps, I shall ... hmm ... pay a visit to ... the ... Bennet family.
Yes, that is it. I will pay another visit to Miss Bennet and her family and
reserve sets for the ball.

After several minutes, the servant returned to report Miss Bingley
had left half an hour ago to spend the afternoon shopping. Bingley was
secretly relieved and champing at the bit to go visiting. "Too bad. Well, I
might as well go out myself, then. But please tell Caroline it is imperative
I speak with her when we both return this evening."

It seemed to be quite the thing that particular day for young ladies
to be seduced by the lure of London's fine shops, because Bingley was
informed Miss Bennet, Miss Elizabeth, and Miss Lucas had departed
an hour ago to do just that. The young man was then at a loose end
and ordered his driver to take him to one of the clubs in which he held
membership. When the coachman looked askance at him, Bingley testily
said, "I am apparently in no mood to make wise decisions today, so you
shall decide for me. Quickly man! Where shall I spend my afternoon?"

Ellis Fleming encountered the same situation when he called at Darcy
House to pay court to Miss Darcy. Georgiana had accompanied her
mother, sister, and aunt on a shopping expedition to purchase some last-
minute feminine frippery for the ball. Fleming then ordered his carriage
driver to take him to Whites, where, to his astonishment, he found his
friend, Fitzwilliam Darcy, uncharacteristically quite in his cups.

"Flemin', what are you doin' here, man? Why are you not payin' court
to my shishter ... sishter ... shi ... Georgiana? You should not washte
a minute, you know; or shome bracket-faced, bottle-headed braggart
might shteeeal her away. Whoosh! Jusht like that." Darcy flung out his
arm and knocked over his empty glass.

"Good God, Darcy. What are you doing here alone, dipping rather
deeply? I have not seen you on the cut since Cambridge. What troubles
you, my friend?" Fleming took a seat next to Darcy and shooed away a
servant about to fill another glass.

"Did you not hear me jusht now? Go find my shish ... Georgiana,
and do not allow her to be shwept away by shome shmilin', shwaggerin'
shwine of a shoulder ... sholdjer ... shol ... "

"Darce, are you trying to say some smiling, swaggering swine of a soldier has been sniffing around your sister?"

"Mosht certainly not! I would never shtand for it. I am merely shpeakin' hypo ... hypo ... er, ... theo - ret - ic - a - lly."

"And you are doing a very poor job of speaking thusly, my friend. Plus I rather doubt whether you are able to stand at all. Let us get your intoxicated self home, shall we?"

"No. I wanna go shee Missh Libazith."

"I beg your pardon? You want to go do what?"

"Not what, who. Whom? What wash the queshtion?"

"Darce, why are you in such a state?"

"Brraaandy."

"Who?"

"Not who, Flemin', what. Braaandy is a what, not a who. Well, I shupposhe Braaandy could be a who, but ... "

"Darcy, why have you been drinking?"

"Missh Bizzy Lennet ... Missh Libbaziff ... Lizzabiff ... LisshyBit ... DeeeelisheyBit ... " Ellis Fleming rolled his eyes, took his friend by the arm, and discreetly escorted him out of the club and into his waiting carriage. The fresh air revived Darcy somewhat. He took a deep, cleansing breath and exhaled stale brandy. "Flemin', you are an intelligent bloke. What, exactly, ish a hanson barberin'?"

"Darcy, you are usually quite an articulate fellow. Nonetheless, when you are tap-hackled, your speech becomes rather unintelligible. What, in blazing hell, do you mean by 'hanson barberin'? Can you use it in the context of a sentence?"

"Shhhure. Um. Ah, yesh. Mr. Darshy, are you sho-and-sho's hanson barberin?"

Ellis knit his brows and shrugged. "Well, I suppose the first part could be the name Hanson; and the other obviously means barbering. What else could it be? So in your example, perhaps the person is asking whether you are somebody's barber by the name of Hanson. But *I* would certainly not trust you to braaandish a razor just now."

"Extraordinarily shtrange. I am shure my name wash mentioned during the introduction to the poppet. Cute ash a button, he wash. Bizzylith and I could have had adorable shildren together."

"Now whatever are you going on about, Darcy?"

"The delightful wee tot."

"Darcy, my friend, as delightful as the brandy might have been, I wager you drank much more alcohol today than just a wee tot."

"Good God! Shurely one so young ash Mashter Robert ish not allowed to conshume shpiritsh!"

"Darcy?"

"Yesh, Flemin', my dear old friend?"

"Please be so kind as to shut your gob."

The Bennet carriage sat outside No. 89 Pall Mall. Miss Bennet, Miss Elizabeth, and Miss Lucas had been inside for well over an hour browsing through each of the four departments of Harding, Howell & Co.

"Lizzy, look at these beautiful ornamental combs. They would look very well with your dark hair and nicely complement either one of your new ball gowns." Jane and Charlotte had both attempted to cheer up the uncharacteristically glum Lizzy Bennet all afternoon.

"Oh, Jane, what does it matter? I no longer even wish to attend the ball if he thinks I am engaged to marry Lieutenant-Colonel Dun. I still cannot believe Mr. Darcy overheard us. Are you certain it was the reason he departed so hastily?"

"I am afraid so, my dear sister. During one of the many lulls in our conversation, everyone heard your suitor's happy exclamation. A stricken expression overtook Mr. Darcy's face, he muttered some nonsensical excuse, and then fled the room. Regardless, Lizzy, we can very easily clear up any misunderstanding when we see Georgiana and Anna at the ball."

"Yes, I suppose you are right … about both the solution and those lovely hair accessories. I may even consider the matching beaded reticule." Elizabeth smiled rather unenthusiastically and joined her sister and friend as they made several purchases and then exited the department store.

When they stepped through the front door, Jane said, "Lizzy, are those not the two ladies we met at the Royal Academy?"

Elizabeth glanced in the indicated direction and saw Miss Caroline Bingley and Miss Sarah Dalrymple walking toward the entrance. The two women were dressed in their usual gaudy finery, quite inappropriate for daywear. It was obvious they had already spotted Jane and Elizabeth, because Miss Bingley pointed and began to whisper in her friend's ear. By the store's front door, the Bennet sisters waited to exchange polite acknowledgments with their acquaintances; and they fully expected to introduce Charlotte to the ladies. To their surprise, however, the Misses Bingley and Dalrymple lifted their noses, looked the other way, and blatantly pretended not to notice them. As they passed by, Miss Bingley was heard to say, "We may have to find another place to shop, Sarah. I believe this establishment's standards have dropped to an unacceptable level."

Jane and Elizabeth were mortified and hurt. As much as they disliked London society, they had never before been subjected to the cut indirect. They hastily made their way to the waiting carriage and asked to be driven home; yet it would not be the home Lizzy craved at that moment. She desperately wished to leave the city and return instead to Hertfordshire and their beloved country estate. Nevertheless, Elizabeth was the first to recover from the shock. "What have we done, Jane, to deserve such treatment? Charlotte, I am truly sorry you had to witness that rebuff." She shook her head and looked to her sister. "I admit I do not at all understand why we were snubbed in such a manner."

Jane took her hand and gently said, "Lizzy, darling, you *do* know why. Georgiana and Anna told us that day at the shoe shop. Remember? Miss Bingley has set her cap for their brother. You have his admiration, and she does not. It is merely envy and jealousy on her part, so please do not take her foolish renouncement personally. You are usually such a confident person. Please do not allow such misplaced snobbery to cast any doubt on your own mettle. You and I are certainly not to blame for another's rudeness."

Elizabeth regained her spirit and managed to smile and arch a brow. "Really, it is of *slight* consequence, Jane; and I shall simply put it out of my head … at least until my dream of a cottage on a cliff becomes reality." Charlotte just had to ask how that was relevant and laughed when her friend flippantly replied, "I shall invite Miss Bingley to *drop over*, of course."

Caroline Bingley crowed, "Oh, Sarah, that was just priceless! My only regret is, in looking the other way, I could not see the expressions on their faces. Hopefully I shall never have to suffer another encounter with those intolerable Bennet chits again. Still, if I do, I shall take great delight in giving that upstart Miss Eliza the cut direct by staring her fully in the face and pretending not to know her. Ooh, merely the thought of it makes me wish to have such an opportunity. It would be just what she deserves. Imagine having the gall to curry favour with the elite Darcy family. Who does she think she is, Sarah? If I get my way, that daring dairymaid will never set foot at Pemberley again; and when I marry its heir and am that grand estate's Mistress, … What? Why are you giving me that look, Sarah? What is that supposed to mean? Oh." She whispered, "Is there someone behind me?" Her friend nodded; and Miss Bingley mouthed the words, "Who is it?" Miss Dalrymple turned white and then red and was quite speechless. She only managed to shake her head and continue to stare, bug-eyed, past Caroline's orange-clad shoulder.

With a sense of absolute dread, Caroline Bingley slowly turned around and nearly swooned at the sight that met her astonished eyes. Following her friend's example, she turned ashen and then crimson. Caroline's mouth opened and closed like a landed fish; however, no words passed her pale, thin lips. She waited in vain to be acknowledged by her superiors, and the foreboding silence dragged on for what seemed an eternity. The icy stares she received sent frissons of fear up and down her spine, and Miss Bingley prayed the esteemed ladies facing her would, at least, be merciful. The unnerving silence was finally broken by, not words, but the swish of four expensive silk dresses as they brushed past the two future pariahs of society.

Miss Anna Darcy, Miss Georgiana Darcy, Lady Anne Darcy, and

her revered sister-in-law, Lady Rebecca Fitzwilliam, wife of the Earl of Matlock, regally swept out the front door of Harding, Howell & Co. The respected ladies, in the wake of their significant leave-taking, left behind not only the gaping Miss Bingley and Miss Dalrymple but also the dozens of important members of le bon ton who had witnessed the cut direct. Tongues immediately began to wag, and gossip spread like wildfire among 'the Upper Ten Thousand'. Caroline Bingley knew at that moment her prospects within polite society were forever ruined.

The Darcy women entered their carriage in stunned silence, and Lady Anne reeled at the potential impact of their unprecedented renouncement of an acquaintance. She had raised her daughters to be genteel, gentle, generous girls; and she almost felt sorry for the other two young unfortunates who had become the victims of their noteworthy, and very public, cut direct. Almost.

Lady Rebecca Fitzwilliam, however, had no such qualms. As an influential member of 'the Beau Monde', she knew the repercussions of her action and had no regrets whatsoever. "The unmitigated nerve of that Bingley harpy to dare align herself with your family and, by extension, my own noble one!" She saw the stricken face of her sister-in-law and said, "Anne, do not dare give those two conniving, name-dropping, wheedling sycophants another thought. They are unworthy of your concern. Caroline Bingley has been a thorn in our side since Fitzwilliam and Richard befriended her brother. When she could not win your son, she tried for my James and even Richard; and now she has been dangling after your Fitzwilliam once again. I do admit I rather like the amiable Charles Bingley. Still and all, I cannot abide his social-climbing, upstart, nouveau riche ... *mushroom* of a sister."

Georgiana quite agreed with her aunt; nevertheless, she also felt remorse for their actions, until she remembered Caroline's vitriolic words spoken against Elizabeth.

Although quite sickened by what she and her family had done, Miss Anna attempted to lighten the mood in the carriage. "I am afraid Miss Bingley's character is not of a very high *morel* standing and she certainly has *mush-room* for improvement."

Her exasperated mother sighed and said, "Anna Darcy, now is not the time. Your newly acquired sense of humour is fast becoming a *pun*ishment for us all. Do, please, have some compassion for our poor nerves."

Charles Bingley, back in his study, impatiently waited for Caroline to return; and he was not in a very receptive frame of mind. He still had not reserved a set with Miss Bennet for the ball. He fretted over Colonel Fitzwilliam's intentions toward her. The uninformed coachman had chosen Boodles, where none of his friends had gone that afternoon; and he worried Caroline might have exceeded her allowance by making unnecessary orange-hued purchases all day. A knock interrupted his fit of pique; he bade the intruder, "Enter."

In proper form, Fossett, the forbearing foyer footman, forged ahead and formally announced, "Miss Bingley has returned, sir. However, she is unwell and wanted you to know she is indisposed and regrets being unable to take dinner or meet with you this evening."

"Oh, really? Well, we shall just see about that." Bingley jumped up from his chair, donned his discarded coat, stomped out of the study, marched upstairs, and pounded on the door to his sister's apartments. "Caroline, open this door, right now. I need to speak with you."

"Go away, Charles."

His sister's voice had an unusual quality to it, so he asked, "Caroline, are you truly unwell? Open the door, please." Bingley had seen his sister disgusted, angry, disappointed, aggressive, contemptuous, and even, on occasion, frightened and sad. However, he had only once before, in their adult life, seen her cry; and that was years previously, at the death of their parents from scarlet fever. Therefore, when the key turned in the lock, the door opened, and he saw her red, blotchy, tear-stained face, he was truly alarmed. "Good God! What is the matter?" Caroline hesitated, but her knees trembled under her; and she sat down, unable to support herself. She looked so miserably ill it was impossible for Bingley to leave her. In a tone of gentleness and commiseration, he said, "Let me call your maid. Is there nothing you could take to give you present relief? A glass of wine? Shall I get you one? You are very ill, sister."

She burst into tears and for a few minutes could not utter a word.

Bingley, in wretched suspense, could only say something indistinctly of his concern and observe her in compassionate silence. He passed Caroline a pristine handkerchief and considered how else he might comfort her. They had never embraced, and he felt awkward even considering such contact.

At length, she got up, paced, and spoke. "Oh, Charles, my humiliation cannot be concealed from anyone; and I know very well that nothing can be done. I have not the smallest hope. It is in every way horrible; and I am so very, very sorry, brother."

When his sister began to weep again, Bingley became increasingly worried. *Fiend seize convention! Caroline needs me.* He disregarded their past differences and indifferences, wrapped his arms around her bony shoulders, gathered her against his chest, and let her tears soak through his waistcoat and shirtfront. Deep, gut-wrenching sobs wracked her body; she whimpered and repeated, "I am so sorry. I am so very sorry, Charles." He murmured and stroked her hair and felt tears sting his own eyes in empathy with such overwhelming sorrow.

When she had cried herself out, she withdrew from his embrace and plopped down on the bench at her vanity table; one glimpse at her reflection in the mirror was enough to make her swivel around and face the other way. It was not her swollen, blotchy features that disgusted her so much but rather the evidence of her own miserable existence. She shook her head, took gulps of air, and yet would not look her brother in the eye.

"It is over, Charles. It is all over. I tried so very hard to fit in, but now it does not matter. I have ruined everything, and I am so, so sorry for you. I do not care about myself, but I would do anything to protect you from what is about to happen. Perhaps you should send me away somewhere … far away from here. I hate it, Charles! I hate this place and this society. They never accepted me, not really. I truly did try, though. Perhaps that is the problem. I tried too hard. Oh, how could I have been such a bird-brained goose?"

"Caroline, please tell me. Whatever it is, we will get through this together. I am here for you. Allow me to help."

"I do not deserve your kindness, brother. Nonetheless, you would certainly find out soon enough anyway; so I will confess before the gossip reaches you. If you wish to be rid of me afterward, I will write to our relatives in Staffordshire and see if they will have me."

"Good God, Caroline! Has some man … Have you been compromised in any way? Is that the cause of your dolour? Are you … are you with child?"

"Charles! Most certainly not! My goodness, I was beginning to think my problem could not be more wretched. That said, I suppose there are others in worse situations."

Her brother crouched down in front of her and held her hands. "Tell me then, you silly goose. I promise not to be angry. Regardless, I need to know what has happened so we can start to work on a solution."

Caroline took a deep breath through her mouth, released it, and said, "I gave someone of our acquaintance the cut indirect and was dealt what I deserved, the cut direct."

She hung her head in shame but quickly raised it when Charles snorted and said, "Is that all?"

"Charles, you do not understand. I was, quite rightly, given the cut direct by the Lady Matlock and the Darcy family."

"*Darcy* renounced you?"

"No, it was the ladies of his family … Lady Anne, Miss Darcy, and Miss Anna, in company with Lady Matlock, at Harding, Howell & Co. this afternoon. The store was crowded with members of the ton. I am ruined, Charles; and you will surely be shunned as well."

"Darcy will not allow that to occur, Caroline. He is a true friend; in fact, he warned me this might happen. I should have spoken to you sooner. When I consider I might have prevented this if I had but explained some of his concerns to you, I am grieved, indeed, by my procrastination. Wretched, wretched mistake."

"You are certainly not to blame for my foolhardiness, brother. Be that as it may, I do not understand. About what did Mr. Darcy warn you? He could not possibly have known I would give the cut indirect to those Bennet women."

"Caroline, no! Do you mean to tell me you cut the angelic Miss Jane Bennet? How could you?"

"It was not Miss Bennet I was trying to insult but her insufferab ... her sister, Miss Eliza - beth. They are merely countrified yokels who are on close terms with *servants*, Charles. I know you met them at Pemberley, but are you actually acquainted with the family?"

"Not as well as I would care to be. The Bennets are not yokels, Caroline. They are wealthy, fashionable, respected members of the gentry, who own a townhouse here as well as an estate in Hertfordshire. They and the Darcy family have been on quite friendly terms lately. Now, tell me exactly what happened earlier today when you were shopping."

His sister described what occurred outside and inside the department store. Charles suggested they should together visit the three families involved and apologize to the ladies. "However, Caroline, we shall not grovel. We still have enough self respect not to stoop that low."

When Caroline became agitated and protested she could not possibly face them again, her brother tried to soothe and comfort her. "I will be right beside you; and I will do most of the talking, if you wish. Even so, I insist you give an honest and heartfelt apology to Lady Matlock, the Darcy ladies, and both Bennet sisters. I still do not understand your antagonism toward Miss Elizabeth, though."

"I am embarrassed to admit it; however, Mr. Darcy seemed to be paying such an undue amount of attention to her that I became rather ... He was never mine, was he?" When Charles sadly shook his head, she continued, "Then the correct word would be envious rather than jealous. She seemed to be a nobody from nowhere who immediately had his admiration, whereas I had been trying for so long for even just a crumb of regard from the man."

"Caroline, are you truly in love with Darcy?"

"Love? What has *love* to do with it? He is a handsome, respected, eligible young man who happens to be heir to a vast fortune. I admit, without hesitation, I am more in love with the idea of being Mistress of Pemberley than with the man who comes along with it. I very much regret losing whatever connection we may have had with that grand estate. I miss the north. Perhaps it would be best for me to go live in Staffordshire. We do not belong in this society, Charles. Why have I been trying so hard to fit in? Oh, why did our wealth have to come from *shoes* of all things? How low and shoddy!"

"Caroline! Was that a pun?"

"Whatever do you mean? I most certainly would never stoop to that insufferable form of so-called humour. I have *some* dignity remaining after all, brother. As I was saying, although I knew we were low-born, I thought if I emulated the attitudes I observed in our betters, I might gain their acceptance. Foolish, foolish girl!"

"Ah, but Caroline, are they really our betters? They may have vast amounts of wealth, distinguished bloodlines, noble lineage and titles, and be more fashionable. For all that, are they truly better people? Some of the young ladies with whom you have been associating are vile, vain, and vacuous. I wish you could be friends with people like the Bennets. No, do not give me that look, sister. *They* are the women you would do well to emulate."

"Am I really so unattractive and unappealing, Charles? What can I do to improve? Please help me."

"Your snobbish attitude has probably been a defensive strategy used to deny feelings of insecurity. We shall work on boosting your confidence and self worth. Be that as it may, we first must choke down some rather unsavoury tripe."

"Of what are you speaking, brother? Truly, I have no appetite for dinner tonight."

"No, my dear sister, I refer to the fact we must soon eat humble pie."

PART IV

Perfumed, Polished, and Perfectly Pleasing

or

Scents and Sensuality

A tribute to Austen's *Sense and Sensibility*

Chapter I

A Romantic Triangle Becomes a Wreck-Tangle

Fitzwilliam Darcy had sobered considerably by the time he and Ellis Fleming approached his townhouse. The two young gents quietly entered and evaded detection, except by a few curious yet scrupulous attendants. Fleming ensured his friend was comfortably settled in the library and said, "I shall leave you now; however, I have been invited to dine with your family this evening, so I will return in several hours. Promise me you will not be making indentures in the meantime. You have had quite enough to drink already this afternoon, Ditzwilliam Farcy."

Darcy waved his friend away and clumsily removed his cravat, coat, and shoes. He stretched out on a cozy couch in the hope of sleeping off the effects of more than just a wee tot of brandy. While in the middle of a strange dream, in which Elizabeth was both his wife and the Exchequer Minister, the library door flew open with a bang that sounded like a gunshot through his stupor. He jolted upright, which made the room spin wildly. "What the … "

Georgiana gasped "Oh!" upon entering the room. "Sorry, brother. I did not realize the library was occupied. Have you seen Barb Thorne? She has escaped again from Anna."

"Chancellor?"

"I beg your pardon? Fitzwilliam, are you unwell?"

"Ah, no. Yes. Pardon? I fell asleep, you see."

"You are behaving rather strangely. I asked if you have seen Anna's hedgehog."

Darcy groggily grinned as he remembered a fragment of his dream in which he and the beautiful Chancellor of the Exchequer had been waltzing. He muttered, "I dreamt I was actually holding her in my arms."

"You have never liked holding hedgehogs. Yet you had your hands on Barbara in a dream?"

"No, on Elizabeth. Who is Bar ... Wait ... Georgie, did you just say *hanson barberin*?"

"No. I said 'hands on Barbara in ... ' oh, never mind! Truly, brother, you are not speaking coherently." She frowned and marched over to determine whether he was feverish but was appalled to find, instead, that he reeked of alcohol. "Fitzwilliam Darcy! Have you been liberally imbibing sufficient amounts of spirits to actually be inebriated at this hour of the day?"

He sheepishly admitted he had, indeed, consumed a quantity of alcoholic beverages at his club. As the intoxicating dream of dancing with Elizabeth faded like a wisp of smoke, he immediately remembered the underlying cause for the drinking binge. Darcy instantly became melancholy, slid back down, and reclined with his forearm over his eyes.

Georgiana sensed her brother was troubled by more than the effects of alcohol and tried to cheer him. "Why are you having a fit of the blue-devils? I should think you would be in high spirits at the prospect of spending tomorrow night in the presence of a certain young lady of our acquaintance. Have you already reserved a set or two with Elizabeth, brother? I hope you secured her for at least the first, supper, or final set; or perhaps you have been sly enough to ask for two of those. Mr. Fleming has requested all three sets from me; still, I wish ... "

Miss Darcy was startled when her brother bolted up, reeled across the room, and stared out the window. When the library stopped tilting, he spoke with a soft but raspy voice. "Have you not heard, Georgie? Your friend has accepted Lieutenant-Colonel Dun's marriage proposal."

She collapsed onto the vacated sofa and gazed at her brother's back as he rested his forehead on the coolness of the windowpane. "No! That cannot be true, Fitzwilliam. You are certainly mistaken."

"I was there, dearest; and I heard his understandable elation upon receiving her positive response."

Georgiana was aghast. "Are you telling me you were actually present during such an intimate moment?"

"Well, I was not present in the same room with the couple, of course. Despite that, I could not help but distinctly hear the end result. In fact, the whole household probably heard the fortunate braggart's happy exclamation. That insufferable, carrot-topped, red-coated blowhard could hardly contain his ecstatic enthusiasm at having won such a woman." He hung his head and muttered, "I certainly cannot blame him for such ardour."

Miss Darcy walked over to her older sibling and gently placed a hand on his arm. "I am so very sorry, Fitzwilliam. Yet I can scarcely believe Elizabeth would willingly enter into such an engagement. I was positive her affections were directed elsewhere. Oh dear, shall it be painful for you to face her at the ball?"

"Do not be concerned about me, Georgie. I will don my usual stiff upper lip and flinty mask, be a perfect gentleman, and ask the dear lady to accept my best wishes for her health and happiness. That said, I know I shall never experience felicity without her in my life. Excuse me now, please. I wish to be alone for a while." Darcy fetched his coat and shoes and staggered out of the library, forgetting he had also discarded his cravat, which had fallen beneath the chesterfield.

Georgiana was sorely disappointed and more than a little annoyed. *How could Elizabeth possibly be so confoundedly blind? She and Fitzwilliam are absolutely perfect for one another. I simply will not believe she agreed to become that officer's wife until I hear it directly from her. I must do what I can to repair my brother's broken heart and re-pair him with Elizabeth.* Miss Darcy also left the room; however, she rang for a carriage, donned a bonnet and spencer, collected Pug-Nacious and Dust Bunny, and exited the townhouse. She was on a mission to the Bennet home and totally forgot her previous undertaking, which had been to locate Barb Thorne, the hedgehog. From beneath the sofa, a white linen cravat stealthily made its way across the floor of the library and crept into the hallway.

Charlotte Lucas had already taken her leave and members of the Bennet family separately pursued a variety of activities. Jane arranged dried flowers while she compared Mr. Bingley to Colonel Fitzwilliam, Mrs. Bennet visited the Gardiners, Mr. Bennet efficiently took care of a pile of correspondence in his study, Mary was at school, Kitty and Lydia were on an outing with their governess, and Robert napped in the nursery. Alone in the sitting room, Elizabeth put the finishing touches on a watercolour painting that had been a work in progress for several weeks. She stood back, appraised the canvas with a critical eye, and was surprised when a footman announced her visitor. "Georgiana! What a pleasant surprise." She quickly turned the easel toward the wall so her friend would not notice the likeness of a certain young man in clinging clothing.

"Good afternoon, Elizabeth. It is nice to see you again, but I do not have much time before I am due to return home for dinner. May I urgently request a few moments of your time for a private conversation? The puppies are in the carriage, so perhaps you could join me while I take them for a short walk in the adjacent park."

Lizzy was puzzled by her friend's cool demeanour as they set off briskly with a footman trailing behind. Dust Bunny and Pug-Nacious sniffed the many interesting scents along the way. Due to the late afternoon hour, the ladies encountered few others on the paths of the small public garden not far from the Bennet townhouse.

"I am so glad to have this opportunity to speak with you, Georgiana." *It is very important you tell your gorgeous brother I am not betrothed.* "I have something of great import to impart."

"You need not bother, Elizabeth." *How could you accept that insufferable, carrot-topped, red-coated blowhard?* "I am already well aware of your shocking news."

Lizzy was taken aback and wondered how word had reached her friend. *No matter ... as long as Mr. Darcy knows the truth.* "Oh. Well, good."

Georgiana continued, "I must admit I was surprised at the result of Lieutenant-Colonel Dun's proposal." *You and Fitzwilliam were perfect together. How could you accept another?* "I wonder why you made such an ill-advised decision."

Elizabeth gasped and felt her heart sink to the pit of her stomach. *Do you think I should have accepted Dun's offer? Does your brother not care for me as I do him?* "You do not approve of my response to his proposal?"

"To be perfectly honest, my friend, no." *Simpleton. You would have been so much happier with my brother.* "In fact, I believe you have made a colossal mistake regarding your future happiness."

"Georgiana, was I wrong to presume that your bro ... "

Her friend interrupted, "Oh, how could you disappoint him in such a cruel way, Elizabeth?" *Fitzwilliam loved you ... loves you. He is inconsolable.* "The poor man is absolutely desolate and heart-achingly heartbroken."

"How could you possibly know his feelings?" *You met Lieutenant-Colonel Dun at our dinner and glared at him throughout the meal. How and why are you suddenly privy to his sentiments?*

"He told me himself; and if I recall correctly, his exact words were, 'I know I shall never experience happiness without her in my life.'" *That's how I know his feelings, you selfish, heartless girl.*

"Under what circumstances were you in his presence? Why would he even express sentiments to you he never even mentioned to me?" *This is insane. Why was John spilling his soul to you?* "When and where did you encounter the man?"

"I left him just now to come here to see you, Elizabeth." *My brother could hardly express his love to you when Dun beat him to it. Why is it so difficult for you to understand his hurt and his need to confide in me?* "He apparently spent the afternoon drinking to drown his sorrow over losing you and was sleeping in the library when I happened upon him."

"He was sleeping in the library?" *Has the world gone mad? I cannot make sense of any of this.* "Which library?"

"The one at our house, of course." *You are such a bacon-brained goose, Elizabeth Bennet.*

"What on earth was he doing at your home?" *Argh! Why was John Dun at your house, of all places in England?*

"I just told you." *Perhaps this is all for the best. You are certainly addlepated, so my brother is better off without you.* "He was sleeping after having consumed too many alcoholic beverages."

Elizabeth shook her head in disbelief. *If Lieutenant-Colonel Dun is intoxicated and sleeping it off at Mr. Darcy's house, then I am surely Queen Elizabeth.* "In your home?"

"No, I believe he said he was drinking at his club. Be that as it may, the where is unimportant, Elizabeth. What is important is that … "

"Excuse me. I beg to differ, Georgiana. I cannot begin to comprehend why, of all places in the entire world, Lieutenant-Colonel John Dun is, or was, sleeping in *your* library."

"*He* was not! I am speaking of my brother. Fiend seize it, Elizabeth, why would your foul fiancé be at my home?"

"That is what I have been asking *you*! Wait, wait, wait … your *brother*? My … *fiancé*?"

"If you had a speck of sense at all, my brother *would* be your fiancé!"

The two ladies stood, arms akimbo, in the middle of the path, glared at one another, and tried to unravel their tangled conversation. Elizabeth sorted through the strands, finally realized the misunderstanding, and arched an eyebrow at her friend. "Georgiana, let me be rightly understood. I do not presently have, nor have I ever had, a fiancé. Lieutenant-Colonel Dun did make me an offer; however, I declined and … "

"You *declined*? You declined!" Miss Darcy clapped her hands and then gave her friend a hearty hug. "Oh, Elizabeth! Of course, you declined; and it is wonderful news, indeed. I beg your pardon, but I must return home on business that cannot be delayed. I have not an instant to lose. There is a rather dejected, heartbroken young man there who desperately needs cheering; and I now have exactly the information with which to do the job. Thank you."

"Georgiana, please wait. I would just like to clarify one point. This dejected, broken-hearted young man you mentioned … You are, actually, speaking of your *brother*, are you not … the one I hold in the highest regard?"

"Of course I am, you silly goose. I speak of none other than Fitzwilliam

Darcy, my beloved brother who will, no doubt, some day make you my cherished, bacon-brained sister."

Elizabeth blushed but rolled her eyes and said, "Oh, Lud! Just what I need … another bossy, interfering, older sister!"

The Bingley siblings were not having much success in their eating of humble pie. The Lady Matlock had received them coolly, listened to Miss Bingley's stuttered apology, and informed them she would have to curtail their visit, as she was going out.

At the Bennet household, they were only able to meet with Miss Bennet, as her sister was on an outing with Miss Darcy. Jane grudgingly accepted Caroline's expressions of regret but succinctly explained that since Elizabeth had been the intended victim of the cut, Miss Bingley would have to seek her sister's absolution at another time. When they were back in their carriage, Caroline reminded her brother he was supposed to do most of the talking and gently chided him for, instead, spending his time staring in tongue-tied adoration at Miss Bennet.

At Darcy House, the Bingleys did manage to make two apologies at once; Lady Anne and her youngest daughter were kind and merciful. Caroline was dismayed she would have to return again to gain Miss Darcy's forgiveness. When Charles asked to see his friend, he was told Darcy was indisposed. As the Bingleys left the townhouse, Charles said, "I hope Darcy is actually indisposed and is not avoiding me." He quickly added, "Not that I hope Darcy is indisposed, I just meant … "

"Charles, I know what you meant; and I am sure Darcy is not avoiding you. Speaking of avoiding, I truly wish to be away from London for a while. I have already written to our aunt and uncle; and with their permission, I will travel north and spend the winter months there. I promise to call on Miss Elizabeth and Miss Darcy before I depart, but please allow me to leave this place soon. I need some time away to reflect and decide on my future … if I even have one."

As the Bingley carriage drove away from the Darcy townhouse, Georgiana alit from hers and ran up the front steps. The footman waiting to receive Miss Darcy's outerwear was left empty-handed until the young lady spun around and thrust two little dogs at him. She then bounded up the stairs in a most unladylike manner, pulled off her bonnet and spencer, handed them to a passing chambermaid, and asked, "Where is my brother?" Upon being informed he was in his room and was not to be disturbed until dinner, Georgiana muttered, "Oh, really? Well, we shall just see about that."

The usually impeccable Fitzwilliam Darcy had fallen asleep on top of his bed, still clad in wrinkled shirt, breeches, and waistcoat; he would have been horrified had he known his state. The left side of his face rested on a ribbed cushion that was damp from the drool that seeped from his open mouth; and his lusty, forceful snores echoed in the hallway. A concurrent incessant pounding in his aching head and on his chamber door rudely awakened him, and the blasted banging finally ceased but was immediately replaced by Georgiana's raised and excited voice. "Fitzwilliam, open this door, right now! I urgently need to speak with you."

A muffled mumble of "Go away!" was ignored by the impatient young lady.

"No, brother, I most certainly shall not. I have news of the utmost importance to reveal to you. Please, Fitzwilliam, I promise it is of the happiest nature; and you will be pleased, if you would just … open … this … confounded … door!" She fruitlessly pushed on the oaken panel with her shoulder, jangled the knob, and nearly fell to the floor when the portal suddenly burst open.

Fitzwilliam caught her but snapped, "Why are you constantly cutting up my peace today, Georgiana? What does a man have to do to be allowed a restorative nap this afternoon?"

Miss Darcy grinned hugely at her dishevelled sibling and said, "It would take more than just a nap to restore you to some semblance of order, brother; and such testy manners and slovenly appearance do little to tempt me to reveal what I have just learned."

Red diagonal lines crossed the left side of Darcy's face, his eyes were only half open, and hair was plastered to one side of his head but puffed up on the other. "Georgiana, was I rudely awakened merely for the purpose of being subjected to ridicule? I thought you said there was urgent news of a happy nature. The only words that would truly be joyous to me right now would be those telling me I may go back to sleep ... or those informing me dunderhead, dung-beetle Dun has been found guilty of treason."

"Brother, do you not get *tired* of sleeping? Seriously though, you should have compassion for the poor Lieutenant-Colonel and the misfortune he has suffered at Elizabeth's hand."

"His misfortune!" repeated Darcy contemptuously. "Yes, his misfortune is great indeed. Imagine having won Elizabeth's hand and having to spend the rest of his life with such a wife! How*ever* shall he bear such tribulation and woe? Nonetheless, by all means, let him have my compassion as well as my woman."

"Tsk, tsk. Well, perhaps now would be an opportune time to offer you my compassion for having to spend the rest of *your* life with such a woman as Elizabeth Bennet."

Fitzwilliam snorted and scoffed, "There is no other woman such as Elizabeth Bennet."

"Sometimes you are as thick as two short planks, brother. You do not deserve her." She turned her back on him and said, "Apparently, neither did Dun, poor man."

"Georgiana, my mind must still be somewhat befogged right now, because it sounds as if you are saying she is ... unattached." Darcy gently turned her around but could scarcely breathe as he awaited his sister's response.

"I just spoke with Elizabeth ... " Darcy was suddenly fully awake and alert. He hung on every word his sister excitedly uttered. " ... and she *is* absolutely unattached, single, eligible, unengaged, in love with you, unencumbered, and as free as a bird."

"Good God! Did you just say she is in love with me and unfettered? But is it certain, absolutely certain?" When his sister eagerly nodded, Darcy's headache and heartache suddenly vanished and he felt ten feet tall instead of his usual six feet, one and a half inches. "I shall go to her at once! I must not lose her again. It must be settled between us immediately. Miss Elizabeth Bennet's days of being unattached, single, eligible, and unengaged are numbered, Georgie." He stumbled around in search of his cravat, coat, and shoes.

Georgiana quickly snatched the coat and shoes from the heap on the floor while her brother fumbled around under the bed. She hid the items away in his dressing room and returned to find him in the middle of the room looking around in bewilderment. "You forgot 'unencumbered,' Fitzwilliam. However, if you arrive at Elizabeth's home in your current state, you will surely *be* an encumbrance. 'Fools rush in where Angels fear to tread.' So please give her some time; and by all means, do not go to her looking like *that*! I hope she never has to suffer such an unsightly sight after you two marry. Ugh! You are certainly no Bond Street Beau right now, brother, trust me."

Georgiana wrinkled her nose and pretended to shudder. He grinned sheepishly before she continued, "It might be romantic to let her know your feelings tomorrow night at the ball, when we are all perfumed, polished, and perfectly pleasing; but that is all the advice you shall cajole from me. I do have my own courtship to enjoy, you know. I must go now and make myself beautiful before Mr. Fleming arrives." She turned away and started toward her own chamber.

"Georgie? Wait."

"Yes, brother?"

Fitzwilliam Darcy took two long strides that brought him to her side and he bent and kissed her cheek. "Thank you, and you do not have to *make* yourself beautiful. You are already truly, and naturally, beautiful in every way."

"Oh, Jane, you are truly, and naturally, beautiful in every way; and I am sure Mr. Bingley would agree. Thank you for handling his sister's visit so well. Still and all, you should not have had to endure that misery alone. I am very sorry I was not here with you. However, Miss Darcy and I had a rather … *interesting* conversation while you were entertaining. I will tell you more of it later. Suffice it to say I expect her brother will begin courting me now that a certain army officer is out of his way. I may only have one charming suitor at tomorrow night's ball while you, dear

Jane, shall surely have to contend with at least two very attractive and amiable young men vying for your attention. Do you hold any special regard for either?"

"Lizzy, I realize how much you are in love with Mr. Darcy and you seemed to know the moment you first saw him. I have not the luxury of coup de foudre, if there is such a thing as love at first sight. You are fortunate to know your heart's desire so well, but it was not a bolt of lightning for me. I admit I am attracted to both Colonel Fitzwilliam and Mr. Bingley; still, I am uncertain. In Derbyshire, Mr. Bingley almost irritated me with his fawning attentions while the Colonel seemed indifferent. Now the boot is quite on the other leg, as they say; and of late my feelings have been shifting about pretty much. If I could combine Mr. Bingley's sweetness with Colonel Fitzwilliam's magnetism, such a man would be quite irresistible."

"Yes, one has all the appearance of goodness and the other has a very good appearance. Take your choice, Jane; nevertheless, you must be satisfied with only one. Perhaps the selection will come down to which of your gallant gentlemen is the better dancer, for they will both want to stand up with you tomorrow night and sweep you off your feet."

"Lizzy, do be serious. Such an important decision cannot rely on such a contest. Oh, how is one to decide between two such remarkable men … two such remarkably handsome and very appealing men? Did you notice how well they looked that day at Pemberley … when we first met? My goodness, the Colonel is a fine specimen of dazzling masculine beauty, is he not?"

"I thought you were not looking then. You certainly scolded me twice for staring."

"Well, I did sneak a few glances while you were ogling Mr. Darcy. I must say, Fitzwilliam's clothing was clinging in a most provocative manner."

"Well, that certainly settles it, Jane. Their names are just too similar. We must avoid confusion; therefore, you shall simply *have* to choose Mr. Bingley."

"How have you arrived at that nonsensical reasoning?"

"I have no idea whether you were referring to Fitzwilliam Darcy's or Richard Fitzwilliam's provocatively clinging clothing."

Fitzwilliam Darcy stepped from the tub and donned a silk robe that clung provocatively to his damp body. He was then shaved and dressed with the assistance of his faithful valet. By the time he left his chambers, he felt no lingering affects from the afternoon's indulgences. He joined his father in the drawing room while they waited for the ladies and their guest, Ellis Fleming.

"Ah, Fitzwilliam, recovered, are you?"

"I beg your pardon, Father?"

"I heard you were sick as a cushion this afternoon … something to do with gross overindulgence and being ape-drunk and on the cut at Whites, I believe."

"Yes, well, I am unsure how you came about that exaggerated piece of on-dit, but I assure you I did not make a cake of myself at the club. Fleming fortuitously arrived before I could actually accomplish that and accompanied me home."

"He is a fine fellow, that Fleming; and I will have no hesitation when he asks for Georgiana's hand."

"Speaking of asking for hands, Father, I should inform you I intend to make an offer of marriage to Miss Elizabeth Bennet in the near future."

George Darcy scowled at his son and walked across the room to gaze out the window. "You can do better, Fitzwilliam. You know I want you to marry a woman with a title or at least a vast amount of wealth. You may be infatuated with a vivacious young beauty from a decent family; however, you can have your pick of the country's very finest ladies. Why settle for less? Do not be so hasty in making such an important decision."

"I very nearly lost her by being slow and careful, and I will not take such a risk again. Miss Elizabeth *is* my pick from the country's finest women. I would certainly not be settling for less, because she is everything I desire in a wife, and more. Why would I want to marry some snobbish, vain, mean, empty-headed woman of the haut ton just because she has a title when I can have a modest, kind, natural, witty, intelligent, and caring lady?"

"Miss Elizabeth will bring very little to a marriage, for I happen to know her dowry is a mere £12,000. You should aim much higher, son. You certainly could have your pick of the many daughters of nobility dangling after you."

"The woman I want to marry is bright and corky compared to the dull, timid, and apathetic young women I have usually encountered in the upper sphere. My experience has been that the accomplished females of our so-called polite society are anything but polite."

"She is outspoken and feisty. You would not get along."

"I admit Elizabeth can be quite assertive and lively and has a teasing nature. Still and all, compared to the respectful, compliant fawning which I usually receive, I find I actually prefer and appreciate such a happy, independent spirit."

Fitzwilliam had not noticed his mother enter the room and was startled when her voice came from behind him. "I know you are merely playing the devil's advocate; nevertheless, did you notice, George, not once did he mention her physical attributes? Any man would be proud to have such a beautiful ornament on his arm. However, our son has the good sense to appreciate Miss Elizabeth's more important qualities. I have often heard prospective daughters-in-law do not usually meet the high standards mothers expect for their sons. Elizabeth Bennet must be exceptional, indeed, for I heartily approve of your choice, Fitzwilliam. Please disregard these tears. I am very, very happy for you, not to mention you have also made me proud to have reared such a fine young man."

Fitzwilliam took his mother's hand and gently kissed her knuckles. "Thank you, Mother. I have you to thank for my good sense, while the only thing I inherited from Father is good looks."

Mother and son exchanged grins.

"All right, all right. Two against one is not fair play." George Darcy smirked, displaying his dimples, so like his son's. He crossed the room and shook his heir's hand. "Congratulations, Fitzwilliam. If you will be half as happy in your marriage as I have been in mine, you will be blessed, indeed."

The young man suddenly realized they were all jumping the gun somewhat and asked for their patience while he wooed their daughter-in-law-to-be.

In the smaller family dining room, Mr. George Darcy and Lady Anne faced one another across the length of the table. At the Master's end sat his two daughters; and the Mistress had her son to her left and Ellis Fleming, her potential son-in-law-to-be, at her right.

Miss Anna observed the happy faces of her sister and Mr. Fleming, who were seated next to one another; however, because Anna was beside her brother, she failed to notice the grins and smirks that frequently appeared on his usually serious face.

Fleming did not. "Well, my friend, I am glad to see you are in better *spirits* than the last time I saw you. If you were to actually say something, I am sure your articulation would be much improved as well."

"Sorry, Fleming, I was woolgathering. Did I miss something? Were you truly saying something witty and intelligent for a change?"

Ellis looked at Georgiana and said, "There it is again, Miss Darcy. Did you see that smile? Why on earth is your brother so pleased with himself this evening?"

"I believe he received some joyous news this afternoon, Mr. Fleming; and perhaps … "

Georgiana's comment was interrupted by a scream, the shattering of china, and muffled curses. A footman was ordered to investigate; and when Disher returned, he reported there had been a bit of an accident on the way from the kitchen to the dining room. During the altercation, a tray containing the next course had, unfortunately, ended up on the floor.

Lady Anne excused herself to speak with the housekeeper and cook. When she came back, she looked pointedly at her youngest child and said, "The poor man was startled by a cravat scurrying between his feet. Anna, perhaps you should go retrieve the mischievous neckcloth before it causes further pandemonium. My apologies, everyone; but the next course will be somewhat delayed. Mrs. Burnham, however, has another dish almost ready; and it will be delivered momentarily."

Miss Anna hurried from the room. As she searched the hallways, she was able to catch the tail end of the cravat disappearing into the drawing room. The piece of linen was unhooked from Barb Thorne's quills, and the little hedgehog was gently deposited in Anna's bedchamber.

When the calamity was made known to Mrs. Susan Burnham, she and her underlings immediately scrambled to improvise another dish to serve while the ingredients for the ruined course were prepared again. An efficient and thrifty cook, Mrs. Burnham was very careful with her available resources. She often poached eggs, shaved chocolate, welched on rabbits; and even her pastry was stollen. She considered her options for a moment; and then a savoury sauce of ale, mustard, and spices was quickly mixed together with melted cheese and served over toasted bread. Mrs. Burnham put the Welsh rabbit, or rarebit, on the tray; and the rattled footman was ordered to be more careful. Just as 'toad in the hole 'is not really a toad, Welsh rabbit contains no hare; so the kitchen workers hurried to have the meat course ready as quickly as possible.

Miss Anna returned to the dining room just as a footman was serving the rarebit. "Um, what have we here, Disher?"

"I believe it is called Welsh rabbit, Miss."

"Rabbit! I cannot possibly eat rabbit. Oh, Mother, I wish you had permitted me to bring my rabbit, Stew. I miss Herr Stewart most desperately."

"Anna, you cannot even keep track of Barbara Thorne's whereabouts; and we have just suffered through the consequences of that carelessness. Calm yourself, child. The dish is meatless, and I believe its name is supposed to be ironic. Peasants were not permitted to hunt game on estates and often had to settle for cheese instead of rabbit or other meat."

Ellis Fleming said, "Miss Anna, you really should try it. Rarebit is delicious." He suddenly smirked at his friend. "A rare, delicious bit ... DeelisheyBit ... LisshyBit ... Lizzabiff ... shall I continue, Darcy?"

George Darcy cleared his throat. "No, thank you, Mr. Fleming. I think we all get the picture."

"Mr. Darcy, sir, I did not ... "

"Quite all right, young man. Perhaps a change of subject would be best, though."

For a while the diners ate in reserved silence, and the promised meat course was soon served. Ellis Fleming was a talkative sort, however; and he was rather uncomfortable with the lull in conversation. "I say, Darcy, ... er, Fitzwilliam, did you ever discover why someone called you 'hanson barberin?'"

Miss Anna choked on the sip of watered wine she had just taken. All the same, she managed to inquire, "I beg your pardon, Mr. Fleming. What did you just ask my brother?"

"Do you mean when I mentioned 'hanson barberin?'"

When both Anna and Georgiana turned red, their brother was instantly intrigued. He narrowed his eyes and suspiciously asked, "Do you girls know a barber named Hanson?"

The sisters looked at one another, giggled, and both truthfully answered in unison, "No."

"But you two do know something! You look so innocent that butter would not melt in your mouths. Despite that, your blushes reveal otherwise. For once and for all, what in *bloody hell* is the meaning of that confounding expression 'hanson barberin?'"

"Fitzwilliam George Darcy! Watch your language while ladies are present."

"Sorry, Father, but these two *imps* hold the answer to that intriguing question asked by little Robert when we dined with the Bennets recently. As you may remember, all conversation ground to a halt when that bloody, er, ruddy Lieutenant-Colonel Dun strutted in. Sisters, what, exactly, did the poppet mean when he asked me, 'Are you Libazeth's hanson barberin?'"

Georgiana squirmed and, if possible, turned even redder. "It has to do with Anna's questionable choice of reading material and very vivid imagination. Since the expression's origin is her responsibility, I should let my dearest sister explain."

"Georgie, no!" Miss Anna was utterly mortified. "I cannot possibly."

Lady Anne sighed and gently set down her knife and fork on her plate. "Anna Darcy, what gothic nonsense have you been reading?"

The young lady cast down her eyes and muttered, "It was not a gothic novel, Mother. It was a Viking pirate saga Miss Bingley loaned me months ago. Oh. I probably should have returned it when she was here earlier today."

Georgiana was shocked. "Are you saying Caroline Bingley had the nerve to show up here after the scene at Harding, Howell & Co. and what she did to Elizabeth?"

Fitzwilliam's knife and fork clashed onto his plate. "What has happened? What has Miss Bingley done to Eliz ... Miss Elizabeth?"

Ellis Fleming spent the remainder of the course wishing for the lulls in conversation he usually abhorred. His friend was clearly upset by Miss Bingley's treatment of Miss Elizabeth. All the same, Darcy was also somewhat amused that the ladies of his own family had given the nasty woman the cut direct. When the discussion on that topic closed, Fitzwilliam then brought up again the 'hanson barberin' subject.

"So, Anna, you were reading a trashy pirate novel; and ... ?"

"Oh, fiddlesticks! Fine, brother. But I am warning you and Mr. Fleming right now ... the tables are about to be turned, and you two will be the ones humiliated."

The two young men looked at one another with alarm and thought back to all the many possibilities that could result in their humiliation. "Perhaps another time, then, Anna dearest. Let us forget all this nonsense and unpleasantness and enjoy the rest of our meal in peace," suggested her brother.

Miss Anna was clearly annoyed. "Not so hasty, if you please. Forget about enjoying your meal in peace. You wanted to learn the meaning, so learn you shall ... in piecemeal. It is not 'hanson barberin,' unless you are three years old and cannot pronounce the words *handsome barbarian.* The 'handsome' part was not of my making, while I am responsible for the 'barbarian' half. I swooned upon seeing Mr. Bingley, Richard, and the two of you that sweltering day at Pemberley. I thought four freebooters had arrived at our estate to pillage and plunder and ... well, you get the picture. Shall I go into detail for Mother and Father of the shocking sight Georgie and I, not to mention our two new friends, witnessed that awful afternoon? I cannot imagine why someone in the Bennet household obviously added the word 'handsome,' for you were all most shamefully scruffy and inappropriately attired in front of us that day."

Georgiana knew her sister's assessment was accurate. Be that as it may, she also understood her own attachment to Mr. Fleming was not the only relationship that blossomed because of the fateful encounter on the lawn. She glanced sideways at her tall, dark, and handsome young man and saw him blush for the first time. Anna's prediction had been bang up to the mark, and the two gents were humiliated and even redder than the ladies. Nevertheless, nothing could ruin Fitzwilliam Darcy's good humour and optimistic hopes that evening.

"Fitzwilliam, remind me I wish to have a word with you later tonight."

"Yes, Father."

Not even that.

Chapter II

In Which Darcy is Dashing and Elizabeth Horses Around

"What about this one, sir?"

"No, no, Knott, the green one."

Fitzwilliam Darcy watched in amazement as his valet, Crispin Knott, put the green coat away and held up the brown one again.

"Knott! I said the green one."

Knott had served the fastidious young gentleman since the heir was eighteen; however, the white-haired valet was quite getting on in years and could be a tad crotchety at times. "With all due respect, sir, I distinctly heard you say 'not the green one.'"

"No. I said, 'No, no, Knott, the *green* one.' Note the pause and the emphasis on the word green."

"I do not recall it being there before, sir."

"Well, it most certainly was."

"If you say so, sir."

Darcy waited, in vain, for the doddering servant to assist him with the green coat. "Mister Knott, would you please … oh, never mind." He knew he really should have a younger man take over the position; but Knott was practically a member of the family, having first served as his father's valet for more than thirty years. Because Darcy was in a hurry to visit Miss Elizabeth that morning, he struggled with the tight coat himself, turned toward the servant, held his arms out to the sides, and asked, "How do I look?"

"Handsome, as always, sir."

Darcy's nerves were frayed. When he checked his appearance in the mirror, he cried, "Knott! Do you not see anything wrong with this blasted cravat?"

The elderly man peered closely at the well-worn, ragged neckcloth, grinned, and said, "Frayed knot, sir."

At the Bennet household, the family had just finished breakfast when a letter arrived from Longbourn's steward. Thomas Bennet scanned the contents and reported, "It seems Whitelaw has hired a new worker by the name of Barnaby Colton." Mr. Bennet had the pleasure of being eagerly questioned by his wife, five daughters, and young son; and it was a cinch to stir-up their unbridled curiosity a bit. "Mr. Whitelaw assigned Colton to the stable and gave the chap free rein; and when Colton was saddled with the responsibility of putting horses on the carriage for the first time, it went off without a hitch. The letter also says the young man recently left a stall door open; and Lydia's pony, Miss Behave, ate all the hay."

Lydia gave the others a baleful look and asked, "Was that the last straw, Papa?"

"Well, let me see. Ah, yes, our steward promptly posted Colton to the fields, where the poor boy has since been busy mending fences."

Catherine sighed and rolled her eyes. Mr. Bennet said, "Kitty, you look as if you did not enjoy the report. Are you not diverted?"

As the most serious member of the family, Catherine felt it her eleven-year old duty to remind her father one should not live to make sport of and laugh at others.

"Never mind, Kitty," her mother said. "Although the mane parts of the tail are quite plausible, I would not put it past-ure father to have embellished certain sections of the letter."

Catherine raised her chin and said, "Well, Mama, the facts can always be verified when we return to Hertfordshire."

Lydia smiled sweetly and said, "Kitty is right. We can hear the whole story right from the horse's mouth."

Mr. Bennet grinned at his youngest daughter and reminded, "But that, Lydia, would be listening to a neigh-sayer."

The conversation jogged Lizzy's memory to the realization she had not yet ridden her horse much during their stay in Town. On the spur of the moment she said, "If you will excuse me, I am going to change into riding attire and visit the mews. I have been neglecting poor Gloriana, so I shall now take her for a short ride in the park. Would you care to join me, Papa?"

"Why, yes, my dear. The weather certainly seems quite stable, and it behooves me to give Zephyr some much-needed exercise."

Before Lizzy left the dining room, she turned to Catherine and said, "We shall not be gone long, Kitty. I promise to help you with your macramé project when I return. In the meantime, practice some of those hitching knots I showed you. Afterward I shall need to start preparations for this evening. Jane, will you please accompany me now while I change? I would like to speak with you about the ball."

When Rachel had helped Miss Elizabeth into her riding clothes and the sisters were alone, Jane asked, "Are you at all apprehensive about tonight, Lizzy?"

"Of course, and I am sure a kaleidoscope of butterflies will invade my stomach again as soon as I see Mr. Darcy."

"I did not necessarily mean that aspect of the evening but rather if you had any reservations about meeting the Earl of Matlock and Lady Rebecca. I have heard they are not as amiable as their youngest son, and I know they would not approve of me as a match for Colonel Fitzwilliam. Oh, Lizzy, I dreamed of him last night; and he was most *incredibly* amiable. You would be shocked, sister, by the content of my dreams; and they occur not only while I sleep, for the strikingly handsome soldier invades my waking hours as well. Please promise you will not allow any private moments to occur between us, for I would not trust myself to behave properly if alone with him."

"Jane! How shocking. Yet it seems we share a dilemma. I asked you to accompany me here in order to request the same sort of favour, except in reverse. I was hoping you would turn a blind eye should Mr. Darcy request a moment alone with me. But what are your thoughts of Mr. Bingley? Do you have similar visions of that good-looking young man?"

Jane sadly shook her head.

"Well, it seems we are destined to have two Fitzwilliams in our family, after all then."

"Lizzy, you are certainly getting way ahead of yourself. I truly have no reason to believe the Colonel feels any affection at all for me, while Mr. Bingley openly wears his heart on his sleeve."

"It is unfortunate Mr. Bingley's sleeve is not attached to a resplendent red uniform coat. If that gentleman wore regimentals, you might see him in a different light."

Rachel returned and informed Miss Elizabeth her father was waiting for her at the rear entrance, which led to the mews behind their house.

"Jane, I must go. Do not worry. I am sure you will make out wonderfully tonight."

She did not hear her sister mutter, "And *that*, dear sister, is just what I worry might happen."

Natty Fitzwilliam Darcy, in his splendid green coat and crisp new cravat, tapped the knocker on the Bennets' door and was admitted by Sharp. His request to see Miss Elizabeth was announced, and the young man found himself in the sitting room with Mrs. Bennet, her three youngest children, as well as the governess.

Mrs. Bennet said, "I am sorry, Mr. Darcy; but Lizzy and her father have gone for a ride in the park. However, they should not be much longer, and you are most welcome to sit and wait. Would you care for some tea?"

Darcy smiled weakly, agreed to the tea, took a seat, and twisted his signet ring. If he had not taken the time to change his frayed and knotted neckcloth, he might not have missed Miss Elizabeth. Knott's palsied fingers took an inordinate amount of time to finesse the intricate knot upon which he had insisted. Darcy and his father had both tried on several occasions over the past year to convince the servant it was time to retire, but Knott had been offended. Since neither gentleman had the heart to flatly dismiss the valet, it had all come to naught.

Mrs. Bennet reacquainted Mr. Darcy with Kitty, Lydia, and Robert and introduced Miss Martha Edwards. Tea was served after inane polite conversation about the weather. Three-year old Robert walked over to Darcy, rested his hands on the gentleman's knees, looked up with wide baby blue eyes, and said, "Libazeth is teaching Kitty maca … macamay with yarns, but I cannot knot. Can you make knots, Mither Darthy?"

"I can, indeed, make knots, Robert. Would you like me to show you how it is done?"

The child shook his blonde curls. "No. But when Libazeth comes home, maybe you can do the knotty thing with her."

Darcy had just taken a sip of tea, it went down the wrong way, and he choked while the little boy continued to innocently stare at him. Mrs. Bennet jumped up in alarm. "Mr. Darcy, are you unwell? Your face is an alarming shade of puce." She took his cup and saucer and, in a motherly manner, patted the gentleman on the back. No thanks to her, his breathing soon returned to normal. Regardless, Mrs. Bennet continued to administer assistance.

Miss Elizabeth and her father arrived at that moment; she was astonished, and he amused. Mr. Bennet arched his brow and said, "Lizzy, do you suppose I will get a *pat* answer should I ask what happened?"

His wife explained, "Poor Mr. Darcy choked when Robert spoke to him, though I did not hear the conversation. Robert, did you bother the gentleman about … you know … what we told you never to mention again?"

"No, Mama. I did not axe about the hanson barberin. I promithed not to, 'member? An' a gennelmin must keep his promith."

Mrs. Bennet rolled her eyes heavenward and silently scolded herself for not strictly enforcing the 'children should be seen and not heard' proverb. "Yes, Robert, it is very important to keep one's promises. Come along now, love; it is time for you to return to the nursery."

The poppet was whisked away as he loudly protested. "Can I not stay? I promith to be a good boy. And, Mama, I weally did not axe him if he is Libazeth's hanson barberin."

Darcy coloured up at the reference. He desperately *wanted* to be Elizabeth's; and although 'handsome' was flattering, 'barbarian' was not.

He stole a quick glance in her direction, and Lizzy's mortification was also evident. The quick glance turned into a long, admiring observation of her loveliness. Sparkling, intelligent eyes had been brightened by the recent exercise, and chestnut curls escaped from a bonnet that exactly matched the green of his coat and her riding habit. Her cheeks glowed, his heart tingled, and he could not tear his eyes away.

Elizabeth dared to steal a quick glance at Darcy, who had risen when she entered the room. It was supposed to just be a quick glance; still, she could not look away despite her embarrassment. Fitzwilliam Darcy was incredibly dapper and arresting, standing tall in his tight-fitting green tailcoat, white shirt, and intricately knotted cravat. He wore a brocade waistcoat, light-coloured breeches, and high black boots. Elizabeth was thrilled to be in his company again and would have rushed to his side if propriety allowed. Instead she reluctantly excused herself to change and promised to return quickly.

Miss Edwards, Kitty, and Lydia curtsied and took their leave of the two gentlemen. Martha had decided to accompany the girls on a quick stroll in the garden because she assumed her employer would want to speak privately with the visitor. The scuttlebutt amongst the servants was that Mr. Darcy was dangling after Miss Elizabeth and mistakenly assumed she had become betrothed to Lieutenant-Colonel Dun.

Mr. Bennet sat in a chair across the room and observed the gentleman caller whose eyes had followed Elizabeth as she left the room. "So, Mr. Darcy, what brings you here on this fine morning?" *I already know the answer, you rapscallion. You are setting wheels in motion that will carry Lizzy away from us. Please spare me a bit more time to adjust to the inevitable.*

"I have come to call on Miss Elizabeth, sir." *I will not spare any more time. I would apply to you for her hand this minute if only I had her consent. Nonetheless, you must be prepared for the inevitable. Although today I will settle for asking Elizabeth to stand up with me at the ball, very soon I will be asking her to stand up with me in front of a clergyman.*

"Pardon me for speaking plainly, Mr. Darcy; however, the last time you were here to visit my daughter you hardly spoke two words together and departed in quite a dudgeon. I hope whatever caused your bristles to be set up has been resolved to your satisfaction." *You acted too hastily upon overhearing Dun's words, young man; and I hope you are not prone to rash decisions and reckless behaviour in other aspects of your life.*

"Mr. Bennet, I sincerely apologize for that unacceptable behaviour. I erroneously believed someone had thrown a rub in my way; yet as it turns out, my plans have, in fact, not been spoiled after all. I confess I jumped to a wrong conclusion, and I hope to avoid any further misunderstandings in my determined course of action. Therefore, sir, I humbly apply to you for permission to court Miss Elizabeth. I have not yet sought her approval; but since you and I are speaking plainly, I believe you should know of my good intentions. If my prayers are to be answered, your lovely daughter … "

Mr. Bennet spoke loudly to cover the other man's words. "Ah, here is my lovely daughter now, Mr. Darcy. Lizzy, do come and join us. Your mother should return any minute. Miss Edwards and the younger girls are in the garden, and I believe Jane and Mary are practicing in the music room. If you will pardon me for just a moment, I must fetch Whitelaw's correspondence from where I left it in the dining room. I will not be gone long. Oh, and Mr. Darcy, I should tell you I have decided to grant my permission." Before he exited he gave the visitor a pointed look. *I trust you to be alone with my precious daughter for a few moments. Use your time wisely.*

Darcy acknowledged Mr. Bennet's look with a slight nod. *Thank you and I will not betray your trust.*

Elizabeth glanced around the room and contemplated where to sit. The point became moot when Mr. Darcy stepped forward, their dark eyes locked, and he kissed her bare hand, sending thrills to the tips of her fingers, toes, and other places in between. He did not release his hold on her hand or sever eye contact as he spoke in his deep, rich voice. "Miss Elizabeth, it is a great pleasure to be in your presence again; and I am very sorry I displayed such deplorable manners the last time I was in your home. Although you did not witness the worst of my behaviour, I am sure you heard of it. Georgiana explained what actually transpired, and I beg you to please forgive me."

"Mr. Darcy, of course you are forgiven. I am sorry you were put into such an uncomfortable position. All the same, you must know my own position, at that time, was extremely uncomfortable as well. Turning down a marriage proposal is not something I would ever care to repeat."

He smiled, dimpled, and squeezed her hand. "That is, indeed, very, very good to hear, Miss Elizabeth; I hope you keep that thought in mind the next time a man asks for your hand." He could not help it; he raised that hand to his lips again, gave her an intense look, and took a step forward.

Elizabeth blushed and thought the room was overheated until she noticed there were no flames in the fireplace grate. She snatched her hand from his and reluctantly, breathlessly said, "Mr. Darcy, sir, my family may return at any moment. Perhaps we should be seated."

He took possession of her hand again. "Not just yet, please. I have two requests to ask of you." *Will you please be my wife? Can we marry tomorrow?* "Most importantly, Miss Elizabeth, may I have the great privilege of being permitted to court you?"

"Well, I am somewhat embarrassed to say, sir, I assumed you had already been doing so since you first arrived in London." Her intelligent eyes sparkled, her brow arched, and a pert, saucy smile sent his blood racing.

He smiled back at her and said, "Answer the question please, Miss Elizabeth."

"Very well, Mr. Darcy. Yes, you may continue to do what I already thought, and hoped, you were doing this past fortnight. I would actually like that, very much, indeed." *My goodness, but you are an attractive man, especially when you smile at me in that manner. I believe I should revise my favour and ask Jane not to allow you and I any time alone at the ball.* "Would your second request have anything to do with my dance card for tonight's event, sir?"

"I remember telling you at the art exhibit our minds think alike, and you have just proven my statement's veracity. Miss Elizabeth, if propriety allowed it, my name would be on every space of your card; and I am already jealous of all those blanks that will, undoubtedly, fill far too rapidly for my liking. Before that happens, will you please reserve for me the supper and last sets for this evening?"

"You may consider them yours, Mr. Darcy." *You may consider my heart forever yours as well, dear sir.*

"Thank you, Miss Elizabeth. I do believe, for the first time in my life, I shall actually look forward to attending a ball." *Is it improper for a courtship to last a matter of hours before it becomes an engagement?*

The sounds of her family in the hallway made Lizzy start to snatch back her hand again, but not before Darcy turned it over and placed a lingering kiss on her racing pulse, thereby making her knees weak and her cheeks red. What effect it had on the gentleman was a private matter.

When Mr. and Mrs. Bennet entered the room together, Lizzy was seated on the sofa while Mr. Darcy stood directly behind her. Mrs. Bennet took one look at her daughter and said, "Lizzy, I did not notice before, but your colour is quite high. I hope you were not galloping Gloriana around the park."

"Not at all, Mama. We rode at an appropriately sedate pace, although she and I long to fly across the fields at home. I do miss Longbourn, yet I must admit London has much more appeal on this visit than at any time previously."

"Mr. Darcy, do sit down, sir. Are you enjoying your stay in Town as well?"

"Yes, Mrs. Bennet; and I quite agree with your daughter. The city suddenly holds a certain attraction with which I could not bear to part right now." He moved from behind the sofa, chose a chair facing Lizzy, and gazed into her beautiful, dark, chocolate-coloured eyes.

Bows and curtsies were exchanged as Jane and Mary entered the room; and when Mr. Bennet asked Darcy if his latest endeavour had been successful, his answer was that in the short term it had, but the long term was yet to be determined. The ladies assumed the two were discussing business, and they began to speak of more important issues. "Jane, have you chosen between the blue silk and the silver satin yet?"

"Yes, Mama, I have selected the blue. Lizzy, have you finally decided on the primrose? Lizzy? Lizzy!"

"Hmm? I beg your pardon, Jane. Did you say something to me?"

Mr. Bennet cleared his throat and said, "Excuse me for interrupting your riveting discourse, ladies; however, I have an announcement to make. I have sanctioned a courtship between two people present in this room … present, at least in body if not in mind, for it seems Mr. Darcy and Lizzy can scarcely tear themselves away from one another's eyes for even a moment."

The couple grinned and accepted the polite comments and teasing from the others. None of Lizzy's family had been surprised; they also assumed a courtship was already underway, despite the brief hiccup caused by Dun. As much as he wished to stay near Elizabeth, Darcy realized he should depart and allow his lady time to get ready for the ball. If Georgiana was typical of other young ladies, many hours were required to prepare for such an evening. He gave precise directions to Matlock Manor and took his leave after another opportunity to kiss Elizabeth's hand.

Lizzy attempted to assist Kitty with her macramé project but was all thumbs when she tried to tie knots. Her mind was more agreeably engaged. She had been meditating on the very great pleasure of advancing from courtship with Mr. Darcy to actually tying the knot with him.

Because the Darcy and Fitzwilliam families were co-hosting the ball, the dance cards featured both their impressive crests embossed on the silver and gold silk covers. Jane opened hers and sighed at all the blank spaces next to the titles of the pieces to be played. She gasped as she read the name of the final one. "Oh, my! Lizzy, do you realize the final dance is to be a waltz?"

Elizabeth sat by the fire with her eyes closed as Rachel towel-dried her hair. Her eyes flew open and she said, "Goodness, I would not have believed the staid Earl of Matlock and Lady Rebecca would allow such scandalous activity under their roof. I am glad Mama insisted on our learning to waltz last season, for Mr. Darcy has requested my final set in addition to the supper one."

"You are very fortunate, indeed, sister. I admit to being quite envious. My dance card has not one gentleman's name on it yet. Other than

Colonel Fitzwilliam, Mr. Bingley, and Mr. Fleming, I am unsure if I will even be acquainted with any other young men tonight."

"Since nobody can ever be introduced in a ballroom, you shall surely be a wallflower all evening, poor Jane. It must be an awful burden to be so unattractive, unapproachable, and unappreciated. Perhaps you should just remain at home." Lizzy had closed her eyes again under Rachel's ministrations and was totally unprepared for the cushion that sailed through the air and landed in her lap.

"Knott, have you ordered my bath for precisely seven o'clock?"

"Yes, sir."

"Have you ensured all pieces of my ensemble are crisply starched or pressed, as necessary?"

"But of course, sir."

"You have not starched my trousers by mistake again, have you?"

"Certainly not, sir, only your collar and cuffs."

"You will not be offended when Bladen is summoned, instead, to perform my barbering?"

"I understand, sir. You need a steady hand this evening. It would not do to have unsightly nicks and cuts on such an important night."

"Important night? What do you know, Knott?"

"I know naught, as usual, sir. Be that as it may, there is some interesting scuttlebutt below-stairs amongst the servants. There is talk you will soon no longer be fiancée-free."

Part V

A Pickle of a Tight Spot
or
Dill-Emma

A tribute to Austen's *Emma*

Chapter I

Whining, Dining, and Having a Ball

From the moment the Misses Jane and Elizabeth Bennet entered Matlock Manor, they were swept up in the glamour of a private ball given by a member of the Peerage. The public rooms were festooned with garlands of flowers, greenery, and ribbon; and illumination was provided by hundreds of beeswax candles reflected in strategically placed mirrors. A multitude of handsomely clad fashionable people milled about, chatting and sipping fine wine, while a quartet of professional musicians played background music.

"Oh, Lizzy, it is all extremely refined and sophisticated. The guests are so very polished and stylish, and their elegant attire is certainly all the crack."

Elizabeth was preoccupied with attempting to espy a certain gentleman and said, "Yes, but fashion is something that goes in one era and out the other." Because she was comparatively petite, Elizabeth stood on tiptoes and craned her neck to look over the milling crowd. "Do you happen to see the Darcy family yet, Jane?"

A liveried footman took their cloaks; and as the Bennet sisters waited their turn in the receiving line, lively Charles Bingley approached and bowed. "Miss Bennet, Miss Elizabeth, what a delight it is to see you both again. Miss Bennet, I confess I have been anticipating your arrival in the hope of securing at least one set. If you are not otherwise engaged, may I request the honour of standing up with you for the first? And Miss Elizabeth, may I have the pleasure of the second set, as well as a moment of your time for a brief conversation before we enter the ballroom?" When the ladies expressed their consent to all his requests, the fellow smiled broadly, bowed again, and walked to the entrance to await Elizabeth.

It was then their turn to be received by the evening's hosts and hostesses. Jane and Lizzy were presented to the Earl of Matlock and Lady Rebecca before being introduced to the Earl's eldest son, James, the Viscount Wentletrap, and his wife, Lady Isabelle. After making the acquaintance of the Earl's niece, Miss Anne de Bourgh, the rest of the party was already well known to the Bennet sisters.

Next in line was Colonel Richard Fitzwilliam in his dazzling red uniform, and Elizabeth supported her sister's arm as Jane took an unsteady step forward to curtsy and receive his courtly bow. "Miss Bennet, I skipped a heartbeat upon first sight of your loveliness tonight; and I expect your dance card is already filled. If not, may I request the first set?" When Jane informed him she was already engaged for the first, he requested the supper set; and she accepted. He then boldly asked whether her final dance was already spoken for and was elated to be able to secure that one as well, especially since he knew it was a waltz. The striking officer then requested Miss Elizabeth's first and was surprised to learn his cousin had not snatched her up for the opening set. He was very pleased with himself for having been granted the good fortune of standing up with two such beautiful women.

The Bennet sisters then moved on to the co-hosting family; and Elizabeth felt, before she even saw, Fitzwilliam Darcy's eyes riveted upon her. The debonair gentleman was impeccably attired in a double-breasted black cutaway tailcoat and trousers. His silver and gold brocade waistcoat was square-cut at the waist, and a snowy silk cravat was artfully tied over the high collar of his white linen shirt. In Lizzy's opinion, the irresistibly handsome Fitzwilliam Darcy was a swell of the first stare and could easily shine down everyone else; and she only had eyes for him.

Jane and Elizabeth were enthusiastically greeted by Georgiana and Anna and warmly so by their parents. Fitzwilliam Darcy politely addressed Miss Bennet, asked to stand up with her, and was granted the third set. When it was her sister's turn, he boldly kissed her gloved hand and said, "Miss Elizabeth, my love … -ly lady, you are positively breathtaking tonight, as usual. I need not ask whether you are well, for it is plain to see you are the very picture of health and vivacity. The supper set cannot arrive a moment too soon; until then, I hope you will enjoy the evening ... but not too much." The corners of his eyes crinkled, and dimples appeared as he smiled at the woman he loved.

Elizabeth was stunningly beautiful in a gown with a low-cut form-fitting bodice, short puffy sleeves, and gracefully flowing skirt. The dress was a buttery primrose silk encrusted with tiny, shimmering clear glass spangles that caught and reflected the candlelight. A band of narrow braided gold trim was tied under the high waistline, and its tasselled ends cascaded to the hem. She wore white above-the-elbow gloves and a gold chain with a small diamond pendant. Her chestnut curls were elaborately upswept and dressed with ornamental combs, and a ringlet hung charmingly down one side of her neck. Around her wrist she wore a pretty fan and a small beaded reticule that matched the combs. Completing her ensemble, pale yellow embroidered satin slippers peeked from beneath her well-designed dress.

Miss Jane Bennet's periwinkle blue gown was roller-printed with silver vertical stripes and had a plunging v-neckline. The elegant creation was pleated in the back for fullness and ease of movement, but from the front the slinky silk moulded to her curves as she walked in soft silver slippers. Her blonde hair was intricately entwined with blue ribbons and piled atop her head, with a few ringlets framing her lovely face. Jane's only accessories were long white gloves, silver earrings and necklace, an ornate fan, and a reticule that matched her gown.

The two ladies headed toward the ballroom. Darcy saw Ellis Fleming step up to them, bow, and begin a brief conversation he assumed would include requests for dances. Fleming then escorted Miss Bennet inside while Bingley offered his arm to her sister. He noticed the latter two in earnest conversation and correctly guessed his friend was profusely apologizing for Caroline's behaviour. Darcy craned his neck until he lost sight of Elizabeth in the crowd; he sighed and returned his attention to the last few guests as they filtered in.

Darcy had secured his cousin, Anne de Bourgh, for the opening dances; and as they entered the ballroom together, he was dismayed to see his other cousin, Richard Fitzwilliam, was hovering near Elizabeth.

He knew Fitz had been promised her first set and was fine with such an arrangement. What he did not like, however, was the army of other red coats and the sea of blue naval uniforms that surrounded them. The officers, all clamouring to be introduced to *his* Elizabeth, annoyed and agitated him greatly. As they passed through the throng, Darcy heard far too many young men asking acquaintances if they could perform an introduction to the 'dark-haired beauty with the fine eyes'. Twice he heard ribald commentary on her other strong points, and twice he had to restrain himself from planting some bloke a facer. "Come, Anne, there is someone I would like you to become better acquainted with before we take our places for the first set."

"Do you mean the 'dark-haired beauty,' the 'lovely lady with fine eyes,' the 'tempting armful,' the 'sultry siren,' or the 'ravishing wench with the ample dairies'?'"

"Anne Catriona de Bourgh! Your mother would be disgusted. By the way, what are you doing in Town? How ever did you escape?"

"I cannot talk of Mother in a ballroom; my head is full of more pleasant things. Let me just say we had another quarrel, I accused her of living in the Middle Ages, she discovered resistance is feudal, and I am now rebelling by staying at Matlock Manor for an undetermined duration. Enough of unpleasantness, tell me about this young lady who is causing such a stir this evening. I assume you are well acquainted with her."

"I am, indeed, Anne." Darcy's face became suffused with pure love and happiness, and his cousin was intrigued.

"By the look of bliss on your face, her name must be Trudy Light."

"That was truly groan-worthy, Anne. You have already met, and I know you are aware her name is Miss Elizabeth Bennet; however, I fully intend to change it to Mrs. Elizabeth Darcy as soon as may be."

"Upon my word, Fitzwilliam! Have you actually finally found your ideal woman? You held out for perfection for so long, I despaired you would ever encounter that quintessential lady."

"I have come to believe in a quote I heard recently but cannot remember the source: 'Love is not finding a perfect person; it is seeing an imperfect person perfectly'. There she is, Anne, in the yellow dress, the woman who stole my hea … Well, bloody hell! Why is Viscount Chalcroft kissing her hand and leering in that obscene manner?" Darcy pulled his cousin along as he cleared a path toward Miss Elizabeth, and Anne giggled at the image of him as the white knight bent on a rescue. Miss de Bourgh looked down at her own rather prim and proper pastel pink gown and thought, *No knight would ever rescue a damsel in dis-dress.*

The opening strains of La Belle Assemblée March halted Darcy in his tracks. He was relieved of his rescue duty by Colonel Fitzwilliam who offered Miss Elizabeth his arm and claimed her for the first set. Fitzwilliam Darcy and Anne de Bourgh took their places in line, as did Charles Bingley and Jane Bennet, as well as Ellis Fleming and Georgiana Darcy. As the dance began, Anne was again amused by her usually stodgy cousin's infatuation with the lady in yellow. His eyes hardly strayed from Elizabeth Bennet's position in the formation, and he nearly took a wrong turn.

"Fitzwilliam, you will have to do better than that absurd display. Tell me, have you secured Miss Elizabeth for the final set?"

"Hmm? Oh. Yes, I have, as well as for the supper set. Why?" The movements of the dance separated them, and he had to wait for her answer.

Moments later, Anne said, "You do realize the finale will be a waltz, do you not?"

"What? A waltz! Oh, God!" Darcy's face was positively panic-stricken.

"Cousin, I know you learned the steps. We were instructed together last year, along with Fitz and Georgie."

"Well, yes. However, I have certainly not practiced since then." Again they moved apart, and Darcy became annoyed with the separation.

As soon as they were reunited, his cousin sought clarification. "You have never waltzed with a woman, except that one time with me?"

"Of course not, Anne! The shocking waltz is hardly accepted by our society. When or why would I have done so? What on earth were our aunt and uncle thinking by including such an indecent activity? Confound it! Why did my parents not inform me we would be performing that confounding dance?"

"Then, you do not approve of such physical contact, my prim, proper, prudish, and priggish cousin? Do you not wish to hold your Miss Elizabeth Bennet in an embrace, one hand upon her waist, and glide across the floor with her?"

Darcy groaned, "Oh, God, yes!"

"Then I suggest you find yourself a partner and practice before making a spectacle of yourself on the dance floor."

"Will you help me, Anne? Please ... dearest, loveliest, favourite female cousin, Annie." Darcy gave her his irresistible, smouldering look, which usually worked uncommonly well on members of the opposite sex. In spite of that, his cousin was unaffected and unmoved.

"When? My entire dance card is full, and I even had to turn down numerous requests. So many men, so little time."

"It must be the lure of Rosings Park. What gentleman in his right mind would want to stand up with such a shrew?"

Miss Anne de Bourgh pinched his arm as she circled; and she reminded Darcy that since he was currently engaged in the activity, he must be quite out of his senses, which, she added, was no surprise to her. When their set ended, he escorted his cousin from the floor and asked if she required refreshment.

"Wine not? Please take your place in the punch-line, Fitzwilliam. But be punch-ual, and do not keep me waiting. I do have a bevy of handsome suitors waiting for the pleasure of my company, you know." As he walked away, she added, "And find out whether or not the punch contains any alcohol. I will want *proof*!"

Darcy shook his head, grinned at his cousin's teasing, and dutifully headed for the punchbowl. He found himself next to Viscount Chalcroft, the ignoble cad who had been leering at Elizabeth. The bloke's pun-gent cologne and crude remarks made Darcy want to punch the cad in the face; but he thought of the impeccably proper and gentlemanly behaviour of his boxing instructor who said, 'If a pugilist wants to get married, he will have to worry about the ring'. Thinking of a ring made him think of proposing to Elizabeth; thinking of Elizabeth made him think of the waltz; thinking of the waltz made him panic. He frantically sought Georgiana in the crush of people standing around waiting for the second set, and he finally caught sight of her pale blonde hair and lilac gown. He hurried back to Anne de Bourgh, thrust a cup of punch at her, executed a poor excuse for a bow, and strode over to his sister and her suitor.

"Excuse me, Fleming. May I have a private word with you, Georgie?" The siblings moved away to a corner; and Georgiana was amused when her brother urgently said, "I desperately need a refreshment course, Georgie. Will you assist me?"

"Brother, why on earth do you need *my* help to obtain a drink? Simply ask a servant."

"No, no! I need a quick refresher course in the art of dance, specifically the blasted waltz. For some unfathomable reason I completely forget how the bloody hellish thing is done."

"Fitzwilliam, why are your knickers in such a knot? Calm down, and watch your language. I am sure Elizabeth would be more than happy to comply with such a request for assistance."

"I cannot ask *her*. She is the reason my knickers … never mind! Will you please give me a hasty review? I am sure my recollection of the waltz will come back quickly. I absolutely must re-learn the proper steps before the last set, for I have asked Elizabeth to stand up with me. Therefore, it is imperative I neither be humiliated nor humiliate her."

"Ah, yes, my perfectionist brother cannot possibly be seen as lacking in any manner. I am truly sorry, Fitzwilliam; but my dance card is entirely full. The second set is about to begin, and I have promised it to Lieutenant Christian Westfall. Now there is someone who truly needs some dance instruction. You shall be fine, brother. That said, *my* feet might not fare so well. Please do not worry yourself so."

Abandoned and forlorn, Darcy sighed and stood alone after Westfall claimed his sister. He sourly wondered how he had gotten himself into such a pickle and just how he was going to extricate himself from the dill-emma.

"Mother, how could you fail to inform me we would be ending our ball with the scandalous waltz? Our family shall be ridiculed for such decadence. Why, even Lord Byron, of all people, is opposed to a dance in which couples actually embrace."

"Oh, Fitzwilliam, stop being such an old-fashioned prig. It is all the rage on the continent and will undoubtedly soon make its way to London as well. My brother and Lady Rebecca like to be trendsetters, plus I have a sneaky suspicion your aunt also wants to defy the patronesses of Almack's. Our guests tonight, for the most part, are forward-thinking people who will not be offended. In fact, I imagine some of them will actually take great pleasure in causing a sensation. Why do you so strongly object, my dear? I would think, as a young person, you would want to boldly *embrace*, if you will pardon the pun, a daring new vogue … and a certain lady."

"Well, I am certainly surprised my uncle even agreed to this. The Earl of Matlock should have been more defy-aunt. Perhaps it would be wise to simply cancel the risqué number before it is too late and replace it with something more socially acceptable. Ah, Father, there you are. What is your opinion of the scandal we shall surely cause tonight?"

"George, our son seems to believe we are all going to the inferno in a hand-basket tonight because we have included the waltz on our agenda."

The senior Darcy was in an ebullient mood, having bent his elbow with his highborn brother-in-law earlier. "I understand your concern, Fitzwilliam, my boy. All the same, I am by no means of the opinion, I assure you, that a ball of this kind, given by the Earl of Matlock and us, to respectable people, can have any evil tendency. Bloody hell, we are certainly not going to Netherfield (hiccup), excuse me, I mean the Netherworld in any sort of basket, son. The waltz is not wicker (hiccup), excuse me, I mean wicked enough to send us to perdition's pit. In fact, I am so far from objecting to dancing myself that I shall take this opportunity to solicit my wovely life (hiccup), excuse me, I mean lovely wife for the scandalous waltz."

Lady Anne smiled fondly at her slightly foxed husband. When their beloved son sighed and set his jaw, she examined Fitzwilliam's face closely and tried to understand the true reason for his opposition. "Oh, my dear. Has some other man asked Miss Elizabeth for the last set? Is that the cause of your dilemma?"

His ploy had not worked. Fitzwilliam Darcy knew when he was beaten, yet he would not stoop so low as to ask for his mother's or his aunt's assistance. "No, no. I assure you, if we are to imprudently proceed with this waltzing business, the lady I am courting will be standing up with none other than me. Mother, Father, please excuse me. I have pressing business to which I must attend."

As she watched him stride away, Lady Anne shook her head at Fitzwilliam's stodginess. *To what pressing business could you possibly have to attend at a ball? Oh, Miss Elizabeth, you shall be very good, indeed, for my straight-laced son.*

Fitzwilliam Darcy had made it the study of his life to avoid situations in which he might appear flawed; and as a perfectionist, he was exceptionally sensitive to criticism and ridicule. He set extremely high standards for himself, derived satisfaction from always being in control, and would not relax until his persistence paid off. *I do not want her last dance to be one of mortification. What if I am awkward and have to apologize instead of attending? What if I often move wrong without being aware of it? I do not wish to be the cause of all the shame and misery a disagreeable partner can give.* His youngest sister was his last hope. Anna had performed the music while the dance master instructed the family group the previous year, and Darcy reasoned she could perhaps remember the basics of the waltz and steal away with him for a few moments of rehearsal.

"Anna, dearest, loveliest sister, remember the time I covered for you when Georgiana's frog accidentally, er, croaked because of what you did? You toad me you would owe a favour; and since I find myself stuck in the mire tonight, I need you to return the service now."

When he had explained his predicament, Anna said, "Fitzwilliam, you are, indeed, a stick in the mud. Just come clean and tell Elizabeth. She is very understanding and will not think poorly of you. I cannot help, because I do not know how to waltz either. I will have to return the favour some other way, some other time. I am sorry, brother."

Darcy wished he had other female relatives from whom he could call in furth-er favours, but he was out of options. The prestigious gentleman felt pressed for time. He pressed his fingers against the pressure in his aching head, compressed his lips, and repressed his feelings. The pressing business of pressing someone into assistance had to be suppressed while he pressed on through the oppressive crowd.

While Elizabeth capered with Ellis Fleming, Darcy danced the same third set with her sister. His depression eased with each fleeting glimpse of an impressive yellow dress, nut-brown curls, and expressive eyes.

Lizzy Bennet's dance card was full. She had opened with Colonel Fitzwilliam and stood up with Mr. Bingley for the second set. Her fourth was promised to a naval officer, Captain Rumbold, whom she dreadfully expected would live up to his name. Then she would stand up with the author of A Comedy of Fencing Errors, Mr. Ray Pierre Witt. Following would be the eagerly awaited supper dances, when she could finally be with Darcy. After the meal she was committed to sets with Colonel Myles Forward, Mr. Hugh Mayne, Lieutenant Landon Sand, Viscount Chalcroft, and Mr. Bernard Lorne before she could rejoin Mr. Fitzwilliam Darcy for the final dance. As she moved up the set with her current partner, she said, "Mr. Fleming, there is something I have been meaning to ask you."

"Then ask away, Miss Elizabeth; that is, unless you want to know about Darcy's behaviour at Cambridge. I will not cry rope on my good friend."

"No, sir, I would never expect that of you. Nonetheless, I must admit you have certainly piqued my interest; and I am now wondering what deep, dark secrets you will not reveal. You might, however, be able to appease my curiosity on a different subject because of your family background in the manufacture of timepieces. When the first clock was invented, how did they know to what time to set it?"

"Ha! A very good question, indeed, Miss Elizabeth; and I am embarrassed to admit I have no good reply. Perhaps they used a times table. Now I have a riddle for you. Tell me how I should refer to a lovely lady who misplaced the watch I recently gave her."

"Hmm, my first instinct would be to say late, as she simply must have lost track of time. Though I shudder to even think of referring to her as the 'late lovely lady.'"

"No, Miss Elizabeth, I would describe her as a timeless beauty. Speaking of Georgiana, do you know she agreed to stand up with me for not only the first and supper sets but the last as well?"

"My, my, Mr. Fleming, you will certainly set tongues wagging by dancing together three times this night. I hope you are prepared to tie the knot, for imminent matrimony will be assumed, you know. We shall all then refer to your lovely lady as Mrs. Fleming."

"To some, marriage is a word; to others, a sentence. All I will admit is for me, the word has a nice ring to it, as does 'Mrs. Georgiana Fleming' and I am prepared." He patted his coat pocket and smiled.

Further along the line, Fitzwilliam Darcy asked his partner if she was aware the final set was a waltz. Jane Bennet replied in the affirmative and admitted she was eager to finally put her dance instruction to practical use.

"Has Miss Elizabeth also learned?"

"Oh yes, Mr. Darcy. You need not worry. We were both taught to waltz last season, and we have often practiced since then. Lizzy shall not embarrass you, sir."

"Oh, good. Wonderful news, indeed," he said unenthusiastically. Darcy was so desperate, he was on the verge of asking Miss Bennet to accompany him to an empty room and reacquaint him with the dance.

Good God! What am I thinking? The scandal of the waltz would be nothing compared to being found in a room alone with the sister of the woman I am courting. I am engaged for the next set with the unbearable wife of my unbearable cousin, and there is no possible way I am seeking Isabelle's assistance. I would rather stick a needle in my eye than hold that harridan in an embrace. A solution shall surely present itself during supper, and I need to concentrate on a more important dilemma ... how, where, and when to propose to Elizabeth tonight. Will such a woman even accept a supposedly genteel gentleman who has not the crucial ability to dance with style and grace?

The long-awaited supper set arrived, and suave Fitzwilliam Darcy moved across the ballroom floor with unconscious style and grace to claim his lady. He smiled down at her and said, "Miss Elizabeth, I believe you kindly promised to stand up with me for this set. Shall we?" He offered his arm, and Lizzy curled her hand around his sleeve. They were finally together, and Darcy proudly escorted his sweetheart to the line of dancers. Colonel Richard Fitzwilliam was already in formation with Jane Bennet, and Ellis Fleming and Georgiana Darcy stood in place as well.

They were all pleasantly surprised to be joined by a very merry Charles Bingley and his partner, who both suddenly stopped laughing and looked rather guilty when they caught sight of Darcy. Bingley glanced at Miss Bennet and the Colonel, and he could not be deceived as to her behaviour to Fitz. Looks appeared on both sides that spoke of a particular regard, and Bingley realized nothing had occurred between himself and Miss Bennet that could justify his own conceited hopes. Although he conceded to his rival for her affection, Bingley was not as heartbroken as perhaps expected. He and his partner delighted in each other's company; and Charles was very glad to have, at the beginning of the ball, secured her for the all-important last set as well.

The musicians began to play. Darcy and Elizabeth briefly clasped hands and with that motion became cocooned in their own private world. Unsure which of them initiated each touch, they moved more closely together than the steps required. Shoulders purposely brushed, hands lingered, hips or thighs briefly connected, and eyes remained locked until the last possible moment before separation. Nearby friends and relatives had to speak several times before being acknowledged by the couple.

"I missed you," he whispered near her ear as they revolved around one another, both physically and mentally.

"I missed you as well; although I did as you suggested, Mr. Darcy, and have enjoyed my evening thus far … but not too much. I wish this set would last until the final one. I have no desire for other partners and admit I am very much looking forward to waltzing with you, sir."

"Ah, yes. About that … " They were separated by the movements of the dance, and he did not complete the thought.

For Darcy and Elizabeth, the two dances seemed to last mere seconds instead of half an hour. Before they knew it, they were walking toward the elegantly set tables for the elaborate supper, although neither had much appetite for the vast array of food available.

At least three other couples that had just danced the supper set experienced a similar attraction. Miss Darcy and Mr. Fleming had, of course, been in a courtship for several months and would actually become engaged before the night was over. Two other budding relationships had just bloomed during the ball; the growing attachments would prove to be no less binding.

The friends met at a stylishly set table with eight places. Each gentleman seated the lady with whom he had just danced, leaving the chair next to her empty until he could return. Fitzwilliam Darcy, Charles Bingley, Ellis Fleming, and Richard Fitzwilliam grinned at one another as they rushed back from the buffet. The gents were buffeted and bumped by other chaps who also balanced glasses of wine and plates of delicacies, all in a desperate hurry to return to their lovely supper partners.

Jane Bennet looked across the table at her sister with a smile of such sweet complacency, a glow of such happy expression, as sufficiently marked how well she was satisfied with the occurrences of the evening. Elizabeth said, "Well, Jane, you look very pleased; and if I am not mistaken, you stood up for every set so far. I find it rather diverting, since earlier today you thought you would end up a wallflower tonight. Although my dance card is full, some of the gentlemen have left much to be desired. I certainly do not understand how Captain Rumbold attained his rank and am certain only garden tools rival his intellect. While Mr. Ray Pierre Witt may have been sharp, I believe I foiled his plans to get me alone in a corner. I do hope all your partners thus far have been intelligent, well behaved, and graceful."

"Oh, yes, Lizzy. My last partner was especially skilled at the dance, very good-looking, and charming. He inquired if it hurt; and when I asked to what he referred, he said, 'when you fell from heaven.' He was very attentive and really has the most marvellous smile." Jane blushed and added, "He also asked me if I had a map."

Georgiana asked, "Why would *he* need a map in this ballroom?"

"He said he kept getting lost in my eyes." Jane sighed and added, "Is he not clever and romantic?"

The young lady who had just danced the supper set with Charles Bingley snorted and said, "But Miss Bennet, I thought you just stood up with Colonel Fitzwilliam. Surely you are not describing *him* in such a complimentary manner?"

"Yes, Miss de Bourgh, of course I am referring to your chivalrous cousin."

Anne de Bourgh snorted once more. "Ah, yes, Colonel Stud-muffin strikes again."

Jane blushed anew, stifled a giggle, and asked, "Did you just say Colonel *'Stud-muffin'*?"

Miss de Bourgh rolled her eyes. "Um, yes. Perhaps I should not have revealed knowledge of that nauseating moniker, so please do not repeat it. I tell you, it has turned me off muffins completely. I am totally at a loss to comprehend the attraction, but apparently he has a following of admiring females who refer to him with that rather dubious pet name. Ugh! Anyway, you Bennet sisters really are quite a *combination* yourselves. I am sure both Fitzwilliam and Richard thought they were *safe*; yet you thieves have surely *stolen* their hearts. Have they asked for *locks* of your hair yet?"

Elizabeth laughed and replied, "Well, I do know of a handsome 'barberin' who could also be a robber if he is good at cutting locks."

A deep voice behind Lizzy startled her. "Ah, Anne and Miss Elizabeth. I know you were introduced in the receiving line, but I have wanted you to become better acquainted with one another all evening. I am glad you have finally had the opportunity to converse. You share a common uncommon sense of humour, and I am sure you will get along like a house on fire. Now, what were you ladies discussing with such hilarity?" *As if I did not know, Miss Lizzy Bennet. Will I never hear the end of it? I do believe I have an unreasonable fear of what might come out of your brother's three-year-old mouth. In what manner do you suppose our own adorable but naughty children will embarrass me? I cannot wait for us to find out.*

As soon as supper was over, singing and playing was arranged and they had the great pleasure of seeing Miss Anna Darcy prepare to oblige the company. She was very nervous, her hands shook, and she fumbled with the music sheets. When Elizabeth saw her distress, she joined the young lady at the pianoforte. She soothingly said, "Anna, please allow me to help. May I turn the pages for you?"

"Oh, yes, Elizabeth, thank you. It will be of great comfort to have you beside me. I have never played in front of quite so many people before."

Anna played splendidly and received an appreciative round of applause; when Lizzy returned to her table, she received an appreciative smouldering look from the performer's splendid brother. The other three ladies had been in the process of excusing themselves when Elizabeth arrived, so Georgiana asked if she would care to join them while they freshened up a bit. The four gentlemen stood as the ladies departed; and the Colonel invited Darcy, Bingley, and Fleming to the library for a glass of port. Only the latter gent declined.

Chapter II

Darcy's Evening Goeth from Werther to Better

While Darcy stared through a window into nothingness, Bingley took the opportunity to quietly speak with Fitz. "I want you to know, my friend, I bear no grudge and wish you and Miss Bennet much happiness."

"Whoa, Bingley! Of what are you talking, man? You speak as if Miss Bennet and I have come to an understanding."

"Have you not? You and the lovely lady have the same look of particular regard as can be seen on the faces of Darcy and Miss Elizabeth as well as Fleming and Miss Darcy. I do believe Jane Bennet has found the man who perfectly *Fitz* her idea of an ideal beau."

"I would very much like to believe you; yet what would such a beautiful woman as Miss Bennet see in me, a second son and soldier? I have nothing much to recommend me and certainly do not expect any attachment on her part. I admit I have witnessed some admiring glances from the lady; however, I believe it is merely the impressive red coat. Some women are undeniably attracted to a uniform. Oh, I *do* wish for her affection, though. Egad, but the fairer sex are difficult to understand, and … Bingley? Bingley, where did you go?" Muffled muttering came from the depths of the bookshelves, and Colonel Fitzwilliam went in search of his friend.

"Fitz, are these books supposed to be arranged in alphabetical order by author?"

"Yes, I believe so. But Bingley, what are you after, man? We have to return to the ballroom shortly. Are you planning to read out there instead of dance? That sort of behaviour will be frowned upon, you know."

"No, of course not. Just give me a moment. Would Johann Wolfgang von Goethe be shelved as 'V' or 'G'? Nope, not under 'V.' Out of my way. Where is 'G.'"

"*Gee*, I do not know, Bingley. Would you like me to summon a *page* to assist you; or here's a *novel* idea … try after 'F', as in … "

"Aha! Here is *The Sorrows of Young Werther*; now I just need to find the right passage."

Darcy joined them and awkwardly said, "I need some assistance but am rather embarrassed to admit … "

Bingley held up his index finger. "Wait just a moment please, Darce. I need to read this quotation to Fitz: 'We love a girl for very different things than understanding. We love her for her beauty, her youth, her mirth, her confidingness, her character, with its faults, caprices, and God knows what other inexpressible charms; but we do not love her understanding. Her mind we esteem if it is brilliant, and it may greatly elevate her in our opinion; nay, more, it may enchain us when we already love. But her understanding is not that which awakens and inflames our passions.'"

Darcy waited several moments. Bingley and Fitz appeared deep in thought; so he cleared his throat and said, "Pardon me. As I was saying earlier, I need assistance but am rather embarrassed to admit my quandary. Bingley, as I see it, you owe me a favour."

"I probably owe you a multitude of favours, Darcy. So how may I help?"

"Firstly, I need a scheme to arrange a private moment with Miss Elizabeth tonight; secondly, I … I do not … remember how to waltz." The other two chaps stared expectantly at him and patiently waited for further elaboration. Darcy stared expectantly back and impatiently waited for their agreement. "Well? Will you assist me?"

The Colonel scratched his head, rubbed his chin, and said, "Ah … just how, exactly, do you imagine we are to help you remember, cousin?"

Darcy rather testily answered, "You bloody well know how to waltz, Richard. You were there when we learned."

"Yes, my point exactly! *We* bloody well learned. How can you not remember?"

"Perhaps it will come back to me once I begin. Be that as it may, I cannot risk making a fool of myself in front of everyone, especially Miss Elizabeth. I know it is a lot to ask, but could one of you please provide the music and the other show me the steps?"

"Egad, Darcy! Here? Now?"

Tetchy again, Darcy replied, "No, Bingley, out in the middle of the street six hours from now."

"Well, what benefit would that be to you?"

Darcy closed his eyes, hung his head, and counted to ten. "Yes, Bingley, here. Yes, Bingley, now."

Colonel Fitzwilliam thought the whole situation hilarious. In spite of that, he could tell his serious, perfectionist cousin was perfectly serious. "But, Darce, there is no instrument here in the library. How do you expect us to provide waltzing mus … Oh, no. Under no circumstances. I simply refuse to either waltz with you or sing. This is ludicrous. Count me out."

"Richard, I simply abhor having to stoop low and resort to extortion. That said, I would not hesitate to cry rope to your sister-in-law. She will, no doubt, be horrified to discover you were the one responsible for spreading those ridiculous rumours about her extraneous body parts. Or maybe it is time your mother be told of the rather sweet-smelling, sandy-haired adolescent chap who broke her favourite, and quite expensive, perfume bottle and blamed it on a clumsy servant all those many years ago."

Colonel Fitzwilliam nonchalantly buffed his fingernails against his red-coated chest and inspected them for shine. Darcy frowned at his cousin's unconcerned demeanour. "Is your father yet aware of a particular wild, drunken escapade in Brighton involving … " He glanced at their mutual friend who was eagerly awaiting further enlightening details. " … er, never mind. We must guard Bingley's innocence from such indelicate imagery. However, shall I let James know who absconded with his collection of risqué etchings?"

The unaffected military officer rolled his eyes toward the ceiling, folded his arms, shook his head, and whistled a tune between his teeth.

Unfortunately for his cousin, it was not a waltz. Darcy scowled until his face lit up with sudden inspiration. "Aha! Did Aunt Catherine ever discover who placed her hand in warm water while she slept and caused her to p ... "

"I will hum! Bingley can be the lady."

"Could we not flip a coin, Fitz? Or draw straws?" Charles Bingley petulantly whined, "I do not want to be the lady either. And what happened in Brighton? I want to know!"

Georgiana Darcy noticed her father and Mr. Fleming in earnest conversation and wondered about the subject of their discourse. The gentlemen shook hands, both suddenly turned to look at her, and the younger of the two approached.

"Miss Darcy, your father has kindly permitted me to request a few minutes of private conversation with you. Would you care to accompany me and take the air?"

She agreed and asked for a moment to first fetch her shawl, but he insisted on retrieving it for her; when he returned, he gently wrapped it around her shoulders and offered his arm. They decided on a quick stroll in the garden. As soon as they were on the path and assured some privacy, Fleming stopped and stood in front of Georgiana. He gazed into her beautiful azure eyes and caressed her soft cheek with the lightest touch.

"Miss Darcy, you are the picture of loveliness standing here in the moonlight. I have been head over heels in love with you from the moment you poked Darcy with your frilly pink parasol and called him bacon-brained. I admired your pluck as you stood up to your brother and the way you tried to protect your sister and friends that fateful day at Pemberley. I could go on and on, for I love everything about you; but time is of the essence, and I must do this quickly before your father runs out of patience."

Fleming paced a few steps and carelessly raked a hand through his hair. Georgiana gazed at the thick, glossy black waves that swept the collar of his white shirt; and she longed to run her own fingers through the feathery strands. She admired his broad shoulders in his tight coat, the deep blue of which matched his tantalizing indigo eyes. He stopped pacing and returned, standing very close and speaking very softly.

"A very, very wise American scientist, politician, and author said, 'Dost thou love life? Then do not squander time, for that's the stuff life is made of.'[1] Miss Darcy, I do love life; and I do love you. I do not care to squander any more time. Will you share with me the stuff of which life is made? Will you consent to be my wife?"

"Oh, of course, Mr. Fleming, yes! I would very much love to be your wife."

"Then why these tears, Georgiana?"

"Do you not know a lady sometimes cries when she is very happy?"

"I hope I never, ever, make you sad, Georgie. Still and all, how shall I ever be certain? If you cry when you are happy, do you laugh while you are sad?"

"Teasing, bacon-brained man! If I had my frilly pink weapon, I would surely poke you with it."

"I would settle, instead, for your calling me Ellis and, perhaps, sharing a … kiss … may I?"

Their first kiss was gentle, sweet, and brief. Ellis Fleming was more than a little intimidated by his fiancée's powerful father and did not want to be caught snogging. He suddenly remembered the ring in his coat pocket; and, with her permission, he slipped the small sapphire band onto her dainty finger and kissed her hand.

He said, "The inscription reads 'G ~ Yours for all time ~ E'. Thank you, my dearest lady, for making me the happiest and luckiest man in the entire world. I would prefer to stay here alone with you all night, though I do not believe your father would approve. Shall we return and share our good news?"

The blissful couple entered the ballroom just as Georgiana's father was about to search for them. They related the joyous news to George Darcy, who made the happy announcement to the entire assemblage.

---

1   *Benjamin Franklin (1706-1790) ~ Poor Richard's Almanac (June 1746)*

"Are you looking for someone, Miss Elizabeth?"

"Yes, Mr. Fleming. I am looking for Mr. Bernard Lorne."

"Ah. Well, I am sorry to report he became rather drunk as a wheelbarrow and had to be carted away to his carriage. But why are you looking for Lorne?"

Georgiana had been speaking with an acquaintance and joined the other two in time to overhear her fiancé's final question. "Ellis, Elizabeth certainly does not look forlorn."

"Oh yes, Georgiana, I was actually looking for Lorne," said Elizabeth.

"But why? Whatever is the matter?"

"There is nothing the matter. He did ask me to stand up with him for the next set, though."

"Who did?"

"Good grief, my friend. Since you became engaged, you have also become somewhat addlepated. We were speaking of my looking for Lorne, remember?"

"Yes, and I am concerned you feel forlorn."

"Georgiana, I do not feel for Lorne. I hardly know the man. You know very well my regard is only for your brother; and, Mr. Fleming, just *what* do you find so amusing, sir?"

Mr. Bernard Lorne did not turn up for the second last set, which was just as well, because Elizabeth Bennet needed to find some privacy. She searched for her sister and saw Jane in conversation with Lady Anne, Anne de Bourgh, and Anna. *If Mr. Darcy and I ever marry and have children, I shall definitely refuse to christen any daughter of ours 'Ann.' Enough already.* She made her way over to the ladies, curtsied, excused herself for interrupting, and asked Jane to accompany her.

"Jane, I need to find some privacy, or I shall simply have to tie my garter in public."

"Elizabeth Bennet, you would not dare do something so extremely shocking and improper."

"Well, most certainly not. But look." She lifted her skirt a few inches so Jane could see the stocking and broken ribbon pooled around her ankle. "I am forlorn, but not for Lorne, and not engaged for this blasted set after all. However, it is unthinkable I might have to sit out the next set and a chance to waltz with Fitzwilliam 'handsome barbarian' Darcy. Please come with me and stand guard while I fix this blasted hosiery. Did you happen to bring any extra ribbon?"

"Yes, in my … Oh, no! Where is my reticule? I must have left it on the chair during supper. Lizzy, ask one of the footmen for directions to the library, as there should be no one there during a ball. I am just going to fetch my bag and shall be right behind you. Oh, and Elizabeth Frances Bennet, do not say the word 'blasted'; it is terribly unladylike of you. Now go! I must make haste to find my blasted reticule. I do not want to miss a chance to waltz with another handsome barbarian named Fitzwilliam." The pert, saucy smile so often associated with her younger sister was, in this instance, instead displayed on Jane's normally angelic face.

With a servant's assistance, Elizabeth quickly found the door to the library. She quietly opened it a crack, peered inside, and promptly pulled it shut while she questioned both her sanity and her eyesight. *Good God. Was that … ? No.* She scoffed at herself. *I could not possibly have seen the scene I thought I did. Perhaps I need a pair of spectacles.* The intrepid Lizzy Bennet again eased the door ajar, took another peek, and was stupefied by the spectacle of the pair in front of her. None other than the very proper Fitzwilliam Darcy was, indeed, holding Charles Bingley in an embrace. There was no mistake. Her handsome barbarian's right arm encircled the other good-looking hooligan, and Mr. Darcy's hand rested on the back of Mr. Bingley's waist. *Remain calm, Lizzy old girl. Remember the sayings of Publilius Syrus: 'The eyes are not responsible when the mind does the seeing' and 'A suspicious mind always looks on the black side of things'. Surely Mr. Bingley can logically explain the black side of things my suspicious mind sees, and then Mr. Darcy and I shall put this behind us and move forward.*

" … and now move your left foot gracefully forward. No, Darce, your *other* left foot!"

Colonel Fitzwilliam became tired of humming the waltz tune and stopped to take a breather. In the silence, a feminine gasp was heard from the direction of the door; the three gentlemen froze in position.

Darcy: Good God. Was that … ? No. I could not possibly have heard what I think I just heard. Fate would not be so unkind. Would it? He slowly turned around.

Bingley: Fiend seize it! To hell with this! I am out of here! Sorry, Darce. He quickly headed for the door.

Fitz: I would probably relish this as a comical dill-emma was I not involved in the same pickle. With a sour expression on his face, he fumbled in his pocket for the key to the library and followed his friend.

Bingley's face was flaming as he curtly bowed to Miss Elizabeth and mumbled what might have been an apology. Elizabeth stepped aside to allow him to pass and was surprised to see Colonel Fitzwilliam hard on his heels. The officer also bowed abruptly and muttered something unintelligible as Lizzy moved farther into the library.

The unmistakable sound of a key being turned in the lock from the outside caused her to reach for the doorknob. Elizabeth's frantic assault on the immovable object proved futile, and she said a silent prayer. *Good Lord! I cannot possibly remain in this room with only Mr. Darcy, although I would certainly like to hear his explanation ... and perhaps a declaration of his intentions.* Lizzy turned to face the other occupant and hoped this turn of events might turn out to be a turning point in her life. With her back pressed against the door, she watched the gentleman turn in her direction.

In the hallway, on the other side of the same portal, the red-coated officer had second thoughts about locking the lady in the library. On the one hand, he wanted to do a good turn for Darcy; on the other, he knew he should allow Miss Elizabeth a chance to escape from the room, his cousin, and her fate. His loyalty to family, he decided after a moment's hesitation, was the key point in favour of Darcy. Colonel Fitzwilliam was no turncoat. He turned away and quickly strode down the corridor.

Jane Bennet was surprised to pass Mr. Bingley in the hallway without any sort of acknowledgement from the gentleman. He was alarmingly coloured up and in an obvious state of mortification. *Well, that is very peculiar! Oh, dear, I hope it is nothing serious.* As Jane neared the library, she turned her head to watch the poor chap hurry toward the ballroom. When she turned back ... *OOF!* She found herself up against a solid, crimson-coated chest, encased in a pair of red-sleeved arms of steel, and surrounded by a very alluring masculine scent. Jane was breathless, not due to the impact, but because the chest, arms, and scent belonged to the body of none other than *her* handsome barbarian, Colonel Richard 'Stud-Muffin' Fitzwilliam.

The good-looking army officer considered himself one very lucky man, indeed. He had helped his cousin with two dilemmas, was not the one discovered in Darcy's embrace, and was now the one embracing the incredibly gorgeous Jane Bennet.

"Miss Bennet, I am most dreadfully sorry. Are you well? I have not injured you, have I?"

Truthfully, Fitz was not dreadfully sorry at all and had not released his clutch.

They were so close she could feel his deep, resonant voice rumble within her. Jane glanced up into captivating hazel eyes that darkened as he gazed back.

She breathlessly whispered, "The fault is all mine, sir. I believe my head was turned. I am not at all injured and should probably go to my sister now. She is in the library, is she not?" Truthfully, she did not wish to be released from his emboldening embrace.

"Yes, but perhaps it would be prudent not to disturb Miss Elizabeth and Darcy just yet. I believe my cousin has a very important matter to discuss with your sister."

He smiled down at her, and Jane nearly swooned. *I do feel a bit weak; so perhaps remaining in his strong, protective arms just a little longer can be justifiably ... justified.*

Why does it feel like the most beautiful woman in the world is in my arms? "Jane, why does it feel like the most beautiful woman in the world is in my arms?" *Good God Almighty, please, please tell me I did not just repeat that inanity aloud.*

"You are not allowed to address me in such a familiar manner, sir. You are far too forward. Are you, perchance, a trifle disguised, Colonel?"

"I am not drunk, dear lady, just intoxicated by you." He winced slightly. *Oh God, I am a Colonel of corn!* But still he would not release her.

"Gracious! You are oddly audacious."

"Madam, may I be frank?"

"I would prefer you be yourself, Colonel," Jane saucily replied. "I was under the impression your name was Richard."

"Miss Bennet, heed this warning," he growled. "You are dangerously playing with fire with your teasing and calling me by my first name. You give everyone the impression you are very perfectly demure, yet here you are addressing me in a familiar manner and being rather forward. I know I have been the recipient of your admiring glances. Tell me, is there more behind those tantalizing looks than just appreciation for this uniform? Do you have any affectionate regard for the man beneath the red coat?"

Jane blushed but steadily looked him in the eye as she brazenly whispered, "What the eye does not admire, the heart does not desire … Richard."

Colonel Fitzwilliam groaned and then instinctively, heedlessly claimed her mouth; Miss Bennet definitely did not wish to be released from his warm embrace, ever. The couple was oblivious and did not hear the approaching soft footfalls and swish of expensive silk gowns.

Lady Anne Darcy: "Nephew!!! Miss Bennet??? Oh, Lord!"

Miss Anne de Bourgh: "Whoo-hoo! The fat is in the fire now. I mean, tsk, tsk. Shame on you, Fitz!"

Miss Anna Darcy: "Cousin! (Gasp!) Jane! What are you two doing?"

The military officer groggily disengaged his lips from the intoxicating osculation, and his passion-filled eyes suddenly opened wide as he became conscious of his surroundings and the scorn of three female relatives. Still, he did not release Jane from his protective embrace as she hid her flushed face on his chest.

"Richard Cosmo Fitzwilliam! Unhand Miss Bennet this minute! Be a good soldier and march into the library while I send for your father. Anna, please go tell your uncle he is needed immediately. Anne, please escort Miss Bennet somewhere and ascertain whether she was … under duress."

"Pardon me, Lady Anne. There is no need. I can assure you right now that I was under no duress. I am thoroughly ashamed of my conduct, but please do not blame your nephew. The fault was not the gentleman's."

The Colonel protested, "Miss Bennet! The fault was most assuredly mine, and I most willingly take full responsibility for my ungentlemanly actions."

"Richard, I told you to wait in the library."

"Um. I cannot go in there right now, Aunt Anne."

"Whatever do you mean?"

"Uh … well, it is currently occupied."

"By whom?"

Sorry, Darce, old man. "Your son is in there."

"Well, I shall certainly just boot him out of there." Lady Anne jangled the knob, yet the door remained closed. "Richard, why is this room locked? You just informed me Fitzwilliam is inside. Is he unwell?" Lady Anne narrowed her eyes at her nephew, who at once looked anywhere but at his aunt's face. In an ominous voice she said, "Is there, by any chance, someone in there with my son?"

The normally brave military officer cringed and said quietly, "Miss Elizabeth Bennet is in there with him, ma'am."

The lady swooned and would have crumpled to the floor if not for her quick-thinking, fast-acting niece, Miss Anne de Bourgh.

Behind the closed library doors, Fitzwilliam Darcy slowly turned to determine whose feminine gasp he heard before his fickle fiend of a friend fled and the military officer deserted. When he beheld Elizabeth, he experienced mixed feelings of relief as well as intense humiliation. There she stood, with her back pressed against the door, as she stared at him with huge eyes. He held his hands out in supplication and said, "It was not what I think you think. I think."

"Well, Mr. Darcy, that is probably not quite true; because I certainly do not know *what* to think. Though I believe I just saw Mr. Bingley in a position in which I was rather hoping to find myself later tonight."

"Miss Elizabeth, I shall not bear false witness. I … I do not bear waltz fitness."

She stepped away from the door, paced a few steps, and unthinkingly ran gloved fingers through her hair, dislodging a ringlet Rachel had so carefully arranged. "Mr. Darcy, are you a trifle foxed? You are not at all speaking in your usual articulate manner."

"I apologize, madam. I assure you I am stone cold sober. I hope you and I shall always be straightforward with one another and avoid any further misunderstandings. The simple, unvarnished truth is I am not an accomplished waltzer. I did not want to be an embarrassment to you or, heaven forbid, humiliate myself. I did actually learn the steps last year but was not a great proficient."

"Sir, the dance is just now making its way to our shores; so none of us are truly proficient … well, with the exception of some young officers like Lieutenant-Colonel John Dun perhaps. He spent some time on the continent and learned to waltz there, but … Mr. Darcy! Did you just … growl, sir?"

"Please tell me you did not waltz with Dun."

"Oh. Very well then, sir. I will not tell you."

"Miss Elizabeth, the waltz is considered quite immoral, you know, because of the … close … embrace … madam, what are you doing?"

She stood directly in front of him and had reached for his right hand. "I am offering my services as waltzing instructor, unless you would rather recall Mr. Bingley to continue."

"Who? I do not *recall* a dance instructor by that name."

"Very good, Mr. Darcy. Now, move in a bit closer. Closer. Stop! My goodness! Back up a bit, sir."

"Must I?"

"Yes!"

He reluctantly complied but rakishly smiled at her.

"There. Good. Now, sir, take your right hand … and … very good. See. You know just where to put your hand. Oops. Ah, Mr. Darcy, that is no longer my waist … Perhaps this is not such a wise course of action … Oh! My! Very, very good, sir. You move so … wonderfully and … masterfully. You are actually making it difficult to concentrate when you look at me in such a manner. Whew! It is rather hot in here, is it not? Sir, I really do think it would be best if we return to the ballroom now, before we … ah … Mr. Darcy, I can certainly guide you through these steps while on the dance floor, although you really do not require instruction at all. It is quite easy … and beautiful … and … my goodness! You are a very apt pupil, sir. I believe you could teach me a thing or two. Oh, how did we end up so close together again? Mr. Darcy, we simply must return to the ballroom now, so we can put this rehearsal to practical use."

"Not just yet, my love."

They had stopped dancing but held their positions. Fitzwilliam Darcy prepared in the highest spirits for the conquest of all that remained unsubdued of her heart, trusting it was not more than might be won in the course of the next few moments. He smoothed her wayward curl back into place, and then his hand slid down to cup the side of her face.

"I grow impatient with this drawn-out courtship, Elizabeth. I need to know, for certain, you will forever be mine. You were quite right earlier today. I *have* been courting you for the past fortnight; and although it may be somewhat unconventional, those elapsed two weeks shall have to serve as our official courtship. Since parting with you this afternoon I have struggled to find a perfect way to propose, yet words utterly fail to express what I feel for you. You deserve the sentiments of a poet, but I refuse to employ another man's words." He roguishly smiled at her and continued, "Although I did toss around the idea of discovering what a certain army officer said during his failed offer and then saying the complete opposite. I thought that way I might be assured of a positive response."

"Oh, Mr. Darcy! Sir, how dare you bring up the thought of another man during such an intimate moment; and you were doing so splendidly up until that point."

"I was?" His other hand had found its way to her face as well, and his long thumbs caressed her rosy cheeks. "Then please immediately forget that nonsense. You must allow me to continue in the previous vein and tell you how ardently I admire and love you. For love you I do, Elizabeth Bennet, with all my heart and soul, and always will. You are the most beautiful woman, both physically and intellectually, I have ever beheld. I love your wit, your joie de vivre, your kind and caring nature, and the way you look at me … like you looked at me on the lawn at Pemberley, and the way you are looking at me right this moment. Please say it means you return some measure of what I feel. Please say you will make me the happiest of men by consenting to be my wife and the mother of my children. Elizabeth, my one and only love, please say you will marry me."

Elizabeth moved even closer, raised her right hand to his face, and dazzled him with the full force of her smile. "I return equal measure of what you feel, Mr. Darcy. In fact, my cup runneth over with love for you. We must be the two most fortunate people in the world to have formed such a strong attachment in so short a time, and I truly do not know what I did to deserve such happiness. Most matches are made for wealth or connections; so I can scarcely believe my fondest wish of marrying for love is coming true, for love you I do, Mr. Darcy."

The gentleman reminded himself to remain a gentleman and settled for a chaste kiss on her forehead. She felt his lips curve into a smile against her skin as he said, "Answer the question, please, Elizabeth."

"Oh, but Mr. Darcy, if you will review your *engaging* proposal, which I shall probably spend the rest of my life doing, you will find there was no actual question. Perhaps you should have consulted the book for advice on how to make an offer."

"I am almost afraid to ask. What book, madam?"

"On Bended Knee by the author Neil Down."

"God, how I love you, you impertinent little minx!" Fitzwilliam Darcy lowered himself and, on bended knee, gazed up at her, and said, "Miss Elizabeth Bennet, will you please marry me?"

"Yes, Mr. Darcy, I would very much love to marry you and be your wife; and if you can bear my teasing, I shall most willingly bear your children."

Chapter III

The Night Their World Whirled

The general consensus of the Quality guests at the lavish ball given by the esteemed Darcy and Fitzwilliam families was that the extravagant event was going extraordinarily well. Matlock Manor was done up in Town bronze; and it glittered with candlelight, crystal, and costly gem-encrusted jewelry that adorned the ladies. Attendees were fashionable, musicians superb, dancing refined, supper delectable, and conversation sophisticated. Miss Anna Darcy had played the pianoforte brilliantly, and her proud father had happily announced to the assemblage the engagement of his elder daughter, Miss Georgiana Darcy, to Mr. Ellis Fleming. There had been warm rounds of applause for both the sweet young performer and the handsome couple; and then anticipation grew as most of the company eagerly awaited the grand finale, which was to be the controversial new dance, a waltz.

Behind the scenes, pandemonium ruled as the manor's servants pandered to guests' requests, some mannered and others ill mannered. Young pages were paged to assist footmen, who were run off their feet with many servile feats. The butler whined about the wine cellar's rapid depletion as attendees were wined and dined; and he was glad the ball would soon wind up. After supper was served, the chef, his assistants, and their tempers finally stopped steaming, stewing, and simmering. Unfortunate scullery maids would labour until daylight before they were all washed up.

Above and beyond the overworked servants, a few other occupants of Matlock Manor had not exactly enjoyed the night's proceedings. Lady

Anne Darcy had collapsed outside the library; and Miss de Bourgh had summoned Lady Rebecca's efficient French abigail, a pretty maid by the name of Mademoiselle Frances Atwarre, who brought the English patient around with smelling salts. Miss Anna Darcy had fetched her uncle; and after his sister recovered from her swoon and related the sordid story of Richard and Miss Jane Bennet, the Earl dispatched an express message to a home several blocks away. Lady Anne left her brother to deal with his youngest offspring while she headed back to the library and an ordeal involving her eldest.

A sheepish Colonel Richard Fitzwilliam was escorted to his mutton-chopped father's study, where he was raked over the coals and lambasted for unseemly behaviour and its ramifications. As a soldier, the officer was used to standing in formation to receive information; so with the best intention, not to mention apprehension, without pretension he stood at attention to defend his own contention.

Jane had been taken aside by Miss de Bourgh, and Anna soon joined them and tried to comfort her friend while the raised voices of her uncle and his son filtered down the hall from the vicinity of the Earl's study. Miss Bennet was absolutely mortified, guilt-ridden over her shameless conduct, and torn between wanting to flee and the need to take a stance with Richard while he faced the music, even if she did not particularly care for the tune. "Oh, Anna, I am so sorry for causing such turmoil; and I believe it would be preferable for me to leave now. I should fetch my sister from the library; and regardless, we really must warn Mr. Darcy and Lizzy before … "

Anne de Bourgh interrupted, "No, Miss Bennet. Please do not go in there. I have every reason to suspect you would barge into the middle of a marriage proposal. At least I *think* that is what Fitzwilliam and your sister are doing behind closed, locked doors … although Aunt Anne has just returned and obviously has visions of another sort of engagement." Three heads turned to watch a determined Lady Anne Darcy as she fumbled with a large ring of keys confiscated from her disgraced nephew. She finally found the one to open the locked library, and it soundlessly turned in the keyhole.

There had been uproar at another London townhouse when a messenger arrived with a dispatch requesting the immediate presence of Mr. Thomas Bennet at Matlock Manor.

"Thomas, you are not leaving without me! If something has happened to one of our precious girls, they would want their mother in attendance. Oh, my dear, what do you suppose is the matter? We should never have permitted Jane and Lizzy to attend that ball without a chaperone."

"Come along then, lovey, but do not agonize yet over the reason. Our daughters are in good hands with our Darcy friends. Whatever has transpired, I am confident it must not be of a serious nature." His face underwent a change as he muttered, "However, if even one *hair* on their beloved heads has been harmed, I may become quite *barbarous*."

As they hurriedly entered their carriage, Mrs. Bennet had dramatic visions of the last legion of handsome barbarians plundering and pillaging at Matlock Manor.

The anxious Mrs. Bennet might have been comforted had she known that in Matlock Manor's library at least one handsome barbarian was not engaged in any plundering or pillaging; and although Mr. Bennet felt confident his beloved daughters were in good hands with their Darcy friends, he might not have been comforted had he known where one of those hands had touched Lizzy during a waltz run-through. In fact, 'run through' might very well have been the action taken against the young man. Said fellow was actually making a valiant attempt to keep himself under good regulation by maintaining a safe distance from the temptation of his fetching fiancée while he enjoyed the pleasure of her exclusive company. Darcy searched the shelves for a book of sonnets by Shakespeare, in love with the idea of reading one or two to his future wife. As he ran his hand along the spines, the title Lost Empires, by Zan Tium, diverted him until Elizabeth reclaimed his attention.

"Mr. Darcy, I wonder why Jane has been delayed for such a stretch of time. What now seems ages ago, I opened the door to this room seeking a moment of privacy; and my sister was supposed to meet me here directly. With her help, I need to repair … something … before I am able to return to the ballroom."

"Elizabeth, may I be of assistance?" He walked over and stood toe-to-toe in front of her.

How can a man look so divine, smell so heavenly, but have such a devilish twinkle in his eyes? "Good heavens, absolutely not, sir! I mean, no thank you, Mr. Darcy."

"Dearest, loveliest Elizabeth, we are betrothed now. Could you not call me Fitzwilliam rather than 'Mr. Darcy' or 'sir' whenever we are alone?" She nodded; and he continued, "We have been fortunate to have this time in private. However, we really should return to the ballroom now. I would certainly not want to miss the opportunity to finally waltz with you after agonizing all evening about doing so. What may I do to help you?"

"Perhaps you could locate my sister and send her to me, sir, ... Fitzwilliam."

"Sir Fitzwilliam? I do not believe you are entitled to bestow that title, my love."

"Teasing man!"

"Never fear, milady. Sir Fitzwilliam, the advocate for missing sisters, shall set forth immediately on a quest for his true love's lost sibling." Darcy kissed Lizzy's forehead again, purposely strode across the room, and yanked at the doorknob. "What the ... ?"

"Oh, I completely forgot. I do believe your cousin locked us in on his way out."

"We are locked *in*? That insolent, insufferable instigator and his insupportable interference!"

"Yes, how insupportable. Instead of leaving, you loitered and got locked in the library with Lizzy. Lousy luck, hmm?"

Darcy quickly returned, slid his hands around the column of her graceful neck, gently stroked his thumbs against her smooth skin, and gazed into her fine eyes. "Elizabeth, time alone with you has been priceless and precious; and I suspect I shall have to thank Fitz for it. Nevertheless, until your father has sanctioned this betrothal, we must be circumspect. You are the best thing that has happened in my life so far; and were I to circumvent propriety and give in to my lustful, licentious longings, lady, your lovely, luscious lips would be long-lastingly locked with mine in a lascivious, lingering, loving kiss."

"Oh, my! Well, then. Yes, I do see the point of your alliterative circumlocution, sir. Under the circumstances, we must certainly not circumvent propriety but instead should practice circumspection. In order to circumscribe limits, perhaps we should retreat to the circumference of the room to avoid circumstantial evidence should we be discovered. Oh, where is that insufferable, interfering instigator with the blasted key; and what has detained dear Jane? Regardless, before we are rescued, Fitzwilliam, would you please avert your eyes while I attempt to repair my ... "

"Are you sure I cannot be of assistance in the repair of your ... ?"

Lizzy closed her eyes and grew dizzy as she envisioned Darcy's long fingers slowly and sensually smoothing her stocking up along her calf, stroking her sensitive skin, and taking their time to tenderly tie the garter's broken ribbon around her trembling leg. When her wayward thoughts reached a fever pitch, she teetered on the edge of reason and breathlessly replied, "N-no, th-thank you. It would be more prudent if I tend to this myself. Now turn around please, Fitzwilliam."

The gentleman most willingly complied. Lizzy raised her skirt and fumbled with a frayed knot on the broken ribbon. When the door unexpectedly burst open, she faced her future mother-in-law and was caught, red-handed, securing her garter, with the right side of her gown hiked up to her thigh while Fitzwilliam Darcy stared intently at the proceedings in the mirror over the mantle.

As the two young ladies entered the ballroom together, Anne de Bourgh glanced at her cousin, frowned, and said, "Anna, were you not supposed to have retired to one of the guest chambers by now? In fact, your mother and I were escorting you there when all hell ... er, when we encountered Richard and Miss Bennet."

Her younger cousin giggled and replied, "Yes. With all the mayhem and trauma, Mother has conveniently forgotten my curfew."

"Well, as your slightly older and much wiser relative, I suppose I should probably remind you it is long past your bedtime, young lady. That said, I shall not mention it if you do not."

"Thank you, wizened old wise woman. With such aged wisdom in your possession, can you foresee what betides Fitz and Jane? I admit their situation worries me, Anne. What do you suppose will happen?"

"I am sure the details are being hammered out amongst the occupants of our uncle's study as we speak. However, I have every reason to suspect you will very soon gain not only Mr. Fleming as a brother, but also Miss Elizabeth as a sister, and her sister as a cousin. My goodness, our family is growing by leaps and bounds."

"Oh! Speaking of leaps and bounds, I have recently heard from Pemberley that my rabbit, Herr Stewart, is actually a fraulein. Still, it is merely haresay until she produces babies. Would you like one if that happens … or should I say *hoppens*?"

Miss de Bourgh rolled her eyes and sighed. "You really do need to go to sleep, Anna. You are obviously overtired. But I shall indulge you and play along. You know Mother would pull her *hare* out if I brought home a pet."

"What would Aunt Catherine do if you brought home a certain handsome, blonde-haired, blue-eyed pet? Look, Anne, he is coming our way."

"Who? Oh. Why would I take Mr. Bingley to Rosings Park, you silly goose?" The two young ladies giggled as he approached.

Charles Bingley's face had gradually diminished from the crimson of the library to a nice rosy hue, and his eyes twinkled as they settled on Miss de Bourgh. "Ladies, I hope I am not interrupting the secret laughter of women, but I was wondering whether you know the whereabouts of Fitz or Fleming. I believe I know where to find Darcy, but I seem to have misplaced my two other best friends."

Anne de Bourgh said, "Locate Georgiana, and you will undoubtedly find her fiancé. They have been inundated with an accumulation of congratulations in anticipation of their upcoming affiliation. The other gentlemen, I believe, are also with their intended brides. Something is in the air, Mr. Bingley, and I would be surprised if the parson's mousetrap has not snared at least another of your circle of friends this magical evening. As perhaps the only remaining eligible bachelor of your coterie, you are welcome to remain with us, sir. If I am not mistaken, which I seldom am, you and I shall soon be standing up together again anyway."

Charles Bingley admired the girl with a pearl earring peeping out from beneath her light brown curls. She looked charming in her pretty pale pink gown; and he spoke honestly when he said, "I am very much looking forward to that dance with you, Miss de Bourgh. I have not had the pleasure of waltzing since … " The young man suddenly and inexplicably coloured up again and amended his statement. "I have never before had the pleasure of waltzing with such a lovely young lady as yourself, madam."

"I am duly flattered, sir. Do I understand, however, that you have, indeed, already embraced another for such a decadent reason?"

Bingley gulped and his face matched the red of Fitz's brilliant coat. "I … well, ... I *have* learned, after all."

"Perhaps Darcy should have sought your expert advice, then. As you know, my poor cousin has been worried sick all evening about humiliating himself during the waltz."

A distinguished, middle-aged gentleman approached the party; and he wondered why Bingley was so highly flying his colours, until George Darcy's eyes grew wide at the sight of his sixteen-year-old daughter still in the ballroom during the wee hours of the morning. Anna was not yet out and was supposed to have retired immediately following her performance after supper. He promptly sent her off to bed and then inquired if any of the party had recently seen his wife. Anne informed him her aunt had briefly suffered from a fainting spell, was fully recovered, and most likely with Fitzwilliam and Miss Elizabeth in the library. The gentleman bowed and took his leave.

What was a mother to believe, especially having just witnessed the libidinous actions of another male relative? Darcy's mother had entered a locked room that was occupied by two people of the opposite sex who were obviously besotted with one another. They had been alone for far too long, not to mention the fact Miss Elizabeth was caught as she re-dressed in a single man's presence. Lady Anne hoped the problem could be redressed in private. "Well, then! Am I to assume congratulations are in order? I insist you tell me a wedding has at least been discussed. Fitzwilliam George Darcy, I am shocked and disappointed by your behaviour, as well as that of your rapscallion cousin, Richard. I put the blame on your reading about that libertine Valmont. My dear son, I know you wish to marry Miss Elizabeth. Even so, could you not have waited?"

"Why should I have waited? Elizabeth has made me the happiest of men, Mother." His chest puffed with pride as he said, "She agreed quite willingly."

Lady Anne turned a gimlet eye toward her future daughter-in-law; however, before she could start to ring a fine peal over her for anticipating their vows, the young woman thrust her skirt back down and spoke. "*No!* No more misunderstandings! Pardon me, Lady Anne, for speaking thusly. But it is not what you think … that is, if you think what I think you think. I came to repair my … *garter!*" Elizabeth reddened; but her eyes flashed as she continued, "Your son was here with Colonel Fitzwilliam and Mr. Bingley. Both of those gentlemen immediately departed when I entered, and your nephew locked us in. Fitzwilliam has made me an offer of marriage, and I have most ecstatically accepted. Yet that is all that has happened in this room. I am a gentleman's daughter who was taught right from wrong by my parents and governess, Nannie MacFee. I am a graduate from the very proper St. Trinnean's Seminary for Young Ladies and am most certainly not a woman of easy virtue!"

The young man finally gained realization of the conversation's content. *Mother never did approve of my reading Valmont and said the book would be a bad influence. Then she found me alone with Elizabeth and assumed we … Good God!* He was aghast and only managed to stutter, "Mama mia! Did you actually think … ? How could you possibly assume … ? We most certainly have not … !"

George Darcy entered the library. Upon witnessing his wife's evident embarrassment, the younger lady's overt outrage, and his son's apparent agitation, he calmly stated the obvious. "There appears to be a bumble-broth brewing hereabouts. My dear Anne, I was informed by Anne you earlier experienced a fainting fit. Are you well now?" The gentleman gently supported his wife's forearm and put two and two together. "You three appear at sixes and sevens. Tell me at once, what is amiss with Miss Elizabeth and Fitzwilliam?"

"My dear husband, there is nothing truly amiss. The only bumble-broth is I foolishly leapt without looking, to a very wrong conclusion, which, I am vastly embarrassed to admit, made me actually swoon for the first time in my entire life. As you can see, I am fine and do not need your support with which to stand. Notwithstanding, your son and Miss Elizabeth do have important news to impart."

"Well, they may have to stand in line. I just met the Earl, Richard, Miss Bennet, and her parents in the hallway. Your brother is soon going to announce to our guests the engagement of his second son to Miss Elizabeth's elder sister. Perhaps we should be there for … "

"WHAT?! Excuse me, sir. But … my sister is to *marry* Colonel Fitzwilliam? My *parents* are here? Good Lord! What has transpired while we were alone in here, Fitzwilliam?"

Before her husband could also jump to a wrong conclusion, Lady Anne said, "Go stand in that line to make an announcement, George. There is another engagement of which our guests should be informed. Fitzwilliam and Elizabeth are to be married as well. We are to gain a regular out-and-outer as a daughter-in-law. Is that not wonderful news?"

"Indeed it is, my dear. Congratulations to you both." The gentleman kissed Elizabeth's cheek and added, "You are very welcome to join our family, young lady. I can tell from the unrestrained look on his face you have made our Fitzwilliam euphoric with your acceptance." He shook his son's hand and said, "Shall we proceed to the ballroom and make the joyful announcement before the waltz begins? We most certainly do not want to miss being involved in the upcoming scandal about to take place under this roof."

Fitzwilliam raised a hand and said, "Wait. Once again we are all jumping to a conclusion. I must first speak with Mr. Bennet and gain his permission for the honour of his daughter's hand. And when did you last see your father, Elizabeth?"

As soon as Lizzy entered the ballroom with her fiancé and future in-laws, she spotted her mother and father and rushed to join them while Fitzwilliam and his parents followed at a more sedate pace. Pleasantries were exchanged; and when Lizzy inquired about her sister's sudden betrothal, her mother gave the pat answer, "I shall explain later." Mr.

Bennet and the junior Darcy walked a short distance away for a few moments of private conversation and returned just in time to applaud the happy news of Colonel Fitzwilliam's engagement to Miss Bennet.

When the applause died down, George Darcy consulted briefly with his son and then stepped forward to make his own announcement. "Ladies and gentlemen, may I have your attention for just another moment, please. I know many of you are anxiously and eagerly waiting to partake in the onset of a bold and exciting new trend. We will very soon be ending our evening together in a most beautiful, albeit controversial, manner. However, before we start the music, I have an especially important announcement. Earlier you learned of the engagement between my daughter, Georgiana, and Mr. Ellis Fleming; and we have all now just heard the happy news about my nephew, Colonel Richard Fitzwilliam, and Miss Jane Bennet. Obviously, there is something in the air tonight. Or perhaps it is in the smuggled … er, imported French wine." Polite laughter followed, and he continued, "Love is evidently all around us at this assembly, because I am very proud to tell you of the betrothal of my son, Fitzwilliam Darcy, to the charming and Original, with a capital 'O,' Miss Elizabeth Bennet."

Murmurs of surprise, envy, and glee gave way to jubilant applause as George Darcy beckoned the happy couple forward. Many in the crowd were astonished to see Fitzwilliam Darcy in such high spirits and actually beaming; and more than a few female hearts were set aflutter as he turned to his fiancée, gazed lovingly and passionately into her eyes, raised her hand to his lips, and then possessively tucked it into the crook of his arm. His father raised his hands to quiet the crowd as he continued, "Thank you all for attending tonight; and now, family and friends, let us celebrate these three joyous betrothals … with a waltz! Lord Matlock, please escort your lovely wife to the dance floor. Lady Anne, shall we? Musicians, let the music, the waltz, and the gossip begin."

The Earl of Matlock led Lady Rebecca onto the dance floor to start the controversial new sensation. George Darcy and his wife followed; and then other daring couples, bold enough to try the intemperate waltz, began to leave the sidelines and joined them.

Fitzwilliam Darcy proudly escorted his radiant fiancée through the throng of relatives, friends, and acquaintances bent on offering hearty congratulations and best wishes. The newly betrothed couple graciously smiled and courteously thanked everyone, but they were bound and determined to find an available spot on the dance floor. Since they had already embraced and waltzed in the privacy of the library, they were eager to do so for a second time and gave not a thought to holding one another in public once they again became cocooned in their own world. The handsome young gentleman in the black tailcoat and trousers, snow-white shirt and cravat placed his gloved right hand on the yellow silk covering Elizabeth Bennet's tiny waist. He inhaled her heady perfume and gazed into the sparkling, intelligent eyes of the woman who would soon be his wife. The strains of the beautiful waltz music began, and they stepped into the romantic dance in perfect rhythm. Darcy and Lizzy moved as one, smoothly and surely. As they glided and twirled, the candlelight caught and reflected the tiny, glittering spangles on the lady's shimmering dress. The gentleman's coattails billowed, and the hem of Elizabeth's flowing gown swirled and floated around her as they circled the dance floor. The dazzling couple outshone all others, not only with their grace and style but also by the blissful expressions on their smiling faces.

The majority of dancers were understandably tentative, uncoordinated, or downright clumsy; and some were embarrassed by their obvious ineptitude. But frequently overheard expressions of apology were also oft times accompanied by peals of laughter and gaiety as ladies and gentlemen tripped, toes were trod upon, and couples collided. Darcy and his bride-to-be had silently found a rhythm all their own as they held each other and elegantly waltzed around the room. Elizabeth felt as though she were floating while she matched the exemplary lead provided by her tall, strong, debonair partner as he moved with style and grace. Her head was delightfully dizzy, and her body tingled wherever it made contact with his. Breathless with exhilaration, she wished the waltz would never end.

With a tear in his eye, Mr. Bennet watched his two beautiful daughters as they moved around the dance floor with their dashing fiancés. Although he occasionally frowned when a male leg came into contact with that of Jane or Lizzy, he thought the waltz was actually quite graceful and not in poor taste at all. He turned to his wife and said, "Frances, my love, would you do me the great honour of dancing the remainder of this set with me?"

"Why, yes, Mr. Bennet, you devilish old coot. I would very much like to give this new dance a *whirl*."

No longer under the watchful eye of his future father-in-law, Colonel Fitzwilliam pulled Jane a bit closer than the accepted distance for a waltz. "My darling girl, I am so sorry you are being rushed into this engagement without an actual courtship. You deserve so much better. Truly, do you have any regrets?"

"Absolutely not, Richard, not a single one." She smiled and then amended, "Well, perhaps one regret."

"Tell me, and I will do everything in my power to make it right."

"I regret we were interrupted earlier, and I do not mean being caught. That goes without saying. I just wish we had been able to continue ..." Jane blushed and lowered her eyes. When understanding dawned on the Colonel, he immediately manoeuvred their position to a set of open doors leading to a conveniently close balustrade and waltzed his fiancée outside. They stared into one another's eyes for a few seconds before he dipped his head and did everything in his power to erase her one regret.

Similar to another newly engaged couple, Fleming and Miss Darcy moved together with perfect timing. Azure eyes gazed into indigo eyes as time stood still for the young lovers. The glowing, fair-haired lady was completely focused on the tall, dark, and handsome man who held her in his embrace while she recalled the first time they met. Georgiana had been attracted to Ellis even then, and it was quite obvious theirs was not the only attachment formed on Pemberley's lawn one sultry summer afternoon.

"Georgie, my dearest heart, you suddenly have a rather mischievous glint in your eyes. May I ask what is running through that very pretty head of yours?"

"You may ask; and I may tell you sometime, but not now. Oh, Ellis, this has been the most wonderful night of my life! I am to wed the most magnificent man in the world, and my two best friends will marry my brother and my cousin. 'Tis too much! By far too much! Oh, why is not everybody as happy?"

"Well, I am, most certainly." He remembered there were other people in the room; and he took a quick glance at them before adding, "And if I am not mistaken, there are lots of other joyful people here as well. Just look at all the beaming faces surrounding us, Georgie. Like your father said, love actually is all around us tonight."

Charles Bingley and Miss Anne de Bourgh may not have been as well coordinated as Darcy and Elizabeth, but at least they did not tumble down like several other unfortunate colliding couples. Bingley and Anne merely laughed away their missteps and awkwardness and waltzed on. They spoke on many topics and found they truly had much in common. Both had a close female relative with 'issues', and those ladies had caused considerable embarrassment over the years. They also discovered those same women, coincidentally, had equally set their caps on Fitzwilliam Darcy. Bingley's sister had pursued Pemberley's heir hoping to become Mistress of the estate he would someday inherit, and Lady Catherine aggressively promoted a match between her daughter and nephew.

"Miss de Bourgh, I have often heard Darcy and Fitz make mention of you in a most complimentary and affectionate manner. Why would you not want to wed someone like Darcy? He is handsome, I suppose; wealthy, certainly; and quite intelligent, really. Is that not what a girl wants in a husband?"

"We are more like brother and sister than cousins, Mr. Bingley. Besides, Fitzwilliam is far too taciturn and staid for my liking. Although I appreciate the importance of being earnest, I prefer being in the company of more fun-loving, frivolous people."

"I am frivolous, and I love fun. For all the years I have known Fitz and Darcy, I am rather surprised our own paths have not previously crossed, Miss de Bourgh."

"Well, sir, I am seldom permitted to spend time in Town. So, unless you have crossed Rosings Park's pathways, it may be pathetic but not really surprising our paths never crossed until tonight."

While they danced and enjoyed being in one another's company, Mr. Bingley and Miss de Bourgh discussed literature, the arts, items in the newspaper, and the latest gossip.

"Miss de Bourgh, have you read the novel about the musician in treble? It was a real cliffhanger."

"Oh, Mr. Bingley! You ruined it, sir. You were supposed to say *clef*-hanger."

"Oops. Drat! Sorry. Just the same, I did hear of some treble at the new music store on Bond Street. It was robbed, and the thief made away with the lute. Speaking of loot, have you heard Miss Pearl Loyne is suspected of stealing a brooch from Miss Plaist?"

"Oh, dear. What happened, Mr. Bingley?"

"They could not pin it on her. They did, however, pin a famous writer for stealing an idea for a stage drama; and he is now considered a playgiarist."

"Tsk, tsk. Before writing his final version of the play, he should have had a pre-text."

"Yes. I suppose authors' lives are punctuated with good writing periods. Nonetheless, in my opinion the fellow should have been more pen-sive. My sister, Caroline, usually mends my pens for me, but she will soon be going away to live with our aunt and uncle. I suspect my handwriting shall suffer, and it is already nothing to write home about."

"Mr. Bingley, to write with a broken pen is pointless." Anne gave him a teasingly coy smile and exaggeratedly batted her eyelashes. "I mend pens remarkably well, sir."

"Do you know, Miss de Bourgh, you make a good point for furthering our acquaintance? Please allow me to ask you a question point-blank. May I please call on you tomorrow?"

"I hope you make a point of it, sir."

Whenever Bingley and Anne stepped on the other's toes, they apologized for the misstep. Step-by-step, they became accustomed to dancing together; and it was a step in the right direction. When they parted, the young gentleman had a spring in his step as he silently recited from Alexander Pope's *'An Essay on Man'*: *'Hope springs eternal in the human breast: Man never is, but always to be blest'*.

Miss de Bourgh made a mental reminder to jot down her feelings later.

Her daily journal was like a confidante, and she had named the diary 'Brigette Johns'.

An avid reader, Charles Bingley recalled a section of a letter from Werther, the main character, to his friend, Wilhelm, in the book *The Sorrows of Young Werther* by Wolfgang von Goethe: *'Never had I danced more lightly. I felt myself more than mortal, holding this loveliest of creatures in my arms, flying with her like the wind, till I lost sight of everything else; and--Wilhelm, I vowed at that moment that a girl whom I loved, or for whom I felt the slightest attachment, should never waltz with another, even if it should be my end!'*

A duchess, who was quite stricken in years, exchanged curtsies of common courtesy with Miss Elizabeth and complimented her. "I have been most highly gratified indeed, my dear Miss Elizabeth. Such very superior dancing is not often seen. It is evident you belong in our first circles. Allow me to say, however, your handsome partner does not disgrace you. I hope to have this pleasure often repeated, especially when certain desirable events, my dear young couple, shall take place. Three upcoming weddings in one family! What congratulations will then flow in. Have you two set a date yet?"

Darcy replied, "Your Grace, Elizabeth and I plan to marry before Christmas. We will then journey to our estate in Northumberland and spend at least a month in the country."

"Winter in the North Country! Brr!" The elderly woman shivered. "How will you keep warm?"

Darcy and Lizzy did not have to say anything. Their eyes, which were locked on one another, and their blushing cheeks painted a picture that spoke a thousand words. The duchess smiled fondly at the couple. "Oh, yes, … to be young again and in love! But let me not interrupt. You will not thank me for detaining you from the bewitchment of one another. I believe your bright eyes are upbraiding me. I am done to a cow's thumb anyway and shall soon take my leave. Enjoy the rest of the waltz, my dears."

The latter part of this address was scarcely heard by Darcy. "That interruption has made me forget of what we were talking, my dearest, loveliest, loveable Lizzy."

"I do not recall we were speaking at all. Her Grace could not have interrupted any two people in the room who had less to say. We have tried two or three subjects already without success at keeping our train of thought, and of what we are to talk next I cannot imagine. Just keep looking at me the way you have been, hold me, spin me, and waltz me around the room, Fitzwilliam. I never want this dance to end. I am surely in heaven here and now."

"We will be in sheer paradise when we arrive at our estate, my love. What think you of living in the rugged wilds of the North with me?"

"What are rocks and mountains to the man I love? I would follow you to the ends of the earth, Fitzwilliam. Oh, what hours of transport we shall spend! You give me fresh life and vigour."

"Elizabeth, you already have enough life and vigour for three people, which is fortunate. We have a lot to accomplish in the next two months. Northumberland may not be another country, but the climate is quite different up there. You must prepare and shop for a cold winter … warm boots, gloves, scarves, hats, muffs, and a pelisse or two. To plan ahead is pre-fur-able."

"Will I have to witness the return of your frosty disposition?"

"Elizabeth, when we are alone together up there, ice-olated, just the two of us … "

"Fitzwilliam! Just the two of us? Shall we not have servants? Am I to do all your cooking and cleaning? What have I gotten myself into? What have *you* gotten yourself into? I cannot cook, sir. We shall be not only cold but hungry too. This will not do!"

"Elizabeth, are you getting cold feet already? There is a whole household of servants, my love … an excellent chef, housekeeper, butler, footmen, and maids galore. There is a fireplace in every room, and a thousand acres of wood to fuel them. We have trunks full of blankets, bricks for warming, and cozy beds in our chambers. We shall be neither cold nor hungry, and I promise to keep you warm."

"I am quite warm right now, so perhaps we should waltz often while up north."

"That can be arranged; and it is, indeed, a very good idea. As you are already aware, I tend to forget if I do not practice."

"Practice makes perfect, Mr. Darcy; and I know you do strive for perfection."

Part VI

Nervous Fiancée
or
Bride and Pre-Jitters

A tribute to Austen's *Pride and Prejudice*

Chapter I

The Mourning After the Night Before

Matlock Manor, the morning after the ball, had been completely put back to rights by the household staff. There was no evidence hundreds had been revelling there only hours previously, except for the fact a fair portion of the company was, in fact, still under the Earl's roof. The family wing and guest chambers were all quiescently occupied, and those carousers who feared they might suffer from being hung over in the morning simply circumvented the problem by sleeping well past noon.

Fitzwilliam Darcy stayed overnight because he and his cousin, Colonel Richard Fitzwilliam, planned to call on their brides-to-be as soon as propriety allowed; and it was of relative importance the ladies upon whom they were to call just happened to be sisters. The two young men hoped they might be the first to break their fasts but were dismayed to find Richard's elder brother, the Viscount Wentletrap, still attired in his evening clothes, slumped at the table. Upon observing his sibling's unkempt appearance and fragile condition, Fitz made a point of speaking more loudly than necessary. "Well, well, Darce, look what the early bird left us. Brother, I am surprised to discover you here, all bright-eyed and bushy-tailed, after the batch of blue ruin you imbibed last night."

The wretched, bleary-eyed man flinched, forced some coffee down his throat, and retorted, "Yes, well, I may have bowed to the porcelain altar of my chamber pot; but you two cork-brained buffoons will soon be paying a much, much higher price."

Darcy sat several places away from his loathsome cousin, who was decidedly green around the gills. He knew he should ignore the cynic.

Nevertheless, like the bird sitting on a perch, he smelled something fishy and asked, "What cause have you to make such a caustic remark, James?"

"You *have* heard of sacrifices made at the altar, have you not?" He sniggered unpleasantly and continued, "Love may be blind; but, believe me, marriage is a real eye-opener and a rather nasty matter of wife and debt. A man needs a mistress just to break the monogamy."

With neither rhyme nor reason, his affronted brother sat back in his chair, glared and declared, "James, you may be the all-important heir, but beware and have a care. I am aware your intent is to scare; but I swear by the air I breathe, you err. How dare you unfairly compare your patched-up affair and sorry excuse of a marriage ensnared to that which the fair Miss Bennet and I will e'er share. We shall be a rare happily wed pair, for she is the answer to my every prayer. Jane Bennet is an angel!"

"Ha! You are lucky then. Unfortunately for me, Isabelle is still alive. Oh, do not give me that superior look, Darce. Your love for Miss What's-Her-Name is also an obsessive delusion that shall soon enough be cured by marriage."

Darcy very much looked forward to wedding his lovely fiancée and proving James wrong; and so he argued, "A man is incomplete until he marries."

The Viscount slapped his palm on the table, winced, and cried, "Absolutely! For then he is quite *finished*! Have you not heard An Ode to Marriage? He goes to a-dore. He rings the belle. He gives his name to a maid, and he is taken in."

Darcy rolled his eyes and said, "I am truly sorry you are unhappy, cousin. Having often witnessed the sharp words you have spoken to your wife, I actually pity … "

"Yes, yes! My words *have* to be sharp. It is the only way to get them in edgeways when that piece of baggage is raising a breeze. Excuse me, I am unwell." He quickly scraped back his chair and fled the room to kneel and pay homage once again at his porcelain altar.

Fitz shook his head as he watched his unfortunate brother stumble from the room. "Poor James. He has made his bed, now he must lie in it."

Darcy calmly buttered a muffin and added, "Yes, when he married Isabelle, he increased his lie-ability."

"Ha! Someone here has been spending too much time with a certain family fond of wordplay. Speaking of our future in-laws, after last night's … state of affairs, I am uncertain of my reception in their home. I shall have to meet soon enough with Mr. Bennet to discuss a settlement. Still and all, what Jane and I really need right now is a chance for a lengthy, private conversation about our future together. Since I do not believe Jane's parents trust me so far as they could throw me, perhaps it would be best if you suggest a joint walk in the park with our lovely brides-to-be."

"Just what *was* the state of affairs to which you refer? Despite what you told Bingley in the library last night, I had not an inkling any attachment or understanding had been formed between you and Miss Bennet until the announcement of your rather sudden engagement."

Colonel Fitzwilliam squirmed uncomfortably in his chair and refused to meet the other man's eye. Darcy set his knife down, wiped buttery fingers on a napkin, and glared at his cousin. "Richard, please do not tell me you acted in an ungentlemanly manner toward my virtuous future sister."

"Fine, I will not tell you. I must admit I obviously not only lost my heart to Jane Bennet but apparently my head as well. She is … " Darcy smirked at the lovesick expression on heroic Colonel Richard Fitzwilliam's face and hoped his own countenance never showed such sappy emotion. " … absolutely intoxicating. Not only is my Jane beautiful, kind, warm, serene, and generous; behind that demure surface, she is also rather brazen, has a diverting sense of humour, and is quite … passionate." At Darcy's look of alarm, Fitz's infatuation gave way to sheepishness as he continued, "We were delightfully and obliviously engaged in a rather erotic kiss when Aunt Anne, Anna, and Anne unfortunately happened upon us. I had a fine peal rung over me by my father, then Mr. and Mrs. Bennet arrived, and subsequently Jane and I became … otherwise engaged as well."

At once both appalled and envious, Darcy wondered if his Elizabeth might be receptive to an amorous kiss. He was quite confident she also had a passionate nature but was uncertain if she would be willing to allow him a taste of it before their wedding.

"Well, once again, please accept my congratulations, Fitz. I obviously do not need to tell you Miss Bennet is a lovely woman. In fact, I am not sure you deserve such a treasure. Although it is certainly none of my business, do you regret being forced to marry her?"

"Good God, man! No, of course not! I was first attracted to her beauty and gentle nature at Pemberley. Back then I assumed Bingley and Miss Bennet had fallen in love at first sight. Since I, being a second son and soldier, had less to offer her than our infatuated friend, I stepped aside. When I later came to realize she admired me, I feared it might only be the uniform that attracted her regard. I was wrong. We are *not* being *forced* to wed. We are in l-l-l- … " The fearless soldier gulped and turned red. " … in l-l-l … We are, in l-l-light of the situation, very fortunate to feel as we do for one another; and the engagement is very much to our mutual satisfaction."

Darcy smirked and said, "Yes, well, thank you for (*ahem*) en-l-l-lightening me. Now, eat something. I wish to be underway as soon as possible, and I will suggest a walk in the park. As much as I enjoy their company, I also look forward to some time with Elizabeth away from the rest of her family. Being with her is, well, a walk in the park, a piece of cake, easy as pie … "

"Enough! I am hungry and suddenly crave something sweet."

"Shall we have the carriage brought 'round, then?"

Fitz nodded. The two young men grabbed some pastries and scarfed them down on their way to visit two sweet ladies at the Bennet townhouse.

Because of the lateness of the hour – or earliness, depending on how you looked at it, as dawn had been fast approaching when Mr. and Mrs. Bennet escorted their two eldest daughters home from Matlock Manor – there had not been much discussion in the carriage. That would come later, especially for Jane. The four rang for their servants to help them undress, tumbled into bed, and slept fitfully for about five hours. The day of reckoning dawned for Jane before breakfast when she was summoned to her mother's private sitting room.

"Jane, come have a seat here." The woman patted the settee beside her. "I wish to speak with you regarding your unbecoming conduct last night."

The young woman sighed, bowed her head, and contritely said, "Yes, Mama. Again, I am truly sorry for causing so much turmoil."

When Jane sat next to her, Mrs. Bennet reached for her hand and held it for the duration of their conversation. "It is all water under the bridge now, my dear. Still, I want to discuss how you feel about the consequences of your reckless actions. You know your father and I always wished for you to enter into marriage only for the right reason. So tell me, have you actually formed an attachment with Colonel Fitzwilliam so quickly?"

Jane raised her head and smiled brightly. "Oh, yes, Mama! I have admired his character and appearance for some time now. But last night, Richard and I felt an immediate attachment."

Her mother frowned, but her tone was mildly teasing. "Yes, I heard about your attachment … at the lips and several other points of contact, I believe."

Jane coloured and said, "I apologize for such abandoned behaviour. As was earlier explained to Lord Matlock, Papa, and you … Richard and I simply … collided. Once I was in his arms, oh Mama, I never wanted to leave. I cannot explain the way he makes me feel."

"Believe me, Jane, I understand completely. Your father and I were young once, you know; and it appears the apple does not fall far from the tree."

"Mother!"

"Just be careful, my dear. Your handsome Colonel has spent time on the Continent, you know."

Jane knitted her brows. "What in the world are you implying?"

"Well, Richard Cosmo Fitzwilliam is … cosmopolitan." She leaned in and whispered, "He is a man of the world and may have Roman hands and Russian fingers. You may be tempted to anticipate your vows."

"Oh, Mama, really!"

"Very well, I will say no more at present. We will have a further talk before the wedding. In the meantime, I just need to know if you have agreed to enter into this marriage willingly."

"I truly do love Richard; and, despite his career, we will be very happy together. Please do not worry about me. I have every reason to believe he and I will have a loving relationship like you and Papa share, which is everything I have ever wanted."

Mrs. Bennet kissed her daughter's cheek and smiled. "Then I am very happy for you, indeed. Your father and I were very fortunate to have found one another." She patted Jane's hand, still held in her own. "I shall not worry. Worry causes falling hair; and when the going gets tough, the tufts get going. Now, are you ready to get going and face your father and siblings at the breakfast table?"

When the two women joined the others, Mr. Bennet lowered his newspaper, looked over the top of his spectacles, raised his eyebrows, and said, "Ah, there you are, Mrs. Fitzwilliam-to-be. You, my dear, are marrying into quite a family. Come have a seat and prepare to be diverted by some gossip in an article on the society page. Listen to this: *'Marriage Mania, Midnight Madness & Immoral Missteps at Mayhem Manor ~ The town is in an absolute uproar the day after a ball given by a member of the Peerage; and the Marriage Mart has suddenly been deprived of three of the country's most eligible bachelors as well as three very beautiful, young, and nubile women.. '"*

"Papa?"

"Yes, Lydia?"

"What does new-bile mean?"

"Nubile means … ah … ask your mother."

"Mama?"

Mrs. Bennet scowled at her husband and replied, "It means marriageable … among other things. That definition will suffice for now. Continue, my dear Mr. Bennet. You read uncommonly well. Still and all, perhaps you could censor further descriptive words deemed inappropriate for young ears."

"Thank you, Fanny. I suppose I deserve such praise as well as such censure. Where was I? Ah, yes. *'Parents of le bon ton are bemoaning the significant loss of six desirable matches for their sons and daughters after the announcement of a trio of upcoming weddings. One very disgruntled matron complained the few families involved were being rather selfish by snatching up so many desirable young partners. "'*

"Papa?"

"Yes, Lydia?"

"If a pig loses its voice, is it disgruntled?"

"Perhaps you should ask the aforementioned miffed matron. Were she a male I am sure she would be a boorish, boring boar. Now, here is where it becomes interesting. We learn the identities of the eligible bachelors and beautiful maidens. *'The ball's two hosting families have, indeed, secured enviable brides and a bridegroom to add to their already illustrious bloodlines. A wealthy young landowner from northern Derbyshire has used his time wisely and won the hand of the eldest daughter of an eminent family from that same county; that young lady's handsome elder brother, heir to their vast estates, has become betrothed to a Hertfordshire beauty; and that woman's lovely sister is engaged to a dashing Colonel, the second son of an Earl.*

As was hinted by one of the hosts during the ball, perhaps there was something potent in last night's wine; and that must also be the reason the evening concluded in such a shocking manner. No mere outmoded minuet was danced last night at Immorality Manor; instead many couples, both married and, more alarmingly, single, dared to defy propriety by embracing in public for the wicked waltz. The patronesses of Almack's are scandalized as are many of the haut ton who had not been invited to the controversial ball. Imagine! A dance in which members of the opposite sex face one another and the man places his hand on the lady's waist. Shocking! Had not the majority of Polite Society been in attendance, one might wonder at such debauchery. "'

The family started to speak all at once until silenced by an announcement that Mr. Darcy and Colonel Fitzwilliam had come to call on their fiancées. Both gentlemen were welcomed warmly, much to the Colonel's relief; and they were invited to join the Bennets while they finished breakfast. The visitors gratefully tucked into a fresh batch of currant scones and washed them down with fragrant coffee while Mr. Bennet continued to read articles from the newspaper.

"Well, it is a coincidence we are enjoying these scrumptious scones. Here is a story about a landlady, Mrs. Lottie Lyes, who had a couple of struggling poets for tenants. The poor fellows got behind in their rent; and when the landlady was unable to have them evicted, she decided to do away with the purse-pinched versifiers. The awful woman baked a large scone laced with arsenic, invited the rhymesters down to her parlour, and served each chap a cup of tea and half a scone. The poison worked as advertised; but, of course, crime does not pay. Mrs. Lyes was soon afterward arrested, and at the trial she pled innocent to the charge of killing two bards with one scone."

Mrs. Bennet gently chided her husband. "My dear, I never quite know whether or not to believe half the things you read aloud. Colonel, I assure you the scones you are now eyeing rather suspiciously are quite safe. Mr. Darcy, I hope you will not change your mind about marrying Lizzy; yet I feel it is my duty to warn you she does take after her father. And Robert, darling, why are you now diligently picking the currants out of your scone?"

"I think these are arse-nits, Mama."

"Oh, Robert! Eew!" Disgusted and disgruntled, Catherine Bennet threw her half-eaten scone back onto her plate.

Mrs. Bennet smiled apologetically at her guests and said, "Poppet, you can stop nit-picking. These scones do not have any arsenic. Perhaps you should eat your Jam Roly-Poly now instead, dear. Mr. Bennet, please kindly refrain from reading such thought-provoking news whilst we are eating a meal."

Catherine asked to be excused, as she had suddenly lost her appetite. Her father, who had just taken a mouthful of his own Jam Roly-Poly, agreed with her and said, "That is one way of pudding it, Kitty." Of course, he who talks with his mouth full is speaking in-gest.

Colonel Fitzwilliam, who wanted to be alone with nubile Jane, prodded his cousin, who was seated across the table, by kicking him on the shin. When that did not have the desired effect, he caught Darcy's eye and winked at him for a considerable time, without making any impression. The other gentleman was preoccupied with thoughts of stealing a kiss from nubile Elizabeth. When at last Darcy did observe his cousin, he very innocently asked, "What is the matter with your eye, Fitz? For what purpose do you keep winking at me? What am I to do?"

"Nothing, Darce, nothing at all. And I most certainly did not wink at you. Why would I wink at my oblivious and obtuse male cousin?" He then sat still five minutes longer; but, unable to waste such a precious occasion, the Colonel suddenly proposed their walking out. Mr. Bennet had paperwork to attend, Mrs. Bennet was not in the habit of walking, and Mary reluctantly could never spare time from her studies; however, the others agreed an outing to the nearby public garden would be quite a pleasant way to spend the morning after the night before.

Mrs. Bennet rang for Alice and Miss Edwards to accompany the children; and her husband also ordered Baines, one of the footmen, to go with the party. *I was your age once, young men; and I would be foolish to trust you alone with my precious daughters before they actually become your wives. Three children, a governess, a nursery maid, and one footman should be sufficient chaperones to keep the four of you out of mischief.*

The ten-person entourage that set off for the park was of a far greater size, by about six people, than Colonel Fitzwilliam had envisioned; however, he decided to make the best of it and gallantly offered his arm to his fiancée. The smitten couple whispered, lagged behind, and tried to allow the others to outstrip them; yet one of the servants always waited patiently. The officer and his lady then increased their pace and attempted to outdistance the rest of the group. In vain had they hastened, for Baines, the long-legged footman, with his gangly, ungainly gait, made a gain upon them in the lane and proved to be the bane of Jane.

She hissed, "Fitz, I insist we persist. I have missed being kissed and shall enlist my sis to assist with our tryst."

The Colonel caressed her gloved hand as he spoke in an undertone. "Baines will not be dismissed, but a well-placed fist might make him desist. Thunder and turf! What you have done to this soldier, my dear? It is obvious I am quite *violently* in love!"

"Richard, that expression, 'violently in love', is so hackneyed, so doubtful, so indefinite, it gives me very little idea. It is as often applied to feelings that arise from a half-hour's acquaintance as to a real, strong attachment."

He stopped, turned to face her, and gazed passionately into her eyes. "My lovely Miss Bennet, if we ever manage to evade our chaperones, you will be kissed with such a real, strong attachment it will leave very little doubt about the undeniable violence of my love."

Jane blushed but continued to look him in the eye. "Sir, I do admire your single-mindedness, constancy, and uniformity."

"Aha! So it was, indeed, my uniform that initially attracted you."

"Not at all, Colonel. I have this clinging memory you were not, in fact, wearing your red coat when we first met."

"How then did it begin? I can comprehend your going on charmingly when you had once made a beginning, but what could set you off in the first place?"

Jane lowered her gaze to his chest, and the flush spread to her own. "I … I dare not make such a confession. Pray, do not ask me."

"Hmm. So shy, demure Jane has suddenly returned, I see. Miss Bennet, I am a military man who has ways to make people give up their confidences. Be forewarned, I am determined to solve this enigma; however, I will not force the issue now. But this deep, dark secret of yours shall be revealed in time. Perhaps I shall have to kiss it out of you. Good God, you were correct. I do, indeed, have an idée fixe."

"Yes, Colonel Fitzwilliam, sir; and that fixation is one of the many, many things I admire and love about you."

The happiness which her reply produced was such as he had probably never felt before; and he expressed himself on the occasion as sensibly and as warmly as a man violently in love can be supposed to do while being chaperoned by his cousin, three of his fiancée's sisters, a three-year-old boy, a governess, a nursery maid, and a gangly footman.

The public garden near the Bennet townhouse was neither as large nor popular as Hyde Park; still, it was a favourite promenade for the fashionable people in the neighbourhood. Its ornate wrought-iron fence and gated entrance surrounded lush lawns, massive hardwoods, coniferous and fruit trees, shrubs, flowerbeds, vegetable plots, fountains, and statues. There was a large pond in the middle of the park with a bridge leading to a small island, upon which sat a music pavilion. Carriages were not permitted, and the garden provided a tranquil atmosphere amidst the bustle of the city. As the group of ten entered the park, the children hurried to the designated play lawn, which they knew had an excellent area especially marked for playing marbles.

In another part of town, a visitor who had already lost most of her marbles paid a call at Matlock Manor. The Earl was informed his unexpected guest was waiting in the sitting room. The nobleman took a deep, steadying breath and said a silent little prayer before he entered to greet his ignoble, ignorant, and ignominious sister.

Lady Catherine de Bourgh was the elder of the three Fitzwilliam siblings; and, to the detriment of her considerable vanity, it showed. The Earl of Matlock and Lady Anne Darcy were still quite handsome despite their mid-life status; however, their older sister had not aged as gracefully. Catherine had always been a self-righteous, conceited woman; and she loathed the crows' feet and other wrinkles that seemed to multiply daily on her hollow-cheeked face.

She had been as blonde as her sister, Anne, as a child; but to Catherine's disgust, her hair had become quite lacklustre and mousy when she reached adolescence. This affront crimped her style, and an unfortunate maid tried to help by giving her a fashionable cut; but hell hath no fury as a woman shorn. Not someone to tangle with, Lady Catherine gave her servant the brush off; and the two parted ways. Although she at first hated the new short style, it soon grew on her. Lady Catherine had then attempted to lighten her locks by drenching them with a harsh solution of potassium lye, which she learned Parisian ladies had been doing. Years later, when the first strands of grey had the audacity to appear, Lady Catherine thought she would dye. Instead, she got to the root of the problem; and the offensive items were immediately plucked from her head. Initially she worried about going bald; yet, for every one painfully pulled, three more colourless, wiry ones seemed to sprout. Therefore, she stopped pulling her hair out. The colour, she proclaimed, was thereafter to be referred to as 'platinum;' and woe betide the poor soul who dared call it grey.

Although she was quite spry, Lady Catherine walked with an elaborately carved cane. The item was useful as a weapon with which to poke and prod people, and she brandished it expertly. The woman was nearly as tall as her brother but had a more bony build, which she continued to clothe in black bombazine despite the fact Sir Lewis de Bourgh had been dead more than ten years. Always a bit touched in the upper works, the death of Lady Catherine's husband intensified her peculiar outlook on life; and so she continued to willingly wear the widow's willow. Her only concessions to fashion were the outlandish lifeless birds, freakish feathers, and peculiar plumes her bizarre bonnets oft-times flaunted.

"Good afternoon, sister dear. What brings you to London? Surely you have not come all the way from Kent simply for a friendly visit. In fact, I do not believe you have ever done such a civil thing in your life as pay someone that sort of courtesy."

"Where is my daughter, Henry?"

"I was not aware you had a daughter by the name of Henry. Surely, you are not addressing *me* in such a familiar manner."

"Oh, get stuffed, brother! And stop calling me Shirley. Where is Anne?"

"Which Anne? If you mean our lovely sister, I imagine she is at her home. I have not seen her since the ball."

"A ball do you call it? By all accounts, you should more accurately describe last night's event as a disgusting and distasteful den of debauchery, deviance, dissipation, degeneracy, and depravity. Why was I not invited? If I find out, however, that my Anne was in attendance at such an orgy, there will be the devil to pay. Heaven and earth, Henry! Of what were you thinking?"

"Just now I was thinking you, madam, are demented, deranged, and disturbed."

"I am most decidedly disturbed, distressed, distraught, and dismayed by all this corruption. I demand you tell me at once! Where is my daughter?"

"You may ask questions which I shall choose not to answer, and that was one of them."

"This is not to be borne, you egregious earl! You cannot keep me from my own flesh and blood. Nevertheless, that is not the sole reason for my visit. I insist on being satisfied, and you can be at no loss to understand the reason of my journey hither. A report of a most alarming nature reached me via the newspaper this morning. I learned, in addition to having the gall to introduce the wicked waltz last night, it was announced your son, our nephew, and our niece are all engaged to be married. I know the rumours must be scandalous falsehoods, yet I instantly resolved on setting off to Town to insist upon having these reports universally contradicted and retracted in the papers."

"Catherine, the reports are not merely gossip. Richard, Fitzwilliam, and Georgiana are, indeed, quite happily betrothed."

"No! A match between Darcy and this Hertfordshire hussy can never take place. Pemberley's heir is engaged to Anne. They are both descended from our noble line, Henry. We must keep all that splendid Darcy fortune in the family."

"When will you cast aside unmitigated avarice for the Darcy fortune and irrational jealousy of your own sister? For once and for all, Anne did not steal George away from you. He has always been a perfectionist and recognized your flaws upon first acquaintance. Pemberley and the other Darcy estates and wealth are lost to you just as surely as Rosings will be because of Lewis' will. Perhaps instead of a match between Anne and Fitzwilliam, you more wisely should have promoted one for her with Richard. Nevertheless, have no fear, Catherine. My second son is a generous man and will, no doubt, allow you to live in the dower house when he inherits Rosings on the eight-and-twentieth anniversary of his birth. By the way, since that day quickly approaches and he is now engaged, we should inform him of the legacy. It is, indeed, unfortunate Lewis died before you could produce a male heir; even so, you shall certainly not be cast out into the hedgerows. Of course, this is all speculation on my part and contingent on your behaviour over the next few months. I have been in favour of committing you to Bedlam each time you have one of your episodes, although the rest of the family has strongly objected to such harsh treatment. Behave yourself, and you may be allowed to stay out of the asylum; the decision is yours, sister dear."

"You would not dare be so cruel and callous to your own sibling. In any event, Henry … What in perdition's pit was that?"

"What was what? Are you hallucinating again, Catherine? Do you see pink elephants?"

"No. That. It sounds like laughter … Anne's laughter! To what wickedness is my daughter now being exposed in this unholy, heathen house of hedonism?"

Lady Catherine de Bourgh stormed off and followed the sound of female giggles and male guffaws to the drawing room, where she was horrified to find Anne and an unknown young man sitting together on a sofa. Her daughter's companion, the elderly Mrs. Ann Teak, quietly sewed in a corner and was overlooked by the enraged woman. Anne and Bingley abruptly stopped laughing upon Lady Catherine's sudden appearance; and the gentleman stood, then quickly stepped back as far as the sofa would allow when the harridan advanced upon him and flailed her deadly looking cane in his direction.

Ann Teak made her presence known, but Lady Catherine was not placated. "Mrs. Teak, you are dismissed. Permanently. Anne, go pack your belongings immediately." The walking stick was held against Bingley's chest as she addressed him. "And you, whoever you are, how dare you have designs on Miss Anne de Bourgh of Rosings Park. Well, speak, man. Who are you?"

"Ma'am, I am Charles Bing … "

"Mr. Bing, do you know who I am? I am Anne's mother and am, therefore, entitled to know every teeny-tiny, minuscule detail of her life. Now, who are you, and what are your intentions?"

"Mother, please allow me to introdu … "

"Anne, are you still here? What did I just tell you to do?"

"Well, if you cannot remember, I do not believe I should have to tell you."

"Obstinate, headstrong girl! Who is this male person?"

"Mother, this is Mr. Charles Bing … "

"Yes, yes! You have both now told me his name. Be that as it may, who are you, Charles Bing? Who are your parents, uncles, and aunts? What are your bloodlines, wealth, and connections? What is your business here? Let me be rightly understood, Mr. Bing. If you dare have the presumption to aspire to a match with my daughter, I must tell you such an understanding can never take place. No, never! Contrary to popular belief," continued the contrary harridan, "Anne is engaged to my nephew, Fitzwilliam Darcy. Now what have you to say?"

Charles desperately tried to remember all the questions fired at him but was saved from having to say anything by the arrival of Miss de Bourgh's uncle. The Earl of Matlock informed his sister that Mr. Bingley was a guest in his home and had been so on numerous occasions, as he was Richard's good friend. He then asked her to kindly refrain from further interrogation of the chap and inquired if she needed to be escorted to her carriage.

Anne saw the terrible transformation begin when her mother's face contorted with anger; and the fast-thinking young woman grabbed Bingley's hands, placed them over his innocent ears, and held them in place as Lady Catherine de Bourgh began to cuss like a sailor. Her profanity continued until she was all s-worn out, had worn out her welcome, and was escorted to her waiting carriage.

Chapter II

Cato, and Caroline, and Catherine! Oh, My!

"It hardly seems fair, Elizabeth," said Darcy petulantly. "Fitz and your sister only have one chaperone while we have five. Tell me, have you heard the expression 'two's company, three's a crowd?'"

She nodded.

"Well, what is four and five?"

"Nine?"

"Actually, I believe 'four's too many, and five's not allowed.'"

"Well, sir, do you know why six was afraid of seven?"

"No. But I wager you are just itching to tell me."

"Six was afraid of seven, because seven eight nine." Darcy looked serious, so Lizzy rolled her eyes and explained. "Seven *ate* nine, as in consumed, devoured, partook of … Oh, my! I suddenly feel like Little Red Riding Hood. Why are you staring at me in such a wolfish manner, sir?"

"What fine eyes you have, Elizabeth."

"All the better to see you with, Mr. Darcy."

"Mr. Darcy is your father-in-law-to-be. Will you not call me Fitzwilliam when we are alone?"

"With five chaperones, we are hardly alone, Fitzwilliam."

He glanced at the others, noticed they were all engrossed in the game of marbles, and took advantage of the opportunity to move closer to Elizabeth on the park bench. Darcy slid his arm along the top of the seat behind her and contemplated pulling her into an embrace and stealing a kiss. He was just gathering enough courage to make a move when they were startled by cries of alarm from the children, and they hurried over to the grassy field where Kitty, Lydia, and Robert had been playing under the watchful eyes of Alice and Baines. One of Kitty's marbles had rolled far out of bounds; and when Elizabeth and Darcy reached the others, they saw with dismay Lydia had discovered a dead sparrow. The little girl was kneeling by the body of the bird; she lifted teary eyes, looked at the gentleman and asked, "What happened to it, sir?"

Darcy squatted down to the little girl's level and explained the sparrow had died and gone to heaven. Robert ran to Darcy, climbed onto his knee, almost threw the man off balance, and raised his arms to be picked up. When Darcy complied, Robert asked, "Did God throw the birdie back down, Mither Darthy?"

One advantage of not having animals in the house was the Bennet children had not suffered the loss of a beloved pet. Darcy had experienced such heartbreak more than once; so, as his mother had done for him, he explained it as best as he could to the youngsters. "Death is a part of life, and most animals have a shorter lifespan than humans." He said the sparrow was probably old or ill and no longer needed its earthly body. Darcy then suggested they bury the bird in the woods and sent Baines off to find an implement with which to dig a small hole.

While they waited for the footman, Robert was a source of non-stop questions. "Will he be happy in heaven? Will he fly around again there? Will he meet God? Will he be with other sparrows? Will he find something to eat when he gets hungry? Will he sleep on a cloud?" When Kitty suggested a name be chosen for the poor creature before it was buried, Darcy decided 'Willie' would be a good choice; and the others agreed.

When the deed was done and an improvised eulogy delivered by Kitty, Robert was instructed to gently refill the hole with soil. Darcy crafted a cross from two twigs bound into formation with long blades of grass, and he placed it into the ground at the head of the grave. At his suggestion, Lydia picked flowers and added them to the memorial; Darcy kindly did not mention they were weeds that made him sneeze. Elizabeth hugged her siblings and needlessly worried they might be upset for quite some time; however, the children soon completely forgot the incident and skipped away to return to their game of marbles.

"Mr. Darcy, I mean Fitzwilliam, you will make a very fine father some day."

"Am I so trans-*parent*, Elizabeth?" He smiled and kissed her hand. "If our children are as adorable as your brother and sisters, my love, we shall be blessed. I very much look forward to experiencing parenthood with you, for I know you will be an absolutely perfect mother." They stood toe-to-toe, looking into each other's eyes, and envisioned their future together until Baines cleared his throat and Alice suggested the children move along to the pond to feed ducks and geese.

The servants had each been given strict orders not to allow the two couples any time alone. Miss Edwards had assumed the duty of chaperoning Colonel Fitzwilliam and Jane, who had decided to take a stroll. The governess trailed along behind as the engaged couple led her along the garden path.

"Achoo! Oh, Miss Edwards, I have foolishly forgotten to put a handkerchief in my reticule. Would you please return to my sister and ask if she has a spare one I may borrow?"

Although young, the governess was not born yesterday. "There is no need, Miss Bennet. I have a clean one right here." She handed a prettily embroidered linen cloth to the unappreciative other lady.

Jane rolled her eyes at her fiancé. "Thank you, Miss Edwards. Oh, look! Perhaps Kitty, Lydia, and Robert would care to join us, for I see there is a puppet booth set up on the other side of the pond." Jane pointed across the water to where children were sitting on the grass, laughing at the antics of Punch and Judy. "It would be a shame for my sisters and brother to miss the show. Please fetch them, Miss Edwards. The Colonel and I will wait right here for you." Jane smiled sweetly, and the governess could not believe the angelic Miss Bennet would allow any impropriety to occur in the short time it would take to follow orders. She gave a quick curtsey and hurried away.

Richard Fitzwilliam did not take time to look a gift horse in the mouth. He was more interested in much, much sweeter lips. "I have always appreciated a good Punch and Judy skit; yet, strangely enough, today I do not care for such entertainment. I much prefer the farce you just performed, Jane. Will you walk with me off the beaten path?"

Jane was a bit skittish. "But, sir, I told Miss Edwards we would wait right here. Truly, it was not pretence. I do want my sisters and brother to enjoy the puppets."

"As do I. However, we can just take a short jaunt through these trees and return before the others arrive. Dearest, I will not act against your wishes. The decision is yours. We will remain rooted to this very spot if that is what you desire."

Jane considered her options for a moment; still and all, what she desired was looking at her so disarmingly, she could not resist. "Very well. But just for a brief duration. We must be back here prior to the rest of our party."

Richard grinned, snatched her hand, and pulled her off the path behind a thicket of evergreen trees. The two wasted no time but did lose track of it.

Because the others were headed toward the pond anyway, Miss Edwards soon met them on the path. Alice was concerned and drew her aside to inquire why Martha had abandoned her post as chaperone. The governess assured her the couple would be the epitome of propriety and would be found waiting out in the open by the pond exactly where she left them.

When the three children heard about the puppet theatre, Lydia and Robert ran off in different directions to get around the water, eager to not miss another minute of the show. The little boy had not gotten far before he fell and scraped his knee on the gravel; and Alice immediately hastened to care for her charge while Baines and Kitty chased after Lydia, and the governess anxiously hurried back to her chaperoning duty.

Elizabeth made sure her brother was not seriously injured and agreed when Alice decided it would be best to take the sobbing toddler home. Darcy volunteered to carry Robert, but the nursemaid assured him she was used to lifting the poppet. In her concern for the child, she did not give a second thought to leaving the lovers alone.

The gentleman turned to his beloved and said, "Well, Elizabeth, it seems I am to once again enjoy the privilege of your exclusive company. When last we were alone, you accepted my proposal; so I wonder to what you might agree this time." *Perchance, a kiss on your luscious lips?*

"Do you have something specific in mind, perhaps, sir?" *Perchance, a kiss on my receptive lips?*

"Indeed I do have a goal in mind, madam." He slowly raised her hand to his lips but did not stop looking into the windows to her soul. Elizabeth's heart rate increased as Darcy kissed her knuckles, her palm, and then peeled back a bit of her glove to touch his lips to her racing pulse. She tore her gaze away from his intense regard and rather breathlessly asked, "Have you reached your goal yet, sir?"

"Not yet, Elizabeth, but I am getting warmer."

As am I. "Fitzwilliam, we cannot possibly continue in this manner on a public path. As much as I am enjoying your … oh! … touching attentions, I must beg you to stop. *Oh, do be quiet, Lizzy!*

"I am sorry, love. I did not intend to make you uneasy, and you are quite correct." Darcy gently tugged her glove into place. "Please forgive me." He was about to offer his arm when he was distracted by three young lads as they chased a small creature through the trees just off to the left of the path. "Here! What are you boys about? Leave off at once! Excuse me, my dear, but I must investigate."

His long strides soon gained on the youths, and Darcy was angered to discover they were after a kitten. The small ginger cat had taken refuge in an oak tree, and two of the boys threw twigs at it to make it come down while the other gripped a low branch and attempted to climb after the feline.

"Leave off, I said!" Fitzwilliam Darcy was a tall, formidable man and could be quite intimidating when he set his mind to it. The boys took one look at his menacing approach, ditched their plan, and fled the scene of the crime. The gentleman was incensed by such mistreatment of an animal but decided not to give pursuit, as he was more concerned for the welfare of the kitten.

Martha Edwards hastened to the place where Miss Bennet should have been waiting with her handsome officer. She glanced to the left, ahead, and across the pond; but the affianced couple was nowhere to be seen. The governess stomped her foot in frustration at quite literally being led along the garden path by the innocent-looking eldest daughter of her employers. When Miss Edwards looked behind, she saw Baines, Miss Kitty, and Miss Lydia approaching. Not wanting to alarm the girls, she explained the situation to the footman in a low, urgent voice.

Baines was aghast. "Miss Edwards, I am shocked. But is a tryst certain, absolutely certain?"

"Well, no. Nonetheless, I do suspect they have made a May game of me. How are they to be discovered? I have not the smallest hope. It is in every way horrible, and I shall surely be dismissed."

The footman shook his head in silent acquiescence and made no answer. He seemed scarcely to hear her and was walking up and down the path in earnest meditation, his brow contracted, and his air gloomy. His position was on the line as well, for he had been entrusted with guarding the reputations of Miss Bennet and Miss Elizabeth. *Miss Elizabeth!!* He swivelled his head around in search of her pretty face, chestnut hair, deep red pelisse, and matching bonnet. "Miss Edwards, where are Miss Elizabeth and her young gentleman?"

"Baines! I thought they were with you! Please do not tell me we have lost *both* young ladies we were ordered to protect!"

Elizabeth had followed her fiancé off the path and found him pacing back and forth, raking his fingers through his hair, and peering up into the tree. He was distracted from the plaintive mewling of the stranded creature by a twig that snapped as Elizabeth approached. He startled and said, "Ah, Elizabeth. My dear, would you mind very much if I remove my coat? I will attempt a rescue but know from past experience a tight coat can be quite constrictive during such an activity. I know it is improper. Would you be offended?"

"Mr. Darcy, we are engaged; and you forget I have already seen you in far less."

"Oh, God. I had forgotten. Thank you for reminding me, though. One needs a good dose of humiliation now and then."

"You must not feel humiliated, sir. I quite enjoyed seeing you less formally attired."

Darcy smirked and considered teasing her about 'handsome barbarians', but he was curious. "What really was your first impression during that encounter?"

He passed her the discarded coat, limbered up, and hefted himself onto the most easily accessible branch. The kitten stared down at him in alarm for a moment and then climbed up another level. Lizzy admired her future husband's obvious strength as he effortlessly pulled himself higher and higher.

"Here kitty, kitty. Come on, kitty. Come here, sweetheart," he cooed.

Elizabeth was glad Kitty was not present and also thought herself quite ridiculous for being jealous of his calling an animal 'sweetheart'.

"I am still waiting, my love. Please answer the question about your first impression of me," he called down.

She was mollified by the endearment. "Well, I remember thinking you were a buffoon."

Darcy nearly lost his balance as he twisted around to glare down at his beloved tormentor. "Miss Elizabeth Bennet! I cannot believe you thought of me as an ass!"

Because she had been ogling a particular part of his anatomy as he climbed, the young lady lowered her gaze and blushed at being caught. When asked if his second appearance improved her opinion, she spoke honestly. "Yes. I distinctly remember admiring your rich brown hair and brazenly wondering how it would feel to run my fingers through it."

Darcy briefly closed his eyes and imagined how it would feel. "Elizabeth, please. I am trying to concentrate on my rather precarious position here. You, my dear, are proving to be quite a distraction." ... *especially since you insist on standing directly below me. Your neckline is something I can look down on and approve of at the same time.*

"Speaking of precarious, Fitzwilliam, I may be going out on a limb, but I do not think it wise for you to venture onto that particular one. The branch does not seem sturdy enough to support your bulk."

"I assure you I have rescued injured birds and stranded cats from trees more times than you could shake a stick. I certainly know what I am doing."

"Uh, speaking of shaking a stick, the branch you are currently on is quivering in an alarming manner, sir. Please come down and allow me. I am much lighter and am also an expert tree climber."

"Certainly not, madam! If the confounded feline would just cease climbing higher each time I ascend ... here, kitty, kitty!"

CRACK!!!

"Good Lord, Fitzwilliam! Back up and get down immediately before you fall and break your neck."

"You sound like my mother, but perhaps you are correct. This branch does not seem able to support my weight. Can you really climb trees?"

Instead of answering, the intrepid Lizzy Bennet glanced around, saw no one in their immediate vicinity, hiked up her skirt, and gracefully scaled the oak as effortlessly as had Darcy. When she reached his level, she sat on the branch beside him and met his incredulous stare with an impertinent one of her own. The sassy smirk was instantly wiped from Elizabeth's face by the sudden, impetuous brush of his warm lips against hers. It was a quick and chaste kiss; nevertheless it left them both breathless, although Lizzy was already somewhat in that state from her ascent. Darcy pulled away to look into her face, hoping for approbation instead of apprehension. Her cheeks were rosy and her eyes still closed. When she opened them, they were filled with affection and warmth. The couple ignored the mew from above and was about to kiss again; unfortunately, they could not ignore the unexpected singsong taunt from below.

"Lizzy and Darcy, sitting in a tree, K-I-S-S-I-N-G ... "

Jane admonished, "Lydia, stop that! Lizzy, Mr. Darcy, I am sorry. I thought you heard our approach; perhaps you were preoccupied. What on earth are you doing up there in that tree? Whatever your reason, I strongly suggest you come back down before Baines and Miss Edwards arrive here with Kitty. They were not far behind us."

Colonel Fitzwilliam was enormously delighted to discover his fastidious, impeccable cousin in another pickle, especially since he had just managed to get Jane and himself out of one. Fitz considered a little white lie was merely a-version of the truth, and he had charmingly explained to Miss Edwards that they only veered off the main path because he wanted to present Jane with tulips and had not realized those particular flowers were out of season. The military man had, of course, successfully plucked the only two lips he truly sought. As the soldier watched Darcy and Miss Elizabeth both go red in the face, he gloated over having enough fodder in his haystack to needle Darcy for a month of Sundays.

Darcy's haughty mask was in place, and he huffily said, "I will have you know that Miss Elizabeth and I are on a bona fide rescue mission up here. So, Richard, if you were about to say something derogatory, you would most certainly be barking up the wrong tree. Unfortunately, our little rescuee is a tad reluctant and has a most ungrateful cattitude." He frowned up at the ginger ball of fluff crouched several branches away.

The Colonel volunteered some advice. "One of you needs to climb another level higher, reach up, grab onto the kitten's limb … I mean pull down the branch, while the other one cat-ches the little fur ball."

Lizzy protested, "But, Colonel Fitzwilliam, if the person holding down the branch loses their grip, it will spring back; and the kitten will indubitably be cat-apulted into Kent. Your suggestion has the potential to be quite a cat-astrophe, sir."

Darcy agreed. "Elizabeth is right, Fitz. But I am curious. Do you have any other purr-fectly brilliant ideas in your military catalog of strategy for rescuing a cat on a log?"

"Ah … no. You shall just have to purr-severe, Darce; and here's a word of warning about curiosity. They say it killed the cat, and they were not kitten."

"Ha, bloody ha. I think … Elizabeth!!! What on earth do you think you are you doing, madam?" As Lizzy disappeared onto the branch overhead, Darcy was horrified his cousin might catch a glimpse of her ankles, calves, thighs, or … "Richard, turn around at once; and do not even glance up here again. Elizabeth!!!"

Lizzy peered down at him. "Mr. Darcy, before the others arrive we either need to abandon our mission or accomplish it. I have chosen the latter. So when I latch onto Ginger, I will gingerly pass the kitten down to you. Since you are so vastly experienced at this animal rescue business, you can carry the contrary clawed critter to the ground."

"*Ginger,* Lizzy? How utterly uninspired. You, my dear sweet lady, definitely need assistance with the naming of pets." Although he scoffed at the cat's moniker, he agreed to her plan. Darcy scrambled to balance upright on the branch, raised his arms, and prepared to receive the kitten.

Elizabeth glanced down at her fiancé and said, "I did not realize Ginger was to actually become someone's pet; and by all means, he does deserve a more distinguished name and a home. Be that as it may, just whose household do you intend to grace with his presence? Mama and Papa have never permitted us to have animals in our residence. Hmm, I wonder whether they are concerned about household pets taking over the world. Why the puzzled look, Mr. Darcy? Have you never heard of reigning cats and dogs?"

Lydia squealed and pointed. "Never mind, Mr. Darcy and Lizzy! The kitten has jumped down and is now running along the path. Here, kitty, kitty, here kitty!"

"I am here, Lydia. There is no need to call out in that ridiculous manner."

Catherine Bennet gasped as she caught sight of her second eldest sister and the normally sophisticated Mr. Darcy in the oak tree. Her attention was instantly sidetracked by the arrival of Miss Edwards and Baines. One and all were amazed to witness the gangly footman as he gently cradled the little orange ball of fluff in his arms.

Darcy called down, "Baines, there is a proverb that goes, 'You will always be lucky if you know how to make friends with strange cats.' It appears you have been favoured with the friendship of Cato, the Philoso-fur."

Lydia asked, "But why did the cat suddenly jump down and run from the tree?"

"Perhaps it was afraid of the bark," suggested Colonel Fitzwilliam.

Darcy alit from the tree and gently caught Lizzy as she leapt from a lower branch. He reluctantly released his hold on her waist, turned to his cousin, and said, "Fitz, punsters such as you deserve to be drawn and quoted."

Lydia whispered to Kitty, "People tend to tell worse puns as they get older. That is why we call them groan-ups."

Blissfully unaware they were soon to receive an unwelcome visitor, Mrs. Bennet and her two eldest daughters were in the sitting room of their London townhouse busily choosing ribbons, beading, and other trimmings suitable for the brides' trousseaux. The fact that Jane and Elizabeth had made very eligible matches and were truly in love with their husbands-to-be was, of course, deeply satisfying to their mother. Most gratifying was the undeniable fact the gentlemen returned their affection tenfold. However, Mrs. Bennet realized she would be quite melancholy when it finally came time to part with her dear girls; that said, having three more daughters and a son still under her care was, in some measure, a comfort. The woman could not image how bereft she would feel when the last child had finally flown the nest.

"Mama, are you crying?" A soft voice roused Mrs. Bennet, and she suddenly realized Jane knelt in front of her and had reached to clasp her hand.

"Most certainly not, my dear. Good heavens, why would I have occasion to weep? Is this not every mother's fondest wish … to be planning her daughter's wedding? I have been doubly blessed with the duty of overseeing the production of not one but two trousseaux, which, of course, would be incomplete without: 'Dresses for breakfasts, and dinners, and balls; Dresses to sit in, and stand in, and walk in; Dresses to dance in, and flirt in, and talk in; Dresses in which to do nothing at all; Dresses for Winter, Spring, Summer, and Fall.'"[2]

"Speaking of all these purchases of attire, it is fortunate Papa's own clothing has rather deep pockets," said Lizzy.

A modiste in the city was already at work on the young ladies' wedding clothes. When she had been needled for a completion date, the woman had hemmed and hawed before replying. "I am only doing sew-sew. I toile day and night, and eye-let my assistant, Velvet, do the crewel embroidery work. But the darn thread, together with the tight fit of the

2   *From William Allen Butler's "Nothing to Wear"*

bodices, causes much seam-stress. I will not embellish the truth but must tack on a few extra days. So awl things considered, I have a notion you may pin your hopes on the garments being ready five days before the wedding." The Bennet ladies had quickly cott-on to the dressmaker's wordplay; and, without bias, they baste their trust on Mrs. Lovelace and Velvet.

Cato the Philoso-fur was quite comfortably curled up into a cozy little orange ball on Mrs. Bennet's lap. Initially, the lady had flatly refused to allow the kitten admittance into the townhouse; nevertheless, she had been sweet-talked and cajoled, mostly by her handsome sons-in-law-to-be, into allowing the feline into her home. Almost immediately, the little cat had also worked its way into the woman's heart; and the two had become inseparable, except when her three-year-old son was in the vicinity. On those occasions the cat became as nervous as, well, a long-tailed cat in a room full of rocking chairs. It was not because Robert was cruel; in fact, the boy loved the purring pet so much, he showered it with hugs and kisses. Robert had been instructed to hold the kitten gently, but the reluctant and squirming Cato's philosophy differed from what the tot had been taught regarding the difference between gentle and taut.

The day Cato had first been introduced into the household, Mr. Darcy had picked him up and taken a look beneath its tail to confirm the kitten was, indeed, a male. The next morning, Lizzy had happened upon Lydia and Robert kneeling on the floor, struggling to inspect the poor cat's belly. When asked what they were about, Lydia answered, "Well, Mr. Darcy picked Cato up, looked underneath, and then told us it was a boy. It must be written here somewhere, though I cannot find it." Lizzy opened her mouth to explain but was gratefully spared when she glimpsed her father about to enter his study. "Papa, would you please come here? The inquisitive minds of your youngest children need some direction. Please excuse me. I am in a hurry to foist upon myself yet another painful bout of writer's cramp. Being betrothed to the cream of the crop of la crème de la crème has some drawbacks. All the same, there is no use crying over spilt milk, so I am off to answer more letters of congratulations."

Mr. Bennet was finally reconciled to losing Lizzy and Jane, yet not to Cato's status as a permanent fixture in his house. The critter had hissed at him upon first acquaintance, scratched his arm when he benevolently tried to pet its head, and bit the hand that fed it when he had tried, the previous night, to evict the little cat from its place on the bed next to his wife. Thanks to Lizzy's talk of dairy, her father was able to evade the risk of further feline-inflicted affliction as well as the need to point out the pet's private parts to his progeny. His suggestion Cato might care for a saucer of cream was met with enthusiasm, so Lydia and Robert scampered off to the kitchen while the liberated kitten scurried in the opposite direction. Quite proud of his resourcefulness, Mr. Bennet smiled smugly as he returned to his den. The self-satisfied smirk was quickly wiped from his face when he discovered Cato had taken shelter in the gentleman's own private lair, and Thomas Bennet could have sworn the creature was grinning back at him, snug as a bug in a rug, from behind the desk in the comfort of his own favourite chair.

The prospect of a northern journey buoyed Caroline Bingley's sinking spirits to a certain extent; nonetheless, she dragged her feet up the front steps to the Bennet townhouse. Having just eaten a generous portion of humble pie with the upper crust's Georgiana Darcy, the young woman did not have much appetite left for eating crow in front of Eliza Bennet. Saying she was sorry was certainly not Caroline's cup of tea, and she did not want to end up with egg on her face. But a promise had been made to Charles, and she was determined to dispense with the unpleasantness of another apology and depart for Staffordshire with a clear conscience instead of being left to stew in her own juices.

The sitting room discussion of buttons, bows, and beaux was interrupted when Sharp announced Miss Bingley had arrived to visit with Miss Elizabeth. The three women rolled their eyes, and Lizzy asked the footman to bring her guest to them. After greeting the visitor, Mrs. Bennet took her leave. Caroline admired Cato's beautiful gingery-orange coat as it followed its mistress from the room. Refreshments were ordered and served along with polite chitter-chatter before Jane thought of a plausible reason to be excused in order to leave Lizzy and Miss Bingley alone.

Dressed in tangerine but green with envy, Caroline jealously eyed the swatches of fine fabric, lace, and satin ribbon. She washed away the bitter taste in her mouth with a sip of tea, attempted a bright smile, and said, "Miss Eliza-beth, please accept my best wishes. I understand you are engaged … to marry … " Her throat closed up, and the smile crumpled. She took another sip and managed to choke out, " … Mr. Darcy. I regret I will not be available for the happy event, although I realize I would not have been invited anyway. I am departing Town soon for an extended stay in Staffordshire … at Tutbury to be exact. Charles and I have relatives there, and … " Both Caroline and the tea ran out of steam, so she sat silently staring into her cup.

Lizzy took pity and said, "Thank you, Miss Bingley. I hope you will have a most pleasant sojourn in the Midlands. Mr. Darcy and I will be heading even farther north after our marriage, as we are to settle at his family's estate in Northumberland. If you are ever in that part of the country, you absolutely must visit us there." Lizzy remembered her dream of a home on a cliff where Caroline would have been welcome to drop over, and she hid a smile behind her teacup.

"You are too kind. If I were in your position … Well, that point is certainly moot. Simply allow me to say I am sorry for the cut indirect that day at Harding, Howell & Co. as well as for my cutting remarks directed at you during the Royal Academy's art exhibit. If the awful truth must be known, I offer as an excuse my resentment of your … je ne sais quoi. You have a sparkle I totally lack and covet. I almost regret we never became friends. If we had, perhaps some of your effervescence might have rubbed off on me. Most of all, I have to admit I was foolishly jealous of the regard a certain gentleman from Derbyshire bestowed upon you. Women, myself included I confess, have been eagerly pursuing Fitzwilliam Darcy for years. But you alone apparently possess the qualities he seeks. I hope you realize how very, very fortunate you are to have secured Pemberley's heir."

"Thank you, Miss Bingley. I must say, I do not know what I did to deserve such happiness and such a wonderful man. I sincerely wish you the same felicity in making a match some day. Perhaps you will meet someone special during your stay in Staffordshire."

Caroline doubted that would happen unless she was willing to scrape the bottom of the barrel and marry some toothless old codger who was completely bald. She could have bawled right then and there; but she balled her handkerchief into a wad and said, "Again, you are too kind. My behaviour merits the severest reproof. It was unpardonable, yet you are forgiving. However, I cannot think of my rudeness without abhorrence."

"Pish, posh, and tish, tosh, Miss Bingley. You have, I hope, improved in civility since those occurrences; they are simply to be forgotten."

"I cannot be so easily reconciled to myself. The recollection of what I said, of my conduct, my manners, my expressions during the whole of it is now, and has been many days, inexpressibly painful to me. You know not, you can scarcely conceive, how my words and actions have tortured me."

"Then you must learn some of my philosophy, which is to forgive, forget, and think only of the past as its remembrance gives you pleasure. Say adieu to disappointment and spleen and make a fresh start in the Midlands, Miss Bingley."

"I do hope to make some new acquaintances in Tutbury, since I have certainly lost the friends I thought I had here in Town."

"They were not true friends if they abandoned you so quickly." Lizzy drew her bottom lip through her teeth as she contemplated her next words. "This is rather presumptuous, but would you care to correspond with me while you are away? I will give you the directions for this address, as well as for my future residence in Northumberland, if you would like."

For the first time, Elizabeth witnessed a genuine smile on Caroline Bingley's face; and she was amazed at the transformation. The young woman was actually quite attractive when not sneering.

The following day Miss Bingley said a teary farewell to her brother and entered the carriage with the elderly companion Charles had hired for her. In company with Mrs. Ann Teak, who had recently left the employ of Lady Catherine de Bourgh, Caroline settled in for the long journey to Staffordshire. She was completely exhausted from all the packing and apologizing. The clip-clop of the horses' hooves soon lulled her to sleep as they rode the road to the home of the Bingleys' aunt, Mrs. Rhea Piers, and her husband, Bartlett.

London society's gossip mill continued to churn with tittle-tattle about the Earl of Matlock's scandalous ball and the rather sudden engagements of three members of his family. Grist for the mill was the prittle-prattle that Charles Bingley, brother to a young lady recently given the cut direct by the Earl's wife and Darcy ladies, was courting another Fitzwilliam relative, Miss Anne de Bourgh.

Invitations to a celebratory dinner at the Darcy townhouse were as scarce as hen's teeth and, in fact, had only been issued to members of the families involved in the betrothals, plus a few favoured kith and kin. The gathering was being held to pay tribute to the three couples and to celebrate the eight-and-twentieth anniversary of Richard Fitzwilliam's birth. Unbeknownst to the Colonel, he would also learn of his unexpected inheritance before that evening was over.

Mr. and Mrs. Gardiner and their eldest son, Evan, had been asked to attend the dinner; and Sir William Lucas, Lady Lucas, as well as their daughter, Charlotte, had arrived in London from Hertfordshire to stay with the Bennet family, at their request, and accompany them to the celebration.

Because none of the guilty parties involved had seen fit to inform Mr. and Mrs. Bennet of the shenanigans in the park, Miss Edwards and Baines had both been able to keep their employment. The day before the Darcy dinner, the same footman once again accompanied Miss Bennet and Miss Elizabeth to the park near the townhouse. However, on that occasion, Baines did not have the worry of their interaction with frustrating or frustrated fiancés. Those eager young gentlemen were meeting with the Archbishop of Canterbury in order to obtain special licenses so they could marry when and where they wanted, and in two days' time Darcy and the Colonel had appointments with Mr. Bennet and their three solicitors to hammer out details of the marriage articles.

The Misses Bennet strolled with Charlotte Lucas and informed their friend of all that had happened since her last visit. Lizzy was just about to entertain Charlotte with the story of Cato's rescue when she espied a very familiar and handsome red-coated soldier as he approached their party. The three ladies silently admired the man of mettle as the metal of his medals and buttons gleamed in the sun. His burnished auburn hair was tied back with a leather thong, and the young army officer exuded virility. He bowed, tipped his hat, and flashed his warm, gorgeous smile. "Miss Bennet, Miss Elizabeth, and Miss … Lucas, is it not? What a delightful coincidence, ladies. I was just on my way to your house to extend my best wishes. Miss Bennet, I have heard you are to marry Colonel Fitzwilliam." His smile was not quite as radiant when he turned to her sister and said, "And Miss Elizabeth, is it true you will wed Mr. Darcy?"

"It is, indeed, Lieutenant-Colonel Dun. Our marriage will take place within the month. In fact, it will be a triple wedding shared with Jane and Mr. Darcy's sister, who is betrothed to a Mr. Ellis Fleming."

"Ah, well, splendid. Splendid. Please accept my sincere congratulations and best wishes on your upcoming nuptials. Miss Lucas, it is a pleasure to see you once again. Are you staying in Town for the wedding?"

"No, sir. My mother, father, and I are only here for the engagement party tomorrow evening. We will then return to Hertfordshire. Unfortunately, we are unable to travel to Derbyshire for the ceremony."

"Derbyshire? Such a long way! Is that where you will be residing, Miss Elizabeth?"

She laughed and said, "No, Lieutenant-Colonel, my new home will be even farther away. Mr. Darcy and I are to settle at his family's estate in Northumberland."

"My stars and garters, how will you ever keep warm?" Lizzy turned red and wondered why people kept asking such a peculiar question. Dun realized his faux pas, apologized, and then inquired whether he might escort them back home. The ladies readily agreed, and he offered his arm to Miss Lucas.

That young woman thought she had died and gone to heaven. Charlotte had been strongly attracted to the soldier's magnetism upon first acquaintance but knew she did not stand a chance when he only had eyes for Lizzy. With Jane's vivacious sister off the marriage market, her own prospects looked much brighter; and she was determined to secure the Lieutenant-Colonel as soon as may be. Miss Lucas was a firm believer concealment of affection could lead to loss of opportunity; so she latched onto his arm, and her chances, with fervour. *There are very few of us who have heart enough to be really in love without encouragement, so I had better show more affection than I feel. Dun may never do more than like me if I do not help him along. I refuse to dilly-dally and shilly-shally and shall make the most of every half hour in which I can command his attention, starting right now.* The thirty minute walk through the park and along the street to the Bennet doorstep was put to good use; and because Charlotte's personality was quite similar to Elizabeth's, Dun was quite undone, not only by her wit but also by her manner of walking, the tone of her voice, her address and expressions.

When the three ladies arrived at the townhouse with the officer, they invited him in and found Mr. and Mrs. Bennet in the sitting room with Sir William and Lady Lucas. Tucked away in a corner at a small writing desk, Robert knelt on a chair and diligently scribbled on a piece of paper. His fingers were inky, the tip of his tongue was caught between his tiny teeth, and the little boy busily continued his task and ignored the room's occupants. Charlotte introduced Dun to her parents; and when the soldier, from force of habit, took a seat near Elizabeth, Miss Lucas claimed the chair on his other side.

Jane quickly realized she had never seen a more promising inclination, for the young man was growing quite inattentive to other people and wholly engrossed by her equally besotted friend. With every minute it was more decided and remarkable, and twice Jane had spoken to them without receiving an answer. *Could there be finer symptoms? Is not general incivility the very essence of love?*

The others in the room were also exceedingly pleased with the obvious growing attachment between the two young people. Mr. and Mrs. Bennet had assumed John Dun would be their son-in-law one day, had always liked the officer, and felt sorry for him when Lizzy rejected his proposal. They also had affection for Charlotte and hoped she would find the love and happiness their daughters had.

Elizabeth was in full harmony with the idea of such a dynamic duet. If she could help in any measure, she would not refrain from playing a key role in assisting the suite couple to form an a-chord in a quick tempo. Lizzy hoped they would not change their tune, that Lieutenant-Colonel Dun would start accelerando romantic overtures, and that Charlotte would not feel as though she was playing second fiddle. *Perhaps Miss*

Lucas will soon march down the aisle toward her handsome soldier, and it will be music to my ears to hear them say 'I will'.

Because Sir William and Lady Lucas lived in the same area of Hertfordshire as the Bennet family, they had also despaired over the dearth of eligible young gentlemen in and around Meryton. They were, therefore, hopeful; and the fact the Bennets were all quite fond of Dun spoke volumes about his character.

Is that shady character still looking for a place in the sun near Elizabeth? Son of a ... gun! Get away from my loved one, Dun! Darcy and the Colonel had been shown in by Sharp, and Lizzy's fiancé had stopped short at the sight of his former rival. He shook off his initial shock, immediately made his way to Elizabeth, kissed her hand, made sure Dun saw the proprietary gesture, and took a seat on Lizzy's other side. The Lieutenant-Colonel, who was rather amused by the man's possessiveness, considered tormenting Darcy but instead decided to demonstrate his good nature to Miss Lucas.

"Mr. Darcy, please accept my congratulations on having won the hand of a most remarkable woman. You are carrying away one of the country's brightest jewels, but I need not tell you Miss Elizabeth is a diamond of the first water and a cut above the rest. Fortunately, I am a man who can also appreciate the value of a diamond in the rough." Dun cast an appreciative glance at Miss Lucas and continued, "Colonel Fitzwilliam, my heartfelt congratulations to you as well, sir. You are both very fortunate gentlemen."

His superior officer assured him it was true and said, "You need not worry that Mr. Bennet has cast pearls before swine, you know."

Darcy added, "Indeed, rather than being trampled underfoot, our brides shall be put on pedestals."

Dun, who still harboured lingering resentment toward Darcy, decided to get in a snide remark after all. "I would certainly be wary of men who put women on pedestals. They may only want to look up their skir ... " He suddenly remembered they were in mixed company. " ... to look up to them and p-raise them to the skies. I would much rather have my bride walk beside me and share my life than spend her time on a pedestal." Again he cast a fond look toward Miss Lucas.

Mr. Bennet had had enough, so he changed the subject by addressing his son. "What are you doing so secretly at the desk there, young sir?"

"It ith no thecret, Papa. I am writing a thtory."

"Excellent, Robert! You write uncommonly fast, though. Pray tell us what your story is about, poppet."

"I do not know, Papa. I cannot read yet."

The room's occupants chuckled, and Mr. Bennet continued, "Well, do not let that stop you. To quote Johann Wolfgang von Goethe, 'Whatever you can do, or dream you can do, begin it; boldness has genius, power, and magic in it.'"

At that moment, Sharp appeared again in the doorway, this time somewhat rattled. The master of the house sharply inquired, "Yes, man, what is it?"

"A visitor, sir. A Lady Catherine de Bourgh is in the foyer deman … asking to see her nephew, Mr. Darcy. Shall I … Ah, here is the lady now, sir."

She entered the room with an air more than usually ungracious, made no reply to salutations other than a slight inclination of the head, and sat down without saying a word. Mr. and Mrs. Bennet were all amazement, and Sir William and Lady Lucas were obviously excited to be in the presence of a personage of such high importance. With great civility, Mrs. Bennet begged her ladyship to take some refreshment; however, upon being informed there was no fruitcake available, the offer of eating anything else was very resolutely, and not very politely, declined. Lady Catherine did, nevertheless, condescend to accept a glass of sherry; and Baines, who was on duty in the sitting room, was aggrieved and aghast when the woman repeatedly beckoned for refills during her visit. The shocked servant was somewhat relieved to receive surreptitious instruction from Colonel Fitzwilliam to forthwith water down his aunt's potent wine.

After sitting for several moments in silence, the inebriated Lady Catherine very stiffly spoke to her Darcy nephew. "I hope you are will, Fishwelliam. Yet I am mosht shocked, ashtonished, and sherioushly dishpleashed with your shishter, Anna. I expected to find a reashonable

young woman; however, I had to shpend a full half flower of weeding
…   (ahem) half hour of wheedling before she would divulge your
deshtination. Anna ought to have known I am not to be truffled with.
I went to your home with the dead-ermined … (ahem) determined
resholution of carrying my porpoise … (ahem) purpose, and I would
not be dishwaded from it. I have not been used to shubmitting to any
pershon'sh whim, and I have not been in the hobbit of braking … (ahem)
habit of brooking dishappointment. I inshishted on being shatishfied and
would not go awry until she finally volunteered the information mosht
unwillingly. I am ashamed of her! Anna should have more reshpect for
her eldersh. From whom ish she picking up shuch mad bannersh …
(ahem) bad manners?" Lady Catherine cast narrowed eyes around to each
of the room's occupants while she took another healthy swig of sweet
sherry. "I asshumed the gosship in the paper wash all a lack of piesh
… (ahem) pack of lies. But that lady, I shupposhe, ish your intended,
the one hearing bedding wellsh … (ahem) wedding bells." She cannily
pinpointed Elizabeth with her pointy cane.

Darcy very concisely verified the identification. *Unless you scare her
off. Elizabeth, I promise you, I do not take after my aunt! Well, there was
that one time at White's when I thought I lost you; but I swear I will not
go on the cut again.*

"And that woman, Rishard, I shuposhe is yoursh." Again, she
accurately singled out her other nephew's betrothed by indicating Jane
with the now wildly wavering walking stick. The fact the couple had
been found fondling one another's ungloved hands had handily helped
the stewed shrew's shrewd sighting.

"Yes, Aunt. This is Miss Jane Bennet, and I am overjoyed she will
soon become a part of our family." *Oh, Jane, please do not change your
mind! Every family has a black sheep, or a skeleton in the closet, or a
skeleton in sheep's clothing in the closet, or …*

Lady Catherine snorted in a most unladylike manner and tossed
back another glass of watered-down sherry. While the adults in the
overcrowded room felt awkward and uncomfortable being witness to the
woman's shocking behaviour, Robert was intrigued by the elderly visitor.
He scrambled down from his seat, crossed the room, and stood in front of

her. The woman's glazed expression suddenly brightened. "Heaven and earth, look at you! Cute ash a bug! Who are you, little one? What ish your name? Who are your father, mother, aunts, and uncles?"

"I am Robert Bennet, ma'am." The little boy bowed and then said, "You have the same name as Caffrin. But we call her Kitty. We have a kitty named Cato. But Papa calls him Bad-Cat! Why are you called Lady Caffrin der Bug? You are *not* cute as a bug. Why does your skin not fit your face?"

Once again Robert's words caused embarrassment amongst the grown-ups; and those who knew, or knew of, Lady Catherine de Bourgh were frozen in place waiting for an explosion. When the eruption occurred, it was not the sort expected; for the woman threw back her head and howled … with laughter. She thumped her cane, stomped her feet, and thrust her empty glass at Baines so she could repeatedly slap her palm on the chair's armrest. Tears rolled down her cheeks, and she struggled to catch her breath. But when Darcy, the Colonel, and Mrs. Bennet all rushed to her aide, she waved them away.

"Mama? What is wrong wiff Lady Caffrin der Bug?"

"Come along, poppet. Jane, please ring for Alice to take Robert to the nursery."

"I will take him, Mama." Jane scooped up her bewildered brother into her arms. The attention turned back to the esteemed visitor, who was by then snoring softly with her chin resting on her chest. No one noticed the Colonel slip out of the room to follow his fiancée.

Lieutenant-Colonel Dun chose to take his leave during the lull in conversation, but not before first asking permission from Sir William to call upon his daughter while they were staying in London. His request was granted; Dun promised to visit Miss Lucas the next day, bowed, and said his goodbyes.

To Darcy it appeared that, had his aunt set out to ridicule herself as much as she could during the afternoon, it would have been impossible for her to play her part with more spirit or finer success. At least the Bennet family was not of the sort to be much distressed by the folly. Mrs.

Bennet looked at her mortified future-son-in-law and asked, "What shall we do, Mr. Darcy? Should we awaken her?"

"I am unsure. I have never before, in my entire life, known my aunt to laugh. I do believe the unaccustomed outburst has quite exhausted her. She is sleeping like a log, so I suggest we just let sleeping logs die ... Pardon me! I meant sleeping dogs ... er, aunts ... um ..."

They were spared having to make any uncomfortable decision by the arrival of Lady Catherine's nearest relation in the world. Anne de Bourgh entered the room in company with the man rumoured to be courting her; and after the necessary introductions, the two gently roused the lady, spoke softly, and induced her to drink a potion from the bottle Anne had recently begun to carry in her reticule at her suitor's insistence.

Darcy was appalled and intrigued. "Bingley, for God's sake, what on earth are you doing, man?"

"I am not doing this for God's sake, Darcy, but for Anne's, I mean Miss de Bourgh's. Her mother, as you are very well aware, can be quite an ogress and has made her daughter's life miserable at times. I have been all over town these past few days consulting with various physicians, and it has been recommended we give Lady Cat a tonic."

The befuddled woman looked up and, in vino veritas, said, "My bear Mr. Ding, how pleashant it ish to shee you again. And you brought my gritty pearl ... (ahem) pretty girl with you too." The woman beckoned her daughter to lean down and whispered, "I re-cog-ni-shize your dozen Carshy; but who are all thesh other people, and where did they come from? It will be nesheshshary to kindly ashk them to leave now, becaush I need to take another nittle lap ... (ahem) little nap. Help me up to my chambersh, Annie dear; and remind me to have the drawing room re-decorum-ated. I do not recall it being sho devoid of pretendshush garrishnessh before."

Lady Catherine was sound asleep again and softly snoring as several of her own footmen were summoned to gently carry their mistress to the waiting de Bourgh carriage. Anne apologized profusely to both the Bennet and Lucas families for her mother's non compos mentis and then ordered that Lady Catherine be immediately taken home to Rosings Park and put to bed. Anne then ignored her cousin Darcy's scowl as he watched from the doorway while she and Bingley entered another carriage and drove off together without a chaperone.

Darcy scowled yet again when he entered the sitting room. Miss Jane Bennet had returned, and he noticed she was suspiciously wearing a high-necked fichu that had not been part of her frock when she carried her brother upstairs to the nursery. She and Fitz were both peculiarly flushed and somehow managed to give the impression of guilt and smugness concurrently. Consequently Darcy somehow managed to appear both shocked and rather envious at the same time.

Chapter III

Upun My Word, Mr. Darcy!

The two fiancés were daily visitors at the Bennet townhouse. The gentlemen regularly arrived before breakfast, were invited to stay for dinner, and remained as late as proper. They agreed to dine with their future in-laws again that particular evening, so Mrs. Bennet hurried off to speak with the housekeeper. Lady Lucas retired to her guest chamber for a rest, and Mr. Bennet challenged Sir William to a battle of wits over the chessboard in the study. Charlotte and the two engaged couples headed for the mews, as the men were interested in seeing Elizabeth's mare, Gloriana, and her father's gelding, Zephyr. Charlotte felt like a fifth wheel on a carriage but chose to walk with her best friend and the Colonel.

Darcy tucked Lizzy's hand into his arm. Dun's presence had set him on edge, and the visit from Lady Catherine had nearly sent him over it; so he was relieved to be away from the house for a while. "Elizabeth, I am so sorry about my aunt. She is … " He glanced ahead to the mews that housed the horses of her neighbourhood. " … un*stable*."

She looked up to catch him smiling down at her and squeezed his arm. "Please do not apologize for something beyond your control, sir. Georgiana and Anna hinted at your poor aunt's malady, and I just hope Mr. Bingley and Miss de Bourgh can finally get her the help she needs. Lady Catherine will always be welcome in our home … oh, I mean the Bennet home … and I hope in *our* home as well, Fitzwilliam."

"Thank you, my dear. You have not yet seen Aunt Catherine at her worst, but I appreciate your consideration. She can be dreadfully embarrassing, and certain members of our family want her committed to Bedlam. But the dear lady *is* family; and so, yes, she will always be welcome in our home. I do like the sound of that, Elizabeth … *our home*; and I grow impatient to make you my wife." He steered them toward the door and his thoughts away from impropriety. "Are the wedding preparations proceeding well on your side? Mother and my sisters are frantically coordinating arrangements between here and Derbyshire, and I am jealous they will most likely monopolize your time tomorrow night. Fleming has wisely suggested a relaxing stroll at Vauxhall Gardens the evening following the dinner to give everyone a breather from all the planning. Would you like to accompany me?"

"The preparations are proceeding well; I look forward to being your wife. I will assign you a few minutes of my precious time tomorrow night, and it would be my pleasure to visit the pleasure garden with you. After all, sir, Vauxhall's pathways are famous for romantic assignations, are they not?"

The stunned expression on Darcy's face was well worth her embarrassment at having so brazenly flirted. He stopped short and stood staring down at her in awe. Elizabeth soon became a tad nervous over the ardency of his look. "Well, here we are at the mews, sir. Are you ready to meet Gloriana, 'The Faerie Queen.'"

Having read a portion of the incomplete epic allegorical poem by Edmund Spenser about good versus evil, Darcy knew it was actually written in praise of the intelligent and powerful Queen Elizabeth of the Tudor dynasty. Gloriana, as her name would suggest, represented Glory in the mythical 'Faerieland' inhabited by Arthurian knights, each representing a virtue: holiness, temperance, chastity, friendship, justice, and courtesy. Although Arthur was supposed to be the embodiment of all those virtues, Darcy considered his own queen, Elizabeth, possessed them in good measure as well.

The other Gloriana was a sorrel, well over sixteen hands high; and once again, Darcy looked at Lizzy, a woman of just under average height, in astonishment.

"Do not look so surprised, sir. Even with a mounting block, I still require assistance gaining my seat."

"So, you use a block to mount; but how on earth do you get down from Gloriana?"

"Oh, Fitzwilliam, really. Are you sure you want me to answer such an irresistible question?"

His brows knit while one of hers arched. Because of the nerve-racking position of that one eyebrow, Darcy rather hesitantly said, "Yes. How *do* you get down from Gloriana?"

"One does not get down from Gloriana, sir; one gets down from a duck."

Fitzwilliam Darcy was an intelligent man, but he did not appear to comprehend her joke –perhaps because he was an intelligent man. He blankly stared at her. She sighed and said, "Fitzwilliam, did you honestly expect Gloriana to be a mere pony?"

"She is glorious, Elizabeth … as are you, albeit *down*right silly as a *goose.*"

She playfully swatted his arm. Darcy glanced around for the others, who were at Zephyr's stall; and although he longed for much more, he only dared put his arm around her and quickly brush his lips against her soft cheek. His deep voice vibrated near her ear. "Lizzy, I want to rain kisses upon you but must keep a tight rein on my desire; you reign over my heart, my faerie queen, and I am your loyal subject."

Elizabeth saw the others approach, so she tore her eyes away from the intensity in his. "I have been thinking about The Faerie Queen and the Arthurian legends, Sir Fitzwilliam; and I, your queen Elizabeth, have a challenge for you."

"Once again, I am almost afraid to ask. Nonetheless, ask I shall, since it is what my queen desires. What is this challenge?"

"I challenge you to a duel of punnery."

"There is no such word, your majesty. But since you have thrown down the gauntlet, I must pun-derously accept." Darcy peeled off his kid gloves, flung them to the ground, and silently dared her to do the same. Elizabeth followed suit and boldly stripped off kid gloves as well. The temptation was too great. Her fiancé quickly snatched both her bare hands and kissed them ardently, and repeatedly, while gazing into her fine eyes.

"Ahem!" Colonel Fitzwilliam suddenly appeared next to Darcy. With arms crossed over his chest, he lectured, "Youn-g-loves, now is not the time, and here is not the place, to dispense with decorum."

Lizzy blushed but cried, "Ooh, another contestant! Please join us, Sir Richard. We are about to engage in a battle of puns relating to King Arthur."

Darcy whined, "Elizabeth, you did not previously mention the puns had to conform to a certain theme. You most certainly have an unfair advantage, madam. In fact, I now suspect you have come to this tournament equipped with a prepared arsenal of quips."

"Are you conceding defeat already, Sir Fitzwilliam?"

"Upun my word, I am not! Let the pun and games begin."

His cousin groaned and opened his mouth to protest. Elizabeth, arms akimbo, said, "Colonel, kindly save your groans for after my opponent's puns. Following mine, however, laughter will be most welcome and appreciated."

When the officer asked how they would determine the winner, Lizzy suggested Charlotte would be an impartial judge.

"But I want to play too!"

Jane solved the problem by saying, "I shall not be joining the challenge but will decide the victor. I require a great deal of forethought before forming a pun. I am far too slow."

Quick as a wink, her fiancé was beside Jane; and when she looked up at him, Colonel Stud-muffin winked and whispered, "I disagree, love. I happen to know you are rather fast."

"Richard!" Jane hissed, "You are incorrigible."

"Only because you incorrige me, sweetheart."

Elizabeth shook her head and objected, "Jane, there is no way you are going to be impartial where the Colonel is concerned. I believe the only solution is to return home and have our father adjudicate."

Darcy doubted whether Mr. Bennet would be unbiased. *Good God, what has this woman done to me? Here I am worried over such nonsense as a punnery contest ruling. Where is the old Fitzwilliam Darcy who would have scoffed at such folly? That perfectionist would never have*

lowered himself to partake in a situation where he could be ridiculed,
and that poor man would have missed out on so much joy.

His cousin was thinking along similar lines, and he marvelled at the fate that had so fortunately brought the Bennet ladies into their lives. Darcy had always been lively enough in company of his immediate family and very close friends but extremely reserved in public. Miss Elizabeth was perfect for him and had already been the cause of more smiles on Darcy's face in the short months of their acquaintance than had ever been cracked in his entire life. Colonel Fitzwilliam knew instinctively Mr. and Mrs. Fitzwilliam Darcy's marriage would be a benchmark of conjugal happiness, as would his own with dearest, loveliest Jane.

Of course, once the five returned to the townhouse and explained the contest, Mr. Bennet wanted to participate rather than adjudicate. Lydia also insisted on being included, so straws were drawn to form teams and to determine which went first. Elizabeth was paired with Colonel Fitzwilliam, Lydia with Mr. Darcy, and Charlotte with Mr. Bennet. Their audience, consisting of Sir William, Lady Lucas, Mrs. Bennet, Jane, Mary, and Kitty, would decide the winning team by the volume and duration of applause each pun earned.

Lydia and her partner went first. After consulting with Mr. Darcy, she stood and offered, "Sir Mount had a bad dream about his horse. It was a *knight-mare.*" This earned smiles and a polite round of applause for the little girl. Darcy was proud of Lydia, as she had come up with the premise on her own and just needed help with the phrasing. She reminded him so much of Lizzy, both in looks and temperament, that he felt he was being allowed a glimpse of what his betrothed would have been like at seven years of age.

With his collaborator's approval, Colonel Fitzwilliam, being a military man, stood at attention and pronounced, "When a knight in armour was killed in battle, his gravestone said *'rust in peace.'*" Predictably, Jane clapped the longest and loudest for her beloved fiancé and sister.

Mr. Bennet held off and allowed Charlotte to fire their first salvo. "A knight put his *arm-our* 'round his lady." Sir William and Lady Lucas hoped Lieutenant-Colonel Dun would be their daughter's knight in shining armour and heartily applauded her choice.

At Lydia's nod of consent, Darcy smugly fired back, "A knight courting his lady wore a suit of *amore*." Groans were heard amongst the sparse clapping, and he knew he would have to do better next round and avoid Italian words.

Jane was jealously relieved when her sister stopped whispering close to Richard's ear. Lizzy stood and proclaimed, "King Arthur had a Round Table so no one could *corner* him." A smattering of applause and groans caused Elizabeth to sit back down in a huff. She crossed her arms, glared at her father, and silently challenged him.

"Thank you, Lizzy, for mentioning that very special table. It made me think the knights facing each other at King Arthur's Round Table disagreed a lot because they were *diametrically opposed*." That pun initially went over all but Sir William's head; and he was the only one to clap until the rest of the audience caught on and joined in the applause.

Darcy was out of his depth and relied on his little companion. Luckily, Lydia remembered a recent discussion between their governess and Kitty; and she was able to put forth, "The Dark Ages were so named because there were so many *knights*." The youngest member of the contest beamed as her audience clapped.

Colonel Fitzwilliam thought his partner's brilliant offering would put them in the lead, and the appreciative round of applause Miss Elizabeth received gratified him. Her pun was 'Old knights in chain mail never die. They *joust shuffle off their metal coils*'.

Lydia tugged on Mr. Darcy's sleeve and asked him to explain. "It is a play on words from Shakespeare's *Hamlet*, Miss Lydia. The quote is: 'What dreams may come, When we have shuffled off this mortal coil, Must give us pause.' And I am afraid we will have to try very hard to top that pun, little one."

"But I still do not understand it, Mr. Darcy."

"Remember in the park, when you found the sparrow?" When Lydia nodded, he continued, "Well, the bird had divested itself of its mortal coil. It no longer needed its earthly body, because it had died. Do you understand?" Again she nodded; and Darcy smiled and said, "Good. We are to be brother and sister, you know. So you must never be afraid to approach me if you have a question. Now, let us hear what our other opponents are saying."

"Miss Lucas, do you happen to know which monarch of medieval England was famous because he spent so many knights at his Round Table writing books?"

Charlotte clasped her hands under her chin and gazed in rapt wonder at her friend's father. "Why, no! Oh, but please do enlighten us, Mr. Bennet."

"It was King *Author*, of course." Their opponents thought the two were unfairly hamming it up, but the audience groaned and reluctantly clapped.

Susanna Palmer, the housekeeper, tiptoed into the room, curtsied, and spoke softly to Mrs. Bennet, who then announced dinner would soon be served. "I have advised Mrs. Palmer to keep the first course of stew and biscuits warm until we end the final round. I suggest each team must now present two puns per turn, so we can finish here before we all shuffle off our mortal coils due to starvation."

Bloody hell, this is entirely too much pressure! Fiend seize it, as Bingley would say! Egad, why am I fretting over this inanity? Who would believe Fitzwilliam Darcy, heir to Pemberley, Northumbrella, and the famous Darcy fortune would be involved in such folly? The gentleman from Derbyshire looked around at his new family and realized he had never been happier, and he anticipated spending many more days and nights in such a manner. *Knights!* After a quick consultation with his teammate, he announced, "When those around King Arthur's Round Table had insomnia, there were a lot of *sleepless knights.* So the *straight-edged ruler* decreed his men must, thereafter, practice *joust at knight.*" Darcy could not keep the smirk off his face as he sat down, crossed his arms, and stared defiantly at his wife-to-be while the audience cheered and clapped. *There! Just try and trounce that trenchant triple treasure, Miss Lizzy Bennet.*

Elizabeth stared back and was determined to outwit her future husband. She and her resolute partner, Colonel Fitzwilliam, planned their strategy and launched their volley. "One evening, the roundest knight at King Arthur's famous table, *Sir Cumference,* discovered Sir Lancelot's moonshine operation; and together with his companions, they shattered the *still of the knight*."

Applause was loud and long; but when it finally petered out, Mr. Bennet and Miss Lucas were ready to retaliate. The gentleman allowed the young lady to present the final pun of the competition. "When King Arthur found out about Queen Guinevere and Sir Lancelot, he knew how to deal with the *sworded* truth. He banished Sir Lancelot to Egypt, where the disgraced knight opened a very successful *camel-lot*."

It was hard to determine whether the sustained applause was intended for that final pun or whether the audience clapped in appreciation of the end of such a pun-ishing contest. However, the six judges were all in agreement the challenge had clearly ended in a three-way draw; and Mrs. Bennet quickly shooed everyone out and into the dining room. Along the way she beckoned Lady Lucas aside and said, "I do not usually join in when Mr. Bennet, Lizzy, and Lydia are engaged in their silly wordplay. Be that as it may, I do have a couple of my own to add to today's theme."

"Fanny, I know you do not share your naughty puns with your family. Pray tell, what do you have for me today?"

Mrs. Bennet waited until the others had passed and whispered, "Queen Guinevere nicknamed her favourite beef-cake lover *Sir Loin*." The two ladies snickered; and then she added, "King Arthur never let any of his personal musicians go swimming immediately after eating for fear they would get *minstrel cramps*."

Mrs. Bennet had not noticed Mr. Darcy and Lizzy had returned to check why the hostess was missing from her own table. The young couple overheard the last pun; and Darcy said, "I do not get it."

His future wife turned red and muttered, "You are very fortunate, indeed, sir."

Mr. Darcy would never have groused aloud; however, he had been disappointed to discover the first course was to be lamb st-*eew*. Elizabeth learned of his dislike but knew he was too much of a gentleman to voice his opinion. "Fitzwilliam, please do not despair. I will simply have our cook prepare another dish for you. You do not have to eat the lamb."

Her fiancé sheepishly said, "No, under no circumstances. Please do not go to such bother on my account. Really, my revulsion is too much ado about mutton. I will simply eat the lamb stew. It is time I overcome my dislike. I shall conquer this. I shall."

"You are very brave and gallant, Sir Fitzwilliam. I had no idea this day would be such an historic one."

"I am afraid to ask … "

"Why, today Fitz-William the Conqueror shall engage in the Battle of Tastings."

Conversation at the table eventually turned to the Colonel's appreciation of the fine horseflesh stabled at the mews; and Sir William commented on the exhilarating sight of Miss Elizabeth on Gloriana racing across Longbourn's meadows against Zephyr, ridden by her father. "But true magnificence, Colonel, would be Bennet's pride and joy, his grey Arabian stallion. Khaldun Kahleil is an incredible creature; even I, an unskilled rider, can appreciate his spirit and endurance." He paused to pass the basket of freshly baked bread, biscuits, muffins, and scones back to his host.

Mr. Bennet thanked Sir William and said to Jane's future husband, "Well, son, you will just have to visit Hertfordshire to see Kahleil, although he is currently at a neighbouring estate rather than at Longbourn. You see, I hire him out to stud. Muffin, Colonel?"

The very ladylike Miss Jane Bennet uttered a very unladylike snort, followed by a giggle, and "Excuse me!"

Mr. Bennet raised his eyebrows and asked, "Was it something I said?"

The engagement dinner held at the Darcy townhouse was a memorable evening for the family members, relatives, and close friends who gathered to celebrate three love matches and the eight-and-twentieth anniversary of the birth of Richard Cosmo Fitzwilliam.

Before the other guests' arrival, the army officer had been summoned to his uncle's study where Lord Matlock, Lady Catherine, and their family solicitor informed him of his inheritance. When Sir Lewis shuffled off his mortal coil ten years previously, he had been the final male member of the de Bourgh line. His will stipulated should his marriage produce no male heir, Rosings Park would be bequeathed to his wife's closest untitled male relation not already in possession of an estate upon that man reaching the responsible age of eight and twenty. In his widow's opinion, the stipulation was an heir-brained one; and although Lady Catherine did not have the willpower to contest the testament on Anne's behalf, her disapproval was clearly evident. The mournful expression on the woman's face was a dead giveaway – which, coincidentally, might also morbidly be considered the definition of a will.

Wealth can be a rather touchy subject; so when the Bennet family arrived, Colonel Fitzwilliam, who was still reeling from the disclosure of his legacy, requested a few private moments with his fiancée in order to inform her of their sudden good fortune. Jane was elated by Richard's information but not by reason of his newly gained riches. The young lady was, in actuality, more relieved by the fact her husband-to-be would soon resign from his dangerous soldiering occupation. That he was also very well endowed was a just another advantage to which she could look forward. The Colonel's heart filled with joy, knowing his bride cared more for his safety than for property; and because love can also be a rather touchy subject, the happy couple took advantage of their privacy before joining the others. The well-endowed officer was warned, however, to not dare leave another brand on her skin, as Jane had not the foresight to bring along the high-necked fichu she had used to previously cover the mark he had left behind.

At the massive dining room table, between courses, announcements were made and toasts were given to those being honoured that evening. The Earl of Matlock made public the news of his second son's good fortune; and, with the vintage champagne contributed to the festivities by Mr. Edward Gardiner, he proposed a toast. "The Fitzwilliam family motto is 'Let your desires obey your reason'. Yet I am proud Richard had reason to obey his desire for gaining the hand of such a lovely young lady as Miss Bennet. So, let us now pay tribute to his good reason, the anniversary of his birth, his inheritance, and his engagement." The Earl lifted his glass and looked to where the Colonel and his beautiful fiancée sat side-by-side. "To quote an Irish blessing, 'May the saddest day of your future be no worse than the happiest day of your past'. Ladies and gentlemen, to Richard and his Miss Jane Bennet!"

The others lifted their drinks into the air; and replies of "Hear! Hear!" "Three cheers!" and "Hip, hip, hurrah!" were heard around the table as guests touched glasses.

Lord Matlock then gestured to his eldest son, Viscount Wentletrap, who rose and and happily announced Isabelle was finally expecting their first child. Everyone was pleased by the news, and many were especially gladdened to see the usually surly James smile and kiss his wife's hand. The two exchanged an affectionate glance, and again glasses were raised in congratulation. It is a truth universally acknowledged that a new baby in the family means many changes are necessary; and five months from that very evening, the couple became doting parents and a much more loving couple upon the birth of a healthy heir.

Next, George Darcy stood and said, "I have heard it said 'Anyone can catch your eye, but it takes someone special to catch your heart;' and I have first-hand knowledge this is true." He gazed fondly at Lady Anne and then continued, "I am delighted to welcome into our family the two extraordinary young people who have captured the hearts of my son and my eldest daughter. Marriages made for love are surely heaven sent. Then again, so are thunder, lightning, hurricanes, and hail. So, may all their troubles be merely tempests in teacups. Family and friends, please join me in toasting the upcoming marriages of Miss Elizabeth Bennet to Fitzwilliam and Mr. Ellis Fleming to Georgiana." Best wishes and the sound of clinking crystal filled the room.

Between the fourth and fifth courses, Mr. Bennet arose and said, "First, I must mention both my future sons-in-law are as fine fellows as ever I saw; and I am prodigiously proud of them for choosing such remarkable women for their brides. As I grow older, my lovely wife often reminds me I am an incurable rheumatic; so I wish to pay tribute to our three happy couples by quoting Homer: 'There is nothing nobler or more admirable than when two people who see eye to eye keep house as man and wife, confounding their enemies and delighting their friends.' May you long confound your enemies and continue to delight us with your love." He was about to raise his glass but remembered to add, "Oh, and if a stalemate is ever a problem, I hope you will be as patient as my dear Mrs. Bennet, who frequently has to listen to me tell the same jokes over and over."

With the various wines served during meal courses, and all the champagne toasts, Charles Bingley, seated next to Anne de Bourgh, had become a wee bit foxed; but he stood and proposed his own toast to his three friends and their fiancées. "'No sooner met but they looked; so sooner looked but they loved; no sooner knew the reason but they sought the remedy; and in these degrees have they made a pair of stairs to marriage.' William Shakespeare wrote those lines, and I just recited them from *As You Like It*. But why is it we recite at a play and play at a recital? Sorry. I became lost in thought, and it was unfamiliar territory. In fact, I spent half my time here attempting to come up with something witty to say, so I am obviously a half-wit. Please do not pore over my words, but pour more champagne, and let us drink to my very fortunate friends and their poor, unfortunate brides."

After dinner, the ladies left the gentlemen to their port and made their way to the music room, where the prodigiously accomplished Miss Mary Bennet entertained them with Beethoven's *Pathetique*. Servants carried in trays of sweets, tea, coffee, and hot chocolate; and Mrs. Bennet, who was especially fond of the latter beverage, remarked, "Men are like chocolate … sweet, smooth, and usually head right for your hips." She immediately blushed upon realizing she was in very refined company but was gratified when all the other women laughed, even Lady Rebecca Fitzwilliam and the medicated Lady Catherine de Bourgh.

The gentlemen did not linger in the dining room but joined the ladies during the second movement of the sonata. When Mary's exemplary performance was completed and appreciatively applauded, Fitzwilliam Darcy asked his betrothed if she would care to take a stroll in the garden with him. The night was crisp and clear, and he wanted to spend time with her under the stars and perhaps share a kiss. He helped Elizabeth bundle up in her pelisse and said, "You realize, love, when we reside in Northumberland during the winters, we may have to forsake the great outdoors for the grate indoors. The weather will be colder than that to which you are accustomed. While we can, let us take advantage of this fi-nite and do some stargazing."

They walked in the garden, arm-in-arm, away from the light of the windows in order to better see the night sky. Darcy settled Lizzy in his arms with her back against his chest and spoke softly near her ear.

"Among your other amazing accomplishments, are you also an amateur astronomer, Elizabeth?" When she shook her head, he pointed toward to a point of light in the sky and said, "That, my dear, is the dog star."

"Are you certain, Fitzwilliam? I do hope you are not teasing me, for this stellar lesson must be absolutely Sirius." She turned to face him, and he knew he was about to be teased by the glint in her eyes, the arch of her brow, and the sassy smile he loved so much. "Hmm, Mr. Darcy, I wonder what would be the correct term for a mutual physical force attracting two bodies. But again, the gravity of the matter must not be taken lightly."

"Ha, hardy har. I thought you said you had no knowledge of astronomy."

"Well, my father did teach me a bit, sir. So allow me to test your own stellar knowledge. Which constellation is also an Irishman's drink?"

Darcy searched for a possibility, but having Elizabeth in his embrace distracted his thoughts. "I shall probably kick myself when I hear this. What is the answer?"

"*O'Ryan's Belt*. Really, Fitzwilliam, your knowledge of heavenly bodies is certainly not a force with which to be reckoned."

"I must not decide on my own performance." He wrapped his arms firmly around her and continued, "However, you were correct heavenly bodies have a very strong attractive force, Lizzy."

She giggled and said, "Why do I have the feeling you are no longer speaking of celestial objects, sir?"

"You are a very quick learner, sweetheart, and I am starry eyed. Astronomy lesson over – anatomy lesson next. Kiss me and discover the affect you have on my poor heart. It races whenever you are near, and … "

A footman's "Ahem" cut through the night and pulled the young lovers apart. "Excuse me, Miss, but you are needed inside. Lady Anne and Miss Darcy request your opinion on some wedding arrangements."

The chaste kiss he had bestowed upon Elizabeth amongst the branches of the oak tree in the park had merely whetted Darcy's appetite for more, and he had anticipated and planned for their first passionate one to be that evening under the stars. An embarrassed and contrite footman, who stood fifteen feet away, could hear the gentleman's frustrated sigh.

Elizabeth felt the exasperated exhalation ruffle the curls atop her head. "Sorry, Fitzwilliam. We were lucky to have those few moments alone. There are still many last-minute details to be considered before we all leave Town for Derbyshire."

"I fail to understand why you have to be so personally involved. Our mothers, together with Mr. and Mrs. Reynolds at Pemberley, are taking care of all the preparations for the ceremony and celebration."

"I do not believe I have ever seen you pout before, Mr. Darcy. You look like a spoiled little boy, and I hope our sons will look just like their father."

"Sons, Elizabeth? How many children do you foresee in our future? Similar to your parents, we may be blessed with five lovely daughters before an heir arrives."

"If such is the case, we shall simply have to keep trying. As I said before, practice makes perfect, Mr. Darcy; and I know you do strive for perfection."

Bingley had not corresponded with his sister during the first two blissful weeks of her absence. To be perfectly honest, due to being so wrapped up in rapt attention to Anne de Bourgh, he had not given much thought at all to Caroline. So when a letter finally arrived from Staffordshire, Charles was only a trifle curious why it might be in his aunt's slapdash and slipshod handwriting rather than his sister's fastidious penmanship; however, he was more than a trifle peeved, grieved, and discontent with its content.

> *Dearest Neffew,*
>
> ***Smudge****thing has ocurd of a most serious nature;* ***blot*** *I am afraid of alarming you, so be assured your uncle and I are find. Please excuse the way I right, which has been described as* ***smudge****lar to yours; we both have a tendency to mispell, leave out half our, and* ***blot*** *the rest. Today I am under pressure and am at present tense. The bumble****bloth*** *relates to your bacon-brained sister, for* ***smudge*** *has fled to Gretna Green in Sotland with a fiend of yours, a George*

Wackhim, from nayboring Derbyshire.

Bingley's heart raced while he paced and thought with distaste, *Fiend, indeed! His name, dear aunt, is actually Wickham. Just the same, if he has in any way compromised Caroline, whack him is what I shall surely do!* Steps were retraced, and he braced himself as he sat and faced his sister's disgrace.

*Although we were surprised by the actual elopement, the match itself was not holy unexpected. The young **blot** presented hisself to us at the assembly here in Tutbury the night falling Caroline's arrival, and your uncle and I remembered his name as being that of one of your Cambridge fiends. His familyarity with you, in addition to your sister's prays of his home on a fine estate, led us to believe he was off good character and fairly flush in the pockets. Therefore, we **smudge**sequently aloud Wreakharm to call on Caroline, and Mrs. Teak chaperoned during his visits. We all assumed the growing attachment ...*

Attached growth, more like, Bingley thought as, with the utmost impatience, he instantly turned the page over and continued to learn how Wickham had wreaked harm and havoc on his family.

*... would follow the normal coarse of curtship and engagment. Obviously our conjecture was **blot** and naïve. The two rascals fled Saturnight about twelve o' the clock but were not missed till yesterday morning at eight while we ate. Caroline did **smudge** a few lines informing us of her intention, and your uncle immediately departed in poorsuit.*

*My dear Charles, I wish this may be more intellijibble; **blot** my head is so bewildered I cannot answer for being coherent. I have just now been advised by express post there is reason to fear cork-brained Caroline and her lecherous lover are not gone to Regretna Green at all; and we are now anxious to be assured a marriage between your **smudge** and the **blot** has, in fact, taken place. Unable to locate the rapskillions, your Uncle Bart did discover George Wreckhart is not an astute owner after all, but rather the son of an estate stewart. Imagine our surprise! The Darcy family of Pemburly is* *certainly well respected in this region and very much **smudge**. My husband visited and spoke with the senior Mr. Workhim, who has no knowledge of his son's enloopment. Apparently the young rake was on an important errant for his parent and is expected to return to Pem**bloty** tomorrow. Your uncle is staying at an in inn Lamptown awaiting the arrival of the wretched wastrel and our poor retch of a niece. Whatever the outcome, your sister has now been brought to point non-plus and will have to become riveted to your fiend. If convenient, nefpew, I earnestly beg you to come here as **blot** as possible. Hopefully it will not be long before Caroline reappears.*

Your loving aunt,

Rhea Piers.

Charles Bingley flung the ill-written pages onto his desk, restlessly paced back and forth again, raked both hands through his hair, and exclaimed, "Holy heaven and bloody hell! I have been a friend to that fiend for years, so I know him too well to doubt his intentions. How dare the cad dally with my dear sister! I shall now have to commit Wickhamicide."

He suddenly remembered Fossett was lurking in the hallway and kept further thoughts to himself. Although he would not put it past Caroline to deliberately engage in an elopement, he had difficulty believing his sister would pass up the opportunity for a fine wedding with an attendant and all its attendant finery. But, perhaps, in her current fragile state, neither her virtue nor her understanding would preserve Caroline from falling an easy prey.

I, who knew what he was, should have warned my relatives of Wickham's rakish character. But since Tutbury is a three-quarter-hour ride from Pemberley, how could I have known they would even meet? This chiding and chastising myself for being chary is uncharitable. Chivalrous Charlie, old chap, you must take charge for a change, make choices, chart your course, and give chase. My chief concern is the cheerless challenge of keeping Caroline's chastity in check from chicanery. Once achieved, I can then cherish choking that churlish smirk from the cheeks of my cheating, checkered chum.

"Whew! I am glad to get that off my chest."

Charles was such a charming, chipper chap, he chafed at not being cherubic. He settled on the chintzy chesterfield in the chilly chamber with the chipped chimneypiece and chatted with his churlish valet, childless housekeeper, and chubby coachman. While chugging tea and chomping on a chewy chunk of cheese, he cheerfully churned out chores to those chosen servants.

Preparations for their master's departure immediately got underway; the feat was a fait accompli following forty-five minutes of feverish, frenetic frenzy. Fossett, the forbearing foyer footman, finally heard, "Fetch me a few books at once. Quickly, man!" Bingley was Tutbury bound within an hour, literary works in hand. The chosen literature consisted of two volumes on loan to him from Miss de Bourgh; and at the last minute, Bingley thought to have his dear Anne advised of the sudden, but unavoidable, departure.

Once settled as comfortably as possible in his equipage, he looked at the titles and chose The Excursion by Sally Forth instead of Primitive Transport by Orson Carte. But Bingley could not concentrate. His mind was more agreeably engaged as he meditated on the very great pleasure that a pair of strong fists could bestow on the face of a handsome skirt-chasing roué.

Unfortunately, his sudden departure would not make one whit of difference in his sister's witless affair. By the time Bingley appeared at Mrs. Rhea Piers' Staffordshire doorstep, Caroline's fate had already been sealed with a kiss in a Lambton chapel in the neighbouring county of Derbyshire.

Before the journey to Pemberley, a hiatus was needed from all the harried purchasing, planning, packing, and preparing for the triple wedding. George Darcy, Lady Anne, and their three grown children, along with Elizabeth Bennet and Ellis Fleming, traveled in two carriages to Lambeth, on the south bank of the River Thames. The Darcy family possessed season tickets to Vauxhall Gardens, so the entire party was admitted to the pleasure garden without having to pay the admission fee of three-and-sixpence. Their plan was to stroll around the grounds for a while and then watch the fireworks display as soon as darkness fell. However, the evening became increasingly foggy; and because of the weather, it was doubtful the spectacle would take place that night.

Darcy and Elizabeth sauntered along without direction and soon lost the others. There was too much to be thought, felt, and said, for attention to any other objects such as people, statues, or the increasing drizzle. They soon discussed their first meeting; and the gentleman said, "Lady Catherine was of infinite use, inadvertently, of course. Had Mother and Father not been urgently summoned to Kent, my arrival at Pemberley would have been delayed until much later in the day; and I would certainly have missed your visit. Such a scenario is unthinkable to me now."

Elizabeth added, "Let us not forget we also have Dust Bunny and Pug-Nacious to thankfully acknowledge. Had they not escaped from the music salon at that particular moment, Jane and I would not have encountered Georgiana and Anna. By the time you appeared, we would have already departed. It is certainly a bit unnerving to realize so much rested on such an insignificant incident."

"I absolutely believe we were destined to be together, Elizabeth; and somehow, somewhere, someday our paths would have eventually crossed."

She disagreed. "I am not so certain. The Bennet family usually prefers to remain in Hertfordshire; and I cannot conceive any reason for you ever ending up in our neighbourhood, unless to attend one of our infamous Meryton assemblies. If such had been our fate, you would have shown up impeccably dressed and made an entirely different first impression."

"We have already discussed this on more than one occasion; nevertheless, I am still wretched that I appeared before you in such an ungentlemanly manner. First impressions can be vitally important, and I sincerely regret the one I made was as an asinine barbaric buffoon."

Elizabeth smiled up at him and said, "I must impress upon you a more impressive impression could not, in any possible way, have been made upon me. I am in no humour at present to give consequence to your intolerable belief your buffoonish, barbaric appearance was not handsome enough to tempt me."

His astonishment was obvious; and Darcy looked at her with an expression of mingled incredulity, mortification, and desire. "This revelation is … stimulating. I was certainly very far from expecting my emergence to make so strong an impression. I had not the slightest idea at the time of it being ever felt in such a way and have long been most heartily ashamed of my attire that afternoon."

"Come now, Fitzwilliam. I cannot easily believe it. I know you saw me staring quite brazenly and appraisingly, and you must have thought me devoid of every proper feeling. Then I teased you most unmercifully when Jane and I were first invited to dine at your townhouse."

"Well, I admit I caught you eyeing me rather blatantly; and although I strived to be perfectly calm and cool as a cucumber, my feelings were quite the opposite. I assure you such warm regard was entirely mutual."

"Oh, please do continue and give a faithful account of your vigorous admiration upon first beholding me."

"Are you fishing for compliments, my love? Very well, I shall indulge you this once. At first sight, I wondered how I could possibly withstand such beauty; and when you first raised those sparkling, intelligent eyes, I was well on the way to being lost. I could not resist such impertinence; and then you proved the liveliness of your mind, and I … I thought it wrong to be so instantly attracted to my younger sisters' friend. Nonetheless, I could not stop thinking about you and … desiring you. Forgive me, Elizabeth, but you are a very beautiful woman. When you dined with my family that first evening here in London … well, you must realize the effect you had on me, for I acted like a blushing, stammering schoolboy with a crush."

Darcy looked at his fiancée with great fondness as the corners of his eyes crinkled and dimples appeared. "Miss Elizabeth Bennet, since most serendipitously making your acquaintance, I have been a hanson barberin, a buffoon, a cork-brained mooncalf, an alliterate art admirer, a riled rival, a green-eyed monster with the blue devils, a befogged and besotted sot, an old-fashioned prig in a pickled panic, a dancer not bearing waltz fitness, locked in an embrace with Bingley, locked in a library with you, afraid of what might come from the mouth of a three-year old babe, a sparrow's undertaker, out on a limb, a mortified nephew, Sir Fitzwilliam,

Fitz-William the Conqueror, and a purveyor of puny puns … all in a span of less than three and a half months. Whatever shall become of me once we marry and spend the rest of our lives together?"

"Oh dear. Fitzwilliam, are you getting cold feet?"

"Most certainly not! I have no intention of walking around with brr-feet. In fact, I have been quite swept off mine by you, Elizabeth. I am head over heels in love and not the sole owner of my heart any longer."

"I am relived you have not changed your mind, sir."

"There is nothing wrong with the one I have, madam."

The heavy moisture in the evening air had begun to bead on their clothing and eyelashes; and not being one for mist opportunities, Darcy said, "Speaking of cold feet, we can return to the carriage now if it is too damp and chilly for you."

He very much favoured the idea of being enclosed and alone with Elizabeth; but when she shook her head, he immediately opened his umbrella and was glad, at least, to have an excuse to draw her closer against his side.

"I am fine, Fitzwilliam. Moisture is good for the complexion; and I will not melt, you know."

Five minutes later, she was melting. In order to fully bring Elizabeth under the shelter of his umbrella, Darcy had pulled her tighter; and his hand remained on her waist. Lizzy glanced up and found him staring at her rather intently. To be precise, Darcy was gazing at his fiancée's dewy mouth, wondering whether or not he should dare attempt a stolen kiss. Because of the lateness of the season and the foggy weather, there were not many others wandering the lanes. His decision was further influenced by the fact Elizabeth had previously mentioned that the pleasure garden's paths were well known as ideal for romantic assignations, so he opted for boldness and steered her toward a massive horse chestnut tree. When they were under its autumn-gold leafy protection, he lightly brushed his lips across the top of her gloved hand. Darcy entwined their fingers, never losing contact with her magnificent eyes, took another step forward, closed his umbrella, and rested it against the trunk.

"Elizabeth, there is something I have desired to do all evening and, in truth, ever since I first laid eyes on you. I long to finish what we began amongst the branches of a certain oak tree in another park before we were interrupted."

His impassioned, smouldering gaze caused a shiver of excitement as well as a quiver of nervousness, which Lizzy attempted to conceal with a flippant remark. "Cato is now living in the lap of luxury, so our rescue mission was successfully completed."

"As you are well aware, I am *not* referring to the kitten; and you are shivering from the cold." Darcy repeatedly stroked her arms from shoulder to elbow and back again as he gently brushed his lips against her forehead. She sighed and closed her eyes when he placed light kisses across her damp, rosy cheeks. His deep voice rumbled, "Elizabeth ... Lizzy ... Lizzabiff ... Lisshybit ... Deelishybit."

She nervously giggled. "Sir! In what manner did you just address me?"

Darcy smiled down at her and longingly stared at her mouth. "I believe, madam, I referred to you as Deelishybit, a rare, delicious ... " He interrupted himself to place a quick, teasing peck on her luscious lips and then another on her delectable jaw. His long eyelashes flicked against her sensitive skin, and the sensation matched the fluttering in Lizzy's heart. Darcy whispered sweet nothings and then gently held her head with both hands while he tenderly kissed her eyelids. Elizabeth melted into his warm embrace and steadied herself by grasping the lapels of his greatcoat. He took another step forward, and her back made contact with the tree. Darcy dipped his head and ignited new sensations as his lips found her earlobe and then nibbled up and down her neck.

Again she shuddered as he whispered near her ear, "May I kiss you properly, sweetheart?"

Laughter threatened to bubble up as she nervously replied, "Properly, sir, or improperly, I hardly know the diff ... " Her words were abruptly cut off, and Elizabeth Bennet suddenly felt the world around her disappear into an overwhelming, mind-boggling explosion of colour, sound, and sensation; and she belatedly realized the fireworks had commenced at the very same instant Darcy's mouth claimed her own with tremendous passion and fervour.

As for the gentleman, he was not as inexperienced as his innocent fiancée; and their first real kiss definitely left something to be desired ... more of her. Fitzwilliam Darcy had never felt anything that even came close to that earth-shattering smouldering smooch. When they finally surfaced for air, he marvelled that his timing had been so well synchronized with the onset of the fireworks display. He breathlessly exclaimed, "My God, Elizabeth, that was ... positively ... astounding!"

Elizabeth finally opened her eyes as he spoke; still all she could manage was to nod in agreement and utter, "Oh, yes!"

After being far too occupied to keep track of time, the engaged couple discovered at last, on examining their watches, it was way past the hour to join the others. Darcy grasped Lizzy's hand as he led her out onto one of the lanes.

"Um, that is the wrong path to take, Fitzwilliam."

"It most certainly is not, my darling. I have an impeccable sense of direction, and this lane will indubitably lead us back to the agreed meeting place."

When their course did not indubitably bring them to the assigned spot, the disoriented gentleman looked around in bewilderment. "Perhaps my faultless sense of direction is a bit hazy this evening because of this confounded fog." He motioned for her to take a left turn down what Lizzy was sure was another incorrect pathway.

After going around the bend, Elizabeth said, "Fitzwilliam, your sense of direction is, indeed, impeccable. We have just completed a circuit and have returned to the exact spot from which we left not ten minutes ago. Are you ready to admit you have lost your way hereabouts in the lanes? We can always solicit someone for direction."

"Absolutely unnecessary! We have not passed another soul; and, furthermore, I realize precisely where we are now, so we most certainly do not require anyone else's assistance."

"Well then, which avenue will lead us to your family?"

After leading her along the garden path, the two lovers ended up at a dead-end. Darcy took advantage of another golden opportunity to thoroughly kiss Elizabeth yet again ... and again ... and again.

"Fitzwilliam, as much as I have enjoyed the benefits of privacy with you, we really must return to the others at once. It is certainly becoming quite late. How do we find our way out of here?"

"I am unsure. Kissing you has obviously left me befogged."

"It is not my fault you do not have the foggiest idea where we are."

"I admit my senses are somewhat clouded this evening."

"So you finally admit to being mist-ified and lost?"

He sheepishly nodded.

Despite several hit and mist attempts, Elizabeth finally guided her fiancé in the right direction; and the two met up with the rest of their party. Georgiana and Anna waited beside one of the carriages while George Darcy, his wife, and Ellis Fleming paced back and forth in the cool, damp night air.

"My dear Elizabeth and Fitzwilliam, where have you two been wandering?" was the question they received from Lady Anne as soon as they appeared and from all the others as they approached the carriages. They only said in reply that they had wandered about till they were beyond their own knowledge; however, the guilty couple coloured up as they spoke and awakened suspicions of the truth.

Fitzwilliam Darcy put his foot in his mouth and further raised their skepticism when he changed the subject. "I am sorry we did not join you at the appointed time. All the same, I hope you enjoyed the magnificent display of fireworks as much as we did. Tonight's pyrotechnic spectacle was truly … breathtaking."

Anna gave her brother a puzzled look, Georgiana giggled, Lady Anne sighed, and a smirking Ellis tried to warn his friend with an 'ahem', a frown, and a slight shake of his head.

Elizabeth inquired, "Mr. Fleming, did you not consider it a most dazzling extravaganza of stimulating sight and sound? Why, it was almost beyond belief."

Feeling somewhat awkward, Ellis scuffed his foot and said, "Well, yes, Miss Elizabeth. Beyond belief is definitely one way of putting it."

George Darcy scowled at his son and announced the evening's fireworks had been cancelled due to inclement weather.

Lizzy Bennet and her fiancé turned matching shades of pink. Fitzwilliam Darcy tugged at his cravat and again changed the subject by saying, "Ah, yes, how unfortunate. Speaking of inclement weather, it is regrettable the cooler temperatures at this time of year cause more and more people to burn coal. The fog we are experiencing tonight is not only natural but man-made as well, because of all the smoke."

"Where there is smoke, there is fire," remarked his frowning father, "and perhaps smoke and mirrors, as well. Somehow you two magically managed to conjure up your very own personal fireworks. Fitzwilliam, I hate to dis-*illusion* you; nevertheless, as soon as we return home, remind me to remind you about proper public comportment."

Chapter IV

Aberration, Altar-ation, Fabrication,
Aspiration, and Anticipation

Almost two weeks previously at a country assembly in Tutbury, near the border between Staffordshire and Derbyshire, Miss Caroline Bingley was obliged by a deplorable scarcity of interested gentlemen to sit down for all the dances. She impatiently listened to Miss Endura Chatsworth's blathering until the third last set ended. At that moment Miss Bingley's attention was not at all on her wearisome new female acquaintance but rather on the fascinating young male who had mingled and danced all evening but, to Caroline's frustration, had apparently not been interested in obtaining an introduction to her. He was tall, devilishly handsome, smartly attired, and somehow familiar; but she could not place where she might have seen him previously. Miss Bingley knew he was intelligent and well-spoken, because by then the fellow stood not five feet away conversing with her aunt and an elderly neighbour, Sir Lance Boyle. The three suddenly looked in her direction; and Caroline fidgeted and played with her bracelets while she watched the smiling, swaggering stranger approach.

Sir Lance said, "Miss Bingley, please allow me to introduce to you Mr. George Wickham, the son of an acquaintance of mine and, coincidentally, a good friend of your brother. Mr. Wickham, may I present Miss Caroline Bingley, who is the niece of Mr. and Mrs. Bartlett Piers." The elderly gentleman then introduced Wickham to Miss Chatsworth.

The young man bowed and said, "It is my very great pleasure to meet you both. Miss Bingley, if you are not already engaged for the last set, may I have the pleasure of standing up with you?" He smiled charmingly at her friend and added, "I must apologize, Miss Chatsworth, but not having been introduced to you before, I regret I have already asked for the remainder of the dances with other young ladies."

So, during the last set, Wickham spoke enthusiastically to Miss Bingley about his long-standing friendship with her brother as well as with the esteemed Darcy family, his extensive education at Cambridge, and his thorough knowledge of the grand estate of Pemberley. Caroline was enthralled.

To give credit where credit is due, the hard-working fellow was truly on his way to becoming an exemplary steward. Be that as it may, George Wickham had not abandoned his rakish behaviour. While knowing it was wrong to lead her astray, he could not convince himself to discontinue a seduction. If Bingley had been present, Wickham would never have dared to pursue a friend's sister. Caroline had a lovely smile when she took the bother to do so and possessed a sharp, cutting wit. He admired her audacious fashion sense, and Miss Bingley was certainly handsome enough to tempt him … as were most young women.

And so it was that Caroline met her future husband and was granted her wish of never relinquishing a connection to her precious Pemberley.

Never before the object of such admiration and attention, Miss Bingley let his fawning and flattery go to her head; and Wickham put considerable effort into wooing and weaselling his way in there. He traveled to and fro between Derbyshire and her uncle's Staffordshire estate and picked wildflowers along the way to present to her. With masterly finesse, he smooth-talked his way straight into her heart.

One fateful afternoon as the couple strolled the grounds, Mrs. Ann Teak complained of a terrible headache. Caroline nittered and nattered, jibbered and jabbered without intermission about how much she was grieved, how shocking it was to have a bad headache, and how excessively she disliked being ill herself. She finally insisted the elderly woman go inside to rest and then thought no more of the matter.

Carpe diem! Wickham wasted no time that day and immediately seized the carping young woman in a passionate embrace.

Overcome by the manly smell of shaving soap and his well-placed grope, down the slippery slope Caroline tumbled and breathlessly asked, "Shall we elope and end my forlorn hope?"

Overcome by the womanly smell of jasmine soap and her well-placed grope, down the same slippery slope Wickham tumbled; and, without thought, he recklessly answered, 'yes' instead of 'nope'.

Miss Bingley had dropped all her prior resentment of Elizabeth Bennet and, instead of writing to Charles about her suitor, she took advantage of that lady's kind invitation to correspond. In her letter, Caroline succinctly explained she had never been romantic and wanted only a home at Pemberley. "My dear Miss Elizabeth, considering Mr. Wickham's connections and situation in life, I am convinced my chance of happiness with him is as fair as most people can boast on entering the marriage state. I hope, my friend, once you are settled in the cold northern clime, you will not be blue with envy over my living on the finer Darcy estate. Your also-engaged friend, Caroline." Although usually quite fastidious with her penmanship, Miss Bingley had written the direction remarkably ill; and the letter had been delivered elsewhere and would only catch up with its recipient many weeks later in Northumberland.

The scheming couple met at midnight and headed for Gretna Green under cover of darkness. But Wickham did not get far, neither with Caroline nor with the inadequate spending money he had in his possession. Although very conscientious with Pemberley funds, George had been drawing his own bustle too freely and soon found himself nearly on the rocks. It became necessary to stay at an inn on the second night; and at the lady's insistence, it was spent in separate rooms. Until they were legally married, she refused to give in to any of his further advances. Wickham then had to sheepishly explain to Caroline he needed to return with important estate papers for his father; and because of having to rent two rooms instead of one, his lodging allowance was already spent. They would barely have enough blunt to buy meals on their way back to Pemberley; and after that, he would be run quite off his legs. The trip to Scotland was, therefore, abandoned.

Waiting to leg-shackle the disgraced couple upon their return were Mr. Hugh Wickham, Mr. Bartlett Piers, and the Reverend Mr. Wingrave;

the parson's mousetrap was to clamp down on Caroline and George in a pretty little chapel in Lambton the following evening.

With money provided by her outraged uncle, the uneasy bride, in company with the parson's wife, went shopping the next morning in the small market town for a new dress to wear at her impromptu wedding. Caroline Bingley was in a daze and hardly noticed the pretty ivory gown with palest of blue pinstripes. It was the only readily available option in her size; and the young woman knew she would probably never don it again, for it just did not have enough vibrancy for her taste. Mrs. Wingrave thought the frock was quite fetching and said, "Miss Bingley, orange you glad you could not squash yourself into that appalling pumpkin-pigmented garment? Who on earth would have the ghastly fashion sense and audacity to wear such a horrid hue?" The older woman was mortified to realize her companion was, in fact, already attired in an atrocious carroty creation.

At the chapel later that same evening while waiting for the menfolk, Mrs. Wingrave could not help but notice the bride was extremely fretful. Earlier in the day, the clergyman's wife had the onerous task of explaining certain aspects of married life to the unfortunate, motherless bride. However, the matron correctly assumed Miss Bingley's apprehension was unrelated to that awkward conversation.

When asked the reason for her anxiety, Miss Bingley said, "This is all very sudden. I … am … " Caroline had begun to worry she was about to become a tenant for life with a loose fish. While shopping, she had overheard whispered remarks about George Wickham being quite the rake. Unwilling to admit to Mrs. Wingrave, or herself, that she had possibly made a very grave mistake, Caroline raised her chin and voiced a totally different concern, "I am afraid I will not remember what to do during the ceremony."

"Ah. Well, my dear, it is very simple. You only need remember three things. First is the aisle you will have to walk down; second is the altar where your groom will be waiting; and third is the hymn we will sing during the service." Miss Bingley nervously gulped and nodded her head in understanding.

256 J. MARIE CROFT

When everyone was finally in place, the ceremony commenced. Arm-in-arm with her uncle, Caroline stared straight ahead and softly repeated the three words she needed to remember. As she approached the petrified groom, he was horrified to hear, "Aisle-altar-hymn. Aisle-alter-him. I'll-alter-him." On the other hand, the rest of the tiny congregation hoped it just might be possible.

It was done. Caroline Bingley became Mrs. George Wickham during a wedding ceremony conducted by candlelight. Unfortunately, their passion burned for only a wick. In spite of that, with her marriage Caroline got a new name and a-dress. She should have been pleased by the fact her new address was a cottage on a three-hundred-foot cliff at the very edge of Pemberley's border; and perhaps Caroline was content, or it might have been a big bluff. Regardless, one thing was certain … the Wickhams were a fastidious couple. He was fast, and she was tedious.

Any thought of those two actually reproducing would be almost unbearable and rather inconceivable; so, fortunately for the world, Caroline proved to be quite impregnable. Mr. and Mrs. George Wickham remained childless and childish. Of course, people may only be young once; but they can be immature forever.

While Jane and Elizabeth shopped with their mother and Mrs. Gardiner, Darcy had arrived at the Bennet townhouse and was directed by Baines to the sitting room to await Elizabeth's imminent return. Mr. Bennet read the newspaper while his two youngest children sat on the floor, under the watchful eye of Miss Edwards, the governess. Lydia played with her favourite porcelain doll, Miss Michelle, which Robert's tin soldier was persistently attempting to engage in a kiss.

"Papa, please tell Robert to stop. Mish does not care to be kissed. Gag a maggot, boys are icky!"

"You keep on believing that for another fifteen years or so, Lydia. However, I highly doubt your eldest sister would agree with you about kissing a soldier. I am reasonably certain Jane does not consider Colonel Fitzwilliam the least bit icky. Robert, leave Miss Mish alone."

Darcy was more often at the Bennet home than his own and was already considered another member of the family rather than a visitor. Mr. Bennet nodded as the young man entered the room and picked up a discarded section of the newspaper. Cato the Philoso-fur immediately leapt onto his lap, and Darcy stroked its gingery coat as he perused the articles. After a few moments he commented, "I see the Prince Regent has coined a new phrase. Whenever someone curses luridly, 'Prinny' says, 'He swears like Lady Lade.' I daresay Lady Letitia Derby's profanity could not hold a candle to my aunt, Lady Catherine der Bug … I mean de Bourgh. Her long-winded cusses would make a sailor blush."

Prissy and missish Miss Catherine entered the room, frowned with reproof at the mention of bad language, curtsied to Mr. Darcy, and then said to her sister, "Lydia, as requested, I have done a reproof, edited, and written out a good copy of the foolish folly you and Robert composed."

Mr. Bennet put down his Morning Chronicle and reached for the handwritten sheets containing the story, which was titled The Hanson Barberin. The tale was inspired by Robert Bennet and composed in collaboration with his precocious seven-year-old sister, Miss Lydia. The anecdote was then edited by strait-laced one-and-ten-year-old Miss Kitty, who somehow missed expurgating a certain section pertaining to where a young lady was kissed. Their father settled back in his chair, adjusted his spectacles, and began to read aloud:

> *"Once upon a time there was a handsome barbarian. A barbarian is a barber who works in a library. His name was Mister Daresay because he always said, 'I daresay'. Mr. Daresay loved books. He slept between the covers, wore a dust-jacket, ate from a bookplate, and put a bookworm on his hook when he went fishing. One day his dog-eared hound, Mythter E. Tail, started to eat a spine-chilling mystery novel; and Mr. Daresay had to take the words right out of his mouth.*
>
> *Mr. Daresay did his barbering in the library. He shaved and cut hair for lots of customers who were aristocrats. The library had more nobles than the royal court because of all the titles.*

Mr. Daresay had a good friend who was a Knight. Sir Cular wrote handbills for Mr. Daresay's excellent barbering. Whenever Sir Cular read a book from Mr. Daresay's library, his Page was always at his side. Sir Cular had a sister, Miss Bizzy Lennet. Mr. Daresay and Miss Lennet loved one another very much. One day the handsome barbarian got all gooshy and kissed her in a very private place.

They were hiding behind a bookshelf. They thought no one saw them, but her brother and sisters all did. Mr. Daresay gave each of Bizzy's siblings a pony. Then they all lived happily ever after. The end."

Mr. Bennet cleared his throat and looked over his spectacles to the spectacle of his blushing future son. "Is this enlightening account a product of my children's over-active imaginations; or is it, in fact, based on fact?"

His fiancée had just entered the room and saved Darcy from further embarrassment as she spoke with enthusiasm of the new establishment she, her sister, mother, and aunt had discovered. The combination draper and bookshop had provided hours of material enjoyment as the ladies browsed amongst the text-aisles. Many volumes of ware to wear and read had been ordered.

Red-faced Fitzwilliam Darcy was thankful for the diversion, and he desperately hoped the other gentleman would believe the entire Hanson Barberin story was fiction. Non-friction between Lizzy's father and himself was vitally important. Of course, the notion of him being a scissor-wielding barber was shear nonsense; nevertheless, the truth was he *had* gotten all gooshy and kissed Elizabeth in a very private place, indeed … behind the bookshelves. Drawing on his masterly command of the English language, Darcy said nothing.

The Darcy and Fitzwilliam families were the first arrivals at Pemberley, with the two de Bourgh ladies and Ellis Fleming close on their heels. Bingley showed up early the next day from neighbouring Staffordshire, and the three carriages conveying the Bennets and Gardiners were expected to roll in late that afternoon. The Anglican clergyman, Reverend Mr. Godfrey, was not expected to present himself until the eve of the wedding; and all the guests would arrive following the early-afternoon marriage ceremony. Because the three fiancés had each procured special licenses, their solemnization of matrimony rites did not have to take place in the morning or, in fact, even in the parish church.

The grand estate was in a state of organized chaos. Gardeners, huntsmen, labourers, cooks, maids, footmen, valets, coachmen, and the gamekeeper all had a hand in the preparations. Weeks previously, a steady stream of delivery carts had begun traveling the road to Pemberley from Lambton and London. Although Ellis Fleming and the Bennets were fairly flush in the pockets, it was not every day three members of two illustrious families such as the Darcys and Fitzwilliams were wed in the same ceremony; so no expense was being spared for the special event. Mr. and Mrs. Reynolds directed the flow of traffic as provisions flowed in for the nuptials and a lavish celebration to follow.

Heavy crates of fine wine, spirits, and champagne, courtesy of Mr. Gardiner, were carried to the cellar under the direction and watchful eye of Owen Reynolds. When told where to store the white wine, one footman gave the butler a blanc stare while another servant was ordered to lock up the vintage red wine in a cabernet. Unfortunately, the latter fellow accidentally broke a bottle, and the ruby-coloured liquid ended up on his livery, which earned the young man a scathing look of dis-stain from Mr. Reynolds. The clumsy servant winked at the other footman and said, "This drink is on me."

During the days, hours, and minutes leading up to the wedding, Pemberley's massive kitchen was a very heated place. Tempers sizzled, workers were steamed, and the new chef, Mr. Eggleston, lambasted his cooks. Despite being a cantankerous supervisor who often beat eggs and whipped cream, Mr. Eggleston was undeniably a very gouda chef who created grate delicacies from Cheddar, Cheshire, as well as Wensleydale. Nevertheless, the kitchen workers often referred to 'Eggy' as a munster or some other equally cheesy name. One emotional onion-mincing minion, Mrs. Culpepper, was particularly astir and mixed up; yet she took it with a grain of salt when Eggleston had a beef with her lumpy gravy. He grilled and roasted the poor woman and called her ham-fisted. While Mrs. Culpepper inwardly simmered and stewed, she was inspired to calmly ask what the chef thought about serving honeymoon salad.

Tetchy Eggleston haughtily inquired, "And just what, pray tell, is honeymoon salad, Culpepper?"

"Lettuce alone, sir!"

Eggleston sniffed, lifted his chin, and looked down his nose at the baker, "You need to knead the dough faster, Mrs. Butterfield. It is the yeast you can do, and you should know batter by now."

The baker may have been a gluten for punishment; all the same, when her shift in the kitchen ended, she left with a loathe of bread. The next morning when she started work again, Mrs. Butterfield noticed one of the large fruitcakes she had made days previously had been cut. She was not, however, the only woman one slice short of a loaf. The half-baked guilty party, in her toasty guest bedchamber, chastised her seasoned maid for not having pinched, poached, or purloined another crumby slice; and the harridan's leavened, unsavoury language was most distasteful until the Lady's daughter, Anne de Bourgh, arrived with a glass of laudanum-infused sherry.

It might be supposed he would have been of a disposition in which happiness overflowed in mirth the days before being united in wedlock with Elizabeth Bennet. However, his family, relatives, friends, and servants hardly knew a more awful object than perfectionist Fitzwilliam Darcy on that particular occasion, at his ancestral home with nothing to do but fret. He drove Mrs. Reynolds to distraction with his concern for Elizabeth's comfort while under Pemberley's roof, and he interfered in every minuscule detail of the preparations for the celebration. Darcy vexed Crispin Knott, his elderly valet, when he changed attire no less than four times before finally being satisfied with his appearance the day of her arrival; and he worried and paced because the Bennet carriage had not arrived precisely at the expected hour.

"Fitzwilliam George Darcy!" admonished his mother. "Do cease being such a niggling, nagging, nettling nuisance and simply allow the servants to do their duties without making each and every little triviality into a monumental issue. They are beginning to wonder if royalty is actually expected, and I imagine Elizabeth would be horrified if she knew how you have been absolutely agonizing over her arrival."

Georgiana agreed with her mother. "Really, brother, Elizabeth is quite easily pleased, does not have unreasonably high expectations, and cannot possibly be so very fussy. After all, she *has* agreed to marry *you*."

"My, my, you are rather whimsical in your civility today, Georgie; and my pitiable friend, Fleming, obviously has *extremely* low standards to be willing to wed such a termagant."

"Children, behave! Fitzwilliam, why do you not go for an invigorating walk or a ride to expend some of your jitters? Take Romulus and Remus with you. Your foxhounds have been underfoot almost as much as you and would surely benefit from the exercise. I believe Mr. Bingley, Ellis, James, and Richard are playing cricket on the back lawn. Please join your friends and cousins. Please."

"But what if the Bennets should arrive while I am not here?"

Georgiana was more than happy to provide the answer. "Elizabeth would certainly never forgive such a blatant transgression. You would subsequently be forsaken by her, left at the altar, ridiculed by society, and forced to live out the rest of your miserable existence as a lonely recluse."

"Leave your poor brother alone, Georgiana. He is beside himself. My dear son, you shall not be jilted; and I do believe your father, your youngest sister, this dear, sweet, sarcastic young lady here, and I can all manage the Herculean task of welcoming the royal family to Pemberley without your invaluable assistance. Go. Physical activity will provide a respite from nervous tension."

Darcy obediently called for his hounds and made his way outside but not before he heard Lady Anne mutter, "Your being outdoors will provide a much needed respite for the rest of us, and we shall endeavour to somehow muddle through without your precious guidance."

"I heard that, Mother!"

Darcy and his canine companions took a stroll along the meandering stream, but the young man remained attuned for the sound of carriage

wheels descending the hill or sight of the Bennet equipage crossing the
bridge. With no sign of Elizabeth's imminent arrival, he decided to spare
a few minutes to check on the backyard cricket players. Regrettably,
Darcy and his dogs were about as welcome at the game as they had been
inside the house, for Romulus took great delight in fetching the leather-
seamed ball, thus ending the closely scored match.

When his beloved bride-to-be finally appeared through Pemberley's
front door, roughly forty-seven and a half minutes late, Fitzwilliam Darcy
became overwhelmed by her very presence at his ancestral home; and he
then drove himself to distraction with unbridled thoughts of connubial
bliss. Unhappily for him, Elizabeth was almost instantly whisked away
from his side; and he began to wonder why he had not considered
whisking her away to Gretna Green.

*Our journey to Northumberland would have been much shorter from
Scotland than from Derbyshire, and I would have been spared hearing
any further descriptions of lace and finery from all the females gathered
above stairs.*

Darcy was subsequently besieged by rampant visions of Elizabeth in
satin and lace and deluged with pleasurable fantasies of further wedding-
night conjugal delight.

Upon arrival, Elizabeth had been immediately caught up in a whirlwind
of welcome, introduction to servants, and an inordinate amount of fussing
from Georgiana, Anna, Lady Anne, and Anne de Bourgh. She was swept
away to her sumptuous chambers and presented with her newly appointed
abigail, Ann Cillary.

*Yet another Anne? Surely the number of Annes associated with
Fitzwilliam's family is an ann-omaly.*

Although her opulent rooms were spacious, the bedchamber, sitting
room, and dressing areas were inundated with a flurry of activity as her
trunks were unpacked and refreshments served. Mrs. Reynolds and a bevy
of maids saw to her every comfort; and Lizzy suspected her perfectionist
fiancé was behind all the fluster, fuss, and foofaraw.

The Bennet children thought Pemberley was almost as fine a place as Longbourn, and Lydia and Robert enthusiastically met the numerous Darcy pets with squeals of glee that sent the poor creatures running for cover. When he was denied access to his fiancée, Fitzwilliam Darcy invited the two youngest Bennets to the barn to show them the tabby kittens that had been born in the summer, several weeks before their sisters' first fateful visit to the estate. Darcy cherished time spent with the siblings of his beloved Elizabeth especially Robert, who was adorable, and Lydia, who was a younger version of Lizzy.

The youngsters already loved their sister's tall, handsome fiancé like a brother; and as they walked, Darcy held their tiny hands and envisioned having his own family.

The dark-haired little girl looked up and said, "Mr. Darcy, your family certainly has quite a maginary of animals."

"Miss Lydia, I believe you mean we have a *menagerie*; because I assure you Pemberley's pets, birds, reptiles, amphibians, barn cats, horses, sheep, and cattle are quite real rather than imaginary. In fact, can you imagine an imaginary menagerie manager imagining managing an imaginary menagerie?"

"Good grief, sir. Sometimes I cannot easily make sense of all your wordy words. I may not be able to say maginary min … whatever you said, yet I can spell it."

"Really? Very well, spell it for me."

"I - T."

Tare an' hounds! I am such an easily caught gudgeon. "You are perfectly right, Miss Lydia; and no one admitted to the privilege of hearing your impertinent wit, so like your sister's, can think anything wanting." Darcy then turned to the little boy on his other side. "And you, my fine young man, are much too quiet this afternoon. Is everything well with you, Robert?"

"Yeth, Mither Darthy." The wee tot walked along in silence for a few moments, with his thumb in his mouth, and then said, "Do you hafta kith Libazeth on your marrying day?"

Good God, what now? "Well, Master Robert, that is certainly not a subject a gentleman normally speaks of with another. To kiss and tell is just not proper, you see. That said, I love your sister very much; so, yes, I do hope to … ah, kiss Elizabeth tomorrow after she becomes my wife."

"But why? It hurts to kith on the lips!"

Bloody hell! This is not a conversation one wants to be having with one's three-year-old soon-to-be-brother-in-law. "Ah, poppet, why are you under the impression it hurts?"

Lydia quickly answered, "Oh, I know what he means, sir. That day we caught you kissing Lizzy behind the bookshelves you were moaning and groaning and said '*Oh, Elizabeth!*' as if you were in terrible pain. And then you kissed her neck, and then you … "

"Enough! This is exceedingly inappropriate!" Darcy dropped their hands in order to run his own through his hair but stopped short of pulling it out. *Thank God, we are at the barn. I shall surely be the world's worst father if these two are any indication. The imps have me wrapped around their little fingers already.* "Did you know we have a number of ponies here at Pemberley? Perhaps, if you are both very well behaved today and tomorrow, you might be allowed to choose one to take home with you to Longbourn."

Lydia happily skipped behind the gentleman's back to reach her brother's side. While Darcy hastily strode on toward sanctuary in the barn, Lydia whispered to Robert, "See! I told you it would work."

Darcy and Elizabeth had not been granted a private moment since her arrival, and they both suffered a bereft afternoon of longing for the other's company. Lizzy, agitated and confused, rather *knew* that she was happy, than *felt* herself to be so. She had always imagined being at Longbourn to prepare for her wedding day; and although she was pleased to be at Pemberley again, her life suddenly seemed overwhelmingly unsettled. It was a comfort to be surrounded by the familiar faces of loved ones, friends, and new relations while in strange surroundings; yet knowing she would not be leaving with her beloved parents and siblings when they journeyed home to Hertfordshire was fairly disconcerting. Elizabeth experienced an evanescent sensation she was totally unready to leave her father's affection and protection for that of a man with whom she had been acquainted for such a short time. There was no uncertainty in Lizzy's heart regarding her love for Darcy, yet so much remained for her to learn about the man.

What does Fitzwilliam expect of me? Will I be capable of running our household in accordance with his perfectionist standards? And the estate in Northumberland is so very, very far from home. Silly goose! Northumbrella shall soon be my home. Oh, why does it feel as if I am leaving everything comfortable and familiar for a life full of the unknown? This must be what is meant by cold feet. And what of our wedding night? Silly girl! Every marriage begins with a time of adjustment to the sudden intimacy of living with a spouse, and Fitzwilliam and I will have a week here together at Pemberley before departing on the bridal tour with Anna and Mary. Oh, Jane! Are you having similar trepidations about your own future? I need to discuss these anxieties with you before we part. Will you and I even have such an opportunity for private conversation before the wedding?

Jane desperately wished for privacy as well. She and the Colonel had managed to escape, unnoticed, for a stroll in Pemberley's garden. Miss Bennet, however, did not have any qualms about the wedding night or spending a lifetime with the fine-looking man walking arm-in-arm with her. Jane very much looked forward to becoming Mrs. Richard Fitzwilliam, in every way, and wished he would kiss her then and there despite the risk of being discovered. By doing so in the next moment, Colonel Stud-muffin proved once again he was incredibly proficient at kissing, utterly irresistible, and equally desirous of their upcoming union.

Elizabeth's fiancé, banished from the unbridled goings-on of the bridal entourage, impatiently awaited the chance to see her again. Darcy knew from the expression on his beloved's face before fussing females engulfed her that she was overwhelmed, and he was fraught with the need to comfort her … and to also give an explanation about the pony that would undoubtedly be accompanying her family back to Longbourn.

Lady Anne descended the main staircase and caught sight of her son as he paced and twisted his signet ring. She moved to his side and stilled his nervous actions with a gentle touch on his arm. "Fitzwilliam, Elizabeth and her family are resting now after their journey. You will see her at dinner and may even find an opportunity to steal your bride away for a few moments afterward. It is not unusual, you know, for both brides and grooms to be nervous before their wedding. At least you both have the advantage of knowing, without a doubt, you love one another. That is rare at the onset, and affection often only develops after a couple has been wed for years. Be assured this uneasiness you are experiencing is normal on the eve of your marriage."

"You misunderstand my restlessness, Mother. I have not the slightest hesitation as regards my future happiness with Elizabeth. My concern right now is solely for her enjoyment of tomorrow's events. I wish everything to be absolutely perfect."

Lady Anne sighed. "Of course you do, my meticulous son. I guarantee it shall not be the case, neither during the day of your wedding nor through the course of your lives together. Relax and realize it will not be the end of the world if you have a speck of lint on your coat, a blemish on your face, or a hair out of place."

Without thought, Darcy brushed at his lapel, checked his appearance in the hallway mirror, and ran a hand through his impeccably arranged curls. His mother laughed at his predictable actions, and he sheepishly glanced at her. "Fitzwilliam, Elizabeth will not think less of you should you mumble, jumble, or fumble your way through the vows tomorrow; and in the grand scheme of things, such stumbles are inconsequential. We all make mistakes; and you must learn to not only take lessons from them but to laugh at yourself as well. You are marrying for love, and that is all you need to remember. Lighten up, dear, and enjoy life."

"I am learning, Mother, with Elizabeth's help. What do I not owe her? She taught me a lesson, hard indeed at first, but most advantageous. By her I was enlightened on the subject of lightening up; and although I may not be ready to shrug off being a bumbling, barbaric buffoon, I am making progress."

Dinner was served in the early hours that evening so everyone would have a good night's sleep, and the Bennet children were permitted to be at the table with the adults. Robert was seated next to his mother so she could help cut his meat and clamp her hand over his mouth if he started to blurt something inappropriate. The little boy was behaving well but did manage to upset his cup of milk, which caused his eyes to well up and his lower lip to jut out. Before the child could begin to cry, Fitzwilliam Darcy was quick to intervene. "That is quite all right, poppet. Remember, there is no point in crying over spilt milk. In fact, I am sure Cato cries *for* spilt milk; and you simply must tell me now what mischief the Philoso-fur has gotten into since last I saw him."

The boy brightened immediately and happily launched into alarmingly detailed descriptions of the dead mouse Cato had proudly presented to their visiting minister and the impressive furball the kitten had hacked up for Mary's genteel school friends. Robert then gave an account of the time the little cat had jumped onto their dining room table, in the middle of the second course, the evening surly Sir Lee King was a dinner guest. The poppet was about to give an account of what happened when Lizzy's former roommates from St. Trinnean's Seminary for Young Ladies visited recently when Mr. Bennet interjected, "That will do extremely well, child. You have delighted us long enough."

The two mothers of the three brides had been chatting about their yearning for grandchildren, as mothers of a certain age often do, and had totally missed Robert's eloquent elucidation. "Lady Anne, do you suppose by this time next year one of us might be a grandmother?"

"Yes, I do hope to hear the pitter-patter of little feet again before long. But, Mrs. Bennet, we are practically family now. So, if you please, *Anne* will do just fine."

"Thank you. My name is Frances, but I prefer to be called Franny or Fanny. Actually, I wish for someone to call me Grandmama. Oh, that would sound very sweet, would it not, Lady Anne?"

"My dear Fanny, I have asked you to drop my title. Please, just refer to me as Anne."

"Thank you. I am honoured. In fact, I will be so proud tomorrow that I shall practically be made of honour. Tell me, Anne, are you bringing extra handkerchiefs? I am sure I shall shed more than a few tears of happiness."

From across the table and several seats down Mr. Bennet remarked, "Yes, my dear, it will most assuredly be a day for plenty of eye dew, although I believe the correct response is '*I will.*'"

His wife sighed and looked heavenward. "You see what I have had to endure these many long years? All the same, I cannot complain, as there has been much more laughter than tears. Follies and nonsense, whims, and inconsistencies do divert me, I own; and I laugh at them whenever I can. Nevertheless, I know I shall certainly weep at the ceremony. Oh Anne, we are both losing two very dear children on the morrow."

"Not at all, Fanny. You must look upon the event as gaining two sons. The Darcy family will definitely benefit from the additions of Ellis and your lovely Elizabeth. Goodness, I now feel very foolish about losing consciousness the night of the ball. Elizabeth and Jane are exquisite young women, and you have done a superb job rearing your charming family." Lady Anne smiled fondly at the little boy at Mrs. Bennet's side.

Robert struggled with his fork, knife, and some rather recalcitrant peas while he listened to his mother's conversation. "Mama, what is con-shush-nuss?"

Before Mrs. Bennet could open her mouth to reply, from across the table Lady Catherine de Bourgh responded, "Consciousness, my dear little bug, is that annoying period between one's doses of medicinal sherry."

Fanny Bennet beamed with pride that her son, for once, had not been the one to come out with something rather inappropriate. She was, however, sympathetic to her friend's mortified look.

"Never mind, Anne. Your sister is obviously your own family's joker and is jest having fun with her-elations. Oh, dear! I assure you I am not usually one for wordplay, but lately I cannot seem to help myself. My puns may be sleep-inducing, but I keep *laudanum* anyway."

When Lady Anne indicated it was time for the ladies to remove to the drawing room, her son also excused himself from the table and the men's company. Fitzwilliam Darcy had had quite enough deprivation for one day and was determined to steal away with his fiancée for a few moments. His long strides easily caught up with her in the hall before she entered the room with the women. Mrs. Bennet was on her way upstairs to tuck in her children before she went to the drawing room; and although she glimpsed the couple in the hallway, she turned a blind eye to whatever the two had planned for their final night of bachelorhood and maidenhood. Darcy, drawing near, said to his bride, "Do you not feel a great inclination, Miss Elizabeth Bennet, to seize such an opportunity of taking a walk with your husband-to-be?" She smiled but made no answer; and he repeated the question, with some surprise at her silence.

"Oh," said she, "I heard you before; but I could not immediately determine what to say in reply. I fear my wit has abandoned me this evening, and I am as giddy as a schoolgirl. Yes, Mr. Darcy, I would very much like to seize … whatever it was you wanted me to seize."

Good God! Darcy looked at her face and tried to determine if she was brazen or absent-minded, but he could not read her expression. *You are not the only one affected, Lizzy. This time tomorrow night I will be your husband, and you will finally be … my wife! I am, as Mother described, beside myself.* "Please seize my arm then, Miss Elizabeth, and accompany me to the shrubbery."

Pelisse, greatcoat, gloves, and hats were donned; and they headed for the garden. As they strolled along the path, Darcy said, "Thank you once again, my dear, for agreeing to hold the ceremony here. It means a great deal to my family and me to be away from the prying eyes of society. Had we married in London from the Fitzwilliam and Darcy parish church near Mayfair, St. George's would have been packed with curious members of the ton; and our special day would have been more of a circus than Astley's Amphitheatre."

"I cannot imagine a more lovely location for our wedding, sir."

Darcy smiled with delight and asked, "So, what think you of Pemberley at this time of year, Elizabeth?"

"Your estate is equally impressive inside and outside, as is Pemberley's heir. It is certainly as handsome as I remember, Fitzwilliam, but perhaps not as *green* as during summer. And there is not now that close, hot, heavy, sultry, damp, clinging feeling I recall being present previously."

"You will never allow me to live that down, will you, minx? But come closer, my darling, and discover just how steamy conditions can be in Derbyshire even during late autumn."

That evening the shades of Pemberley were very useful, not for shelter from the sun but for providing cover from prying eyes. After the embrace and kiss that did much to both slake and increase their hunger and thirst for one another, the gentleman hesitantly said, "Elizabeth, I could not help but notice your unease earlier this afternoon. Are you nervous about the ceremony, the celebration, or perchance apprehensive about our wedding night?"

"I admit I am, or was. Yet every moment spent with you finds me less and less worried and more … impatient."

"Lizzy, tomorrow our vows will be made official. Even so, please allow me now to assure you I will *always* love, comfort, honour, and cherish you. And I will forever be faithful."

"Thank you, Fitzwilliam. And I believe you should seal such a fervent commitment with a fervent kiss." Most of Elizabeth Bennet's anxieties were soon vanquished and vanished. She thought the wife of Mr. Darcy must have such extraordinary sources of happiness necessarily attached to her situation that she could, upon the whole, have no cause to be nervous or apprehensive on the eve of her wedding. As the engaged couple disengaged and strolled back to the house, she said, "It was very considerate of you, sir, to provide fireworks again for my first night at Pemberley. That kiss was another truly extraordinarily breathtaking experience, was it not?"

For his part, Darcy looked forward to the following night's extraordinarily breathtaking experience. Like watching fireworks, he had high hopes for interesting shapes, lots of surprises, and banging. An uplifting display could be quite stimulating, but he worried about short fuses and explosive bursts. *Good God, I must return to the house before I combust!*

"Fitzwilliam? Do you not agree, sir?" When he made no answer, she repeated the question, with some surprise at his silence.

"Oh," said he, "I heard you before; but I could not immediately determine what to say in reply. I fear my wit has abandoned me this evening, and I am as giddy as a schoolgirl. But yes, my love, I quite agree with whatever it was you said."

Chapter V

Something Old, Something New, and an 'Omen Pigeon or Two

The night before the wedding, the gentlemen deprived themselves of the pleasure of the ladies' company by secreting themselves away in the library to imbibe and play cards. Nevertheless, giggles, shrieks of laughter, and squeals of delight from the drawing room still occasionally reached their ears and disturbed their concentration.

"Whatever can they be discussing with such hilarity?" Ellis Fleming distractedly sorted through the cards he had been dealt and took a sip of his drink. The young man was still quite in awe of his future father-in-law and formidable uncle-in-law, the Earl of Matlock. Outward calm disguised Fleming's case of nerves, and a third helpful snifter of excellent brandy increasingly caused a shift from tension to a feeling of euphoria.

"No doubt love, romance, and all things *gooshy*, as my son, Robert, would say," Mr. Bennet replied and flicked a card onto the table. "I assure you, gentlemen, any hearts and diamonds being talked of in that other room bear little resemblance whatsoever to the ones being played here. Your turn, Mr. Bingley."

"I think … ," but Bingley's words were drowned out by gales of laughter from down the hall.

Colonel Fitzwilliam rolled his eyes and said, "Have they not heard Shakespeare's line 'Speak low, if you speak love'? Your turn, Bingley. Pay attention, man. Thunder and turf! I swear you are only playing with half a deck."

"Sorry. I am worried about my sister. Anyone can tell the three marriages about to take place tomorrow will be very happy ones. However, Caroline and Wickham ... " Bingley shook his head as his queen of hearts was trumped by Mr. Gardiner's ace, and he felt his sister's happiness might also have been discarded. "In Lord Byron's words, 'Love without passion is dreary; passion without love is horrific.' I am more than a little uneasy and fearful of Caroline's future with Wickham. As you well know, his conduct has not always been quite right."

"Well, Bingley, I suggest you get the upper hand and deal with the black-heart scoundrel. Deck him, if you must; or club the knave with a spade if that would suit you better." The Colonel smirked as he played his trump card.

The soldier's words did nothing to comfort Bingley, but George Darcy's suited him better. "They will be here tomorrow, and you can judge for yourself. But young Wickham would not have tried to elope with your sister if he had not a real regard for her. I hope and trust they will yet be happy, and his consenting to marry her is a proof he has come to a right way of thinking. They will settle so quietly and live in so rational a manner as may in time make their past imprudence forgotten, and I will ensure they live free from hardship while he serves as my steward after his father retires next month."

"Thank you, sir," said Bingley with a sigh. "I do hope any affection Wickham feels for Caroline proves to be more than just a passion interest."

The senior Darcy glanced at his son, who stood at a window. Pemberley's heir stared into the night and absently stroked the head of one of his foxhounds. "Fitzwilliam, come and have another drink. It is normal to be a nervous groom, but do stop fretting and join us. Married life will not be quite so bad, you know."

James Fitzwilliam, the Viscount Wentletrap, said, "Yes, consider, at least, the pleasurable aspects of the marriage bed and the children you will soon beget." He suddenly remembered the lady's father and uncle were in the room and mumbled, "Sorry, Bennet, Gardiner."

Fitzwilliam Darcy began to pace. "I have no hesitation whatsoever in regard to marrying Miss Elizabeth. Life would be unbearable without her, and the money spent for the special license is the best investment I have ever made. I just wish everything to be perfect tomorrow, for her sake."

"Perfection is very hard to attain, young man." Mr. Gardiner gestured for a footman to pour the fretful fellow a drink. "Lizzy has always been an optimistic girl, and she will focus on the positive aspects of the ceremony and celebration rather than on any negative ones. Relax and enjoy yourself tonight."

Colonel Fitzwilliam agreed. "I intend to have a few more drinks to steady my nerves, win a few more hands of cards, and then shuffle off to retire early. I want to be well rested and refreshed tomorrow, as it is the day for which I have been waiting these long weeks."

Fleming, not yet quite in his cups but certainly half-sprung by that time, said, "I thought the date soldiers waited for was March 4th."

"Ah, my friend, you forget I shall be resigning my commission directly after the honeymoon. As stated in Deuteronomy 24:5, 'When a man hath taken a new wife, he shall not go out to war, neither shall he be charged with any business: (but) he shall be free at home one year, and shall cheer up his wife which he hath taken.' It was time for me to resign anyway. I was getting fed up with army food. Tomorrow, however, I plan to be a desserter … a soldier who stuffs himself with wedding cake. Quite seriously though, gentlemen, I have mixed feelings about deserting my brothers in arms during this war against Boney. Be that as it may, I very much look forward to the challenge of becoming an astute estate owner." Colonel Fitzwilliam looked at the man who would soon be his father-in-law and added, "Tomorrow I will be united with a member of a pun-loving family, and I must hone my skill in the use of new weapons. My arsenal will soon only consist of weapons for a literary war, such as the witty zinger and the pithy barb. Gentlemen, the pun is here to slay."

The others groaned, and the Earl of Matlock cast his eyes to the ceiling and shook his head. *This Bennet family fondness for wordplay is quite out of control and obviously contagious.* When the nobleman then asked if anyone was up for a game of billiards, Mr. Bennet stood, wobbled a bit, and said, "I do not have a cue how to play. All the same, I would certainly like to give it my best shot."

Lord Matlock and Thomas Bennet walked unsteadily together toward the billiard room, and the former suggested his eldest son join them. James declined because he liked to play cards, though his father had been nagging him to re-deuce the amount of time spent gambling. Fitzwilliam Darcy knew of the Viscount's checkered past and challenged him instead to a game of chess. The board was set up in front of the fireplace; and while they played, Darcy was surprised to hear his cousin speak glowingly of his expectant wife, Isabelle. Not to be outdone, the groom warmly praised Elizabeth, his lovely fiancée with the sparkling, intelligent eyes. Bingley came over to watch the match; but because of their proximity to the hearth, he soon became overheated and also grew tired of listening to chess nuts boasting by an open fire. If asked for an opinion, Charles would have favoured Miss Elizabeth Bennet as the more beautiful of the two women being discussed. The truth was plain and simple: Isabelle was plain, and her husband was simple.

Before retiring for the night, some of the older gentlemen gave the grooms a few words of advice. Thomas Bennet's speech was a trifle slurred as he said, "Gentlemen, I offer you a small pearl of wishdom that has served this old married man well through the years. Can you guessh the three magic words you must use to ensure a happy and healthy marriage?"

Both were rather reluctant and embarrassed to voice the words aloud; nevertheless, his two sons-in-law, Fitzwilliam Darcy and Richard Fitzwilliam, dutifully gave the obvious answer in unison. "I love you?"

"Excellent answer! Please feel free to shay those words to my daughters often, but the three I recommend mosht are *'You are right, dear.'*"

Edward Gardiner rather gleefully pointed out the fact that had actually been four words and then saluted the three young men with his glass of port. "Here's to a good sense of humour and a short memory."

As they all staggered their way upstairs, Richard asked his older brother whether he had any advice for domestic felicity. James put his arm around his sibling's shoulder and answered, "Sorry, Rich. As far as I know, the secret of a happy marriage remains a secret."

The ladies, having long since retired, were not, however, all asleep in their own bedchambers. Lady Anne engaged an apprehensive Georgiana in a heart-to-heart conversation about matters of the heart and other hearty organs. Jane, Lizzy, Mrs. Bennet, and Mrs. Gardiner gathered in Jane's room for a further discussion of what the brides could expect the following night and during their marriages in general. Mrs. Bennet hoped the physical side of their relationships would be as pleasurable as hers had been with her dear husband of twenty-two years, and she had already given her two eldest daughters separate talks on that aspect of married life soon after their engagements.

During that earlier preparatory tutelage, Elizabeth had been flummoxed. "Mama! You were in the middle of explaining wifely duties and marital relations and abruptly changed the subject. What is this nonsense about not having to settle for only a missionary position? I am getting married and am not at all interested in spreading God's word in a foreign, heathen country. Not once has Fitzwilliam mentioned our taking on such a mission. In fact, he would most likely consider it quite beneath him. Although it may imply we are wrapped up in ourselves, I cannot imagine he and I ever being satisfied in doing such a deed."

Mrs. Bennet had set her straight on the matter but had difficulty keeping a straight face while doing so, and she also assured Lizzy she *could* be rather nicely satisfied in such a position.

Although Lizzy was still a tad uneasy and Jane eager, their mother was more concerned with their emotional well being. "Girls, I am giving you some literature I hope you will consult. The first two are *Sermons to Young Women* by Dr. James Fordyce and *A Father's Legacy to his Daughter* by Dr. James Gregory. Please read both books, and then ignore everything those two pompous asses have instructed, particularly the former. This author, however," Mrs. Bennet held up Mary Wollstonecraft's *A Vindication of the Rights of Woman*, "is an inspiration."

Elizabeth said, "I have already read Wollstonecraft and have even discussed the work with Fitzwilliam. I am entering into marriage with a man who respects women and considers us rational beings worthy of education. Lady Anne has been a strong influence in his life, and he cares very deeply for his sisters and wants them to be well-rounded individuals.

If we are to be blessed with a daughter, I know he will feel the same about her. Fitzwilliam will be an excellent father." Having voiced her thoughts, Elizabeth began to relax again and look forward to a happy life with a wonderful man.

Madeline Gardiner hugged her and remarked, "Lizzy, you are very fortunate to have found such a fine gentleman. Then again, men are like coffee: the best ones are rich, warm … and can keep you up all night long."

Jane and Elizabeth coloured and laughed; and the former exclaimed, "Aunt, I am shocked! But you still have my deepest affection. Lizzy and I are both ever sensible of the warmest gratitude towards you. By taking us into Derbyshire, you have been the means of uniting us with the very special men we shall wed tomorrow. We never wanted to marry solely for status or for the matri-money; and your marriage, and Mama and Papa's, influenced our hope we could really marry for love. Thank you both for setting perfect examples."

Mrs. Bennet exclaimed, "Oh, my dear Jane, no marriage is perfect. We all have our share of vexation, so please do not enter the married state with expectations of perpetual bliss and perfection. Arguments will certainly occur; so take my advice, and never go to bed angry. Just go to bed with him … a lot."

"Mama!"

"I am teasing, Jane. Yet, truthfully, never go to bed angry. Always stay awake and argue until your husband realizes you are right."

"Mother!"

"I am sorry for being so silly. You have found a gentleman who loves you very much, dear; and I am sure your Richard will be a sensible husband willing to discuss, understand, and respect your views."

Jane nodded in agreement and decided to share a story she had recently heard from him. "Although Viscount Wentletrap and his wife are now behaving in a more civil manner toward one another, my future brother and sister-in-law were not always so thoughtful. Richard told me of the time he was traveling by carriage with them to Rosings Park, and the couple said not a word to the other for many miles. Before departing, they had been involved in a rather nasty argument; and both stubbornly refused to concede their position. As they passed a barnyard of mules, goats, and pigs, the Viscountess sarcastically asked, 'Relatives of yours, James?' Her husband replied, 'Yes, my in-laws.'"

Their laughter filtered out into the hallway; and as the Viscount stumbled toward his wife's bedchamber, he wondered what in the world the ladies found so vastly amusing at that ungodly hour of the night.

Elizabeth Bennet was in a bed, under his roof, so near and yet so far. The union would take place in a matter of hours, yet Fitzwilliam Darcy wanted her as his wife then and there. He paced in his bedchamber, restless with unexpended energy, unfulfilled needs, and vascular congestion. Lusty yawns aside, he doubted he would sleep at all that night and knew it would be extremely hard in such a turgid state of frustration. His ravenous appetite was aroused; and although that hunger would not be sated, perhaps there was something he could do about a craving for something sweet and warm. Darcy headed for the kitchen and the desired hot chocolate.

As he had expected, workers were still astir; and loyal Mrs. Reynolds was on hand to supervise last minute arrangements. When the housekeeper inquired why he had not simply rung for a tray, Darcy replied, "Well, in addition to having a hard … time getting to sleep, I was hor … horribly hungry and also wanted to check on preparations for tomorrow."

"Sir, I assure you everything is proceeding as it should. You must not concern yourself with such matters. It is very late, and you should be asleep. Now, what can I fetch for you?" Once his request was made, Mrs. Reynolds prepared his hot chocolate just the way he preferred it and set the mug before her young master at the large wooden table.

"Mrs. Reynolds, will you and Mr. Reynolds be at the wedding ceremony?"

"Of course, sir. Your parents have already kindly requested our presence, and Owen and I are honoured to attend. Now, please excuse me. I really must continue with my duties."

She hurried to her office and went over the list of tasks to be accomplished before she could catch a few hours of sleep. Darcy sipped his warm drink and thought he might abscond with a scone and retire to his bedchamber.

The workers hustled and bustled around the enormous room, nervously glanced at their young master, and wondered why, of all places, he was in their midst on the eve of his nuptials.

Darcy's family, friends, and fiancée were all in their beds, snoozing, snuggling, snogging, or snoring; but the young man did not want to be alone with his wayward thoughts. The servants' chatter, however, did nothing to alleviate his torment; and he caught segments of their conversations as they scurried about the kitchen.

" … and where's the tureen fer that blasted clear meat soup? What's it called? *Consummate?*"

"Nay, it's consommé, *mate.*"

"Ain't there larger punch bowls? I thought we had a *couple.*"

"They're on the top shelf. Careful of your noggin. You don't wanna get *bonked.*"

"Ah, Susie me luv, if yer offerin', I wouldn't mind gettin' *boinked.*"

"Oh, shove off, Randy, and *go to bed!*"

"I've done finished the cider, Kate. Now what should I *make, luv?*"

"Lud, I can't remember what vegetables bloody Eggleston wanted me to pick. Was it potatoes, turnip, carrots, and *ravish?*"

"That's radish, corkbrain! And if Eggy hears you, he'll be givin' you a headache to *sleep with.*"

"Why can't I just leave them apple cores and peelings here tonight? Them horses can wait fer a treat. It's too bloody cold out, the stable's too far, and I don't want to *go all the way.*"

"Oh stop bein' such a baby, and just go *do it!*"

"See this here iron pan? Keep pesterin' me, and it and yer backside are gonna *become intimate!*"

"Well, now, that's a fine way to talk, ain't it? You need to learn gooder social *intercourse.*"

"Don't dare touch them biscuits! I'm savin' 'em *fer Nick, Kate.*"

"AARGH!!!" The astonished servants froze in their places and gaped as Pemberley's heir sprang from his chair and ran out the kitchen door into the frosty night without first donning a coat.

After cooling off in the frigid air, Darcy returned to his lonely bedchamber and attempted to get his mind out of the smutty gutter by familiarizing himself with the beautiful words he would have to repeat during the wedding ceremony. He located his well-worn Anglican *Book of Common Prayer* and found next to it his copy of the 'good book'. He picked up the latter and muttered, "Better yet, I should peruse this one; there are certain passages I should *know, in the biblical sense.*"

The gentlemen had thought the previous evening's female clamour was rather diverting; however, on the morning after the night before, their aching heads wished for quietude and calm. George Darcy was not suffering from the repercussions of imbibitions of spirits but rather from the spirited activity rampant in his home. A giggling bridesmaid, giggling maids, and giggling maidens joined the cacophony of yipping, yapping, and barking dogs. Shrieks of laughter followed shrieks of shock as a wet Maltese, that resembled a drowned white rat, shook itself in Georgiana's chamber; and squeals of delight resounded as the beautiful brides presented themselves to admiring family, friends, relatives, and one another.

Ellis Fleming, Thomas Bennet, the Earl of Matlock, and the Viscount Wentletrap were all a little worse for wear; and Mrs. Reynolds, who was already overworked, was asked to prepare a batch of her remedial elixir. Pemberley's excellent housekeeper had not been bestowed that accolade without having earned it, and the tincture had already been brewed the evening before in anticipation of its requirement. The remedy was in the gentlemen's hands and upset stomachs post-haste; and as the morning wore on, the men's mental capacities proportionally increased from bags of hammers to their normal intensive intelligence.

Mrs. Bennet had heard a new wedding rhyme that was supposed to be lucky, and she insisted her daughters and Miss Darcy should have every advantageous start to good marriages. Therefore, each bride incorporated into her preparations something old, something new, something borrowed, something blue, and a silver sixpence in her shoe.

Georgiana proudly wore her late grandmother's strand of lustrous pearls, and the required silver coin had been sewn into the lining of the left foot of her new pair of dainty slippers. Pretty jewelled hairpins, belonging to her mother, held her blonde tresses in place; and both her silk gown and the ring Ellis had given when he proposed were blue.

Jane and Elizabeth wrapped delicate pieces of lace from Mrs. Bennet's own wedding gown around their fragrant bouquets, and sixpences had been sewn into satin slippers. They donned pearl earrings borrowed from their Aunt Gardiner and blue ribbon garters. The mother of the brides watched as pretty new bonnets with lace veils were carefully placed upon her daughters' coiffed tresses. Mrs. Bennet lovingly kissed her daughters' cheeks and tried her best to hold back tears, to no a-veil.

In Fitzwilliam Darcy's dressing room he and Crispin Knott argued, as usual, over the gentleman's attire. The elderly valet had been chastised over his choice of cravat and knot and was quite put out. "Sir, with all due respect, there is no need for such a tie-rant on your wedding day. Please stop fidgeting and allow me to finish this complicated new knot."

"Knott, I am the one who will actually tie the knot this afternoon. The choice is mine, and I insist upon a white silk knotted in the Oriental. Please fetch that neckcloth; and while you are at it, these trousers have been de-pleated. Please have them pressed again."

Behind Darcy's back, the valet made a face and asked, "Will there be anything else, sir?"

"Well, what do you think about the plain ivory waistcoat? I know you prefer the embroidered one; but I have a vested interest in looking my very finest today. Yes, despite your worthwhile advice, I shall wear the less fussy one."

Knott sighed and peevishly capitulated to his singularly fussy master. "Suit yourself, sir!"

The newest structure on the manicured grounds of the grand estate known as Pemberley was a small wooden chapel with a pretty bell tower. Its construction had been ordered immediately following London's scandalous ball at Matlock Manor, and the local Anglican bishop had consecrated the building just days before the Darcy family returned to Derbyshire. The chapel was a freestanding edifice erected on the vast lawn near a certain seven-foot hedgerow where, one sultry summer afternoon, four handsome young men had encountered four lovely young ladies and three romances had blossomed. The estate's staff had worked long and hard to have the place of worship prepared in time for the wedding. Hugh Wickham, Pemberley's steward, had jokingly mentioned they were all in a steeplechase against time.

On the morning of the wedding, the pretty little building smelled of freshly hewn timber, paint, polish, flowers, and greenery from the orangery. Chimes rang out from its gabled belfry in a most a-pealing and in-spiring manner. A young hawk sat, unnoticed, atop a nearby tree and watched as the group of finely dressed humans flocked to the chapel's front door.

The senior Mr. Wickham had designed, supervised, and physically worked on the construction of the little church; and because Pemberley's exemplary steward was also an accomplished organist, he was asked to play the chapel's small pipe organ during the wedding. Although he had a Bach-ache from so many hours of manual labour, he was honoured to provide the music for the ceremony. Through correspondence, the three brides had selected their favourite pieces from Mr. Wickham's repertoire; and as soon as people began to file into the chapel, he performed *Air on the G String*.

Miss Mary Bennet sat in the left-hand second-row pew with Lydia, Robert, and Kitty. Her youngest sister listened to the pretty piece of music for a while and then whispered, "Mary, is that song by Mozart, the opera-tunist?"

Mary whispered back, "No, Lydia. The composer is Johann Sebastian Bach; and because it is very lovely, please be quiet and appreciate the music."

Miss Lydia tugged at the sleeve of her sister's pretty white frock and asked, "Do you know why Mozart killed all his chickens?"

"Good heavens, Lydia! What a morbid question to ask in church. Oh, very well," she whispered. "Why did Mozart kill all his chickens?"

"Because they kept saying, 'Bach! Bach! Bach!'"

Mary tried unsuccessfully to stifle her laughter, and the prissy Miss Catherine admonished her older and younger sisters with a stern look and a hissed "Hush!" Three-year old Robert Bennet then began to cluck like a chicken just as the Earl of Matlock entered. Kitty was mortified and leaned down to speak into her brother's ear. "Robert, do you remember why you must be quiet in church?"

The angelic little boy with the golden curls looked at Catherine with wide, innocent blue eyes and nodded contritely. Kitty was pleased with him until he took his thumb out of his mouth and said in a very loud voice, "I haf to be quiet 'cos people sleep in church." Missish Miss Catherine wondered whether she might possibly have been adopted, while laughter rang out from the pews behind her.

Hugh Wickham was very proud of the little place of worship that had been built in such a short time. As he played the chamber organ, he looked out over the chapel fondly while he also watched his pews and keys. Upon receiving a pre-arranged signal from Mrs. Reynolds, the organist began a section of Bach's *Wachet Auf* as young Evan Gardiner escorted Mrs. Frances Bennet and Lady Anne Darcy to their seats in the front rows.

Reverend Mr. Godfrey, Fitzwilliam Darcy, Ellis Fleming, and Colonel Richard Fitzwilliam entered the chapel from a side door while Hugh Wickham played Bach's *Largo*. The clergyman led the three grooms to wait nervously, excitedly, and eagerly at the front of the church for the women who would soon be their wives.

Darcy was, as might be expected, devastatingly handsome in a spotless navy blue tailcoat and matching neatly pressed trousers. A pristine silk cravat was neatly knotted in the Oriental style around the high collar of his white shirt, over which he wore an unadorned ivory waistcoat. Fitzwilliam was not at all nervous but rather impatient to be done with the ceremony that would finally make Elizabeth his wife.

The Colonel was impeccably dressed in full regimentals for the final time, as he would be resigning from the army after returning from his honeymoon. His face gleamed, as did his highly polished tall black boots and the brass buttons and medals on his red coat. A sword, encased in an ornate scabbard, dangled on his right side, just in case he had to fight off any barbarians. As he waited for Jane, Richard's feelings were those of triumph at having won such a beautiful, kind-hearted, passionate woman and excitement at the thought of beginning a whole new life with her at Rosings Park.

Raven-haired Fleming had chosen a grey tailcoat with black velvet collar, black trousers, grey linen waistcoat, and a white cotton shirt with a matching linen neckcloth. Mesmerizing blue eyes watched for his bride's entrance as his emotions vacillated between nervousness and thrill. Ellis remembered that on the day he met Georgiana he had desperately wanted to make a good first impression. He unconsciously grinned as he thought, *Who knew that green slime, clinging clothing, and a malodorous stench would appeal to the lovely, refined Miss Darcy?*

Anne de Bourgh entered on Charles Bingley's arm, and the two witnesses walked down the aisle to Bach's *Sheep May Safely Graze*. They parted at the altar with a parting look of unadulterated love, with the lady keeping to the left and the gentleman to the right.

Canon in D by Johann Pachelbel resounded in the little chapel as Miss Anna Darcy entered with Dust Bunny, Pug-Nacious, and Remus. Georgiana had insisted at least some of their pets be involved in the rites; and the Reverend Mr. Godfrey could hardly refuse, although he did request the canines not be permitted to run amok during the ceremony. The dogs had been bathed, brushed, and bedecked; and Anna, who kept a tight rein on the three braided ribbon leashes, made sure the dogs were under restraint.

Some members of the small congregation were surprised pets had been allowed to participate in the solemn Solemnization of Matrimony, but only one person was truly shocked and appalled. Mrs. Caroline Wickham sat, with her husband, on the right-hand side of the chapel; and her expression indicated she had a mouthful of something she desperately wished to expectorate. The unfortunate truth about Mrs. Wickham was the bad taste in her mouth was nothing compared to her bad taste in clothing; and her outlandish orange organza outfit was quite out of place amongst the tasteful soft-hued dresses of the other young ladies in attendance that afternoon.

The silky white Maltese wore a satin ribbon tied in a pretty bow around its neck; and the pale blue collar not only matched the gown worn by Dust Bunny's owner, but it also held Georgiana's golden wedding band. Likewise, Pug-Nacious sported a ribbon of silver similar to Miss Jane Bennet's dress; and the little dog's bow held her ring. Fitzwilliam Darcy had flatly refused to have his Foxhound, Remus, suffer the indignity of a satin ribbon bow. Therefore, Anna had crafted a little drawstring bag from a piece of ivory fabric; and the pouch on the pooch's leather collar contained Elizabeth's wedding band.

Hugh Wickham happily performed Purcell's *Trumpet Tune* as soon as he received Mrs. Reynolds' tacit signal the first bride was ready to make her entrance. Georgiana stood in the doorway a moment until George Darcy proudly took her arm and began to slowly walk his lovely middle child down the aisle. Miss Darcy was a vision in palest blue silk trimmed in delicate ivory lace, and she carried a pretty bouquet of pink peonies.

The Misses Jane and Elizabeth Bennet had jointly agreed upon Clarke's *Trumpet Voluntary* for their processional, and both ladies carried beautiful bouquets of Damask roses wrapped in their mother's lace. Thomas Bennet greeted his two eldest daughters with a smile, but tears quickly welled in the gentleman's eyes due to their beauty and the knowledge he was about to lose those dear offspring to the young bucks who stood at the front of the chapel. With Lizzy in embroidered ivory satin on his left and Jane in shimmering silver silk on his right, he proudly led his beloved children toward the altar and their futures.

The three brides were stunning in their silk and satin creations, and each wore a small lace-veiled cap that matched the colour of her dress. For the most part, the small congregation smiled lovingly upon the beautiful young women. However, Lady Catherine de Bourgh's smile was, more accurately, a laudanum-induced grin. Mrs. Caroline Wickham's smile was obviously forced, while her husband wore a blatantly lecherous smirk. Viscount Wentletrap actually scowled, for his wife had rather rudely nudged him awake from a most delightful dream. The wide eyes of Robert and Lydia Bennet twinkled at the sight of their fairytale-princess sisters on their marrying day, and the trio of grooms absolutely beamed as they watched their lovely fiancées finally enter the chapel and sedately walk toward them.

As the last strains of music faded into silence, the Reverend Mr. Godfrey began, "Dearly beloved, we are gathered together here in the sight of God, and in the face of this congregation, to join this Man and this Woman, this Man and this Woman, and this Man and this Woman in holy Matrimony." The young clergyman was extremely nervous about performing the unusual triple ceremony for the illustrious Darcy and Fitzwilliam families and was worried he would make a clerical error by mixing up the brides and grooms. He wiped his brow with a handkerchief and prayed he would not confuse any of their names and marry the wrong man and woman.

"Richard Cosmo Fitzwilliam, wilt thou have this Woman to thy wedded Wife to live together after God's ordinance in the holy estate of Matrimony? Wilt thou love her, comfort her, honour, and keep her in sickness and in health; and, forsaking all other, keep thee only unto her, so long as ye both shall live?"

The Colonel smiled lovingly at Jane and resisted an overwhelming urge to caress her lovely face. "Yes. Yes, I will."

"Jane Augusta Bennet, wilt thou have this Man to be thy wedded Husband … "

And so it went, with the same being repeated for Ellis Leander Fleming and Georgiana Claire Darcy and also for Fitzwilliam George Darcy and Elizabeth Frances Bennet. The Minister then said, "Who giveth these Women to be married to these Men?"

George Darcy kissed Georgiana's hand and then sat with Lady Anne in the front pew. Likewise, Thomas Bennet kissed both his daughters on their soft cheeks and took his place on the other side of the chapel beside his wife.

Miss Anne de Bourgh gathered the brides' three bouquets to hold and took the opportunity to also momentarily hold the loving gaze of the handsome Charles Bingley.

Colonel Fitzwilliam and Jane Bennet were the first to plight their troth to one another; and then the Minister had the next couple join their right hands.

His hands might have been trembling, but his voice was steady and strong as the next groom fervently said, "I, Ellis Fleming, take thee,

Georgiana Darcy, to my wedded Wife, to have and to hold from this day forward, for better for worse, for richer for poorer, in sickness and in health, to love and to cherish, till death us do part, according to God's holy ordinance; and thereto I plight thee my troth."

After Georgiana, and then Fitzwilliam and Elizabeth all had their turns, the couples then loosed their hands; and Bingley, with Miss Anna's assistance, untied Jane Bennet's ring from the pug's silver bow and passed it to the Colonel. The rites continued until it was the last couple's turn.

Bingley retrieved the wedding band from Remus' drawstring bag and put it into Darcy's waiting palm. The groom passed it to the minister, who blessed it; and then the Reverend delivered Elizabeth Bennet's gold ring back to the groom. After the band had been bandied about, Darcy then tenderly slid it upon the fourth finger of his bride's hand. As he held the ring in place, there was no stony, unreadable expression on Fitzwilliam Darcy's face. Everyone in the chapel could plainly see the look of pure adoration as he gazed into Lizzy's eyes and lovingly said, "With this Ring I thee wed, with my Body I thee worship, and with all my worldly Goods I thee endow: In the Name of the Father, and of the Son, and of the Holy Ghost. Amen."

The couples then knelt, and gasps were heard from the congregation. Before they had a chance to turn around to investigate, Elizabeth and Darcy were shocked when a long muzzle suddenly pushed its way between them. The Foxhound's sweet expression made everyone laugh as Remus proudly sat beside his master and stared adoringly at Darcy. A crimson-faced Miss Anna apologized profusely and quickly took charge of her brother's dog again. The Reverend Mr. Godfrey rolled his eyes heavenward, wiped his brow, and said to the congregation, "Apparently the canine was just following his own dogma. Let us pray."

After the prayer, the minister joined the right hands of each couple and said, "Those whom God hath joined together let no man put asunder. Forasmuch as Richard Fitzwilliam and Jane Bennet, … ah, Fitzwilliam Darcy and Elizabeth Bennet, … and ah, Ellis Fleming and Georgiana Darcy … " *Please God, allow me to have married the correct couples only to one another!* " … have consented together in holy Wedlock, and have witnessed the same before God and this company, and thereto have given and pledged their troth either to other, and have declared the same by giving and receiving of a Ring, and by joining of hands; I pronounce that they be Man and Wife together, In the Name of the Father, and of the Son, and of the Holy Ghost. Amen."

The beautiful service continued; and finally the witnesses, Mr. Bingley and Miss de Bourgh, happily added their signatures to those of the relieved minister and the ecstatic newlyweds into the marriage register while Hugh Wickham performed Bach's *Arioso*.

When chapel bells began to chime, servants from the great house, Pemberley's tenants, and its workers gathered outside the little church for a quick glimpse of the three happy couples and to offer their best wishes before scurrying back to their duties; and neighbours and friends from surrounding estates and from Lambton began to arrive for the celebration.

As the brides and grooms exited the church, a covey of six white homing doves was released by the gamekeeper, while strains of Bach's *Jesu, Joy of Man's Desiring* followed the human flock outside. Ancient and revered symbols of peace, purity and innocence, new beginnings and hope for the future, white doves remain loyal to their mates for life and are devoted partners and parents and also represent unending love, fidelity, and fertility.

Lady Anne Darcy had thought it would be a clever idea for birdseed to be tossed at the newlyweds. The kind-hearted woman was, after all, a nurturing soul who was concerned about her fine-feathered friends as the weather turned colder. However, the flock of doves, the very embodiment of peace and harmony, decided to stage a coo. As the seeds were flung upward at the newlyweds, the gesture attracted a flurry of avian activity over the congregation of finely attired guests; and Mrs. Caroline Wickham was the fortunate recipient of the intestinal contents from several of the released covey. It was, perhaps, not universally acknowledged that good luck would follow such a fowl deed; but some people did have faith in such a belief. The tangerine-togged woman shuddered as a white dove circled, dove, and then perched on her shoulder. As jubilant Colonel Fitzwilliam passed by, he said, "My dear Mrs. Wickham, do not kiss birds; for you might get an untweetable canarial disease."

While Dust Bunny and Pug-Nacious yipped, yapped, and ran circles around the congregation's feet, the young hawk that had been perched atop a nearby tree was not after birdseed but rather the fascinating little morsel on the ridiculous bonnet worn by Lady Catherine de Bourgh. The bird of pray was disappointed to find an ornamental canary on the bonnet was most certainly not worth two in the bush. The raptor also discovered Lady Catherine de Bird had a rather fowl mouth for someone who had just been in a House of God ... her language being more suited to a warship than a place of worship.

Chapter VI

Marital Elations and Relations

It was an afternoon of no common delight to them all. The satisfaction of the newlyweds gave a glow of such sweet animation to their faces as made the brides look more beautiful than ever and the grooms the handsomest young men that ever were seen.

The gentlemen in attendance pronounced Fitzwilliam Darcy to be a fine figure of a man and admired his wife's fine figure. The ladies declared that Elizabeth Darcy had a very agreeable countenance and counted her husband amongst the most agreeable of men, and the newlywed couple was looked at with great admiration for the whole afternoon. As the joyous Mr. and Mrs. Fitzwilliam Darcy mingled with the crowd outside the chapel, the groom worried his proud, loving heart might actually rupture with rapture. His eyes scarcely strayed from his wife; and the ladies, as well as the lady herself, sighed at the adoring, lustful looks he bestowed upon his bride.

As they strolled toward the house, hand in hand, Fitzwilliam smiled down at her and said, "Words utterly fail to express how ardently I love you; for love you I do, Elizabeth Darcy, with all my heart and soul, and always will."

Her eyes shone back at him as she teased. "Hmm, I have heard *almost* those exact sentiments before, have I not? Perhaps you are employing another man's words. Regardless, I assure you I return equal measure of what you feel. In fact, my cup runneth over with love for you, *my husband.*"

"I have heard almost those exact sentiments before, have I not, madam? Still and all, they sound even sweeter today than on the night of the ball, for I esteem my new title of husband very much, *my wife.*"

Elizabeth squeezed his arm and gathered her thoughts. "Fitzwilliam, I am exceedingly elated, enthralled, ebullient, enamoured, euphoric, ecstatic, effervescent, excessively exhilarated, enthusiastic, enchanted, eager, exultant, and earnestly excited." She gave her husband the saucy grin and arched eyebrow combination.

Darcy's own eyebrows shot up. "Egregiously and embarrassingly effusive also! Your elaborate, embellished and exaggerated elocution and euphonic enunciation are eloquent, my exquisite Elizabeth. You exude exuberance; and I entirely, emphatically, and energetically empathize and shall endeavour to emulate your exceptional encomium until enervation exhausts and enfeebles my effectiveness." Darcy smirked as the sassy smile was wiped from his wife's face.

She gazed at him in astonishment. "Egad! You, my esteemed esquire, are the very epitome and embodiment of enriched and enhanced erudite encyclopaedic enlightenment. Equality in education is not encouraged; and while you are emboldened, equipped, and empowered, my English is embryonic and effete. It encumbers me in this entertaining exercise and entirely enables you to effectively emerge from this extemporization in exclusive eminence." *But surely you are done now, husband.*

Fitzwilliam Darcy was nonplussed but allowed it to neither show nor discourage him. "Elizabeth, you enliven, enrapture, and enkindle me and also upset my equilibrium and equanimity. Enough, I expostulate and entreat you! This extraordinary exhibition is evoking an extreme exigency, and I may explode. Let us eschew this epic, exasperating, esoteric embroilment and employ our estimable efforts elsewhere to essentially escape and engage in an enjoyable embrace and exchange explicit expressions of endearment ere our evening is encompassed by everyone else extravagantly expounding on, exulting, exalting, and extolling our enviable espousal." His wife was then on the receiving end of an infuriatingly challenging look.

"Elude and elope … excellent!" exclaimed Elizabeth. They exited the elite estate without explanation, etiquette, or excuse and executed an expeditious excursion to expel and eliminate extraneous elementary emotions. Ensconced under an enshrouding elm engraved with "EB & FD," they were encased, enveloped, entwined, and encircled in each other's arms; and exactly eleven exemplary, engrossing minutes elapsed ere they eventually and elegantly made an entrance as each envisioned an enticing, erotic, and early encore.

The exquisite Mrs. Jane Fitzwilliam was practically giddy with excitement and happiness as she walked arm-in-arm with her gorgeous, red-coated husband across the very lawn where she had first secretly admired his handsome face and masculine physique. Jane felt an overwhelming passion and caring for that exceptionally special man, and tears of happiness suddenly welled in her blue eyes and threatened to spill upon her rosy cheeks.

After the solemnization of his marriage, Colonel Richard Fitzwilliam could not but feel proud Jane had accepted his hand before learning of his inheritance. It was obvious she truly cared for the man inside the uniform, regardless of his excellent connections or wealth; and he was thankful his devotion was reciprocal. Her beauty, faith in him, and delicate gloved hand on his arm provoked feelings of protectiveness, overpowering tenderness, and mounting desire.

After receiving congratulations from the congregation, the three couples had been besieged by well-wishers waiting for them on the lawn outside the chapel. The Colonel had dutifully, respectfully, and enthusiastically kissed and shook hands, bowed, smiled, and thanked everyone; and all the while he strategically planned a tactical manoeuvre to capture a few clandestine moments with his bride, a vision in slinky, silvery silk.

When they finally escaped from the throng, he steered Jane away from Pemberley's front entrance toward a side entry leading to the library. Once inside, he cupped her precious face in his strong hands and just stood there gazing in rapt wonder. *My God, this gorgeous gentlewoman is actually now and forever my wife!* "Jane, sweetheart, I very much long to kiss your inviting lips; yet I am afraid if I begin, we will not be celebrating our marriage in public but rather in an especially private manner."

"Richard! As persuasive as you are, we cannot simply disappear from our own wedding celebration. Surely you are not serious?" She gently pushed him away, uncertain whether he was teasing or in earnest.

"I am seriously considering heaving you over my shoulder and carrying you upstairs this very moment, my enchanting wife."

"You will do no such thing!"

"Oho, what is this now? Another facet of my demure yet passionate, quiet but brazen Jane? Married hardly … " The Colonel checked his fob watch. " … thirty minutes, and already I am met head-on with her shrewish side." Richard could scarcely maintain a straight face yet crossed his arms over his impressive chest and stood his ground.

Mrs. Fitzwilliam tapped her dainty foot and tried to glower at her husband, but her lips twitched and betrayed her amusement.

"Jane, do you have any perception of how beautiful you are with your colour high and eyes flashing in that provocative manner? However, you are right, dear." *See, Mr. Bennet? Already I have made use of your invaluable advice.* "Come, my love, we must now share in the celebration of our nuptials, dance, partake of some fine food and wine … " He waggled his eyebrows. " … and fortify ourselves for tonight."

The Colonel clasped her hand and started to walk in the direction of the door. Jane stopped him by throwing her arms around his neck and kissing him passionately. When they surfaced for air, she said, "Richard, you are my rock; yet every now and then I wish you were a little boulder. I did not mean to imply we must return *immediately*. I cannot imagine we have been missed already, and I do *not* require any fortification."

He gradually backed her into the corner. "Speaking of fortification, mine weakened when I met you. As a soldier, I identified with Shakespeare's character, Benedick, in *Much Ado About Nothing*. I believe his line was 'When I said I would die a bachelor, I did not think I should live till I were married.' You, my bewitching woman, easily invaded the walls of this poor soldier's soul. I had no weapons to use against the capture of my heart; for you laid siege, and it was seized without a fight. Resistance was futile, and I surrendered. But tonight, my lovely Jane … " Richard interrupted himself to thoroughly kiss her before he continued. "Tonight you will finally surrender to me."

Jane breathlessly whispered against his ear, "Tonight, my handsome barbarian, will not be about surrender or submission. I am your wife and you are my husband. Society may not look upon us as equals, yet in our private chambers I expect a harmonious union."

They did not, at that point, return to the celebration of their nuptials in the ballroom as intended. The Colonel and Jane thought they were well secluded and concealed in a corner of the library, so, the snogging newlyweds were startled and mortified to hear an excited voice nearby. "Papa, look! We found them! And Janie and KerFitz are kithing! It does not hurt, though. Mither Darthy told me so."

Dazed and confused, Colonel Fitzwilliam disengaged himself from his wife's swollen lips and slowly turned around to face her stern father and grinning little brother. Robert walked up to Richard, tugged on his red sleeve, and said, "KerrFitz, do you have any ponies?"

Mr. Bennet cleared his throat and said, "And I wonder if you have any *sense*! I understand your enthusiasm, young man; however, this is neither the time nor the place. I recommend you return to the festivities currently taking place in *your* honour and refrain from overtly embracing my daughter in public."

"With all due respect, sir, Jane is now my wife. I apologize for any perceived indiscretion; even so, Pemberley's library is definitely *not* a public venue. Nonetheless, we were just about to attend our celebration. Shall we, my dear?" He offered an arm to his blushing bride; but before leaving the room, he said, "Mr. Bennet, I very much respect your daughter, my wife. Today I vowed before God, you, and the rest of the congregation to love, comfort, and cherish Jane. She is mine, and I am hers, to have and to hold from this day forward; and that is all we were doing here, holding and cherishing one another."

"Yes, well, very good. Carry on then … " He watched them depart and muttered to empty air, " … just not where I shall have to witness it!" Mr. Bennet frowned down at his wide-eyed son and said, "Now, about this business of kissing and ponies, poppet … "

Before Jane and Richard entered the ballroom, the gentleman glanced at his wife's neck and shamefacedly suggested she might want to retrieve a fichu from her room to put on before joining the others.

"Oh, Richard! Not again! Whatever am I going to do with you?" Knowing full well what she was going to do with him later, Colonel Stud-muffin rakishly waggled his eyebrows.

Jane turned to go upstairs; but Richard suddenly caught her arm, frowned, and said, "My lovely wife, did you, by any chance, call me a handsome ... *barbarian* a few moments ago?"

Ellis Fleming's chest puffed with pride as he and Georgiana strolled around the room chatting with their guests. *This beautiful woman, so kind, so elegant, yet feisty, is finally mine; and I am the most fortunate man alive.* He smiled down at her with an expression of deepest respect and affection and felt another thrill of desire as she returned his ardent regard.

The former Miss Darcy hardly remembered the ceremony, or which guests had spoken with her, or how she had responded to them. Georgiana was lost in a blur of bliss and exhilaration. Whenever her handsome, raven-haired husband looked at her, she blushed at the feelings he provoked. Georgiana knew their marriage would be one of mutual love, tenderness, respect, and passion.

It had been a heart-warming wedding ceremony, charged with emotion; and many of the ladies, not to mention a few weepy gentlemen, needed their handkerchiefs before the service was finished. Tears of happiness were still being wiped away during the celebration that followed, and even the pretty wedding cake was in tiers.

Lady Catherine de Bourgh blissfully sat alone at a table near the balcony and watched the world go by. After the hawk and hat debacle, Charles Bingley had been thoughtful enough to inquire whether she required a dose of her special sherry; and the medicated woman was pleased Anne's suitor was so excessively attentive to her needs. *Why, here is my dear Mr. Bing now with a piece of fruitcake for me. So sweet, full-bodied, spicy, rich, spirited, delicious, and sinfully tempting.* She began to cackle hysterically when she could not recollect whether she was, in reality, describing the man or the wedding cake.

After his delivery to Lady Catherine, Charles Bingley fetched two more plates of cake and passed one to Miss de Bourgh as he sat down across from her at a small table near the balustrade. The ceremony had filled the lovesick fellow with hope and enthusiasm for his own future happiness, yet he was concerned about Anne's unusual quietude since they left the chapel. He eagerly watched as she daintily lifted her fork and tasted the fruitcake.

Anne Catriona de Bourgh, who had witnessed the three marriages alongside Mr. Bingley, was pleased to have performed that honour for her relatives and friends. However, she longed for her own special day. *Yes, a beautiful dress, a new pair of shoes, a golden ring, and a Charles Bingley would set me up forever.* She noticed her mother was already going back for a second serving of fruitcake and that her beau was staring. "Mr. Bingley, why do you scrutinize me so? Do I have bird droppings on my shoulder, unsightly nasal hair, or something stuck in my teeth?"

"Anne, you are so elegantly eloquent and classy. I was merely wondering whether you like the fruitcake, for I believe your slice contains a very special ingredient."

Miss de Bourgh scoffed and took another forkful. Bingley's blue eyes grew even wider than usual, and he feared his scheme had been an ill-conceived one. "Ah, perhaps you should not … ingest that particular … No! Anne, do *not* eat that piece!"

"OW!! What in blazing … blazes is in this blasted cake?" She daintily spit a mouthful of fruitcake into her handkerchief and extracted a shiny piece of metal. "This is an outrage! How in Hades did … ? Oh! This obviously does not belong to the baker. It is far too valuable." She turned the unexpected object to and fro in the sunlight. "Is this actually an emerald? How extraordinary! But I could very well have broken a tooth. Heads shall undoubtedly roll over this!"

At her initial exclamation Bingley had risen and hovered by her side. He worriedly wrung his hands as he stuttered, "Miss de Bourgh, I am so, so sorry. I … I thought you would notice it before … I n-never intended for you to … Are you injured?"

"Stop fussing. I am fine. But … *You* are responsible for this? *This* is the special ingredient?"

Bingley glanced sheepishly at her as he sat back down and said, "My father gave it to my mother when he proposed. She always referred to it as her engagement ring … "

"Well, I just about en-*gagged* on it, sir. Why on earth would you do something so bizarre? You, Mr. Charles Bungley, are as nutty as this fruitcake and twice as crumby."

"Please forgive me. It was a cork-brained plan." He reached across the table for the ring, but Miss de Bourgh quickly snatched it away from his grasp.

"Wait. You say this was an *engagement* ring?"

Bingley rubbed his hands up and down his flushed face a couple of times before he loudly exhaled and softly replied, "Yes, and I was hoping it could again serve the same purpose; so I planted it in your slice of wedding cake. It was, indeed, a very crumby idea; and I am certifiably a nut." The abashed young man attempted another grab at the emerald-encrusted band.

"Not so hasty, if you please, Mr. Bingley." Anne held the sparkling ring away from his reach. "Let me rightly understand this. You deliberately implanted a so-called *engagement* ring into *my* particular slice of *wedding* cake because … ?"

Bingley coloured up again and blurted, "Because I am in love with you and want us to spend the rest of our lives together." He calmed and spoke softly once more. "Could we not have our own wedding cake, Annie? Will you please enrich my life by becoming my wife?"

"Oh, Charlie Bing!" She flung herself across the table and her arms around him. "Yes, yes, yes! I would very much love to be your strife … I mean your wife."

Bingley placed gentle kisses upon her forehead and finally the ring upon her finger. "Thank you, Annie. I expect you will, indeed, do an exemplary job of being both my wife and an endless cause of strife for the rest of my life."

Bingley's sister, Caroline Wickham, had suffered through the indignities of the hounds from hell in church and pigeon poop on her tangerine turban with, in her opinion, considerable aplomb. She could not, however, keep at bay her feelings of resentment, envy, and regret when she compared her own simple wedding to the finery on display that day at Pemberley. Her husband, George Wickham, also experienced feelings of resentment, envy, and regret as he leered at the three fine-looking brides. *Darce, Fitz, and Fleming have found women who are more than tolerable and certainly handsome enough to tempt me.* He glanced at his tolerable wife and was tempted to drown his sorrows in the handsome glasses of liquid refreshment slighted by other men.

His father, Hugh Wickham, watched George ogle his friends' brides and felt shame and regret over his daughter-in-law's situation. He planned many lengthy talks with the lad before handing the stewardship reins over to George in the New Year and would impress upon him the importance of keeping strictly to the straight and narrow. For his own part, Hugh Wickham felt justifiably proud of the jobs he had done for the Darcy family in his service to them over the years, the building of the chapel, and even his performance on the small pipe organ that day. He planned to stay in tune with the goings-on at Pemberley after his retirement.

Owen Reynolds and his wife, Pemberley's butler and housekeeper, watched the happy proceedings with relief that everything was going so splendidly. As much as they enjoyed the ceremony and celebration, the couple was glad it would soon be over so they could rest after weeks of preparation for the very special day. Mrs. Reynolds became teary-eyed at the thought of two cherished Darcy offspring leaving Pemberley but was instantly cheered when her husband said, "Esther, you must now anticipate all the little Darcy and Fleming children bound to frequently visit their grandparents here in the years ahead." The housekeeper dried her eyes, planted a kiss on Owen's cheek, and daydreamed of the esteemed estate's future.

Another wistful servant sat in the background and slowly sipped a mug of Pemberley's robust ale. The Darcy men had insisted Crispin Knott attend the celebration after his final duty for the family had been performed, that of preparing the groom for his wedding day. The valet, with a tear in his eye, proudly watched as his former master escorted the lovely Mrs. Fitzwilliam Darcy around the ballroom. Knott had thoroughly trained Bladen, his replacement, and knew the young fellow would serve Pemberley's heir proficiently. Bladen had been a cut above the rest of the candidates for the position and seemed to appreciate it when Knott dispensed invaluable tips on how not to provoke Darcy's pique. The elderly valet advised the lad to wait a few years, however, before putting to use his pointers on how to ruffle the master's feathers and get his goat.

Wine, spirits, negus, ale, and hot chocolate flowed like water, tables were laden with delicacies such as white soup and fruitcake, and Pemberley's ballroom was bedecked with evergreen boughs as well as flowers from the orangery. A string and wind orchestra had been hired to perform from the time the ceremony ended until the last guests departed, and the waltz made its debut to many in Derbyshire. The violinist drew his bow across the strings, gentlemen bowed, and ladies curtsied as the opening strain of waltzing music began. Three newlywed couples led the daring dance, and bystanders were enthralled by the grace and beauty of both the waltz and the young lovers. Other pairs soon followed, including Mr. Bingley and Miss de Bourgh, the Bennets, George Darcy and Lady Anne, the Gardiners, the Earl of Matlock and his wife, and even Mr. and Mrs. George Wickham.

An infatuated Evan Gardiner stood restlessly on the sidelines and wished he could invite a certain young lady to stand up with him; however, she was not yet out in society. He kept glancing at her as she gleefully watched her older sister, brother, and cousin glide across the floor with the partners they had wed that day.

Miss Darcy was, indeed, observing the beaming newlywed dancers. Bright, late autumn sunshine slanted in through the windows, casting a warm glow on the room and its occupants. Anna recalled the candlelit night of the ball at Matlock Manor … Fitzwilliam's dilemma, Richard and Jane's scandalous kiss, Georgiana's bliss, and three joyous engagement announcements. That special evening had been responsible for the love and happiness she witnessed at that moment, and Anna was bound and determined she would only marry for the deepest affection as well.

Miss Bennet was tasked with minding her younger siblings - missish Kitty, wide-eyed-with-wonder Lydia, and little Robert. The boy watched the proceedings with curiosity for a while, quickly became bored, and then wanted to go to the nursery.

Mary said, "Kitty, would you please take your brother upstairs and leave him in Alice's capable hands until it is time for us to depart. I do believe Robert has had quite enough merriment."

The sleepy little boy nodded and muttered, "Yes, I had enough marry-ment for one day."

Kitty smiled, ruffled his flaxen curls, and said, "That is not what Mary meant, poppet."

Before the guests departed, the three brides retrieved their wedding bouquets; and each plucked a bloom to be pressed and saved as a memento of the special day. Georgiana then sought Miss Darcy and handed her sister the arrangement of pink peonies. "Dearest, I want you to have this; yet it does not follow that you must be the next to marry. Promise me you will wait until you are ready and absolutely certain of doing so for love." She caressed Anna's cheek and said, "Whoever he may be, your future husband will be a very fortunate man; and I hope you will be as content as I shall be with Ellis. I love you, Anna, and shall miss you desperately; so you must promise to write often and keep me informed of the further adventures of Barb Thorne and Herr/Fraulein Stewart."

"I will, Georgie … " Anna's eyes welled with unshed tears. " … and you must send me news of Dust Bunny and Pug-Nacious." The younger sister was downcast and lowered her gaze as she spoke. "But I suppose married women have never much time for writing."

"Nonsense! I shall write so regularly, you will quickly become quite sick of hearing from me."

"Oh, no, never! I shall miss you very, very much!" Anna flung her arms around Georgiana and held tight. "When shall we meet again, do you suppose?"

"You know full well that Ellis and I are not going so very far away at all. We will be visiting Pemberley frequently, and you must come stay with us whenever it pleases you. I am delighted you have chosen to accept the offer from our brother and Lizzy, so please write and tell me of your journey. But now, dearest sister, I must start my own journey as Mrs. Fleming. My husband is waiting for me." She offered a hand to her sibling. "Come and wave good-bye, Anna. I want to see your beloved face as Ellis and I pull away from Pemberley."

Across the room Jane Fitzwilliam carried on a very similar conversation with Mary Bennet and passed her the bouquet of Damask roses. Miss Bennet's expression was wistful as she said, "Oh, Jane, there is someone I hope may make me an offer some day in the future. I realize I am far too young yet, but ... "

"Mary! Who is this wonderful young fellow? I know he must be a singular gentleman to have captured your regard. Am I acquainted with him? Is he, perhaps, a brother of one of your seminary friends? I am all curiosity."

Mary smiled enigmatically and shook her head. "I shall not disclose his identity yet, other than to say you *are* acquainted with him. Now go." She giggled and continued, "Your handsome barbarian is waiting for you." Jane kissed her sister's cheek, and they walked hand in hand to where Richard impatiently waited for his bride.

Miss de Bourgh was surprised when she was presented with Elizabeth Darcy's wedding bouquet of roses. "Lizzy, how sweet ... and prophetic too ... albeit a tad tardy. Thank you, cousin."

"A tad tardy prophetically? Anne Catriona de Bourgh, is there something I should know?"

"Well, I am unsure if Charles wants anyone else to be informed as yet. He is asking Mother for permission as we speak. Oh, good grief! She is very fond of our Mr. Bing, so I hope she does not assume he is actually proposing to her."

"Anne! Do be serious. Did Mr. Bingley truly make you an offer?"

"Yes, indeed ... one I could not refuse, complete with an emerald. Do you want your roses back?"

"Silly goose. May I see the emerald?"

Miss de Bourgh held out her left hand and wiggled her fourth finger. "It is an en-gag-ment ring."

"Do you mean an engagement ring? It is very beautiful."

"Well, yes, it is certainly that. However, I almost gagged and broke a tooth because it was in my slice of wedding cake. Ergo, it shall be named en-gag-ment ring from this day forward."

"I would still prefer to call it an engagement ring, Anne; but as Shakespeare said, 'What's in a name? That which we call a rose, by any other name would smell as sweet.' Congratulations, my friend. I am very happy for both of you."

They hugged. "Thank you, Lizzy, and thank you also for the bouquet of roses. The gesture was very thoughtful of you. Speaking of roses, being married to my impeccable cousin shall not be a bed of them, you know."

"Every rose has its thorn."

"Yes, but if Fitzwilliam's behaviour becomes obnoxious, you must promise me to nip it in the bud."

"I cannot, even in my wildest dreams, imagine Fitzwilliam ever being obnoxious. Nonetheless, since we were speaking of gardening, I do remember he once had a green thumb, green hair, green shirt, and … "

The rich, resonant voice of her husband startled Elizabeth, and she jumped. "Ladies, I am almost afraid to ask about your pre-seeding conversation. When you two speak with one another, I never know the ground rules and am always garden my comments. I feel quite green and must pro-seed by trowel and error."

"You heard?" his wife guiltily asked.

"Every word after 'speaking of roses.' Did I miss anything noteworthy prior to that?"

Anne waggled her left hand in front of his face. "I am en-gagged. I have snagged and bagged Bingley."

"Ah! My best wishes then, Annie." He bent to give her a hug and to kiss her cheek. "Poor Bingley! I hope my wretched friend shall take time to smell the roses once in a while." He was duly rewarded by a pinch on his arm.

All guests had at last departed Pemberley except for the six newlyweds and their families. The Colonel's fine new carriage, a wedding gift from his parents, stood at the drive ready to carry its owner and his wife to well-appointed Waterstone Inn, where the bride and groom would remain for ten cozy nights before journeying to London to stay at Matlock Manor while Richard finalized the resignation of his commission. The couple would subsequently travel to Kent and settle at Rosings Park. Leave had already been taken of the Bennets and Darcys, and Richard and Jane stood chatting with the Fitzwilliam family.

Viscount Wentletrap, the Colonel's older brother, had a relatively enjoyable afternoon quaffing more than his share of Mr. Gardiner's generous contribution to the festivities. As he bent to kiss his new sister's hand for the third time that day, he nearly keeled over and took Jane with him.

With quick reflexes, the Colonel rescued them before they took a tumble. "Whoa there, James! Steady, man. Sorry, darling Jane, but I believe my brother is as drunk and wobbly as a wheelbarrow."

The Viscount put his arm around Richard and cheerfully quoted Lord Byron. "Man, being reasonable, must get drunk; the best of life is but intoxication."

"Well, brother, Lord Byron also said, 'The great art of life is sensation, to feel that we exist, even in pain.' The sensation you are feeling now will not exist long, and the pain is certain to come later. Please take good care of this poor sot, Lady Isabelle."

The Viscountess, who was with child and rather exhausted, gently took her husband's arm. She smiled at her brother-in-law and said, "Colonel, you and I have had our differences in the past; all the same, I sincerely wish you and your wife much happiness. Years ago at our own wedding James and I vowed for better, for worse; and we have had quite enough worse, so we are attempting better for a while. Is that not true, husband?"

"Ah, Isabelle, I never knew what real happiness was until I married you … and then it was too late." He winked at his brother and then placed a loud, wet, sloppy kiss on his wife's cheek.

Richard rolled his eyes, patted James on the back, and led Jane over to take their leave of Lord Matlock and Lady Rebecca.

There had been tears and laughter as the Bennets, Darcys, and Fitzwilliams said farewell to the newlyweds; and servants cheerfully tossed shoes, for luck, toward the departing carriages of Mr. and Mrs. Fleming and Colonel and Mrs. Fitzwilliam. Finally Mr. and Mrs. Fitzwilliam Darcy stood alone on Pemberley's front steps and waved as their families pulled out of sight.

Darcy and Elizabeth were to spend their first week of connubial bliss at Pemberley before heading to Northumberland. The Gardiners planned to spend several days in Lambton before returning to London; and the Bennet family, Anna Darcy and her parents, Mr. Bingley, and the de Bourghs would all be guests of the Earl of Matlock at his Derbyshire estate before traveling onward to their own homes.

Alone at last! Darcy tucked his wife's hand into the crook of his arm as they turned toward the entrance hall. "Elizabeth, I could not help but notice you hardly ate anything at all this afternoon. You must be famished, but would you prefer to rest and refresh before we dine?"

She nodded and said, "I admit I did far more chatting, smiling, and dancing than anything else, and it is certainly later than I imagined the celebration would last. But, oh, Fitzwilliam, everything was simply *perfect*! Your parents are the quintessential host and hostess; and I fear, as mistress of your estate, I shall be unable to live up to your expectations."

"Dearest, I do not expect you to be perfect." He smiled at her as they ascended the staircase to their rooms. "Just please understand why I am not."

"Agreed." She nudged him with her elbow, and he nudged back.

"Is everything to your satisfaction here at Pemberley, Elizabeth? Are your chambers comfortable?"

"Yes, and you have asked me that exact same question at least a thousand times since my arrival. How could they not be? I understand, from Anna and Mrs. Reynolds, that my apartments are those normally reserved for the likes of a marchioness or duchess. I am duly flattered and honoured, sir."

"It is true. We once had two duchesses staying here during the same week, and we thought they were going to *duke* it out over which of them would be accommodated in those particular rooms. Fortunately, they did not resort to fisticuffs."

"Finally, a pun! I was beginning to speculate over our lack of knack for wordplay, sir."

"This evening, Elizabeth, shall be reserved for play of a different variety. I will come to escort you to dinner in, say, an hour?" He kissed her hand and left his blushing bride to the ministrations of her abigail, Ann Cillary.

The romantic, candlelit repast was served in a private dining room with a small fireplace and a table only large enough for two place settings. After their hunger was sated, Darcy asked if Elizabeth would care to join him for a short stroll along the river. Never one to pass up an opportunity for a walk, she agreed; and servants fetched their outerwear.

As they sauntered alongside the bourn, the gentleman repeatedly peeked at his fob watch. "Sir, why do you so secretly and frequently verify the time? Do you have an assignation tonight, perchance?"

Darcy startled at being caught, put the timepiece back in its waistcoat pocket, and smiled down at his wife. "As a matter of fact, yes; and the rendezvous must be perfectly synchronized."

She began to solicit his meaning, but her words were cut off when his warm lips claimed hers just as a shrill, whizzing whistle pierced the silence. An unexpected boom made Elizabeth jump; and as she stepped back and opened her eyes, the night sky above the stream was alive with colour. She laughed with delight and clapped her hands. "Fireworks yet again, Fitzwilliam! And finally they are authentic." The impressive display lasted another few minutes, although its splendour was totally wasted on the newlyweds whose senses were more agreeably engaged.

As they ambled back to the house, gloved hand in gloved hand, the gentlemen stopped just shy of the entrance and spoke softly. "Mrs. Darcy,

I just want to reiterate that to have and to hold you from this day forward shall be my greatest pleasure; and I will do everything within my power to keep the promises I made today before our family and friends."

"Fitzwilliam, I promised to love, honour, keep you in sickness and in health, forsake all others, and keep only unto you so long as we both shall live; and I absolutely have no qualms as regards those pledges. I must caution you, however, that I may struggle mightily with the obey aspect."

Less than an hour afterward, Darcy, barefoot and clad only in trousers and open-necked shirt, tentatively tapped on the door to his wife's chambers. Elizabeth had previously dismissed Ann Cillary and, therefore, opened the portal herself. "Come in, Fitzwilliam."

The spacious room, decorated in ivory and gold with burgundy accents, glowed. A radiant fire blazed in the grate, beeswax candles softly illuminated the shadows, a subtle lavender aroma permeated throughout, and chilled champagne awaited. Darcy, nonetheless, noticed not any of those niceties. He only had eyes for the glorious vision standing alluringly before him. Elizabeth's rich, vibrant hair was unbound, her magnificent dark eyes glittered, and her voluptuous curves were clad in the single most becoming, bewitching, and beguiling gossamer piece of clothing he had ever witnessed.

"Oh, my love! This chamber has just been elevated from being worthy of a duchess, for at this moment it is surely occupied by a goddess. My God, Elizabeth, but you are beautiful!" He rushed forward to embrace his bride and met with no resistance. Their kiss advanced from tentatively tender to heatedly intense and deeply passionate within mere moments. Darcy had intended to take his time and be extremely gentle, but Lizzy was wreaking havoc with his control. When he pulled away to search her face for censure or encouragement, he was surprised to see instead her sassy, saucy smile.

"Mr. Darcy, I do believe you have another dill-emma."

"I assure you my only dilemma at this moment is one of willpower," he panted. To what do you refer, Mrs. Darcy?"

"The dill-emma, sir, is the enormous pickle in your pocket."

"Madam! I have no pockets, as you are very well aware. Your teasing is frustrating my self-restraint, you little minx." He rather roughly pulled her close, plunged his hands into Elizabeth's hair and his tongue into her mouth, startling her. "Oh God! Forgive me, Lizzy. Be assured I will not rush you, even though I grow impatient to make you my wife."

"I believe the Reverend Mr. Godfrey has already performed that service, sir."

Darcy gazed at his naive bride with equally immense affection and amusement. "I most certainly trust not, at least in the manner to which I refer, Mrs. Darcy."

Elizabeth become conscious of her blunder and blushed furiously. "You must consider me the most green girl in the kingdom, Fitzwilliam."

"You are my beautiful blushing bride, Elizabeth … a true English rose; and you are expected to be an innocent. As for being green, you must remember the day we first met … I was green, literally. But, Lizzy, I do trust your mother explained … ah … in relation to … relations."

"She did, and she also gave me some reading to do by Fordyce and Gregory to guide me in our marriage."

"Good God. Elizabeth, I attempted to read those books but could not stomach such hogwash, such claptrap, such balderdash. Ah. I see by that certain twinkle you are teasing me. You must allow me the pleasure of putting another kind of passion in those fine eyes of yours tonight." Darcy reached for her left hand, raised it to his lips, and kissed the band of gold on her fourth finger. "I have already wed thee with this ring and endowed thee with all my worldly goods. May I worship you with my body now, Lizzy?"

Afterward

Lizzy's New Home ~ a Moving Experience

The week at Pemberley passed very rapidly for the newlyweds; and before they knew it, the carriage containing George Darcy, Lady Anne, Anna, and Miss Mary Bennet returned to the estate. Kitty, Lydia, and Robert had already returned to Longbourn with their parents and a pony; and Mary brought letters for Lizzy from each member of the family, wishing her well and expressing unending love for their daughter and sister.

Fitzwilliam Darcy had been concerned his bride, who was raised in a rather lively family, might be lonely during the twelve days of Christmas. So, with her consent, Anna and Mary had been invited to travel with them to Northumberland and remain as long as they desired. Invitations had also been dispatched to their northern neighbours in Erethistle asking them to visit on New Year's Eve to meet Mrs. Darcy.

The journey north had been quite a lengthy one, necessitating several stopovers. Fortunately there had been no snowfall, and the roads were in passably good condition. Elizabeth, as they neared their destination, was thrilled to see Hadrian's Wall; and Darcy was delighted to explain the remaining segment in Erethistle's vicinity was one of the region's best. He gladly provided his wife and sister-in-law with information about their surroundings.

"Erethistle has been in existence since Roman times, circa 122 AD; and, in fact, the stone road, Stanegate, is within easy walking distance of Northumbrella. Lizzy, I am sure you will take great pleasure in rambling about; and I shall be more than happy to accompany you on hikes but can assure you the area is quite safe from marauders. As you are aware, Hadrian's Wall was erected to keep out *barbarians.*"

Anna found great amusement in her brother's unexpected banter; and she added, "The barrier worked remarkably well up until a few months ago when a barbaric horde arrived at Pemberley. I always thought the Picts painted themselves blue, yet the barbarians that day were most definitely green-tinged."

The surroundings contained a great diversity of scenery, including several yawning ravines with rivers rushing through them; and Elizabeth cried, "Oh, look! Some of these river valleys are absolutely gorges!"

Anna had, of course, been at her family's Northumberland estate many times; but Mary was completely fascinated by her journey and had never traveled much farther than London. Her nose was pressed against the window as they bypassed the town; and she said, "Please tell me more about the district, sir."

"There are mills and mining in the region; and many of the dwellings are constructed from local stone, as is our own Northumbrella. Ladies, you will be pleased to learn Erethistle is a market town with artisans, shopkeepers, and tradesmen; and our weekly market is held on Mondays. Miss Bennet, before you leave we must make an attempt to visit some of the nearby castles … Stonetrippe, Blinkenought, Hiddenwall, Phelanwell, as well as Quillhill Hall. Ah, Mrs. Darcy, may I direct your attention to the right-hand side, for we are currently approaching our estate."

Lizzy watched for the first appearance of her new residence with great anticipation. The park was very large; and although she saw and admired every remarkable spot and point of view, her mind was too full for praise and conversation. When at last Northumbrella Hall was sighted, her spirits were in a high flutter. *And of this immense northern estate I am now mistress. I hope the strong, stone walls withstand such ineptitude. Please God, let them still be standing this time next year.* The house was a large, handsome building on a prominence that was surrounded by woods and overlooked a vast lawn that led down to a small ice-covered lake.

"Tell me, Fitzwilliam, do you happen to swim in that pond during summer?"

Had Mary Bennet and Anna Darcy not been in the carriage, the young master of Northumbrella might have kissed the puckish smirk from his beloved wife's mouth. Instead he merely grinned and replied, "I have yet to take the plunge, my dear. Perhaps I shall in August; but it deep-ends on whether I might, out of the blue, stumble upon a strikingly beautiful brunette woman with sparkling, intelligent eyes once I emerge. Are you aware one's form appears to the greatest advantage while walking in wet, clinging clothing?"

"Oh! Shocking!" cried Elizabeth. "I never heard anything so abominable. How shall we punish him for such a speech, Anna?"

"Nothing so easy, Lizzy, if you have but the inclination. You must punish him severely; and as intimate as you are, you must know how it is to be done."

Elizabeth arched her brow and gave her husband an impertinent smile. "Perhaps my intimacy with your brother *has* taught me a thing or two, Anna. Beware, Mr. Darcy," she purred. The gentleman shifted uncomfortably, considered himself forewarned, and eagerly anticipated time alone with his sassy wife.

They were soon thereafter at the front entrance of Northumbrella Hall. Darcy was thrilled by the expression of joy and excitement that suffused Lizzy's lovely face, and he unexpectedly swept his bride off her feet and carried her over the threshold. The introduction to staff and the brief tour were both conducted quickly, as Darcy suspected the three ladies would prefer to rest and refresh themselves after their journey. As Lizzy became acquainted with the grand house, she was pleased to see the rooms were lofty and handsomely fitted up with elegant, well proportioned furnishings. "It reminds me very much of Pemberley, Fitzwilliam; and I shall, indeed, be very happy to reside here. But may I visit the stable now? I wish to check on Gloriana."

Darcy was amused his wife's first priority was her horse; and he led Elizabeth outside, not to the stable, but to the pasture, where Gloriana was out standing in a field. A groom had braided the animal's mane and tail so she would look pretty for her owner's arrival; and Lizzy summed up her impression of her contented mare's appearance and her own new home in two words, "Nice plaits!"

Mr. and Mrs. Fitzwilliam Darcy and their sisters had arrived at Northumbrella in time to deck the halls in preparation for the beauty and Christian significance of Christmas. Their steward, Mr. Cringlewood, and the housekeeper, Mrs. Pye, had both the manor and grounds in readiness for the newlyweds and their guests. Nevertheless, there were still a few decisions Northumbrella's new mistress had to make, and Darcy was exceedingly proud of the way Lizzy took charge in an amiable yet efficient manner. Under the direction of its new mistress, the residence was spruced up with evergreens, mistletoe, and a Yule log; and Mrs. Darcy and Mrs. Pye decided on a mouth-watering menu of special festive foods, including roast goose and Christmas pudding, to be served at the family feast on December 25th.

On Christmas Eve, Lizzy put a few finishing touches on the gifts she had brought along to her new home, wrapped the items in handkerchiefs she had painstakingly embroidered, tied them with colourful ribbons, and hid the presents away in her dressing room. Anna and Mary had already retired for the night; even so, the girls, who insisted on sharing a room, could still be heard talking and giggling behind closed doors. Elizabeth found her husband at ease in his sitting room, and they were both surprised when a bemused footman informed them a very special delivery had just been received from Mr. Thomas Bennet of Hertfordshire. The servant then handed a letter to Mrs. Darcy, and she excitedly read her father's words. "Oh my! Fitzwilliam, you must follow me outside to receive Papa's Christmas gift." She instructed the footman to bring their coats, hats, and gloves and requested an extra scarf.

As they exited the house, Elizabeth said, "Now wrap this muffler over your eyes in order to not spoil Papa's surprise. I will guide you along the way." Lizzy led him in the direction of the stable while she explained, "As you may know, my father breeds hounds for hunting; but even the best bird dog is only good to a certain point. Apparently Papa has successfully crossed a Gordon Castle setter and an English pointer; and, just in time for Christmas, you are now the proud owner of ... " Elizabeth unwrapped the scarf from around Darcy's face and beckoned a servant to bring the gift closer, " ... ta-da, a point-setter!"

When the wool was pulled from his eyes, Darcy found himself face to face with an adorable male puppy, about ten weeks old. He reached for the little dog and was so totally enraptured he did not notice Elizabeth had left his side until she spoke behind him. "Fitzwilliam, here are the second and third parts of our gift from Papa. This handsome colt is Majeed, which means noble and glorious; he is yours. My filly here is named Sharifa, meaning honest and noble. These sweet-goers are yearling Arabians - twins out of Yasmina, sired by Khaldun Kahleil. Are they not prime bits of blood?"

"They are magnificent! The point-setter pup is magnificent! Your father is magnificent! You are magnificent! My life is magnificent!" He did not care a few servants witnessed his unrestrained enthusiasm. Darcy gently put the point-setter in an unoccupied straw-filled stall, lifted Lizzy off her feet, and spun her around several times.

"You seem to be in extremely high spirits this blessed eve, husband. Merry Christmas, Fitzwilliam." The newlyweds kissed, oblivious to their smirking audience.

"How can I not be joyful, Elizabeth? Your father already bestowed upon me his most precious gift … your hand in marriage. His generosity is boundless, and I am immeasurably thankful." He settled his wife back down on the ground and ran his hand down Majeed's soft grey neck. "Just wait until Fitz sees this beautiful stepper. I am sure he will be positively green with envy over this fine piece of horseflesh."

"Perhaps not. Papa has also sent another of Kahleil's progeny, a slightly older colt, to Rosings Park for your cousin. On his instruction, the three horses were dispatched from Hertfordshire and began their travels just after the wedding. Longbourn's steward despaired his newest worker, Barnaby Colton, would ever earn his keep; however, the young hand has recently proven to be a top-sawyer. Mr. Whitelaw says he has rarely seen anyone handle horses so superbly. I am sure Mr. Colton is quite fagged to death and knocked-up, so I must ensure he is given comfortable quarters and fed well after his journey." Elizabeth stroked her filly's soft muzzle and said, "You know, Fitzwilliam, there is a Bedouin legend that goes, ' … and Allah took a handful of southerly wind, blew His breath over it, and created the horse. Thou shall fly without wings, and conquer without any sword. Oh, horse!'"

"I had not heard that fable before; but someone once said, 'To ride a horse is to ride the sky.' My own personal favourite equestrian quote is from William Shakespeare's *Henry V*: 'When I bestride him, I soar, I am a hawk: he trots the air; the earth sings when he touches it; the basest horn of his hoof is more musical than the pipe of Hermes.'"

"I do admit I oft' feel that way when cantering across an open field at Longbourn. There are two Arabian proverbs Papa told me. 'The horse is God's gift to mankind' and 'The wind of heaven is that which blows between a horse's ears.'"

Darcy was busy thoroughly inspecting the newest additions to his estate's stable. He expertly ran his hand over each shiny coat; observed posture, muscular development, and spine; checked limbs; and looked into their trusting eyes. Lizzy laughed when he pried Majeed's lips apart to inspect the colt's teeth. "Upon my word, Mr. Darcy! Do you not know one must never look a gift horse in the mouth?"

Mr. and Mrs. Darcy, Miss Darcy, and Miss Bennet ventured out on a crisp Christmas morning to attend the parish church on the sacred holiday. The new mistress of Northumbrella was of great interest to the congregation and was introduced to many of those who would be visiting her home on New Year's Eve.

Mr. and Mrs. Roman Candel and their twins, dark-haired Randall and Miranda, who were only slightly older than Mary and Anna, were invited for an afternoon of ice-skating on Northumbrella's frozen pond. The Darcys' bordering neighbours cheerfully accepted.

When the Candel family arrived, skate blades were distributed to one and all; and the party of eight walked the short distance down the lawn to the lake. Darcy fetched the point-setter puppy, which he and Elizabeth had decided to call 'Balthasar'. They chose the Magi name because the little dog had been one of three gifts from a wise man on Christmas Eve.

Mary Bennet was somewhat bashful at first; but between Balthasar's comical antics on the slippery surface and the cordiality of Miranda and her fine-looking brother, the ice was almost immediately broken; and those three youths skated circles around the others. Randall Candel was quite smitten with Anna Darcy and tried to be of assistance every time she took a tumble; however, the lad realized he was skating on thin ice when gimlet-eyed Darcy scowled at such actions. Elizabeth gracefully glided over to her husband and said, "Fitzwilliam, you could be a good brother and a-sist-her too; the poor fellow is rather taken with Anna and in some way reminds me of a certain cork-brained mooncalf with whom I was once acquainted. In your own words, you were a blushing, stammering schoolboy with a crush. My dear, the young man obviously wishes to embrace your sister. But, as I am sure you agree, no one could ever hold a Candel to a Darcy!" She giggled and skated away just as Darcy's feet flew out from beneath him.

Fitzwilliam tried to catch his lovely, teasing wife; but similar to his sister, Northumbrella's master was not a great proficient on blades. He had already taken more than a few spills and was somewhat irked his graceful spouse had no difficulty keeping her feet under good regulation. His mood was not improved when he tumbled yet again; and Lizzy skated in close proximity to inquire, "Are you not tired of sitting down, Fitzwilliam?" The next time he lost his balance, Darcy landed hard on his backside and hoped his wife had not noticed; however, she was, of course, instantly there to offer invaluable assistance. "Would you like some *ice* for that, sir?" Elizabeth did lend a hand so he could regain his feet and his pride, and she spent the remainder of the afternoon skating arm-in-arm with her unbalanced husband.

When they all had an adequate amount of fresh air, exercise, tired ankles, sore backsides, and teasing, the chilled skaters returned to the house for an assortment of favourite brews. Lizzy ordered a variety of sweets and pastries, tea, coffee, hot chocolate, mulled cider, and Mrs. Cringlewood's delicious wassail of ale, sugar, ginger, nutmeg and cinnamon. As soon as the fire and hot drinks had warmed one and all, Mrs. Darcy suggested they gather around the pianoforte to sing Christmas carols; and after Miss Candel, Miss Darcy, and Miss Bennet had all taken turns performing, Fitzwilliam asked Elizabeth to play next. Lizzy merrily agreed but insisted her husband join her for a duet; and since she was the apple of his eye, he mulled it over and sat down be-cider.

The guests had planned to depart before darkness fell but were having such an enjoyable time that daylight had diminished swiftly without anyone's notice. When servants entered the drawing room to light gas lanterns, Mrs. Candel exclaimed upon the lateness of the hour.

"Mrs. Darcy, we had not intended to encroach on your evening for such an extent. Thank you, my dear, for your splendid hospitality. It was a pleasure to meet you and your charming sister, but we really must be on our way home. Roman, where is that parcel?" Her husband passed her a peculiarly-shaped package wrapped in paper, and Mrs. Candel handed it to her hostess. "Here is a modest gift from our house to yours, Mrs. Darcy. Merry Christmas, and welcome to the neighbourhood."

Lizzy was at a loss to identify the mysterious glass object she had unwrapped but did not want to appear unappreciative. Initially she thought it was a decanter, but it had a hole in both the top of the slender neck and in the rounded bottom as well. "Thank you, Mr. and Mrs. Candel. It is exquisite, and I am positive we will utilize it regularly … whatever its function."

"Oh, my dear Mrs. Darcy, you are delightful! It is a toddy lifter made by a talented craftsman in Erethistle."

Mr. Roman Candel then continued the explanation, "You see, it works similar to a siphon. You simply immerse the bulbous end into the bowl of hot toddy, and the liquid is drawn inside. Once you place your thumb over the hole on top, you can transfer the drink into your glass by releasing your thumb."

Lizzy had grabbed a lit candlestick and positioned it close to the gentleman as he described the procedure. Mr. Candel then searched the wrapping paper for a small card with written instructions about the toddy lifter. In the process, the flame made contact with the man's disorderly mop of dark russet curls. The stench of burnt, sizzling, frizzling hair alerted Elizabeth to the predicament, and she hastily withdrew the candle before it caused a conflagration on Mr. Candel's head. Unfortunately, the tall tallow taper toppled out of its holder and hot wax dripped onto the poor fellow's foot. Fortuitously, his foot was encased in a sturdy boot; and there was no damage done other than a few singed strands of hairs and an unsightly splotch of wax on brown leather. Mrs. Darcy apologized profusely and summoned a servant to remove the globule, but Mr. Candel waved away both her distress and the maid.

The Candel family departed almost immediately following the unpleasant incident but with no hard feelings toward Northumbrella's agreeable new Mistress. As the door closed behind them, Elizabeth flung herself into Fitzwilliam's arms and wailed, "Mama often warned me about burning a Candel at both ends!"

Darcy acknowledged his wife was, without a doubt, keeping relatively late hours. Her commitment as Mistress of the household was taken very seriously, and Elizabeth especially wanted their first holiday season together to be as perfect as possible. As her husband, Darcy had also been responsible for her missing out on a fair amount of sleep, not that she had ever complained about that aspect of her wifely duties.

Darcy kissed Lizzy's crown while he held her in his loving arms and suggested a rest would be beneficial prior to dressing for dinner. Yet when the newlyweds arrived at their chambers, he promptly forgot, or simply ignored, his own recommendation. Although they were soon abed, the couple did not sleep. Later, as they prepared to meet their sisters for the Christmas feast, Darcy made a decision. *Since there is no time like the present, I do believe it is time to present my present.* He fetched the wrapped gift from its hiding place and rapped on her dressing room door. When it opened, he stared in rapt admiration at his beautiful wife while Ann Cillary bobbed a curt curtsey and hastily left the couple alone.

Elizabeth Darcy was garbed in an elegant cranberry velvet gown; and her curls were swept up, exposing the entire elegant column of her creamy white neck. Her abigail had woven a crimson ribbon throughout her lady's locks and also tucked a few sprigs of holly and ivy into the creation. Lizzy's face still glowed from their previous activity, her eyes sparkled, and she dazzled her husband with her brilliant smile. In Darcy's estimation, she was the most breathtaking woman that ever lived; and he stood, rooted to the spot, and gaped at her in silent adoration.

"Fitzwilliam, are you unwell?" Lizzy rushed to stand in front of her statuesque spouse, soothingly stroked his clean-shaven cheek, and brushed several rebellious curls off his brow.

Darcy roused himself and said, "I am in perfect health, dearest, but can scarcely believe you chose to dress in that particular shade this evening."

Elizabeth's hand flew to the base of her throat; she frowned and fleetingly trapped her lower lip between her teeth. "Oh, Fitzwilliam, I am sorry you do not approve of this colour. Mama, Jane, and I thought it looked rather festive when we chose the fabric at Mrs. Lovelace's establishment. If we had more time, I would change into something more appropriate; but as we are already behind schedule meeting our sisters, I am afraid you will just have to tolerate my appearance tonight."

Darcy ardently caught Elizabeth around the waist, pulled her into a tight embrace, and spoke huskily next to her ear, sending shivers down her spine. "You are bewitching this evening, Lizzy; and I burn for you yet again."

"Oh! I thought you disapproved."

"Quite the contrary, my dear. I was merely remarking on the coincidence you are wearing that particular shade of deep red, which looks absolutely ravishing on you, by the way."

"Coincidence? What could be the coincidence?"

"Close your eyes, sweetheart."

Darcy draped the delicate ruby necklace around her throat and placed a gentle kiss on her nape as he fastened the clasp. "Now open those fine eyes of yours, look in the mirror, and behold splendour."

Elizabeth gasped at the vibrant jewels that encircled her neck. "Oh, Fitzwilliam, I have never seen anything quite so beautiful!"

Her husband stood behind her with his hands upon her shoulders and admired the reflection of her perfection. "I am of the same opinion. The gems are tolerably pretty as well, are they not?"

"I was speaking of the jewels. What did you ... oh!" Lizzy blushed as she realized his connotation, and she turned around to face him once more. "Thank you, for both the gift and the compliment. I am gem-uinely awestruck. I never imagined I would own anything quite so ... exquisite. Thank you, my wonderful husband." She stood on tiptoes and placed a soft, sweet kiss upon his lips.

"It is my pleasure, Lizzy. It may not be as dazzling as the nine-hundred-and-fifty diamonds in the tiara Boney gave to his Empress this year; nonetheless, I suspect you would be disgusted by such a vulgar display of wealth. I purchased this bauble the same day I was granted permission to court you, the same day of the ball, and the same day you later made me the happiest man in the world by accepting my proposal. I had intended to present the necklace to you that very night, but it was in my guest room at Matlock Manor. If you recall, we were locked in the library, next my mother barged in, after that it was time for the waltz, and subsequently all other thoughts were forgotten except having you in my arms and knowing you would soon be my wife."

"Yes, for some reason, I do seem to remember the sequence of events from that particular night as well. I assure you I had already crossed the Rubi-con, and there was no turning back; nevertheless, did you intend to entice me with rubies to accept your proposal?"

"Madam! I may be a barbarian, yet even I would not stoop that low. I realize you are teasing me; despite that, I must confess I would have done everything in my power to win your hand. However, if you were the sort of female to be swayed by such a strata-gem, you would not be the Lizzy I know and love. Ergo, it was never my intention to use a bribe to attract a bride. Now, could I entice you to kiss me one more time before we find Mary and Anna?"

"You could." He did. A few minutes later Elizabeth said, "Still and all, Fitzwilliam, please do not suppose I shall be expecting any further lavish trinkets. I am definitely not the kind of wife who would say, 'Husband, you are very rich and handsome; now hand-some over.'" Elizabeth ran her fingers up his chest and then into his hair. Whilst gazing into his dark eyes, she whispered, "Husband, you are a very, very handsome barbarian; now lavish me with kisses again." He performed as requested; and soon after, as they hastily straightened their appearances and rushed down the staircase, Elizabeth light-heartedly admonished, "Fitzwilliam, I am reasonably certain I said *lavish* me with kisses."

"Absolutely not, my darling wife; I distinctly heard you say *ravish*."

They found their sisters waiting good-naturedly in the music salon; and the four proceeded to the dining room where they feasted on an exemplary roast goose and vegetables, followed by Christmas pudding. While the others made their way to the drawing room, Lizzy dashed upstairs to fetch her gifts for Fitzwilliam, Anna, and Mary.

With Balthasar, Romulus, and Remus settled by his feet, the gentleman insisted he be the first to distribute presents to the ladies. Anna received a lovely cameo brooch as well as a recently published three-volume novel, *Sense and Sensibility* by A Lady. Mary thanked him for a mother-of-pearl needlework étui with stiletto, bodkin, thimble, scissors, and needle case. Lizzy was presented with ruby earrings to match her necklace, three packages of pretty personalized writing paper so she could keep in touch with her loved ones so far away, and a book on paint and pigmentation, *The Paint Ingredient*, by Lindsey Doyle.

Elizabeth gifted her husband with a rare 1766 volume of the skillfully-illustrated *The Anatomy of the Horse* by George Stubbs. "My love, how ever did you acquire this book? I have tried to procure it for years. Thank you. Do you remember how I raved about Stubbs' artwork when we were at the Royal Academy exhibition? His paintings of horses are positively brilliant."

"Yes, I did remember. My uncle and Papa searched for that first edition for months. It is advantageous, you know, to have a relation in the import/export trade; and Uncle Gardiner does have many valuable connections." She next rather bashfully handed him another gift, which she had wrapped in a handkerchief painstakingly embroidered with his family crest.

Darcy admired her needlecraft and quoted Voltaire. "Love is a canvas furnished by nature and embroidered by imagination." He untied the ribbon, and a silver pocket watch was revealed. As he turned it over, the light caught the engraving on the reverse, "For my HB ~ with all my love ~ E." Fitzwilliam smiled uncertainly at his wife and said, "This is an exceptionally fine watch, Lizzy; however, I am alarmingly jealous. My initials are FD. Was this intended for some other man? It cannot be your father since his initials are TB. Does HB, perchance, symbolize husband?"

Anna tittered, thereby raising her brother's suspicion. "Oooh no! Please do not tell me it represents ... what I think it represents. I will

not be able to pull this out of my waistcoat pocket. What if someone
questions the engraving?"

Lizzy's eyes sparkled and her sassy smile taunted. "You could always
bestow one of your flinty, imperious glares and say HB stands for ...
um, Huffing Buffoon? Hot-headed Bonehead? Hokey Bloke? Huggable
Bugbear? No? Well, you shall simply have to acknowledge it is from
your wife to her Handsome Bar ... "

"No! Do not say it aloud." He glanced at Lizzy's sister, who was
desperately attempting to stifle her giggles. "Mary ... you *know*? You
do know! Elizabeth! How could you?"

The three females could no longer suppress their mirth and quickly
had the gentleman chuckling as well. Romulus and Remus looked up
but saw all was well and rested heads on front paws, exhaled huge sighs
of boredom or contentment, and dozed. When the puppy, Balthasar, was
unsuccessful in persuading the adult dogs to frolic, he then explored the
large room by investigating every nook and cranny.

"Fitzwilliam, my handsome barbarian, there is another component to
that gift. Open the watch."

"No. I am afraid."

"Oh, for goodness sake! Open it."

Darcy warily opened the cover of the timepiece and dimples
instantaneously bracketed his wide grin. "Lizzy, how beautiful! Who
painted this masterpiece?"

"It is neither beautiful nor a masterpiece. Self-portraits are exceedingly
difficult to portray, so you may remove that miniature and replace it with
a painting of your horse if you prefer."

"Not on your life! The depiction is beautiful, you are beautiful, and the
gift is beautiful. Thank you." He went to her and placed a quick kiss on
her brow.

Elizabeth then gave Anna and Mary the items she had wrapped
in embroidered handkerchiefs for them. Her sister-in-law received a
miniature of Herr/Fraulein Stewart, the rabbit, and Barb Thorne, the
hedgehog; and the lace-trimmed linen was stitched with the initials AD
surrounded by butterflies and flowers. Mary's gift was a hand-painted

fan, and her monogrammed handkerchief was sewn with music notes. Those gifts had been lovingly created by Lizzy's own hand, but she then passed each girl a present purchased in London - a fringed paisley shawl in pastel hues for Anna - and for Mary, sheet music in addition to *Sense and Sensibility*.

Next, Anna handed out her gifts, which proved to be a calling card holder for her brother, a small pearl brooch for her new sister, and a beaded reticule for Mary.

When it was Miss Bennet's turn, she gave her brother-in-law a pair of riding gloves Lizzy had helped select; and Anna received a selection of bottled, scented waters from Longbourn's stillroom. As she handed Elizabeth her gift, Mary giggled and said, "Great minds think alike, Lizzy. Merry Christmas." The others chuckled when Elizabeth unwrapped *Sense and Sensibility*.

The four were at ease to spend the remainder of the evening taking turns to read aloud from the 'lady's' story; and Mary said, "Had I written such a superior work of fiction, I would undoubtedly want my name known. I am fond of this lady's style and hope she pens many more novels in the same vein." They all agreed the anonymous authoress was, undeniably, exceptionally talented.

Before they retired, hugs and gratitude were exchanged all around; and Elizabeth Darcy was pleased her artistic efforts had been worthwhile and appreciated. Her philosophy was 'Love, like paint, can make things beautiful when you spread it; but it simply dries up when you do not use it.'

As they were leaving the drawing room, Anna exclaimed, "Oh, look! Balthasar has left us a present too!" She beckoned a footman to dispose of the offering, but her brother pooh-poohed the suggestion. He was in an especially charitable disposition; and in view of the fact he was going to check on the horses anyway, Darcy simply scooped up the contribution with a section of newspaper and made his way to the stable. Relieved that the puppy was not in deep doo-doo with its new master, Lizzy summoned a maid to scour the stain; and prior to retiring she ensured the boxes of foodstuff and coin were ready to be distributed to the estate's staff and tenants the following day.

The three Darcys and Miss Bennet spent the time between Christmas and New Year's Eve peacefully and in preparation for their open house on December 31st. Elizabeth was surprised to discover a number of her neighbours embraced customs of the Scottish Hogmanay celebration; and the first-footer to cross Northumbrella's threshold after midnight was the tall, dark-haired Randall Candel. The young man was thrilled to have beaten other revellers to the punch and hoped he would, in reality, be the bringer of good fortune to the household. The Darcys received traditional gifts of coal, whiskey, shortbread, fruitcake, and salt; and, in turn, they provided their guests with an endless supply of food, drink, and revelry. The estate's festivities carried on well into New Year's Day, and the merrymakers unabashedly sang Auld Lang Syne until the song was done to a cow's thumb and the cows came home.

Northumbrella's new mistress was very well satisfied with her husband, her home, and her neighbours; and her new family, acquaintances, and servants were very well satisfied with her. Elizabeth's presents and presence cheered the entire household; and Darcy teased her about having a very merry charisma.

Mr. and Mrs. Ellis Fleming had not arrived at Eventide Hall, their estate farther north in Derbyshire, for their wedding night. The newlywed couple enjoyed celebrating with family and friends so thoroughly that they departed Pemberley later than planned. Fleming sent a rider ahead to secure lodging at a reputable cozy inn along the way and to notify his estate's personnel he and their new mistress would arrive the following afternoon instead.

Finally ensconced in their snug room for the evening, Ellis cuddled with his bride and continued to ask for forgiveness. "I am so sorry, Georgie ... of all people to lose track of *time*. I hope you are not having second thoughts concerning me."

"Oh husband, I have, indeed, been having second, third, and fourth thoughts of nothing but you for the past ... " Georgiana checked her timepiece and frowned. " ... however many hours since we wed. Now, please stop agonizing and apologizing. Your man did well to secure this room on such short notice. Ellis, these accommodations are charming, we have enjoyed a scrumptious serving of food, there is a roaring fire in the grate, and I would be grateful if you would cease fussing as regards my comfort. To be honest, I am scarcely aware of my surroundings while I am with you."

They declared their ardent admiration for one another, kissed passionately, and in due course found their way to the large, inviting bed. Alas, Fleming, the son of a clock-maker, was dissatisfied with the mattress and wanted to complain to the innkeeper. His wife, on the other hand, was not in any discomfort and insisted he stop tucking the ticking and talking. Georgiana had a better conception of how they should expend time on their wedding night, and Ellis could not find fault with her excellent way of thinking.

The next day, as the sun climbed higher, Georgiana, who was not a morning person, ignored her husband as he shook her shoulder and coaxed her to arise. She groaned at his chipper tone, opened one eye, and was surprised to find Ellis already dressed, bright-eyed, and bushy-tailed. Mrs. Fleming groaned for a second time and pulled the quilt over her head.

"Georgie, love, it is a glorious morning. Rise and chime, sweetheart. I am eager to take you to Eventide Hall, my family's age-old estate." Ellis pulled the coverlet off his wife and was rewarded with a glower. "Come along, my sugar. I have already eaten but will join you for an extra breakfast. Akin to a clock, when I am hungry, I go back four seconds."

Georgiana snatched the bedcover away from him. "Ellis, are you always so cheerful in the morning? We did not catch much sleep last night. Are you not tired?"

"My dear, Mrs. Fleming, I come from a long line of watchmakers. We are used to working around the clock, so I do not require much slumber." He grappled and tugged the quilt from her grasp. "Ah, Georgie?"

"Yes, Ellis?"

"Last night … ," He smirked as he realized why his wife was so sleepy. "Was I imagining it, or did you, in the throes of passion, refer to me as a handsome barbarian?"

"You were imagining it." Mrs. Fleming's face was flushed as she dove under the covers again.

As with nearly all newlywed couples, Ellis and Georgiana did, after some time, adjust to one another's routine. Within a year, however, they had to adjust to their daughter's routine. Although they were both tickled pink over the birth of their first healthy child, the new mother wondered why people spoke of sleeping like a baby. Ella Helene Fleming, their adorable infant, insisted on waking every two hours, like clockwork.

fterword

In the Darcy Family Way

In the sumptuous master bedchamber of Northumbrella, Fitzwilliam Darcy lounged abed while his wife of two months stood nearby at her easel and observed him.

"May I ask to what this scrutiny tends, Elizabeth?"

"Merely to the illustration of your physique," said she easily. "I am trying to capture it."

"And what is your success?"

She shook her head. "I do not get on at all. My subject is far too distracting."

"I wish, Lizzy, you would not sketch my anatomy at the present moment, as there is reason to fear the performance would reflect no credit on either of us."

"But if I do not take your likeness now, I may never have another opportunity."

"As my wife, I assure you there will be ample opportunities for you to see me thusly; but I would by no means suspend any pleasure of yours. Come here," he warmly invited; and Lizzy put her paints away and climbed back into bed.

Several mornings afterward, Fitzwilliam Darcy, in a midnight-blue silk dressing robe, stood before the easel that held the canvas his wife had completed the previous evening. "Well, this is unquestionably one painting which will *not* be placed in the gallery at Pemberley."

"I am offended, husband. I rather thought it should look well hung next to that of your great uncle, the judge."

"I cannot judge … *is* this a very striking resemblance of my form, Lizzy?"

"Do you not think I did it justice, darling?"

"How near it may be, I cannot pretend to say. *You* think it is a faithful portrait undoubtedly."

"I must not decide on my own performance, Fitzwilliam. But, if you will come back to bed, I may offer many compliments on yours," she warmly invited. The effect was immediate, and a deeper shade of colour overspread his features; Darcy said not a word, cast aside his robe, and climbed in alongside her.

During the third year of his marriage to Georgiana, following the birth of their second daughter, Leanne Georgina Fleming, Ellis worked diligently to write the first book on the production of watches and clocks; and when it was finally published, everyone thought it was about time. The opening sentence was, 'Contrary to popular belief, people who work in watch factories do not stand around all day making faces'.

While doing research for his publication, Ellis Fleming came across the following anecdote. The Tates Watch Company of Massachusetts, America, wanted to manufacture other products; and since they already made the cases for pocket watches, they decided to market compasses for the settlers traveling westward. Although their timepieces were of the finest quality, the company's compasses were so faulty pioneers often ended up in Canada or Mexico rather than California. This, of course, was the origin of the expression, 'He who has a Tates is lost.'

Darcy Ellis Fleming was born in the fourth year of their marriage. Darcy was a happy babe and continued to be good-natured, albeit very active, as he grew into boyhood. In the mornings Georgiana and Ellis watched their son rise; in the afternoons they watched their son shine; and after their son was set for the night, they could finally rest.

Fitzwilliam Darcy entered Northumbrella's west-facing sitting room as the mid-afternoon sun slanted in through tall windows and cast its meagre light on his lovely wife. To him it seemed Elizabeth radiated a warmer glow than that late-February sun. He stood behind her chair, placed his hands gently on her shoulders, and kissed the top of her head. "What manner of project are you working on so industriously there, Mrs. Darcy?"

She bent her head back to look up at his handsome face as he leaned over her. "It is a beaded macramé item for the child of someone I love very dearly. Would you care to lend a hand?" Elizabeth passed him a ball of cream-coloured yarn and demonstrated the particular knots she was using.

Darcy took a seat across from her and smirked as he tossed the ball from one hand to the other. "You are exceptionally skilled at macramé, Lizzy. I very much enjoy engaging in the *knotty thing* with you and look forward to filling our own home with the fruits of our labour produced by such joint efforts."

"I am not entirely naïve, you know, sir." Elizabeth said primly. "Therefore, I do not, for a moment, believe you are speaking of creating knotty macramé projects at all but are just being plain naughty. As such, any labour of love involved will be mine alone; and our first creation should, in fact, be produced, or should I say reproduced, in about six and a half months."

Darcy instantly dropped his smirk along with the ball of yarn. He gaped in wonder at the incredible woman who had been his wife for a mere two and a half months. Elizabeth giggled at the shocked expression on her beloved husband's face and tossed another ball of yarn at him to bring the poor fellow out of his stupor. It bounced off his forehead, and she said, "Well, that was quite a *pregnant* pause, Fitzwilliam. Is this all the reply I am to have the honour of *expecting*? Have you nothing to say?"

Darcy's astonishment was beyond expression. He stared, coloured, doubted, and was silent. Finally he gulped and stuttered, "Are you ... are you ... spinning another yarn, Lizzy? Your mother once told me she does not believe everything your father says, and she also informed me you take after him. Truthfully, are you ... are you ... ?"

"Spinning another yarn in the Bennet *family way?*"

"Elizabeth!"

"Darling, I shall not tease you any longer over such an important issue since you are *expecting* an answer. Prolonging your anticipation would just be *breeding* contempt. Hmm, I wonder whether our excellent cook has finished baking rolls, or if there might still be *a bun in the oven.*"

"Elizabeth!!!"

It was already established Mr. and Mrs. George Wickham did not produce offspring; and their relationship was certainly unequal to the grand passions of the Darcys, the Fitzwilliams, the Flemings, or even Mr. and Mrs. Charles Bingley. Caroline and her wickedly handsome husband got along tolerably well; and Wickham was kept under the watchful eye of his godfather and namesake, George Darcy.

Upon the demise of the elderly Mr. and Mrs. Bartlett Piers, who both succumbed to a virulent influenza, their only male relative, Charles Bingley, inherited their Staffordshire estate. So Charles and Anne sold their London townhouse and settled within a three-quarter-hour ride to Pemberley. George Wickham then also had to contend with and answer to his wife's brother, which was a rather awkward situation since the two young men had been friends for some years. The Bingley brother and sister, whose family had made their fortune in footwear, often made George feel like a heel; and it is a known fact that time wounds all heels. For her part, Caroline realized she was fortunate not to have fallen on hard tines after having fallen for a rake. She was content to say she lived at Pemberley, and Caroline always accompanied her husband when he had business at the grand house. Mrs. Wickham enjoyed walking the grounds, and she particularly liked to spend time in the orangery.

Like her Darcy nephew, Lady Catherine de Bourgh eventually learned to lighten up; and after ten years in mourning clothes, she finally shed her black widow attire and began to wear shades of charcoal, silver, lilac, and mauve, which looked quite fetching with her grey … er, platinum hair.

Lady Catherine's time was either spent in the dower house at Rosings near Richard and Jane Fitzwilliam or with her dear Annie and Mr. Bing in Staffordshire, and the gutter-mouthed gentlewoman spent as little time as possible in society and in sobriety. For a while her greatest joy in life (beside fruitcake, plumes, and laudanum-laced sherry) was when she became a great-aunt, time and time again, to the Fitzwilliam brood, who were always on their pest behaviour in great Aunt Catherine's presence.

The brave Colonel (retired) Fitzwilliam was a wreck the day his first offspring was born. The midwife had been attending another birth ten miles away in a different part of Kent, and Richard was in the midst of a mid-wife crisis when the woman finally arrived fifteen minutes before his daughter entered the world. Jane Fitzwilliam presented her husband with a healthy child every year and a half until their brood reached a total of seven. A baby's sex is a hidden agender until it makes its first appearance; however, the couple seemed to have a set pattern of girl-boy-girl-boy, with Janetta Lily Fitzwilliam followed by Henry Bennet Fitzwilliam, Regan Alexandra Fitzwilliam, Geoffrey Richard Fitzwilliam, Rebecca Frances Fitzwilliam, Cosmo James Fitzwilliam, and Muriel Jane Fitzwilliam.

It was very agreeable to the Bennet family to have Jane settled within so easy a distance of Longbourn. For what was fifty miles of good road? It was little more than half a day's journey and a very easy distance when there was fortune to make the expense of travelling unimportant. When they visited Rosings, Lady Catherine was always especially pleased to see Robert Bennet, her little bug.

During one of their visits Mr. Bennet was surprised when his son asked, "Papa, is Lady Caffrin an author?"

"No, my boy, not to my knowledge. Why do you ask?"

"She complains about having authoritis in her hand. Is that not writer's cramp?"

For several years, Robert Bennet continued to create pun-filled stories; and his writing style was like the little boy himself, short and sharp.

Great-nieces and great-nephews, as great as they may be, paled in comparison to when Lady Catherine's own daughter delivered Catriona Anne Bingley, followed the next year by Lewis Charles Bingley, and then Rosanna Catherine Bingley two years after that. Lady Catherine was positively over the moon and absolutely loved being a granny, even if it meant she had to be very careful not to cuss. To be on the safe side, she adopted and adapted a motto, 'A closed mouth gathers no feet'. Surprisingly, it was not a hard canon by which to live, because at her age, Lady Catherine found actions creak louder than words.

As soon as Richard Fitzwilliam resigned his commission, an opening became available for the rank of Colonel. The former Lieutenant-Colonel John Dun gladly filled the position; and his wife, Charlotte (nee Lucas), was thrilled by the promotion. Their daughter, Mariah Beatrice, was born four months before her parents celebrated their first wedding anniversary. (Charlotte had wasted no time in securing her man.) Mariah's brother, Arthur Wellesley Dun, named for the victorious commanding General in the Peninsular War, arrived almost three years later.

Fitzwilliam Darcy finally beheld true perfection on September 25th, 1812, upon the birth of his first child, an heir, Bennet George Darcy. The proud papa presented his wife with a bouquet of Damask roses and baby's breath, while tears of joy and thankfulness filled his eyes.

Perfection was achieved a second, third, fourth, and fifth time over the years upon the births of their sons George Ellis Darcy, followed by William Robert Darcy, Richard Charles Darcy, and then Thomas Fitzwilliam Darcy.

After five perfect boys and five beautiful bouquets of roses and baby's breath, Elizabeth finally delivered a daughter, Anne Judith Rose Darcy. The flawless baby girl had dark chestnut curls and, at least in her father's totally unbiased opinion, the most captivating, sparkling, intelligent brown eyes ever beheld in the entire history of the entire world; and he was instantly besotted and head over heels in love. Upon Anne's birth, Elizabeth's chamber was filled to overflowing with Damask roses; and the tears in Darcy's devoted eyes actually overflowed onto his cheeks that memorable day.

Despite being thrown into the path of rich and titled men, Mary Bennet happily accepted an offer of marriage from a tradesman's son. She had long ago set her cap for young Daniel Burke, who lived across the street from the Bennet London townhouse.

Randall Candel, the Darcys' Northumberland neighbour, did not win the hand of the lovely Anna Darcy. That honour went to Evan Gardiner, the son of another businessman.

Four years after their elder sisters had so blissfully tied the knot, Miss Bennet and Miss Darcy wed their strapping young tradesmen during a double ceremony in Pemberley's charming chapel. Those genteel ladies, both gentlemen's daughters, saw many changes take place in society during their lifetime; and as they reached middle and old age, those transformations and reformations became more evident. Through diligence and merit, many hard-working tradesmen, like Daniel Burke and Evan Gardiner, became extremely affluent. That wealth enabled them to purchase large tracts of property; and the upper classes finally, and begrudgingly, welcomed businessmen into the landed gentry.

George Darcy and Lady Anne invited their extended families to Pemberley every summer, and the grand estate's manor practically burst at the seams. There were Fitzwilliam and Elizabeth with their five sons and one daughter; the Flemings and the Bingleys each had two daughters and one son; and Richard and Jane brought their boisterous blonde brood of three boys and four girls. In addition, the Bennet family often spent a week or two at the Derbyshire estate, as did the Gardiner clan, Daniel and Mary Burke, Lady Catherine de Bourgh, the Earl of Matlock and his wife, and Viscount Wentletrap with his wife and son.

In the month before Bennet Darcy turned one-and-twenty, his cousin Darcy Fleming was eighteen years of age; and both Henry Fitzwilliam and Lewis Bingley were nineteen. George and Lady Anne Darcy had long ago shuffled off their mortal coils, but Fitzwilliam and Elizabeth continued the tradition of inviting friends and relatives to Pemberley during summer. It was uncommonly hot in Derbyshire that particular season, and the four attractive, virile young men spent a great deal of time swimming and kicking up a lark in Pemberley's piddling pond. That pitiful little lake had been dredged regularly; nevertheless, the lagoon still managed to generate a healthy crop of lime-coloured slime and a particular stench during late summer.

Ella and Leanne, the lovely daughters of Georgiana and Ellis Fleming, had invited a couple dearest friends from seminary to spend August with them at Pemberley. One sultry summer afternoon the four young women took a leisurely stroll around the grounds; and when the beauty and fragrance of the august estate's magnificent gardens had been enjoyed to everyone's satisfaction, they decided to head toward the river and visit the pretty chapel on the manicured lwn near the tall but neatly trimmed seven-foot hedgerow. The two Flemings related the story of how their own parents had serendipitously met at that very spot and about the triple wedding that had subsequently been held in the little church. The four giggled and sighed, thinking it all quite comical yet romantic. As the ladies exited the chapel and opened their parasols against the brilliant summer sun, a bizarre image caught their astonished eyes; and they screamed.

Bennet Darcy paced back and forth in front of the elegant mahogany desk, as he alternately ran a hand agitatedly through green-tinged chestnut curls and twisted the signet ring on his pinkie finger. He had already thrown a coat over the wet cotton shirt that clung indecently to his well-developed torso, but Fitzwilliam Darcy's eldest child's appearance still bore little resemblance to his usual meticulous attire and grooming.

Elizabeth set aside a stack of correspondence on the writing desk that had belonged to Lady Anne and watched in amusement as her strikingly handsome son, so similar in looks and temperament to her beloved husband, continued his rant.

"I simply cannot comprehend him, Mother! I have just utterly humiliated myself out there on Pemberley's lawn in front of four very genteel and, now, traumatized young ladies; and Father has the audacity to consider my situation to be, for some ungodly reason, absolutely, gut-bustingly hilarious. I swear the deranged man is sitting in the study at this very moment actually wiping tears of laughter from his face. Has he gone completely stark raving mad?"

Elizabeth Darcy's beautiful eyes twinkled; and she tried unsuccessfully to stifle a burgeoning impertinent smile as she replied, "Oh, Bennet dear, your father merely considers your dilemma entertaining because it is a perfect example of *his-story* repeating itself."

Finis

J. Marie Croft

J. Marie Croft, a Nova Scotia resident and avid reader all her life, discovered Jane Austen's works later than others but made up for lost time by devouring the six novels and as many adaptations and sequels as she could find. In the midst of reading prodigious amounts of Austen-based fan-fiction, she realized, 'Hey, I can do that'. So now in her spare time (when not working at a music school or on a wooded trail enjoying her geocaching hobby), she listens to the voices in her head and captures their thoughts and words in writing. Her stories are light-hearted; and her motto is Miss Austen's own quote, 'Let other pens dwell on guilt and misery.'

J. Marie Croft is a member of the Jane Austen Society of North America (Canada) and admits to being 'excessively attentive' to the 1995 BBC version of Pride and Prejudice.

She can be contacted at jmariecroft@gmail.com.

Acknowledgements

Family, friends, and colleagues deserve heartfelt thanks for various reasons. From the onset, Dennis, Heather, and Jessica provided much-need support and encouragement. When my family rolled eyes, shook heads, and uttered groans, they *were* just being helpful ... right?

Readers at two Jane Austen fan-fiction websites (Derbyshire Writers Guild and A Happy Assembly) provided invaluable feedback; and although too numerous to name, those on-line friends were ultimately responsible (i.e. to blame) for this book. Author Emma Hox (*Longbourn's Unexpected Matchmaker*) started the ball rolling, and it came to rest across the continent at Rhemalda Publishing. That company's President, Rhett Hoffmeister, merits an ENORMOUS THANK YOU for going above and beyond the call of duty. I'd also like to put in a good word for Rhemalda's Editor, Kara Klotz, who put in a good word or two (or umpteen) for me and deleted those that were ... not so good.

Gregory Watters has my unending gratitude for inspiration as well as for tea caddies, toddy lifters, and Regency glass. Sincere appreciation goes to Elise Besler-Harnish for enthusiasm and assistance, to Lola Doucet for advice, and to Glane Gorveatt for patience.

Finally, Mary Simonsen (author of *The Second Date, Searching for Pemberley*, and *Anne Elliot, A New Beginning*) gets a long-distance hug for being such a dear, generous, obliging lady. Thank you all, so very much, for being there for me while *I* took the plunge.

~ J. Marie Croft ~

Lightning Source UK Ltd.
Milton Keynes UK
16 September 2010
159958UK00001B/238/P